Ocracoke Island is the only major island in the Outer Banks that is not connected to the mainland or any other island by bridge or causeway. The only way on or off the island is by boat.

The North Carolina Department of Transportation maintains a ferry service for regular access to the island.

MAN
OVERBOARD
ON
OCRACOKE
ISLAND

MAN OVERBOARD

ON

OCRACOKE ISLAND

AN OUTER BANKS MYSTERY

FARLEY DUNN

MAN OVERBOARD ON OCRACOKE ISLAND, Dunn, Farley

1st ed.

Subtitle: An Outer Banks Mystery

ISBN: 978-1-957173-41-2

Dedication

My sister spent hours proofing the text in this book. She caught mistakes I never noticed.

Thank you, Cynthia.

And yes, she is who you think she is, one of the characters in this book, although with a different last name.

Introduction

Book 1 in this series, *Dead Body on Bodie Island,* was born from a wedding, a drive halfway across the country, and a weekend on the Outer Banks for a sister who wanted to see one thing: Ocracoke Island.

Book 2 came about because I liked my characters so much that I couldn't not give them another adventure.

The core team from C-District in Dare County, North Carolina, is back, with a host of new people you will come to love, hopefully as much as I have.

This story moves south an island but takes in much of the Pamlico Sound as well. Enjoy my journey as I delve into *Man Overboard on Ocracoke Island.*

TABLE OF CONTENTS

Prologue

THE WIND SCREAMED through the pilings holding up the Avon Pier. In the dead of night, the high-pitched whistles and groans slammed into the sand dunes between the beach and the road and reverberated, increasing the magnitude of the blow's fist into a battering ram of unimaginable proportions.

Sand, turned by the wind into sharp needles, battered unprotected skin, and Lieutenant Diane Turnipseed of the Dare County C-District Patrol Division snapped her collar to stand erect and turned her back to the needles and looked out to sea. Two boats might be out there. One she was certain of, and another she didn't want but would be satisfied to locate.

Smugglers, dope runners, and other wicked people used the vast stretches of unoccupied Outer Banks beaches for nefarious ends and pulled the people of her island down into the depths with them. She would throttle the lot, given a chance, and she'd make no bones of her opinion of them. Still, the beaches of Hatteras Island would draw them in.

"Some things aren't ours to wish away," she said.

"Ma'am?"

Diane jumped. "Taylor?" she called. With the wind whistling through the legs of the pier, she wasn't sure she could make herself heard.

"Yes, ma'am. I didn't catch what you said."

"I need my windbreaker from my truck. Skedaddle on up yonder and haul it down here for me."

"Yes, ma'am." He grinned, a lighthouse of excitement. "We're a team. Whatever you need. I'll be right back."

A team. She let her thoughts dwell on those words. Her C-District Team had grown to include members from Hyde and Carteret counties, a cross-county endeavor to clamp a fist around the nuggins encroaching on the island life she treasured so much. Tonight, even the Coast Guard was present and on her turf, scrabbling away like they belonged on Lieutenant Diane Turnipseed's perfect piece of earthly heaven.

For all sakes, pull your pants up, Diane, she said to herself. *You don't got the sense God gave a minnow. We're all on the same team here ...* She heard Deputy Sean Taylor in her words, and that irritated her even more.

"Taylor!" she yelled, wondering where the sakes the fool deputy had gotten to now.

—— Chapter 1 ——

Midnight Beach Rendezvous

LIEUTENANT DIANE TURNIPSEED snapped her collar to stand erect, and she turned her back to the wind whipping under the Avon Pier. She remembered a much warmer day she'd been under the pier, though it wasn't a particularly pleasant recollection. Sissy Chadwick and her third drunk boyfriend of the month, Jimney Crawford, now in jail for aiding and abetting a crime, had been throwing their empties at one another in a drunken rage. It seemed to Diane that if Avon pulled the pier down, there's be a lot less trouble to go around in the village.

Then, Calvin Skidmore, the owner of Rodanthe Surf Shop, would have to find another place to surf, and he'd likely grouse about that.

She looked up at the underside of the pier, what she could see of it in the dark. Sand whipping along the beach was needles on her skin, but she could just make out the wooden structure, with the legs darkened at the bottom and waiting on the high tide to return, and the spaces between the boards overhead that allowed slivers of moonlight to create a pattern on the sand below.

"Some things aren't ours to wish away," she said to herself, forcing back the undertow of dark and wind.

"Ma'am?" A male voice, one of her C-District Dare County deputies.

Pulled from her reverie, the sound of the sea pounding the beach jarred her thoughts, and she turned to answer, only to be blasted by more sand, this time from a blender slinging salt spray at her.

"Taylor?" she called. With the wind whistling through the legs of the pier, she wasn't sure her voice could be heard.

"Yes'm, Sean here. You said something, and I didn't catch it. You know I'm here to serve, no matter what. Anything you need, name it."

"What I need—" She yelled the words, then cut herself off. What she nearly said was that she needed him back in the car, or perhaps at the sub-station in Buxton, or better yet, back in Raleigh, four hours away. Whatever the location … she just wanted him off the Banks and out of her hair. She took a deep breath, squinted against the building gale, and motioned away from the beach.

"Ma'am?"

"Sean," his first name felt like a knot in her throat as she forced it out, "a heavy windbreaker from my truck. That would help." And give her some space while he retrieved it.

"Yes, ma'am." He grinned, his teeth a lighthouse of excitement at being given something to do. "We're a team. Whatever you need. I'll be right back," and he skipped off with a double jump and jogged into the darkness, his feet leaving dimpled shadows in the sand, his path barely visible in the moonlight.

Diane turned to look out to sea, using her binoculars to

— 2 —

search for the Coast Guard 29-footer she knew to be out there. She caught its outline against the horizon. Aboard were Coast Guard Lieutenant Braxton Sallinger, a muscular man with a closely cropped beard and an ego to match; Deputy Calvin Dingman, balding and fleshy, from up Swan Quarter in Hyde County; and Drone Pilot Deputy Clifton Magruder, an agreeable family man from Morehead City down in Carteret County.

Diane considered that her own C-District team could handle this on their own. No sense in muddying the pond with too many lead-footed frog wranglers, but as her Aunt Lucille once said, what you do for one, they do back for you. Then, it seemed to Diane that Aunt Lucille's "wisdom nugget" was straight out of the Bible, entwined with some of her aunt's own take on the words of the Lord. It was called the Golden Rule within the hallowed walls of the church, and an Aunt Luci-ism everywhere else.

Then, Aunt Lucille had been her own light of goodness in some people's eyes. Diane for one had worshipped her as a girl, and now she lived in her aunt's old beach house. That was, when she wasn't back at home in Elizabeth City in her real house, which was about as often as a nor'easter whipped up a squall and threatened to shut down the islands altogether.

Like tonight.

"Taylor," she yelled. To herself she muttered, "I bet tomorrow's breakfast this is already near a hurricane blow. For all sakes, where's that deputy?" She turned toward the shore to see him striding down a sand dune. She yelled, "There's a walk-through right there. Why'd you not take it?"

"Sorry," he yelled back, and closer, he apologized. "I thought I had my flashlight, but I musta dropped it between here and there. I got lost on the way back."

"Some people got sharks already swimming in their collards." She handed him the binoculars. "Here. Don't drop them while I put on my jacket. I located our boat. See if you can locate the drop-off boat. It's near about midnight, and that's our time."

"Yes, ma'am," Deputy Taylor said, and he traded the jacket for the binoculars. "It's a good thing Clifton included us in Carteret's plan to catch these smugglers. Pardon, ma'am, Deputy Magruder, that's how I should call him."

"It don't change who he is, Deputy, and since this is Dare County, I don't see he had much choice. We're all on a stringer when they got the intel and we got the beach."

"Yes, ma'am. Still, three counties and the Coast Guard!" If a voice could be said to glow, Sean Taylor's did.

"Here's you a question, Deputy. That Magruder, he's what, a drone pilot?" The whistle of the wind tore her last two words away.

Sean leaned in, asking, "What was that, ma'am?"

"A drone pilot, Deputy. A flying camera."

"Oh, yes. He's the best they've got."

"Did you see it flying out there?" Diane threw her hand up into the dark sky, with only the moon and the stars for light.

"Let me see—"

"Shush that." She snatched the binoculars. "Besides being dark, ain't no drone out flying in this wind. It'd be flummoxed and into the sea with the first gust."

Seafoam had begun to build up on the sand, whipping in the wind and spattering their pant legs, and Diane moved up the beach toward the dunes when something pale in the sand caught her eye. She glanced up, located the moon overhead, and dropped her gaze before nudging the item with her foot. Leaning down to pick it up, she held a shark tooth in her grip, and a nice one, slick with enamel on the business end and a rough, porous root like the top of a "T" where it would have anchored into the shark's mouth. She slipped it into her pocket, unsure why she kept it, but feeling it call to her.

Deputy Suzanne DeSantis from Hyde County appeared through the dunes, only she hiked the walkthrough rather than stumbling down the dune face like Taylor had. Diane approved. She was less forgiving with the light the woman held pointed at her feet, revealing jeans over her heavy black boots.

"Lieutenant?" Deputy DeSantis called, or yelled, to be more accurate, as the wind continued to wail, and from more than about three feet, nothing was getting through.

"For all sakes, douse that light, Deputy." Diane moved quickly, blocking the water's view of the woman's flashlight.

"Last I heard, this is how we get around at night," the deputy retorted, although she did cup the light more tightly, dimming its visibility.

"Hold your taters, Deputy. You people put your spoon into my pot, and I'm not having you stir up a mess of muck with that light. Those people out there," and Diane pointed out to sea, "can see that tiny little light from miles out. You got any idea why they picked midnight? Or don't you Hyde County people get out at midnight over on Ocracoke?"

"You want some of my pity pills so you'll feel better?" Deputy DeSantis retorted as she flipped the light off. Even under moonlight, she could be seen looking off, likely gaining self-control in the face of the lieutenant's virulent upbraiding. "Got us a truck back on 12, might be the smugglers' contacts. They said you know them, but we don't believe a word of it. You want to come vouch for them?"

"Let me tell my deputy."

"I'll be in the car. Gray Charger, no markings. You can ride with me." The deputy turned, and in the moonlight moved away from the blustery beach.

Pity pills. And from a deputy. Diane would throttle someone, if she didn't need the cooperation of the Hyde County Sheriff's Department. Despite her claim that Dare County could go this this on their own, they would likely be above their knees about now without the extra manpower. For instance, Jason Romney, new to Dare County and C-District from Carteret County, well, as much as he irritated her sometimes, he was notching up her ladder one contact at a time. The man seemed to have a web of people he could pull favors from in all the surrounding counties. Dingman, especially. The man might come across as swamp rat with no learning, but Swan Quarter was mighty fortunate to have him, like a flea collar on a ship's cat. Turn it loose, and one varmint kept a lot of smaller ones at bay.

Diane found Taylor and handed him the binoculars. "Sean, Deputy DeSantis needs me to verify someone up to the road. You okay on your own?"

"Yes, ma'am. You can count on me, ma'am." He pointed to one eye and grinned. "My eyes are peeled."

"For all sakes … just keep that peeled eye pointed out yonder. Your radio on? Call me if, well—" and she waved one arm out to sea.

"Yes, ma'am. I got this." He clicked the radio unit on his belt, put the binoculars to his face, and turned out towards the water.

Diane was certain the man had no idea what he was looking for, instead just staring into the darkness, but she couldn't be here and in DeSantis' car at the same time, and it was possible, maybe even likely that they had indeed found the contacts who were to retrieve the drop off. A truck? That was telling, so yes, Diane needed to mosey up that direction to see if the fish had found the fire or if they needed to be cut loose and thrown back in. Likely, cooked up and served in court, but that waited to be seen.

DeSantis' light gray was easy to find in the Avon Pier parking area, as with the moon out, it glowed like a beacon. A good reason for black, like Diane's unmarked Explorer. She opened the passenger door, and interior lights came up, but only enough to see DeSantis in the driver's seat and her console area with her equipment out and at hand. Diane dropped inside and closed the door. The deputy started the engine, and Diane had to give her one thing: the headlights remained off.

"I appreciate the ride, Deputy," Diane offered up, a peace branch.

"Yes, ma'am." A peace offering in return, the respect due an officer of a higher rank. "Mostly I'm in town over on our island, touristy issues and stuff. My husband, Teague, down in Beaufort—" She turned the wheel, and a massive gold man's watch flashed on her left arm. "—says I'm a whippersnapper."

"Beaufort … quite a commute on the ferry." The Ocracoke-Cedar Island ferry was over two hours, and the drive across Cedar Island to Beaufort could sometimes add another hour to that.

"Nah, I'm too much whippersnapper for Teague to handle." She laughed, sharp and controlled, almost a bark. "A little distance, well, you understand."

Diane did, and she called him Jason Romney. Except he'd transferred from Carteret to Dare, and now he was on her C-District team. She understood the deputy's meaning, however, that DeSantis and her husband had leaped out of the live well. Maybe not back in the ocean yet, just testing the waters to see if they wanted to be.

Pulling onto the highway, Diane immediately recognized the shape of the truck the deputy and her partner had stopped. Lifted, with fishing rods waving in the air off the back end. What were those fools doing out at this time of the night? "Nubbin" Danny Franklin and "Carrot" Kerry Bertram, teen purveyors of all things obnoxious on the island.

"There." The Hyde County deputy turned on her headlights, what with the dunes shielding them from the water, and the two boys, Nubbin with his hair askew and his clothes stained; and Carrot in orange hair and freckled skin, both stood heads down between Nubbin's daddy's old truck and another deputy's patrol car, white with sheriff slashed down the side in green.

"For all sakes," Diane exclaimed, fighting to keep an exasperated tone from her voice. "You might coulda said it was Nubbin and Carrot."

"You know these two." DeSantis said it hard, a fact and not a question, like she didn't believe it possible, or that she at least should have been warned.

"And their dogs, Simba and Scar." Diane shook her head. What had they done to get stopped *while roaming the highway at midnight?*

"Okay, let's get this moving." DeSantis pulled alongside the boys, put the car in park, and killed the engine. She threw open the door, said to Diane, "Answers, I need answers. Join me, please," and was out and gone.

I could write a book, thought Diane, *and these two would be the clown fish that haunts every page.* She tripped the door latch, pushed the door, only to have the wind fight her. DeSantis, right out. Her door? On the windward side, and the wind was taking no comers. Yet, she forced, the wind buckled, and she was out. The aroma of sea, wet sand, and damp beach grass swirled around her, part of living and working on an island, and was as quickly thrust over the car and into the Sound, only to be replaced by a fresh gust of the same.

DeSantis called to her, "The dogs. Likely an early warning system, we thought. Let them know if someone was coming. But you say you know them." She looked disappointed.

"Sad to say." Diane could almost feel sympathy for the two dejected-looking examples of humanity except for what they had put her through on previous occasions. They were trouble looking for a place to happen.

"This ain't shoofly pie," Deputy DeSantis flung out, the words splattering in the wind, "so let's talk to them. You want to go, or me?"

"You people put your spoon in my pot, so I'll let you have a stir." Diane would as soon throw them in the surf and be done with it. A drug bust ... what else could Nubbin and Carrot find to mess up before the catch was hauled in?

"Okay, moving on." The deputy stepped up to the boys, and when Nubbin started to speak, she held up a hand, palm out, and said, "Talk to the hand," and he shut up like a puckered fish. "Three counties and the Coast Guard taking care of this stretch tonight, and you boys out here roaming this road like you got business out here. It's near midnight. *Midnight.* Open your brain and some knowledge might slip in, you ever think about that? I got me a college degree. What do you got? An old truck and nothing better to do—"

"Deputy DeSantis," Diane interjected, tossing a brick in the roiling pond and hoping to calm the torrent of words.

"Yes, Lieutenant?" The deputy's mouth compressed into a tight line, a predator expression that spoke of anger and frustration. In the glare of the lights from her car, she was a fierce sea goddess about to devour the boys.

"You want to arrest these boys, I'll back you. Do it myself, if you want, but we might oughta stay focused on what's on that beach out there." Diane changed her attention to Nubbin and Carrot. "Boys, I'll bet tomorrow's breakfast your mommas and daddies don't know you're out here. Am I right?"

"Ain't got no daddy," Nubbin groused, his hands thrust deep in his pockets.

"And I ain't got no patience." Diane was, indeed, out of it. "If you tell your story honest, I'll get you on your way home. Otherwise, there's a deputy yonder that wants to cuff you and take you in."

"We heard," Nubbin started, and he looked at Carrot, as if asking for agreement, "that something was going down out thisaways, and here we are. But we're just here for fun, that's all, Officer Turnipseed."

"Carrot, that's how it went?" She looked at him hard.

"Yes'm," he said, cutting his eyes to Nubbin.

"I'm here, Carrot. Nubbin didn't ask you the question."

"Sorry." He shifted his eyes to the ground.

"Sorry, *what?*"

"Sorry, um, ma'am."

"You boys are above your knees. You get in that truck and get on home, and I'll talk to your parents in the morning and ask them what time you walked in the door. Don't think I won't, either. Now, git."

"Ms. Turnipseed?" Nubbin.

"For all sakes, Nubbin, what? I've done said you could go."

"That." He pointed past Diane and Deputy DeSantis toward the beach, and in the moon's glow, the distant sail of a fully rigged yacht pushed south toward the Hatteras Inlet and Ocracoke Island beyond.

"Answers. I see answers," DeSantis said, and she grinned. "Looks like the bad guys are coming in just on time."

From the beach, multiple flashlights appeared, heading toward the highway. Closer, Deputy Sean Taylor, Coast Guard Lieutenant Braxton Sallinger, Deputy Calvin Dingman, and Drone Pilot Deputy Clifton Magruder marched five cuffed men along the highway in heavyweight, rough-looking clothing and black-soled outdoor-type boots.

"Look what the trotline snagged," Sean Taylor called. "We got us a mess of fish to fry."

"You let the boat go?" DeSantis, with dismay and disbelief in her words.

"C'mon, DeSantis. My daddy didn't raise no fool. It's tied

to the pier, a bug in a rug." Lieutenant Braxton Sallinger let out a laugh.

"Somebody's slipping up, Sallinger, and it's not me." She pointed seaward. "There something goes."

Deputy Magruder followed her hand and said, "Hey, Braxton, the lady's right. Down in Morehead, we call that a sailing ship."

Deputy Dingman pulled his cap from his head, ran a hand over his balding scalp, and said, "I'll be ding-danged. Wonder where they're going in the dead of night?"

"Deputy Taylor?" Lieutenant Turnipseed studied the sail, just visible in the yellow moonlight, and she called to him. "You had a look-see down to the beach. Anything I should know about?" She had taken the measure of the five fools marched onshore wearing their iron manacles, although they looked more like stainless steel handcuffs, and she didn't figure they'd planned the operation. They were fish flopping in the net, surprised to be pulled in from the sea, and hoping they would be cut free before they hit the frying pan.

Not likely, she determined, if they had the goods in their vessel secured out on the pier.

"Commitment and respect." Sean Taylor grinned, running up to her, a lightbulb of enthusiasm. "Those guys don't have it. They were yelling and telling us off till Lieutenant Sallinger set 'em straight."

"For all sakes, Deputy, I weren't asking 'bout their school-boy manners. That sailboat out yonder … I'm wanting to keep the fish on the line." With the gusty conditions, it hadn't made much progress, as it was aimed into the wind poorly and the sails were improperly trimmed. Sergeant Mary Wilson would recognize a poorly trimmed sail, but she wasn't here, was she? "Maybe these slimy eels are only a part of the catch. The big'un, that sailboat. Did you look along the beach, find anything washed up?"

"You want me to check, Boss?" Sean fumbled for his flashlight, nearly dropping it while removing it from his equipment belt.

"Hold your taters, Deputy." Diane took a deep breath and looked at Nubbin and Carrot, now sitting on the tailgate of Nubbin's truck, their feet swinging and grins on their faces. With the deputies and Lieutenant Sallinger up from the beach, flashlights were lighted, as no one felt the need to continue to disguise themselves along the road, and the scene was diced into light and dark, with shadows jumping every time someone shifted a light. Deputy DeSantis' headlights were still on, and when people walked through the beams, they painted dark streaks of ink beyond whatever they hit, twisting the liquid night into black streamers whipping in the wind, and people's legs became long, shadowy puddles of velvet darkness.

"Turnipseed?" Deputy DeSantis jostled Diane's elbow. "Last I heard, you got something you're thinking about. You and the deputy there discussing that sailboat. Care to let the rest of us in?"

"Not moving much, is it?" Diane wasn't sure about the woman using her last name, but it didn't seem purposeful, not to make fun, anyway. She'd grown up with that, didn't like it, and wouldn't tolerate it from anyone. Anyway, tonight was for the drug bust, not imagined slights. "Somebody could have dumped something. No one's checked the beach. The deputy and me—"

"I'm with you, Lieutenant." DeSantis turned, called to Deputy Dingman, "Dingman, can you join us?"

"What'cha need, DeSantis?" He was alongside Deputy Magruder, and they were at the bed of Nubbin's truck messing with the dogs.

"You busy, Dingman? I mean, last I heard, the people you

came to haul in done been hauled." Sure enough, the five men from the beach were sitting on the side of the road. The wind was less this side of the dunes, but their clothes still whipped and twisted, masquerading them as dancing marionettes. Three of the men had their heads down, fighting the air tumbling over them and the prickly sand it carried, but with their hands cuffed behind their backs, they were more miserable than successful. "Or, I get it, up on Swan Quarter, you people got maids and butlers to tidy up the loose ends, is that it? Or you want to come earn your paycheck like us island doobies? I need answers, so let's get moving."

"Shucks, Suzanne. Nothin' a taco won't solve." Deputy Dingman laughed, and he turned to Deputy Magruder. "See what we deal with up here? Be glad you're down yonder in Carteret."

"Hey, not no problem." Magruder waved him off. "I got the pups to keep me company. You go keep the deputy happy."

"Okay, you ladies run upon some shingles here? Don't want to ground our boat before we got our lubbers over there booked and locked."

"Deputy Magruder—" Diane stepped in. This was her patrol district, and she didn't intend for that to get away from her, no matter who'd set up this investigation. "—you see anything odd about that sailboat out yonder?"

"It's night. Me, I t'wouldn't be doing that in the dark. But that ain't nothing if they're good at it." He shrugged and spat on the ground, a goop of green tobacco juice that disappeared into the shadows. "Sorry, ladies."

"I might oughta—" Diane looked at the pavement where the spit had landed, and she shook her head and decided to pull up her pants and get on with it. "My Aunt Lucille used to say that when you aim your bow in the right direction, the wind will get you home. That boat out yonder, Deputy, it's not moving, leastwise like it should. Even I can see the sail flopping like an eel out of water. So, the question is, did you big, bad men haul everyone in, or just the shore party?"

"Ooh, Turn-ip-seed!" DeSantis drew the name into three distinct syllables, and she grinned. "Give me an elbow."

Diane scowled at the proffered limb, but she relented enough to smile and shake her head. Instead of bumping the woman's elbow, she pulled out her flashlight, flipped it on, and called to Sean Taylor, "Sean, you're in front. Then DeSantis and me, and Deputy Dingman, you take last." *So you can run away if you get frightened*, she allowed, *without knocking the rest of us off kilter*, but she kept that thought in her head.

Despite Diane's assertation that the yacht was hardly moving, by the time they reached the sand under the pier, it was farther down the shore, with a path like a toddler finding its way down an unfamiliar store aisle, inspecting one side, then wandering to the other and back again, less concerned with the distance traveled than exploring every possible thing along the way.

Swinging her flashlight along the sand, Diane alighted on two craft under the pier and secured to the pilings. They fought for freedom in the wind-driven surf. On the north side of the pier, the smuggler's craft, looking weather beaten and, frankly, like an old shoe dragged from the sand; and on the south, a sleek, functional Coast Guard 29' vessel in orange and black with a central pilothouse, small but perfect for the night's weather conditions. The rising tide would soon eat the sand, and she suspected waders would be a prized possession when it came time to reboard … then, wet pant legs were an option, too. *Talk about being above your knees. Sallinger, don't wait too long.*

Diane smirked, and she turned to Suzanne DeSantis and said, "Those two boys up yonder on the highway? We might could put 'em to work." They'd wanted to come play in the surf.

Well, she was about to dump it on 'em.

"How'ya thinking, Turnipseed?" The wind was still blustery, and Deputy DeSantis leaned in to be heard.

"Hold on," Diane said, and she pulled her radio from her belt. Sean Taylor had vanished into the gloom, and as his flashlight was pointed away from her, even that was now invisible. "Sean, you there? Over."

"It's me. That you, Lieutenant?" The radio thumped, then Deputy Taylor returned with, "Sorry. I dropped my radio. I'm good now. It is you, Lieutenant, right? Oh, sorry, over."

"You thinking someone else told you to turn on your radio, Deputy? What are you doing down yonder, having a party? If so, can you locate Nubbin and Carrot to meander down here and give us some backup?"

"Nubbin and Carrot?" Sean sounded confused. "When we headed down, the deputies up to the road were about to have them call their parents, maybe get someone to come drive Nubbin's truck—"

"Hold your taters, Sean. Them boys said they were here for some fun, so let's give 'em some. Head up, plant a flashlight on 'em, and I'll be waitin'. Tell 'em the tide's arising and they're liable to get their feet wet if they don't scurry on down."

"Yes, ma'am. On the double, Lieutenant. You can count on me—"

"One, two, three—"

"Aw, Lieutenant, you know what I mean—"

"It's not like I weren't listening. You, Deputy, now!"

"Yes'm. Taylor out."

Deputy DeSantis laughed. "You got one of those, too, huh?"

"He's growing on me. Like a barnacle on a turtle's shell. Didn't ask for it and can't flick it off, so might as well learn to live with it." Diane found a bit of camaraderie in DeSantis' biting assessment, and she let herself smile. Down the sand, a light bobbed like a dinghy in the surf, clearly Taylor headed their direction.

"We got Dingman down in Hyde," DeSantis began. "Same story. Okay, let's get this—"

Before the Hyde County deputy could finish, her Swan Quarter compatriot interrupted, his flashlight following Sean Taylor's legs heading back through the cut in the dunes towards the highway, asking, "Where's he going? Thought we were combing the beach for clues."

"Extra feet on the sand, Deputy," Diane said. "Maybe get this done before the sun peeks over the dunes."

"Shucks, just asking, Lieutenant. Now, I don't know this beach like my own backyard, so's things might be normal as cod on a plate, but down there—" He pointed his flashlight south. The tight beam reached a good eighth mile and captured glistening, swirling sparkles hovering just above the sand, with roiling layers of foam blowing off the tops of the incoming waves. It had collected on the sides of the dunes, but in one location, in the center of the sandy beach, something had snagged the foam like a lobster trap on the seafloor. "Thinkin' that might be something."

Activity from the cut in the dunes drew their attention away, when two wildly swinging flashlights appeared, with a final one marginally more in control following some distance behind. The third flashlight dropped to the ground, and Sean Taylor could just be heard saying, "Shoot, not again," before kneeling to pick it up.

"Hey, Officer Turnipseed," one wild flashlight called, leaping forward and planting feet in the sand directly in front of her.

"Me, too," the other flashlight yelled before joining his friend.

"So," Diane began. "You two boys came by just for fun. Did I hear that right?"

"Yes, ma'am," they chimed as one.

"You want to help out?" The admission was important. No coercion. She didn't need *that* complaint from their parents. She winced as their dancing flashlights glared in her face more than once.

"Yes'm," this time with more enthusiasm.

"Simba and Scar, how about them?" It wouldn't do for the two dogs to be off creating havoc while the boys were occupied on the beach.

"We need them?" That was from Nubbin. "The deputy didn't say—"

"I can go up—" Carrot joined him.

"Or just call to them—" Nubbin smacked Carrot's arm with his fist.

"Yeah, that would do—" Carrot.

"Boys!" Diane called it hard to get their attention. It was clear the dogs weren't secured, and that's what she had asked. "The dogs will stay up yonder, even with you down here?"

"Yes, ma'am. They're good dogs." Nubbin nodded reassuringly.

"The best, Ms. Turnipseed," Carrot added.

"Then just you two are all the clamdiggers we need. Those flashlights," and she grasped Nubbin's to steady it, then Carrot's, "are key. You boys got sharp eyes and that might can help us out—"

"Yes, ma'am, the best. Right, Carrot?" Nubbin nudged his friend with his elbow.

"Anything. We can find it."

"That's what I want to hear." Diane shone her flashlight towards Officer Calvin Dingman's mound of seafoam. The first surge of regret at calling in the two rambunctious hoodlums pricked her, and she pushed aside her irritation. The truth was, the teens likely did have sharper vision, and they spent so much time on the island's beaches that they would know what was supposed to be there and what wasn't. "Deputy Dingman?"

"Waiting on you, Lieutenant."

"For all sakes, you hanging over my shoulder?" The man's voice was in Diane's left ear, and she considered that DeSantis had been pegging the truth pretty hard. Dare County might have Sean Taylor, but Hyde County was chucking sand at a furious rate with Calvin Dingman.

"T'wouldn't be how I'd call it, ma'am." The deputy lifted his black cap and rubbed his balding scalp with one hand and nodded respectfully. "Just wantin' to get those guys up there on the highway booked and locked so's we can get on home. What'cha need?"

"These boys, walk 'em down that direction so they can gander a look-see at that." She aimed her flashlight to peg the seafoam in the middle of the beach. "DeSantis, you willing to head north with me?"

"Absolutely. Let's get this moving." The deputy stamped her feet, revealing a higher level of impatience than her words suggested.

"Taylor?" The man was missing again, and Diane probed the darkness with her light. "Deputy Taylor!"

"Here, ma'am."

She turned toward the boats tied to the pilings underneath the pier, and he stood on the bow of the Coast Guard's 29-footer, grinning like an adolescent teen out crabbing in the mud and happy to be there.

"Deputy Taylor, that boat's not ours nor a bathtub toy. I might oughta—" She turned to Deputy DeSantis and shook her head.

"I've got this, ma'am." DeSantis called to Taylor, "Last I heard, Deputy, that's a Coast Guard boat. You signing up?"

"Maybe," he called. "I never got to be on one of these.

Possibly—"

Diane interrupted to put him straight. "You're above your knees now, Deputy." She glanced at DeSantis. "Literally. You willing to make a trade?"

"For Dingman?" DeSantis laughed. "Last I heard, fish in a skillet all cook up the same. We'll keep the one we brought."

"So, that's a big no." Diane's shoulders fell. She called to Sean, "Taylor, make a change and be the man your parents hoped you'd become. Off that boat, and how did you get aboard and keep your feet dry?"

"Long jump, ma'am. I'm good at it."

"Long jump? You? When?"

"High school, ma'am. Took first at state. Want to see?" He backed up, leaned forward, and loosened his pants at his knees. He clapped his hands together and rubbed them briskly.

"You're above your knees on this'un, Taylor."

"Gotta get off," he called, grinning. "Unless you expect me to wade. Give me some space." He motioned, visually pushing them aside with his hands.

Calvin Dingman had yet to move off down the beach, although the lights of the two teens jabbed the darkness as they played at searching the sand. One pushed the other toward the incoming surf, and they both tumbled into a dune before retrieving a downed flashlight and calling out, "We're okay. Just dropped the light," while dancing the flashlights once more.

"I'll be ding-danged," Dingman called to Sean, evaluating the distance to dry sand. "That ain't nothing. Shucks, you give it enough runup, and you can get clean across. Evel Knievel, why, he did Snake River. Bam!" He slapped his hands together, startling both Diane and Suzanne DeSantis. "Right across."

"Yeah, Dingman. I got me a college degree. What do you got? A story about a daredevil, and you can't even tell it right. So, zip the lip." DeSantis traced a finger across her mouth, one side to the other.

"Shucks, Suzanne. What did I say wrong this time?" Dingman spit snuff juice again, this time hitting right at the edge of the water, and an incoming wave ate the green waste.

"Open your brain, Dingman. The man holed his ship before he reached the far shore. How come you can't know that?"

"Cause I don't got a college degree." He had his can of snuff out, and he twisted the top open to pinch out a portion.

"I think you got that right. And that trash you're slipping in your mouth." DeSantis shuddered. "Head on down, Calvin. Those boys down there likely need you."

She was right. Now they were on a dune, and one—which they couldn't see—was at the top, and they heard him yell, "I'm king of the world!"

Diane rubbed her hands over her face, and she shook her head. "I bet tomorrow's breakfast I regret this whole night. Sean, get down here, wet feet or no."

"Yes'm. Y'all all back plenty far? I'm coming in."

Flashlights were aimed at the sand and guiding their move away from Deputy Taylor's impact zone, so no one actually saw him do his runup and leap, but his feet impacted the deck several times in loud, repeated thumps; his flashlight went wild as a hooked fish; and he yelled, "Aieee!" After a few moments of silent flight, his feet slammed into the sand just clear of an especially vigorous wave.

Diane had her light on him by then, and she marveled at the distance and that he had remained upright. Then, he teetered, tottered, and with his arms flailing, slowly fell backwards. A moment later and his clothing would have remained dry, but his backside caught the water just before it receded, and he hit with a soupy splash.

"We, Deputy," she drawled, "drew back plenty far. It's not like we weren't listening, now was it? You couldn't dodge even one little wave. It seems to me someone planted their sharks in the collards, and high tide ain't even arrived yet."

"You're telling me." Sean jumped up and brushed his pants with the hand holding his flashlight, only to make his clothes more pitiful than if he'd left things alone.

"Lieutenant Diane Turnipseed," a voice called from the dunes.

"Turnipseed here," she called back, working to place the voice. "That you, Sallinger?"

"Put your money on it, ma'am. Halsey's here with his dog. Wants to know if he can come down and have a go at that boat we pulled in. You people have anything going on he might disrupt?"

Halsey was Sergeant Zack Halsey from up in Swan Quarter. He was a K9 handler, and his dog, Goldie, was specially trained in drugs, the reason Cynthia Ellison and Toby, C-District's K9 handler and German shepherd, weren't present.

"For all sakes, Sallinger, get Sergeant Halsey on down here. You people need to check the tide tables. This pier's about to be inundated, but then it's your boots you gotta keep dry."

"I got that, ma'am." The Coast Guard lieutenant laughed, less with humor than a challenge, suggesting that he might give in to Diane's authority on Hatteras Island, but the sea was all his. "Halsey," he called. "C'mon, man. You've got a beach down here and a boat about to be swamped. The tide's not getting any lower just cause you got a case of the shakes."

"Shakes?" A tall man, stick thin and towing a golden retriever on a leash, appeared. He held a big flashlight, and in the glow of the massive lamp, his black cap with Sheriff Hyde County in orange and gold hung at his waist, and his hair was topped with a cowboy-style hat with a rolled brim and decorated with a feather. He glanced at the beach, in the direction he'd come from, and wiped his face with a bandana. "Where's the boat I'm to inspect?"

"Ah, Halsey," Sallinger teased. "There's three types of men. The sort that likes a challenge, the sort that doesn't and takes it on anyway, and the sort that turns tail and runs. You a runner, Halsey?"

"Just like keeping my feet on the sand. You know that, Braxton." Braxton was Lieutenant Sallinger's first name. "It's why you're with the Guard and I'm up in Swan Quarter. Goldie and me, we got this, though. I'll get her on it, and she'll take the lead. Just got to get my head around it, that's all."

"That's a good man. You and the dog have a go at it." Sallinger chuckled, then suggested, "Lieutenant Turnipseed there says you might need a pair of rubbers on. Tide's rolling in and ready to get your feet wet."

"Not a thing anyone can do about. Besides, I come fully prepared." Zack pointed his light at his feet to reveal thick Wellies nearly to his knees.

As Sergeant Halsey maneuvered across the sand, Diane joined him. The wind had gotten stronger, and it pummeled them, whipping their hair and clothes, and forcing Zack Halsey to hold onto his cowboy hat. She leaned in to speak to the tall, rail-thin man. "Here's what we got, Sergeant. Deputy Taylor and I—"

"Ma'am, just Zack, if you please."

"What's that?"

"My name. I know that Braxton, well, Lieutenant Sallinger, if you prefer, likes to shake around my last name, but I'm a first-name type, if you don't mind."

"So that's … for all sakes." Diane stumbled on her words, glared at Deputy Taylor, who was grinning with more teeth than a shark, and said, "Our boat is there, south of the pier." She lifted her light and caught the orange and black vessel in the beam. "Yonder on the north side of the pier is the one you want. You might need them Wellies. The tide's done come in two feet just since we've been here. Good luck, um, Zack."

"You people sticking around?" Zack looked dubious each time the waves pushed close to their feet.

"Deputy Taylor—"

"Sean," the C-District deputy interjected.

"*Sean,*" Diane stressed, "can keep you company. Deputy DeSantis and I are headed north. South," the direction she turned her flashlight, "we've got two volunteers. Deputy Dingman is headed down to keep them from flopping overboard, or," and she called to Deputy Dingman, "did you already roll over for dead, Deputy?"

"Ouch, Lieutenant Turnipseed. You done been hanging around DeSantis too long. Nothin' happening around here a taco won't solve. But before I bite into another layer of spicy, I'm gone." The man spat green muck into the surf and turned to head the direction of the two boys.

ZACK HALSEY was halfway to the dope runners' boat, with the black surf whipping against his rubber boots and Goldie in his arms, when a commotion from the southern direction of the beach stirred the air like a sea turtle swimming into a school of anchovies.

"We found something, Officer Turnipseed!" By the voice, it was Nubbin, though all they could really see was a flashlight whipping like a strand of police tape in the wind.

"More than one something," a second voice called, which by the process of elimination must be Carrot.

"Deputy Dingman, stop those boys!" Diane yelled the command, even as the wind sucked the words from her lips. Knowing them, they were bringing whatever it was back with them, rather than leaving it in place for the professionals to observe in situ. Maybe allowing the two teens onto the beach was more muck-up than she had anticipated, though with the late hour and this wind, who could think, much less anticipate what rambunctious ruffians like Nubbin and Carrot might get up to?

By the time their flashlights were close enough to make out the individual boys, Suzanne DeSantis was in front of Diane, and she flashed her light into their faces, startling them, and demanding, "Get it together, boys. You're wild as fish in a skillet. First, what'd you find, and second, did you leave it there?"

"Officer Turnipseed," Nubbin called, as he tried to dart around DeSantis.

"Talk to the hand." DeSantis held up her open palm directly in front of his face. "I'm asking the questions, so zip the lip, and let's get this moving. One, what? You, with the orange hair, what did you boys find?"

"Officer Turnipseed?" Carrot called.

"Nubbin, Carrot, this is Deputy DeSantis from up to Hyde County—"

"Down to," DeSantis corrected, "but I'll let that stand."

"Anyways," Diane shot her a look, "she's been invited to have a look-see at what we got going on, so yes, boys, please answer her questions."

"So, answers. Nubbin—" with a roll of her eyes, "and Carrot, you found what? Treasure, maybe, a downed airplane, perhaps a WWII torpedo?" She turned to Diane with a smirk.

"Give it a rest, DeSantis," Diane muttered. There was still talk in the surrounding counties about an explosion in the dunes just south of Avon that Dare County had never managed to confirm as unexploded war ordnance or not.

DeSantis laughed, a short bark, before turning back to the boys. "Well?"

"There's a jacket—" Carrot began when his friend nodded

and interrupted him.

"One of those things, you know, that ya' wear around your waist." Nubbin did a thing with his hands at his beltline, encircling an imaginary donut.

"To float—"

"Yeah, out of the water, so's—"

"Ya' don't drown." Carrot finished up the back-and-forth muck-up, and the boys looked at each other and grinned, like they'd just ended a tournament and hauled in the biggest catch of all time. Their flashlights finally settled to the sand at their feet, revealing how close the tide was bringing the waves to where they stood.

"Boys, this way." DeSantis motioned with her light for them to move closer to the dunes before she quizzed them once again. "Someone's slipping up here, and it's not me. Am I getting this right? You're talking a life preserver?"

"Yeah!" Carrot jerked his neck in a hard nod, and he turned to Nubbin and repeated, "Yeah, that's how we say it."

"I knew that." Nubbin cuffed his friend's shoulder. He called past Deputy DeSantis, "Officer Turnipseed, I knew that. Carrot just wouldn't shut up for me to have a turn to say it."

Diane had listened to 'em both spout pretty good, two little sperm whales trolling up and down the beach, shouting *King of the Mountain* when they was supposed to be looking for clues on the sand. Still, like a flea collar on a ship's rat, anything that does some good, even if it's just one varmint keeping a lot of smaller ones at bay, well, you couldn't argue with that.

"Did you boys answer Deputy DeSantis' second question?" The deputy acknowledged Diane's support with a raised eyebrow.

"Um," they began, both talking at the same time, and they looked at their empty hands before realizing they only held their flashlights, and they looked back down the beach. "It's back there a ways." They pointed with outstretched arms and grinned.

"You good, Turnipseed? I'm ready to head down and get this moving." DeSantis shifted position, pausing for Diane's signal to step that direction, and her big watch caught one of the boy's flashlights and glinted in the dark.

"You might oughta head on, and I'll follow." Diane didn't even get to shift her feet in the sand when a voice called to her, clear even over the reverberating surf tearing at the beach.

"Officer Turnipseed, hold up there, if you please."

"Halsey, you talking to me?" She searched the opposite side of the pier but couldn't locate him, and she turned back to find DeSantis already moving down the beach, her light swinging back and forth in a controlled pattern; and the boys with their erratic lights putting some real distance between them. DeSantis was already too far away for her to call to, and she couldn't be both places at once. She debated for the barest of moments before taking a deep breath and choosing Halsey. She stepped under the pier and was caught off guard, despite her warning about the incoming tide, to see how far out the boat was.

"Catch this line, Lieutenant," Halsey called. "My Wellies, well, I want to remain dry if at all possible."

"I'll bet tomorrow's breakfast you do." She was yelling, but she also knew the wind was blowing his words to her. Hers were being ripped from her and flung back towards the dunes. She figured Halsey was having more trouble catching her words than she was his, but he laughed.

"Yes, ma'am. I like that. It's coming hard."

It landed at her feet, with two coils still wrapped, and she pulled it up, wrapped it around her arm, and pulled it taut.

"Wrap a piling, ma'am. Then I'll untie down here and pull myself that direction. Yell when you're ready."

"Those boys down there said they found a life preserver. From this boat, you think?" She called the question over the tumbling water but didn't really expect an answer. When she had the piling wrapped, she yelled, "Ready," even though she could no longer see his light. She figured he'd laid it down to free both his hands, which was what any sane waterman would do. The bow of the boat appeared out of the darkness, and the water swirled blackly underneath. Halsey was going hand over fist, over and over, and the boat stopped suddenly with an audible squeal as it impacted the sand. A high wave retreated and left the bow sitting dry.

"That's a good one." Halsey grinned, called, "Goldie, down," and leaped to dry sand. The dog appeared and tumbled down after him. She was unleashed, and she ran into the dunes, likely to do her business. Halsey took the line, unwrapped it from the piling, and moved it to the next one and tied it with a firm knot. "Glad to get my feet on the sand. A life preserver, you say?" He didn't look up when he asked it.

"To tell the story honest, they're down there now with DeSantis. She's the one that'll have the updated story." Diane shrugged, looked for the dog, and saw it returning to the Hyde County K9 handler.

"Found something even more interesting." He adjusted his cowboy hat, pulled a leash from his pocket, and clipped it around Goldie's neck. He knelt, tussled her around the ears, said, "Good girl," and offered her a treat before standing.

"It's not like I weren't listening, now is it?" Diane waited, aware that each of the counties represented on her beach had something to bring to the fish fry, and some of it might be worth eatin' on, if she could just be patient. She did, however, want the man to dump it on her, whatever he was waffling on about.

"How many men you got up there?"

"The dope runners?" They weren't hers, not like someone she'd rounded up and wrestled into a patrol car, but she answered anyway. "Five's what I counted. You seen 'em,

Deputy."

"Zack, if you please."

"Certainly, Zack." Certainly she'd pinch his ears, if he didn't spit out what he wasn't saying.

"The stuff in that boat, ma'am, is set up for six men. Even the lockers for the life preservers. And Goldie and me, we found evidence that six men been on that boat, and recently." He nodded knowingly.

"Like tonight." Spit it out, man, she wanted to say.

"Yes, ma'am, only where's number six? When you asked me that question about the preserver, my mind pictured the inside of this boat, with space for six preservers and only five still hanging there. If that one out there ... well, you get what I'm saying, don't'cha, Lieutenant?"

Diane was pretty sure she did. They might very well have a sixth drug smuggler roaming the beaches on her island with no one the wiser except Deputy Halsey and her. And it was after midnight, the wind was blustering her to death, and she was ready for a shower. *This*, she thought to herself, *is going to be a very long night.*

"Lieutenant Sallinger?" she called at the top of her voice. "You might hold onto your taters while I tell you this, 'cause you're not gonna want to know the kettle of fish Deputy Halsey just dumped on the beach for us to skin and fry."

DEPUTY DESANTIS made it back from her excursion with Nubbin and Carrot, although from her looks, barely. If it were possible to feel empathy for a woman who was as quick, efficient, and as strong a personality as herself, Diane would have bled it out at the point DeSantis barked out a sour laugh, pointed through the dunes, and called roughly, "I told you boys the last time, this isn't shoofly pie. Open your brain for the first time in your life, and you might learn something. Get up to the road, turn in those flashlights, and I don't want to hear another joke from you two."

"They givin' you a run for it?" Diane grinned. She'd been run through the fish ladder so many times by the teens that she forgot how tough it could be for a newbie who didn't know how to reel 'em in and chuck 'em in a fish basket to where they couldn't flop free.

"Absolutely. I'll tell you what, Turnipseed, I know I say fish in a skillet all cook up the same, but those two. If I had those two on my stringer, I believe I'd toss the whole line back in just to be free of them."

Diane laughed but moved into her real question. "Y'all came back with an empty collection pail, so nothing that direction? I got ambushed here by Halsey, and Deputy Taylor is off to the north side of the pier somewhere, though he might be out way-laid in the surf, for all I can tell. I can't keep up with him."

"No, there's something, a life jacket like they said." DeSantis checked her chunky watch and grimaced. "Sure is late to get someone out here, but I'm thinking it might be something. Anyways, I marked it and thought I'd check to see who Dare's got in forensics. Ours is in Swan, and that's three hours on a good ferry schedule, and you and I both know that after mid-night, there's no good ferry schedule."

"Emily Bryant might be available." Diane understood DeSantis' remarks to mean that she wanted photographs. If there was more, a body perhaps, the deputy would have been on the radio getting a team down already. It was a thing, a method understood in police work that didn't have to be filleted and deboned every time it leaped onto the hook. She cautioned, "She's up in Kill Devil Hills. That's an hour from here."

"Better than three. Halsey," she called, "what's with the boat? You moved one of 'em and not the other. And where's Goldie?" She turned to Diane and said, "People from up in Swan

— 29 —

don't get the island thing. Up there's land and people. Down here, the ocean eats everything not tied down. Gotta keep 'em in line."

"You check on Halsey, and I'll round up my deputy." Diane pulled her walkie from her belt and pushed the talk button. "Taylor? Turnipseed here. You got yours turned on? Turnipseed over."

Her handheld unit buzzed, bleeding the sound of the wind, and it replied, "Deputy Taylor here. I'm … I'm sorry, Lieutenant …" Then came the clear sound of someone losing his supper.

"Taylor?" Diane released the talk button, and when nothing came through except the wind, jabbed it again. "Taylor, talk to me!"

"Yes ma'am." She could hear him spit. "I'm back, ma'am. My apologies. That was a rough one, but I'm here to serve, a hundred percent of the time—" and his words devolved into the sounds of upchucking again.

"Where are you, Taylor?" She held the unit to her face and nearly yelled into it."

"Here, ma'am. This way."

A light flashed through the pilings, and she thought, *For all sakes, the man is truly waylaid in the surf. What's he getting up to next?* Then she realized it was coming from the smugglers' boat. She found her way back to the north side of the pier to discover Sean Taylor standing on the bow of the craft, swaying, and about to tumble onto the sand.

"For all sakes, Taylor. What's got into you? Why are you on that boat?"

"Sorry, ma'am. A little green in the gills. Don't want to splash you, so you might stand back a bit."

"You might oughta get down, Taylor."

"Sean, ma'am, please." He smiled weakly, then he held his

stomach and gagged. Nothing came up, and he leaped down and landed on his knees. "Sand, precious sand," he exhaled, rubbing his hands over the damp surface.

"Explain yourself," and she spat out his name for emphasis, "Sean."

"You said to keep the K9 handler company, so when he got on the boat—" He covered his mouth and closed his eyes for a moment.

"You had to follow." She let out a tired sigh.

"You did say—"

"I know what I said." She looked around to see who else might be watching. "Did you learn anything, *Sean*?" Like to use common sense, the kind God gave even minnows?

"I learned I get seasick in the hold of a boat."

"And when Halsey was having me retie the boat? You were down there the entire time?" That she didn't have figured out. It seemed Halsey would have said something.

"I was too embarrassed to tell him I was in the head puking. I said I was—"

"Puking in the head?" Destroying evidence is what he was doing. What was already down that toilet might be the drugs these suckers were trying to flush away.

"I'll be okay now." Sean stood, holding onto the bow, and he brushed off his knees. Then he felt his belt and said in dismay, "My flashlight. I must'a left it in the boat."

"You get up yonder and retrieve it. I've got a call to make to Emily, and likely Hyde County's gonna want to know everything."

"Boss, you can't expect me to climb back on that boat—"

"More'n expect, Deputy. I order you to. That flashlight is county property, and if'n it needs replaced, it's out of your pay. And make sure your belt is fully accounted for when you climb back out. No more forays aboard."

She watched him climb back onto the bow, and she felt no sympathy when he realized he didn't have a light to search for his. His wail of dismay rolled off her like water off a duck's back, slick and fast, and with as little concern for his obvious apprehension and discomfort.

DIANE PULLED out her cell phone rather than her police radio to contact Emily Bryant.

The walkie was useless this far out, and Ashley Dixon at the C-District sub-station in Buxton did go home to her husband, Todd, from time to time, which was where Diane expected her to be at one in the morning. And she didn't know who was on dispatch up in Manteo on Roanoke Island, it being well past midnight, and sometimes it was easier to just dial direct. She tapped Emily's number and steeled herself when it began to ring. Yes, Emily expected to be called before the sun peeked over the dunes, but for all sakes, the sun had barely set the other side of the Sound.

"Emily here." Loud music flashed pinpoints of sound in the background.

"Guess'n you're not in bed." Diane breathed relief.

"Ah, no, um, Lieutenant?" In the background, Emily called over the music, *My boss, I'm pretty sure.*

"Might be spoiling the rest of your evening. And yes, it's me."

"My morning, maybe. Did you notice the time?"

"Let me dump it on ya'. You remember those drug runners we've been wrestling to haul in?"

"The collaboration, right? With Hyde, and maybe Carteret. I don't remember if Beaufort County was in on it."

"Might oughta keep 'em all in the pot, as they're on the stringer. Sheriff Pafford's parked up on the highway—"

"Hyde County Pafford?" Emily laughed. "It's that big, huh?

Are y'all down to the Avon Pier?"

"That's a big yes. And we think we might'a lost a man."

"One of the dopeheads." Emily laid it out, something she was good at. As the county forensics investigator and a sworn deputy, she could nail a situation with a dart gun and rarely miss, that is when she wasn't pranking people just to see them squirm.

"Suzanne DeSantis from Hyde wants photos of some evidence—"

"Sure. Just tape it off. I can drive down first thing, that is unless it's a dead body."

"If you want the story honest, I'd rather have a body. Now I expect we got one running loose on the island. I'd druther the bad guys not be sharing the island with the rest of us. Back to the evidence. The deputy is thinking tonight—"

"Okay, just for fun, Lieutenant, tell me why Suzanne thinks her evidence needs me there tonight. I'll do it if you ask, but it is late. Evidence doesn't go anywhere in six hours, and I'll be up by then. And rested."

"Three words. Island. Beach. Tide." And sand, life preserver, and who knew what else, especially with Nubbin and Carrot involved. Diane closed her eyes for a moment, boxing up and packing away the sounds of the shore just for a bit. Tonight, the wind and surf weren't her friends. Her pillow was, and it wasn't anywhere nearby.

"Hold on, Lieutenant." Emily could be heard talking to someone, explaining why she had to leave.

For a moment, Diane regretted whatever she was disturbing. A party? Late supper? It didn't matter. Whatever, she appreciated the investigator's willingness to jump aboard as soon as she approached the dock.

"Avon. Are you actually at the pier?" Emily's tone had shifted into law enforcement mode.

"You'll find us. We got cars from all over, like a

convocation of crows along 12. Hold for a moment." Diane's walkie was squawking at her, and she picked it up, holding the phone in one hand and the walkie in the other. "Turnipseed here. Over."

"This is Darlene up on the road. You still down there at the beach?"

"You got that right, Sheriff Pafford. How's the situation up there?"

"I already fixed all this. Just threw it in the warsh—" adding an extra "r" in the word, an Ohio thing from her formative years, "—and it's come out fine. Zack tells me we're missing one of our drug runners."

"There's that chance, Sheriff. I'm on the line with my forensic investigator to come out and photograph a clue Deputy DeSantis uncovered."

"She said that." Sheriff Pafford drew in a deep breath and let it out. "You people saw that sail go by?"

"Yes." Diane had no idea where the sheriff was headed, and she kept her input to a minimum until she got a feel for the current. She also glanced at her phone and Emily's name on the screen and wondered how much she was hearing of this. Likely all of it if the wind wasn't scrubbing the sound from the device.

"That boat's made its way down to Ocracoke. Don't ask me how or if it's even still afloat, but my radio says it appears to be empty."

"Empty … as in cargo or," and Diane couldn't fathom she was imagining something so bizarre, "empty as in people?"

"Down south in Kentucky—" as seen from an Ohio native, the sheriff implied, "they say someone's running around like a chicken with its head cut off, and that's how this feels." Sheriff Pafford chuckled, but it ended sourly. "The boat's empty like a freshly scrubbed spittoon."

"Did the captain indicate a problem—" People did sail solo

from time to time.

"Like I said, a freshly scrubbed spittoon. Empty."

"Hold your taters, Sheriff. You're saying that sail we saw out yonder about when the Coast Guard was pulling in their catch just docked in Ocracoke slick-empty, not even a captain?"

"Didn't say it docked, but you're not coloring with the wrong color crown." Crown was how Sheriff Pafford pronounced the wax coloring stick. "Tell me, do you have the authority here, or does this go to Sheriff Kringlebach?"

Morton Kringlebach. Diane winced as she repeated the name in her head. The explosion in the dune that had injured Steven Hill, the medical examiner from Raleigh, well, Sheriff Kringlebach still wanted answers, and C-District hadn't been able to give them.

"Diane? If you want to dodge this deer, I can call him up like I never talked to you. He can road trip me back to you if he doesn't want to get on board with me."

"No." Diane processed and decided. "The sharks'll be in the collards for certain then. I heard once that what's in Vegas sticks in Vegas, and down here in C-District, we do it the same. What's in C-District stays in C-District."

"Not exactly the way I heard it but the point's clear. It's like we say back in Ohio, Miracle Whip, mayo, what's the difference? It's all in the sandwich."

"Meaning?" Diane had never heard that one, not even from Darlene Pafford.

"I deal with you." *And not Morton Kringlebach.*

"I like that color crayon, Sheriff Pafford."

"You and me, both. Now, how soon can that forensic investigator of yours get here? We've got a ferry to Ocracoke to catch, and I want you aboard."

"She's on the line—"

"And in the car," Emily called from the phone. "Twenty

minutes away."

"Thanks, Emily," Diane said into her phone, and to the walkie, "Twenty minutes, Sheriff."

"Okay. Darlene out."

The first ferry to Ocracoke hit the waves about dawn. Diane rubbed her eyes, looked towards the sea, and considered if a bit of shuteye was an option. Then she heard Sean Taylor calling, and she turned toward the dunes and headed that direction.

Chapter 2

Crossing Ocracoke Inlet

DEPUTY SEAN TAYLOR stood alongside his lifted Jeep in the priority line for the Ocracoke ferry. His back tires, courtesy of the Dare County Sheriff's Office and Tire Choice in Manteo over on Roanoke Island, still boasted the manufacturer's vent spews, the rubber hairs found on every new tire. Atop the roof, a slender light bar proclaimed the vehicle for what it was, the deputy's patrol car, although Sean owned and maintained it. Well, except for the back tires, as he had shot them out during a chase when Nubbin Franklin and Carrot Bertram attempted to carjack him and would have if he hadn't taken out the tires as they pulled away. Overhead, swirling, soot-stained clouds, barely visible in the darkness, blanketed the ferry landing, but to the east over the trees, along the horizon, a hint of pink at the world's edge suggested the morning to come.

"Red sky in the morning ..." Sean grinned, already enthused with the day. The old ditty finished up with *sailor's warning,* suggesting bad weather on the way, but Ocracoke! Here he was, with Lieutenant Turnipseed, Emily Bryant, and Sheriff Pafford, all on the same team.

Was it an Impact Team? Like when they had found the dead man up by Bodie Lighthouse? No one had said so yet, but he was here, a part, and ready to serve a hundred percent.

Behind him, Emily Bryant was inside her white personal sedan. She was just visible, as it was dark in her car. He'd offered her his county cruiser to use, but no, she preferred her own, she had assured him, as well as the stipend she received for not driving a county vehicle. Sean didn't receive a stipend for using his Jeep as his patrol car, but then he had a county vehicle, just one he refused to drive.

Behind Emily, Lieutenant Turnipseed and Sheriff Pafford were in separate vehicles, with the lieutenant in her black Ford Explorer, unmarked, and the sheriff in a massive black Dodge truck, also unmarked, but with a slender light bar across the top of the cab. She wasn't an Outer Banker, and while Ocracoke Island might be part of the sheriff's Hyde County jurisdiction, she would be heading back to the mainland and Swan Quarter from Silver Lake at the southern end of the island when they were done.

Deputy Clifton Magruder, drone pilot on loan from Carteret County, would be heading over on a later ferry. With the discovery of the life preserver in Avon, he wanted to wait until full light and hope for a break in the wind. He'd volunteered to show Sean how the drone worked, saying, "Sean, you need one of these," and, "I'll show you how it's done." Was Sean interested? Of course he was and had suggested to Lieutenant Turnipseed that he could wait and accompany the Carteret County deputy over later in the morning. She had started in, "For all sakes—" and Sean had flopped belly up like a catfish. He'd shrugged to Clifton and said, "Maybe when you get to

Ocracoke?" Sean was certain, *certain* there would be plenty of drone-appropriate scenarios that could crop up on Ocracoke. Like that sailboat from the night before. With no pilot? Completely empty? The mystery of it sent shivers of excitement up and down his spine.

He strolled to Emily's car, casually as though monitoring the ferry employees and how long until they would be loading. He also checked on the lieutenant and the sheriff. They were outside Pafford's black truck, talking and ignoring him, about what he didn't know. Emily was more amenable, though she did like to prank him, and that wasn't always fun. If she rolled down her window and wanted to talk, however, he wouldn't mind.

Her window released with a sucking sound, the glass pulling out of the rubber seal along the top, and it dropped about four inches. "Yes, Sean?"

"Hey, Emily. This is exciting." He grinned and rubbed his hands together.

"It's cold. That's why my windows are up. Anything specific, or do you just want to chat?" She yawned and rolled the window down another four inches. "Sorry, Sean. Short night."

"Were you napping?"

"Nah, I just like to sit in the dark waiting on the crack-of-dawn ferry to an island an hour away. Okay, I'm waking up." The window went the rest of the day down, but she pulled the collar of her jacket tighter around her neck. Her hair caught in a gust, and from the water, muffled bird sounds reminded them that they were at the shore, they were surrounded by water, and the weather, if it decided to turn, could do so in a whim—and no human within sight or hearing had any choice in the matter.

"I'm thinking this might be an Impact Team." He leaned in and put his arms on her windowsill and glanced towards the lieutenant and the sheriff. "The four of us and maybe Clifton. That's exciting."

"Magruder?" Emily laughed. "How is he on our 'Impact Team' anyway?" She emphasized the words. "He's from two counties away."

"I know. He offered to show me how to use his drone." He laughed again and said, "You know I'm all about commitment and respect—"

"A hundred percent-type guy. You tell everybody. So, Sean, go on."

"I've got no regrets about being in Dare County, but Clifton offering to teach me—"

"Let it rest, Sean. Spend some time on the sand and get over yourself. Clifton is just a nice guy. He doesn't mean anything by it, just being friendly." She smiled. "Besides, I like you, and we're already on the same team."

"You like to prank me." Sean felt his expression sour.

"Oops, look." She pointed ahead. "Ferry's about to load. I'll see you onboard," and her window began to close.

Behind her, the lieutenant was already in her Explorer, and Sean caught Sheriff Pafford closing the door of her black Dodge. Now alone, and the only one still outside his vehicle, a ferry employee called to him, "You! This Jeep yours? We're loading in two minutes. If you want on, you need to be inside."

"Thank you," Sean called out, jogged that way, and pulled himself inside. "I choose to serve … no regrets … I've got this," he said aloud, as he checked his mirrors and started the Jeep.

But being outside and having to be reminded? And at the front of the line? Where everyone could see? He liked to say he "had this," but sometimes, he wasn't so certain he did.

"YOU THERE, Taylor?"

Sean jumped as his walkie talkie blurted out his name. The boondoggle of having to be told to *get back in his Jeep* while *first in line to board the ferry* had imprisoned him inside his vehicle. He had mentally locked the door and tossed the key into the Sound, and he had no desire to see or talk to anyone. He imagined meeting with Deputy Magruder on Ocracoke, getting a lesson on how to fly a drone, and in his mind, receiving a request from Sheriff Kringlebach to become Dare County's new drone operator. Now, Calvin would know him for a fool who couldn't even board the ferry without tripping over the side and going under, lapels first.

Now, he was parked at the very front of the ferry, and leaving the harbor, shadow-encrusted buildings with windows ablaze had crawled past, whispering accusingly, "I saw that. You can't even drive on the ferry without screwing it up." Out of the darkness, water whipped up over the ferry's bow, and the spray impacted his windshield with a splat. He touched his wiper control to flick it away and felt along his belt in the seat beside him for his walkie. He pressed the talk button and muttered, "I choose to serve no matter what."

"Whoa!" Emily laughed. "That's the saddest 'choose to serve' I've ever heard. You worried about salt water on that pretty Jeep?"

"Hi, Emily. Nah. You saw me back there, right?" He imagined a giant television screen broadcasting his foul-up to everyone on the ferry. They were likely laughing and smirking, and with him at the very front, he wouldn't be able to tell.

"Which part?" She didn't *sound* critical, more curious.

"Not being ready to board."

"I saw. Seriously, Sean, a little get-over-yourself beach time. The ferry crews, well, that's their job, and no one had to wait on you. Hey, I radioed because Diane says Darlene wants to meet with us, but she refuses to walk to your Jeep and get soaked. You need to join us. We'll be up top."

"You all go ahead without me." He pictured the small passenger area on the upper level of the ferry. The ferry to Cedar

Island had copious passenger space, but this one? A couple seats and an aisle for everyone to squeeze down.

"No, we can't." Emily snorted, whether with disdain or laughter, Sean couldn't tell. "Where's your team spirit? The lieutenant requested you along today for a reason. Now, she didn't tell me what it is, but I'm sure she has one. Make her look good in front of Sheriff Pafford, and you'll be two thumbs up in her book."

"Lousy start on that."

"It was dark. No one was watching. C'mon, let's go."

"You were."

"Because you were right in front of me. I'll see you upstairs. Emily out."

Behind him, Emily's interior lights came on, and she stood and waved at him before closing her door. She snugged the neck of her jacket against the wind. Sean's Jeep shook as the ferry impacted a wave, water splatted heavily on the windshield, and Emily ducked as the residue danced across her shoulders. She flipped up her collar and walked purposefully toward the stairs, fully in control of her day and her life, as always, which was something Sean knew he would never manage. He looked ahead, tried to judge the wave pattern, and when he was certain he could get out, close his door, and squeeze past his Jeep and get to the stairs without coming away like he'd been at the helm of a dory in a downpour, he flipped his door release, held onto the door to keep it from banging back, and in the process, caught his foot on the Jeep's doorsill as he climbed out. The extra half minute it took him to correct his stance, protect the paint on his door, and get it closed meant he was unprepared for his morning shower.

He grimaced as the water hit his windshield, then he was soaked.

"Shoot, y'all," he muttered, as he shook his head to clear the water from his face, "I know I'm not in this alone. We're a team, and together, we're a success."

He tried to be positive, but even he could hear his words fall flat. He headed towards the stairs, his right side wet and chilled, but his left perfectly dry. Jekyll and Hyde. The phantom of the opera. Iron Man ... he liked that one. Maybe Clark Kent and Superman. Sean grinned, his attitude shifting from woe is me, to wow is me.

"I got this," he said as he grabbed the handrail and took the steps two at a time. "Commitment and respect, what it's all about. You can count on me, Lieutenant."

He entered the upstairs passenger area to find Sheriff Darlene Pafford seated across from Lieutenant Diane Turnip-seed, with Forensic Investigator Emily Bryant standing just behind them, and all three of them looking at him.

Lieutenant Turnipseed laughed. "Well, have a look-see at that. The shark's done got in the collards and come up swim-ming."

Emily smiled and winked at him. Darlene Pafford fought a grin and looked away, and he shrugged and quipped, "Didn't know if you wanted Aquaman or Arthur Curry."

"For all sakes ... Arthur who?" Diane shook her head.

Emily laughed, said, "I'll explain later, Diane," and motioned for the deputy to join them for the discussion.

Darlene Pafford quipped, "That's a joke, I guess. If so, who dey! I want you to bring me on board before we reach the island. Now, let's look at what we've got." She pulled out a folder and removed two sheets of paper. "Look at this, and two eyes will tell you ..."

The metal plating under their feet vibrated repeatedly as the ferry fought the rough water; and as Sheriff Pafford droned on, Sean's focus drifted. He imagined Calvin Magruder looking at his phone on some social media site and watching a video of him being told off by the ferryman to *get in your vehicle if you want to go on this ferry.* People did that, didn't they? Uploaded random videos? He was brought back to the room with, "And that'll be the deputy's job, some fifteen minutes the other side of the ferry landing." Darlene Pafford looked directly at him. "How's that sound to you, Deputy Taylor?"

Oops, Sean thought, *caught out.* There was only one thing to say. He nodded vigorously and called, "You can count on me, Sheriff Pafford. A hundred percent, you can count on me."

Emily's eyes twinkled, and Sean tried not to freak out. He'd not been paying attention *again.* He could only imagine the prank she would spin out of this, or maybe he couldn't. Dread was a pit in his stomach; and about then, the ferry hit a massive swell, and he closed his eyes, trying to keep the cartwheeling octopus in his stomach inside his stomach.

Rough water. Why did it always do this to him?

"SO," SEAN began, standing beside Emily's car and watching the ferry landing close in. "Fifteen minutes in, that's like across the whole island."

"Sure." She had her window down and was fiddling with her seat belt. "Not quite to the far side but to town, anyway." She looked up and smiled sweetly.

"What did, um, Sheriff Pafford think was so important about what I need to do?" He wanted to ask point blank, but he had been on the receiving end of Emily's biting wit often enough. No need to stick his hand into a Portuguese Man-of-War just to get stung by the tentacles, no matter how beautiful.

"So, I was correct." Emily gloated. "Deputy Taylor was day-dreaming during the meeting with Sheriff Pafford. Did I read that right?"

"Not daydreaming." This was going south, and Sean could feel Emily sorting him into her prank folder, inventing future opportunities to bring him to his knees. Prickles crawled up his back.

"No? Then explain. And make it quick. We're about to dock."

"You know what I'm asking." Sean had his keys in his hand, and he desperately wanted to head to his vehicle, but he also needed to know what he'd agreed to do for the sheriff. He weighed his choices: risk another warning about getting into his Jeep or get on the radio, which everyone would be able to overhear.

"Okay, I give. But only for a donut, cherry-cream filled. The best flavor, by any measure." She smiled again, sweetly. "The sheriff wants you to stop in at Sweet Tooth for breakfast fare and meet up back at the sheriff's office."

"Okay." At least now he knew what was expected of him, but that presented a new complication. Ferries … the reason he'd first applied to the Kitty Hawk police department and not to the Dare County Sheriff's Office was ferries. He didn't like them, or to be more accurate, they didn't like him. Seasickness was not a law enforcement officer's friend. With no bridges to Ocracoke, he'd never been past Hatteras to the smaller island. Once here, he'd expected to trail everyone else rather than ask directions. Now, to have to find a breakfast shop and locate the sheriff's office on his own? He could get lost driving Highway 12 in Kill Devil Hills, and that was where he lived.

"You know where the sheriff's office is, right?"

"Not really." His first time on the island, but he didn't want to have to admit that. "I've heard of Jason's Restaurant. It is near that?'

Emily smirked. "The sheriff's office is on the left just before you get into town. If you see Jason's, you've passed it. Sweet Tooth and the Fig Tree Bakery are just past that on the right. Be sure to get a receipt. And cherry-cream!" She waved and began rolling up her window.

Sean closed his door just as the ferry lurched against the landing, and it locked into place, finally one with the sandy spit of land fronting the edge of the Atlantic Ocean. He expected to be first off, as he was the first on, but ahead of him, Sheriff Pafford and Lieutenant Turnipseed's line took first dibs, and their brake lights flashed once as they bumped from sea to land and moved off down the island.

Off the ferry, Emily took her first opportunity and passed him, waving one hand out her window as she zipped around and left him behind, which Sean took as another personal slap. Everyone else knew where they were headed and didn't care about him. Mired in his self-flagellation, he almost passed Shelby Ellison at the first beach parking area a couple miles in. Shelby was the daughter of Cynthia Ellison, the C-District K9 handler, and Sean knew she lived on Ocracoke, just not where. The surprising part was that she was miles from anything and without transportation that he could see. He braked, turned around, and drove back to the pullout to see what was going on.

"Hey, Shelby," he called, with his window down. "I don't know if you remember me—" She had been a pretty woman, but today she boasted stringy hair, faded jeans so out of date that Sean didn't recognize the style, and a weathered puff jacket in coral tones that had faded to pale pink where it caught the sun.

"Like I care." She looked at him and his Jeep, took in the light bar across the top, and asked, "Did my momma send you?"

"Cynthia? No, I'm here on an investigation, well, what might be one if it turns out to be one."

"That's stupid. You're Sean, right? Are you stupid or just a sheep? Oh, right, they're the same." She jerked her head up and smirked at him.

"Sorry. I recognized you and didn't see your car. I thought maybe you needed help or something, but if not?" He left it hanging, not yet wishing he hadn't stopped, as he liked to help people, but not enjoying more abuse heaped on top of his already lousy morning.

"I was just …" She looked up and down the highway. It was empty. The ferry was only partially filled, and those cars were already well on their way to town. The ones headed north were at the ferry landing and likely loaded already.

No one was heading in to join them.

Sean took a risk and asked her, "Which are you heading?"

"That way." She pointed south towards town.

"I've got room if you want a ride." He glanced at his watch, worked out the time he was adding to his visit to the sweet shop, and made the decision to radio in, ask for requests, and let them know he'd offered Shelby a ride … that was if she could decide what she wanted to do.

She nodded, gave an angry sigh, and said, "Momma should keep her mouth shut about where I live," but she trudged to the opposite side of Sean's Jeep. He dropped his gear in the back floorboard and unlocked her door. Inside, she relented with a grudging, "Thank you."

Sean pulled away and asked, "Did someone drop you off, or?" Again, leaving the question hanging, letting Shelby answer it or not as she wished. When she worked her face but didn't reply, he offered, "I need to stop by Sweet Tooth before my meeting at the sheriff's office, but I can drop you off anywhere."

"I was spending the evening with Jade." She muttered the words, giving them little effort, and she kept her face turned towards the gray Sound chop stirred by the gusty Atlantic winds. The sky was still painted charcoal, likely matching her outlook on life.

"Jade, your daughter, right?" Despite the weather outside, Sean perked up. Mothers and daughters, well, that was a good thing, right?

"'Cept she decided to go off with her friends, so lot of good that did, a wasted trip. Like I care." She tapped the glass repeatedly with the knuckles of her right hand.

"That's rough."

"Yeah, rough. Hey, the Pirate's Chest, you know that place?" She looked at him, her expression brightening. "You can drop me there."

"On the double." He hesitated, then asked, "Is that this side of the sheriff's office or the other side?"

"You really are a sheep, aren't you?" Shelby laughed.

"I just—" Sean took a deep breath, fully aware he could never take this back once he said it, "—never came here before. This is my first time on the island."

"You've not missed much. It's on the other side. I'll show you. I can walk to my place from there." She shifted to halfway face him. "You know where Sweet Tooth is, right?"

"Maybe." Sean hesitated to admit too much. He didn't dislike Shelby, but he'd never heard anything good about her, either.

"You don't. You are truly a dingbatter."

"I live in Kitty Hawk, so I'm not one of those." It was a word Sergeant Mary Wilson used like a cussword, and he didn't want to even repeat it.

"Ha, ha. Only a dingbatter would say that. Hey, I'll show you where the sheriff's office is. You can't even find that, can you?"

"It's on the left." That was one thing he did know.

"This left?" Shelby pointed to the first building they saw, then another and another. "Or that left." She pointed to the right.

"Okay, I don't know." Sean pulled over and idled the Jeep. They were on the edge of town, and a kid about ten was riding a bike. Under the overcast sky, the small town looked deserted.

"Isn't this the whole town? I'm not likely to get lost. Anyway, you're confusing me, so please stop. Okay?"

"Sure, Sheep." She laughed.

"Wait," Sean said, and he studied a sign just ahead. "That's Jason's, so the sheriff's office is—" and he pointed just behind them where he found three cars he recognized, "—there."

"Oh, you're good." Shelby laughed again, this time real. "I'll show you Sweet Tooth on the way to the Pirate's Chest if you'll buy me something."

"Food?"

"Of course, Sheep." She slouched in her seat, relaxing for the first time since climbing into the Jeep.

"I can do that." He looked at his radio. He hadn't called in yet, but then he wasn't late, either. He had time.

SEAN ENTERED the rustic sheriff's office, a nondescript brown building, with one arm cradling a large brown sack with coffees and pastries and the other holding a smaller plastic bag from the Variety Store.

"Late is a word I don't like to use, but you are the world's best example today." Emily materialized to help him with his purchases.

"Where are the sheriff and the lieutenant?" He offered her the smaller bag, saying, "This one's yours."

"In the back office. Cherry-cream, right?" She smiled hopefully.

"Almost." He shrugged and set the bigger bag on a desk.

"How is it almost?" She looked inside and with dismay pulled out a squeeze bottle of cherry ice cream topping. "What's this?"

Sean laughed. "Sweet Tooth only had cream-filled, no cherry, so I stopped at the Variety Store and found that. I thought it a good compromise. No regrets, right? Feet on the sand and all that?"

"Are you pranking me?" She jabbed his shoulder with the unopened container.

"Maybe," he said, grinning. "But no. Since you insisted, that's the closest I could get."

"It would be a good prank, though. You got cream-filled, though, right?"

"And coffees."

"I'll let it slide. Bring that and follow me."

"Oh, Emily, one more thing. I ran across Shelby out towards the ferry, and I gave her a ride into town."

"Oh, you are a sweetie. Two points in your scorebook. You'll make Cynthia happy."

"It's more than that. I got her a donut at Sweet Tooth, and I guess she felt she owed me something for it. You remember that sailboat from last night—"

"Actually, no. I was in Kill Devil Hills where I live. But go on. I did hear about it. That's part of why we're here."

"Well, Shelby spent last night on the beach, and she said that sometime after midnight—"

"Shelby." Emily interrupted with a frown. "On the beach. It got cold last night."

"She had on a coat. Anyway, she watched it sail by last night."

"And that means?"

"Well, Sheriff Pafford never said that it docked here, just that it didn't have a captain onboard. Or anyone on the boat that she knew of, but the point is that maybe Shelby could help us find where it went."

"If she really saw it. You know Shelby has honesty issues. If you mentioned that sailboat to her ..." Emily looked at him as though he might have done just that.

"Never! I didn't, just that there might be an investigation, but nothing about what it might be. Shoot, Emily. I'm not that stupid." A wall heater kicked on, and it hissed as if not believing a word he said.

"Even the heater's on my side." Emily laughed. "You bring that, and I'll carry my cherry topping. Thank you, by the way, even if it's not exactly what I ordered."

Sean hefted the bag, and when Emily opened the door, he stepped carefully through, determined not to spill even one cup of the precious liquid. Inside the office, not large enough by far for four people, he searched for a place to set the coffee, and Lieutenant Turnipseed looked up from the paperwork she and the sheriff were studying and frowned at him.

"Over yonder." Diane motioned toward a waist-high vertical file cabinet before turning back to Darlene and asking, "That how it mighta went? It coulda just passed the island altogether?"

"What passed the island?" Sean whispered to Emily as she shifted a stack of books and another of file folders filled with paperwork.

"The sailboat." She reached into the sack, removed the treats from the top, placed them onto the cabinet, and with both hands, worked out the four coffees in a cardboard tray and separated them one at a time beside the baked goods. She turned them, looking for names, and she said, "Hm. Don't see one with my name."

"You expected Starbucks?" Sean snickered.

"Yes, I did. How do I know what's what?"

"Pranks, pranks."

"You didn't." She blew out her cheeks, picked up one, and sniffed it. "Cinnamon roast, right?"

"If you want. See the lids? The dots tell what's inside. The key's inside my pocket." Sean patted his breast pocket and grinned, revealing a piece of paper.

"Give me that." Emily reached to snatch it away, and when Sean backed up, he bumped a chair, and it launched against an upright filing cabinet which echoed in the tight space.

"Enough chatter," Diane said. "Coffee, please."

"Yes, ma'am," Emily called, taking what was likely the cinnamon roast and choosing another one for her boss.

When she looked at Sean and raised her eyebrows to ask if her choice was a good one for the lieutenant, he grinned and shrugged. "I got the one for the sheriff."

He felt the dots on the lids, paused, and nodded with satisfaction. He grinned at Emily and carried one to Sheriff Pafford. He returned to take the final drink for himself.

"MIRACLE WHIP, mayo," Sheriff Pafford muttered, as she set several papers aside and pulled out Deputy Suzanne DeSantis' keyboard.

"For all sakes, Darlene," Diane said. "What's that mean, anyway?"

"What, the Miracle Whip thing?" She laughed. "That's an Ohio joke. My computer, this computer, it's all county property and there shouldn't be any difference. Ah, here." She clicked a few times and started typing before shuffling two sheets at her side and adding something else to the computer. "Who dey! Making progress."

"That's good, right?" Sean said. They had come to Ocracoke to sort out the events of the previous evening, and he couldn't tell that much was getting done. He wanted his time on the ferry to be worth it.

"You, Deputy Taylor." Sheriff Pafford looked at him expectantly. "You're a man, right?"

"I, um—" The question caught him off guard. "Um, yes?"

"Down south in Kentucky, they call that a half-answer, Deputy. Like, road trip time!" She smiled, taking the edge off her dig. "All the *men* from last night—" the Coast Guard and Swan Quarter people, she seemed to suggest, "—dodged today like a fixed puppy ignoring a playdate. We three women know what we saw, except you, Emily, as you were at a party, the Lieutenant tells me, but you can still have an opinion. Cornhole is open to everyone, even here on the edge of the East Coast. But you, Deputy, you have a mind like a freshly scrubbed spittoon. And we want to inspect it."

"I'm a team player, Sheriff, and I want to serve no matter what, but I have no idea what you mean." He had taken a bite of a chocolate-covered donut while she was speaking, and he had to talk around it, muffling his words. He licked his lips, sipped his coffee to clear his throat, and said, "Sorry. I don't know what a spittoon is."

"He's kinda cute, Diane, like a can of pop just out of the fridge and dripping with the humidity."

Emily moved to his side and quietly whispered, "Don't get close enough for her to lick it off."

"Shoot, Emily. Don't say that." He gave her a quick glare. "I'm sorry, Sheriff. What does me being a man have to do with our investigation?"

"See?" Diane said to Darlene. "We've already got an investigation. We might coulda stayed back on Hatteras and just let the deputy come on over."

The sheriff ignored it all and said, "Tell me what you saw last night. A man's viewpoint, fresh and clean. I'm ready." She adjusted her keyboard and watched the screen.

"Well, Shelby said—"

"Shelby?" Diane shifted in her chair to frown at him. "Shelby Ellison? For all sakes, Deputy, what does she have to do with anything?"

"I gave her a ride this morning." He glanced from the lieutenant to Emily for corroboration. She shrugged, and he looked back to Sheriff Pafford to explain. "She spent the night on the beach and saw that sailboat from last night go by. I thought if we talked to her, she might know something that could help us out."

When the sheriff looked confused, Diane explained, "She's the daughter of one of our officers, Cynthia Ellison."

"Let me get on board." Darlene began typing, and the screen showed, *Shelby Ellison, the daughter of Cynthia Ellison, Dare County officer.* "Now, Deputy, what's important about Shelby Ellison?"

"She might be a witness. She said she saw it sail by last night about the same time we saw it, only a little after, but that would make sense, as it was coming this way and we saw it first." He watched the computer screen to see what the sheriff would type.

Saw sailboat a little after midnight. Sheriff Pafford paused and looked at Sean.

"With no lights." He smiled encouragingly.

With no lights. "I can type faster, Deputy."

"Sorry. That was pretty much all, except that it was weaving back and forth like there was no one piloting it. Oh, and the sails were—" and he frowned, pulling the correct word from the air, "—luffing, I think it's called. Not taut. That's all."

Weaving. Sails luffing. "Heading south? Close in, far out?"

"Yeah, south, and just weaving, she said."

South, just weaving.

"Silver Lake?" Diane asked.

"Likely. Don't think I can dodge this one, though I'd like to catch the ferry up to Swan Quarter. If that boat came in on this island, it would most likely have to be at Silver Lake. Otherwise—"

"You mean it might not be here?" Sean was appalled. Another ferry ride? And what did she mean by otherwise? He could already feel the butterflies that came with a rough water crossing, and with the weather outside, any crossing today would be just that.

"Sean," Emily offered, "the chain of islands extends past this one, but there are no anchorages. No docks, no moorings. Nada on the ocean side for the next fifty miles. Boats dock at Silver Lake, which means navigating through the Ocracoke Inlet to the other side of the island, or not at all, and if it was just weaving when Shelby saw it … are you following me?"

"It couldn't just weave through the inlet. But I thought it was here." He looked at the three women. "Last night, how did Sheriff Pafford know it was empty?"

"Passing boats hailed it with no response." Sheriff Pafford logged off the computer, pushed the keyboard back, and stood. "No time like now for a game of cornhole. Wonder if they have a farmer's market on this island. Any of you know about that?"

"To tell the story honest, Darlene, this is your nesting area, not mine. Let me finish my cuppa blackie, and we can get that direction." Diane put the cup to her lips and nearly spat it out. "Cinnamon? Who's the leaf peeper who gave me cinnamon?"

Emily and Sean did their best to look innocent, while the sheriff looked at the cup in Diane's hand with clear envy in her eyes.

FOR THE SHORT drive to Silver Lake, Sean took his place in the back seat of Diane's black Explorer. He shared with Emily, giving the lieutenant and the sheriff the front. As a first-time passenger in the vehicle, he was surprised at the number of coffee cups littering the floor.

He caught Emily's eye as she opened the door opposite him, and he looked to the floor, asking with his eyes if they should offer to clean them out or let them go.

"Stones on the beach, Sean. Flotsam, jetsam, the work-around residue of a brilliant mind. Just climb in." Emily pulled herself inside, shuffled the empty cups aside with her feet, and settled onto her seat before closing the door.

The lieutenant and the sheriff exited the small office, with the sheriff inserting a key to lock the door. When she saw Sean still outside the Explorer, Diane called, "Before the sun peeks over the dunes, Deputy."

Darlene laughed. "Not today. The overcast will likely hang around till dark. Like they say down south in Kentucky, if the good Lord's willing and the creek don't rise."

"He just needs to make a change and be the man his parents want him to be."

Diane spoke it to Darlene, but the words carried to Sean perfectly well, and he fell into the truck, sending one of the coffee cups tumbling onto the rough parking pad.

"Shoot," he said, looking at it. "Another one bites the dust."

"Don't be lazy," Emily encouraged. "Get out and get it."

He did, and this time, climbing in, he was more careful with his feet. However, when he sat down, a loud farting noise erupted in the truck. Diane and Darlene had just opened their doors, and they gave each other a puzzled look. Emily burst into laughter.

"You are such a mark, Sean. You should have known I would do that."

"You?" He reached under himself and pulled out a rubber fart bladder. "Why, Emily?"

"Why not, Sean?" She reached for it, rolled it up, and slipped it in a small bag at her feet.

"That was you, Emily?" Sheriff Pafford was in her seat and adjusting her position and her equipment belt.

"Technically no, but I did set it up. Sean produced the noise, all by his lonesome."

"So we should thank the deputy for the entertainment." The sheriff accidentally bumped elbows with Diane when the lieutenant pulled her door to, and offhandedly she said, "Please, just an errant elbow."

"Please?" Diane asked as she started the engine.

"Well," Darlene said, "for you islanders, I could say excuse me, but I'm from Ohio." She shrugged. "I don't expect so, but I'm hoping that boat is moored at Silver Lake. If it went south, that's Carteret County. You suppose they have a farmer's market down there?"

"For all sakes, Darlene," Diane said, as she looked both ways before pulling onto the Irvin Garrish Highway curving deeper into the island and towards Silver Lake. "You and your farmer's markets. Another Ohio thing?"

"Who dey!" Darlene laughed. "That means yes. Now, about that boat, we know anyone special in Carteret if that's the way we've gotta go? And to get on board with all this, I figure we're not dodging the deer this time."

"Jason," Emily said, more clearing her throat than actually volunteering the name.

Sean grinned.

"What's that, Emily?" Diane glared at her in the rearview mirror. "Don't be gettin' above your knees. You're likely to be walking in overwash any time about now."

"Jason knows lots of people down in Carteret." Sean became a fountain of information. Jason Romney had evolved into a bit of an icon to the younger deputy, a symbol of what an ideal island deputy ought to be; and it didn't hurt that the tall, salt-and-pepper man could banter with the lieutenant and not take any guff off her.

"Hold your taters, Deputy," Diane began, when Darlene took over.

"No, I want to hear this." Darlene turned in her seat enough to study Sean's face. "I've not met the man, but several of my deputies mention him time-to-time."

"Halsey and Dingman?" Diane snorted and shook her head. Outside the vehicle, they were passing the Pirate's Chest, a large gift and souvenir shop on the right with an expansive front porch. The lights were on, and several shoppers were climbing the steps to go inside. "Those people entering that shop are as likely to help us out with Carteret as Halsey and Dingman."

"Didn't say they would help us out, Diane, just that they mention Jason from time to time. Last name of Romney, right?"

"Yes." Diane growled and didn't elaborate.

"Then, Deputy," and Darlene glanced at Diane before turning her full attention to Sean, "who does Jason know in Carteret?"

"Everyone." Sean grinned, enthused by the interest from the sheriff. "Deputy Magruder, for one. He's the drone pilot from last night—"

"I've met Clifton," Darlene assured him. "I was there last night with you and all the dopeheads we hauled away. He's coming over later, right?" She cut her eyes to Diane, and when the lieutenant kept her attention on the drive and didn't respond, she looked to Emily for her answer.

"Sean hopes so." Emily slipped Sean a wink.

"Stop it, Emily," Sean said. "It's not like that. Drones are cool."

"Okay," she said. "Whatever, it's all beach to me."

"Who else besides Magruder?" Darlene pulled them back to her question.

"I don't know everyone he knows, but he worked there—"

"Enough about Jason. We're here." Diane interrupted the stories as she pulled up at the Anchorage Inn and Marina across the main road running around Silver Lake. She killed the engine. "Any boat grown as big as that'un we saw last night, likely it'd be here if anywhere. And yes, Darlene, if'n we need to contact Carteret, Jason might be a good crab pot to reach into. The man likes to have his spoon in everyone else's pot, so likely he's tugging at the reel if he knows we have an investigation on."

"More specifically your pot, Lieutenant," Emily muttered as she exited the black Explorer.

"Hold your taters, Forensic Investigator. What was that?" Diane twisted sideways to glare at her over the seat.

"You've got ears as sharp as windblown sand, Lieutenant, and I'm not repeating whatever you think you overheard." Emily grinned.

"If that don't shuck all." Diane did slam her door when she exited.

Sean was having fun, and he was about to decide that hanging around Emily might not be so bad after all. He watched the C-District's forensic investigator open her door and climb out, and once she'd closed the door, he opened his to join her.

THE MARINA—in fact everything around Silver Lake—was beautiful. The buildings, docks, and moorings wrapped the small harbor like the inside of a horseshoe, opening out to the Pamlico Sound through a cut in the shoreline that Emily called the Ditch. Birdlife, the rustle of the water against the shore, the clank of rigging against aluminum sailboat masts. Sean berated himself for never making the effort to visit before. He thought he understood why Shelby had chosen to live here rather than on Hatteras like her mother and father.

Except that he wouldn't have … make that *couldn't* have, not with having to ride a ferry every time he needed to go some-place that was more than fourteen miles from his front door. Up to his place in Kill Devil Hills, he was near enough to walk to the beach, yet he could drive his Jeep clear to California and never have to get on a boat even once. He couldn't say that about this place. No one could, and that made him sad, because it really was as pretty a place as he'd ever seen.

"I see that look in your eyes." Emily walked up to stand beside him along a portion of what Sean had determined must be a boardwalk, even if it didn't completely surround the harbor. A harborside pool belonging to the Inn hugged the shore at their side. "Are you abandoning us for Hyde County?"

"Shoot, Emily, I choose to serve in C-District, you know that. Lieutenant Turnipseed deserves my commitment and respect. I wouldn't run out on her like that." Last night, then this morning being asked to join the Team, if he could call it that, to come to Hyde County, even if had required a ferry ride, well, why would he give up the very thing he'd been wishing for?

"Only because you're here and not up investigating a hotel fraud scam." She adjusted her elbows on the railing, looked into the water, and said, "Look, an alligator."

"Where?" Sean leaned forward, only to feel her tap the back of his head with her fingers, causing him to jump.

"Gotcha. No alligators have ever been recorded in the Sound. Sorry, Sean. But look! Your flashlight!" She jostled the flashlight at his waist, although she didn't unhook it. "Don't drop it."

"Stop that!" He grasped the flashlight and stepped back. "If it falls in the water, the lieutenant says I have to pay for it. I'm not made of money."

"Me either. Just having a little fun, so don't abandon the beach just yet. Your equipment is still all attached."

"Sometimes it does come loose." He began checking the attachment points. His handcuffs fell from his belt to his hands, and he barely caught them before they got away. "See?"

"That's you. Sorry, Sean, but it is. You're not careful taking your equipment off and back on. Back to that hotel case, how did all that come out? Did you get things wrapped up?" Before he could answer, she shifted her attention and pointed to several buildings down and across Irvin Garrish where the Hyde County sheriff and the C-District lieutenant were speaking with someone from the marina. "I bet those two come back with every answer we need. They're good, like a beach fire on a cold night."

"Cept when the lieutenant roasts me like a torch."

"You get too close, and a hot fire does that. Now about that hotel case."

"Not wrapped up." A dog off in the distance barked, and the sound of a bell on a kid's bike was bright under the overcast sky. "Not my fault, though. I would have solved it, but Sheriff Kringlebach squelched the investigation. *Waste of department resources*, he said. Lieutenant Turnipseed didn't think so. She thought it was important and that I needed to stay at it."

"In Kitty Hawk, meaning not in C-District, right?"

"Some of it was in C-District, but no, not mostly. But what does that matter? It's still Dare County."

"And the lieutenant really wanted you up there. I know."

"I did help solve who the dead man was, and all because I was working on the hotel case at the Conference Center." He was proud of that. Even Jason Romney had bragged on him.

"Until Sheriff Kringlebach banished you back down here." Emily shook her hair back, turned from the water, and pointed to the source of the bell they'd heard ringing earlier. A young girl with pigtails on a pink bike outfitted with training wheels was pushing at her pedals hard, and every so often, she reached to a bell on her handlebars and gave it a turn. "No wasted effort there, even if she'd not making much progress. Still, she's giving it everything."

"I do that, give my work everything." He said it with pride.

"Okay, you're not getting my point. Let's go see what our bosses have uncovered. Maybe we need to go to Cedar Island, or even Swan Quarter." She winked at him. "On the ferry."

"Are you trying to ruin my day, Emily? And what point? I

didn't know you were making a point. Emily?" She was already moving away, however, and all he could do was follow her. She crossed the main road to the inn's parking lot in front of a car, and Sean was forced to wait. The car slowed as if it wanted to give him access, also, but he motioned for them to go ahead. It was several stops and starts before the car moved on and Sean could join the rest of his "team."

"Sean, you'll like this." Emily motioned him their direction. She had an impish gleam in her eye.

"Deputy," Sheriff Pafford called. "Where've you been? Two eyes will tell you we're meeting here, not across the road. We need you on board, because it looks like our best choice for our road trip is that direction." She pointed south. The Ocracoke lighthouse was just visible across Silver Lake through the trees.

"Road trip? To the lighthouse?"

"For all sakes," Diane Turnipseed barked, "boat ride, Deputy. Down towards Portsmouth Island and more'n likely down to the Cape."

"Cape Lookout?" Sean felt the blood drain from his face. "They don't have ferries down there, do they?"

"For all sakes, yes, they have ferries to the Cape, Deputy. It's not bushwhacker country." Diane Turnipseed shook her head.

"We're just not taking one." Sheriff Pafford confirmed Sean's worst fear. "We'd have to get to Cedar Island for that, and to spend two hours on the Cedar Island ferry only to spend another hour accessing the ferry from either Davis or Harkers Island, then locate transportation back up the coast? We're hiring a boat so we can take a shortcut."

"What can go wrong?" Emily chided him with a laugh. "It'll be fun, something few people get to do."

"On a boat ... across the Ocracoke Inlet, the busiest and only shipping lane through the Outer Banks. No, nothing can go wrong with that, nothing at all." Sean could already feel the bile rising in his throat, and he was forced to swallow it back down.

LOCATING TRANSPORTATION to Cape Lookout proved challenging, especially on such short notice. Most of the deep-sea capable vessels were gone for the day, already on charter, or the private property of "dingbatters" from off island who were currently *off island.*

Diane relented with a growl, saying, "Jason don't got the sense that God gave a minnow, but even a minnow can swim the right direction once in a while. Let's string him on a hook and see if a boat bites."

Jason Romney, however, proved inaccessible, whether by police radio; contacting Karen Midgett, the Dare County dispatcher in Manteo; or on his private cell line. Heading back towards the sheriff's office, as they passed Jason's Restaurant, Sean called out, "Hey, Lieutenant. Stop."

"For what reason?" she barked, hitting the brakes hard.

"For that reason." He motioned to the restaurant's bold, green-and-white sign on the side of the road, boasting Jason's as an invite to stop in, and the white truck next to it.

"It's early for lunch, Deputy," Sheriff Pafford commented, but she glanced at Diane and shrugged. "Your call, Lieutenant."

"A cuppa blackie sounds good. Emily?" Diane took a deep breath, like she wanted someone else to agree to stop.

"I had breakfast," Emily said, raising both her palms to put the decision on someone else.

Sean said, "It's not about lunch. That's Ricky Johnson's truck, the man Jason lives with."

"Understood, Deputy. Ricky's on the island. I can still go for a cuppa blackie." Diane slipped the black Explorer towards the eating establishment and beside the white GMC with the toolbox bed. Sure enough, the door boasted an alligator with

Alligator Remodeling scrawled above it, and in smaller letters underneath, Ricky Johnson's name with his contact number.

"See?" Sean said. "I told you so."

"Calvin will be disappointed." Emily grinned. "I thought you two had a date with his drone."

"Stop it, Emily. Ricky might know where Jason is, and if not, he might know someone with a boat."

"The man's right," Sheriff Pafford said. "It's worth a try."

"Or the Coast Guard," Diane muttered as she put the truck in park and opened her door. "They have boats. Lots of boats. Big boats, small boats …" She was still muttering as she got out and closed her door.

"Just no drones, right, Sean?" Emily released her seat belt and grinned at him.

"No fart bladders, either. I'll see you inside." He chose to ignore Emily's insinuations. He'd finally figured her out. She wanted him to react, so he needed to do the opposite, even tease her back if he got the chance.

That was if he could think of anything to say.

Diane had already located Ricky by the time Sean got into the restaurant. He was at one of the picnic tables in the screened dining area with a plate consisting of a tuna roll and a bag of chips.

"Lucky you found me here," Ricky was saying. "A couple weeks more and this place'll be closing for the season. Won't reopen till Valentine's."

"They got coffee, though, right?" Diane stepped to the door into the main room, and she looked through.

"I believe so. You're Diane, right? The one Jason talks about?" Ricky took a chip, bit into it, and tried to look innocent.

"Never mind that." She frowned. "The deputy wants to ask you something. I'll be right back."

"Sean, how're you doing? Have a seat." Ricky pushed out

the bench across from him with one foot. "Ladies, if you want?" He motioned to even more places they could sit.

"Sheriff Pafford, from Swan Corner." Darlene held out her hand to shake.

"Glad to meet you, Sheriff." Ricky stood to shake the sheriff's hand, and he took Emily's and grinned. "And I know you. You're the prankster I hear about. Emily, right?"

"Only if you have good taste in women."

"She'll fart bladder you. Look under you before you sit down," Sean cautioned with a grin.

"Please?" Darlene said, interrupting the introductions. "Sean says you might be able to help us."

"Sure. How?" Ricky jumped his eyes from Darlene to Sean.

"We can't locate Jason. We need to ask him—"

Ricky laughed. "That's easy. I apologize for interrupting, but Jason's out with Sherrill Jenkins." When no one seemed to recognize the name, he said, "Sharky? Sharky Jenkins?"

"No bells going off in my head," Emily said with a shrug.

Diane was on her way with a cup of steaming coffee, and she said, "Did I hear Sharky Jenkin's name? What's that fool doing now?"

"What I wish I was doing," Ricky said. "I was invited out fishing today, but I'm here ripping out a water line instead. One of the summer houses needs an update for a late-season renter next week."

"Jason and Sharky together on a boat. Can't see no good coming of that." Diane shook her head as she brushed away the steam from her cup of coffee.

"Likely not. What'cha need Jason for? If it can wait, he should be back about two. If not, likely you can get Sharky's boat on the radio." Ricky popped the final bite of his tuna roll in his mouth and began to chew.

"How big is the boat?" Darlene seemed to have formulated

a plan. "Oh, I should ask, if they're fishing, will he need to warsh it down once he brings it in?"

"You're not originally from around here, are you, Sheriff?" Ricky took a drink from his glass. "That's some accent you've got there."

"What accent? I don't have one. Now, down south in Kentucky—"

"Okay." Ricky chuckled and stopped her. "If warsh means wash, yes. I'm gathering you people need a boat, and yes, Sharky hires out. He was free today, the reason he and Jason are out. You want me to give him a call?"

With a sinking feeling, Sean realized what he'd done by stopping here with the lieutenant and the sheriff. They'd found Ricky, and through him, Jason, but that meant a boat. Maybe they'd let him stay behind if the boat wasn't big enough for all of them … and that's when he caught Ricky's answer to a question he must have missed.

"Sure, upwards of twenty. Plenty of room for you four, Sharky, and heck, even Jason. Yeah, I bet Jason would love to go along. I've got to use my radio in the truck. I'll be right back."

Diane watched in dismay as he exited the restaurant, and she said to no one and everyone, "We need the boat. We don't need Jason along."

Sean sat on one of the empty benches. He was preoccupied with *twenty*. He couldn't focus on whether Jason joined them, or even the rest of the C-District force. There was no way he would be allowed to stay behind. He could already feel his stomach churning, and he hadn't even stepped aboard.

"GOOD MORNING, Diane." Jason Romney leaped from Sharky Jenkins' sport fishing boat onto the dock. Salt-and-pepper hair fought to escape a black beanie, and a thick cable-knit sweater gave his shoulders a burly stance. The rear of the boat read *Pamlico Queen* in a flowing script, and recently used fishing gear decorated the deck.

Diane Turnipseed's eyes narrowed, and the sparks between them crackled in the thick sea air. She growled an indecipherable answer.

"Aw, Diane," Jason said. "Let it alone," and he turned to Sean. "My man, I didn't expect to see you out here. Hit me with it. What's got you on the team?"

"You know me. I'm here to serve no matter what. You missed last night. We did a drug bust up in Avon—"

"And the lieutenant let you help?" Jason peered at Diane. "Who's in that lieutenant's uniform? Knock, knock, Diane, are you in there?"

"For all sakes, Jason Romney." Diane spat the words. "You, out there fishing while the rest of us are working … I gotta take someone out with me, so don't get above your knees on me in this."

"I'm only the metallurgist. Until you find metal, I've not got a lot to do, least until my transfer to Dare County is finalized. That's up to Sheriff Kringlebach. He's the one dragging on finalizing my status with C-District." Jason shrugged and called to Sharky. "Hey, my man, I think you and Diane are friends. Come on up and say hello."

Sharky appeared from below tugging on a thick coat, and he nodded at Diane, said, "Diane," and didn't engage with her otherwise. He did concede to share that with the weather, they might get a trifle damp if they were going back out, but he had slickers onboard if they wanted to use them.

"Ricky?" Jason shot a question with the name, motioning back into the boat and asking, are you heading out with us, or are you still needed in town?

"I want to so bad." Ricky took a deep breath, pulled out his phone, and said, "Let me call Mick. He's in Hatteras and he might enjoy a bit of overtime."

"Mick Landers?" Jason clapped Ricky on the shoulder. "Mick always enjoys overtime. He'll be good for it. Investigator Bryant, welcome aboard, if you're willing to share the deck with an off-duty metallurgist." He offered his hand to Darlene Pafford. "You must be the Hyde County sheriff."

"Where's a sweeper? We've got some shredded nonsense coming out of this man's mouth." Darlene laughed. "I'm doing fine, Jason. Calvin and Zack send their love. I heard what you said about off-duty, so no work from you. You can tag along but as an observer only."

"I might could've expected that," Jason said with a good-natured laugh. "Good to meet you, too, Sheriff, and thank you. I promise not to get in your way. Can I at least know what we're going out to find?"

Sean studied Darlene as she scanned the people schooling beside the large sport fishing boat. Ricky was on his phone to Mick Landers, and Emily was with Sharky at a port-side locker choosing a slicker. The dock was filling shoulder-to-shoulder with people, but Sean put off stepping aboard the mostly empty boat as he waited for the sheriff's answer. The water beyond the boat was vying for his attention, and he found himself watching it for possible whitecaps, of which there weren't any, only chop and small waves splashing against the docks. The sheriff glanced at Jason for a moment, gave a brief frown, then turned to the C-District lieutenant and asked, "Diane, if I may?"

"Your island, your call." Diane clearly wasn't happy. "Jason is technically with Dare County and was with Carteret before that—"

"Still Carteret till Mr. Kringlebach turns loose of my paperwork." Jason grinned.

"—so he's not out of his rights to be curious."

"Miracle Whip, mayo to me." Darlene shrugged, and she turned to Jason. "You know anything about last night?"

"Multiple counties working together but mostly that I wasn't invited. Hit me with it."

"We pulled in five drug runners, but Zack found evidence of six on their boat." She gave him a moment to take that in. "Now we have reports of a sailboat with no pilot or crew."

"How are those connected?"

"The sailboat went by under full sail just as we were bringing in the smuggler's craft. Someone named Shelby—"

"Ouch," Jason said. "Shelby Ellison, Cynthia's daughter."

"You know her, then. Good."

"Not good but go on."

Darlene raised her eyebrows. "That's a joke, right?"

"You have to know Shelby, but what about her?"

"She saw it from the north end of the island just after midnight—"

"This island? There's nothing on the north end of the island."

This time Darlene raised her hands in a *don't ask me* expression. "Then, *who dey*, we get a report that a sailboat with no one on board is freshly beached down Lookout Lighthouse way. It started up in Dare County, but you, if you're still with Carteret County, that's good because that's where we're headed. I won't have to call in and get someone to run interference."

"Seems like you've already got intercounty cooperation going," Jason began, "so my justification for being along is sketchy. And I'm not getting how the empty sailboat is connected to your drug bust."

"One of those boats could have a man overboard, as I see it, and I want to find him. The weather last night was rough, and we need to know if they are connected."

"Might could be connected, if you see it that way. And

rough? Just wait for the ocean, Sheriff, if you think last night was rough. Sharky wasn't teasing about needing slickers." Ricky was walking down the dock, and Jason called, "My man, you onboard with us for a wild time on the sea?"

Ricky shot him a double thumbs up, clapped Sean on the shoulder as he walked by, and called, "Sean, not on board yet? We're about to head out."

Sean was pulled out of his focus on the water. It churned and roiled, although he expected that was his stomach as much as what the water was doing. The lieutenant now had a slicker, and Sharky was helping the sheriff select one. Jason had a hose out and was rinsing the open part of the stern, and Emily was on the bow of the boat leaning against a stainless railing and letting the wind whip her slicker around her.

"You, Deputy?" Sharky called to him and held out a slicker.

"Sure," Sean said, and he muttered as he stepped onto the boat, "We're all in this together, and I have no regrets. I signed up to serve, and I'm on board a hundred percent."

Then Sharky started the engine, Jason tossed off the lines, and the boat headed towards the Ditch. Sean found a seat, planted himself, and waited. Who knew how bad this might get, and he'd forgotten to ask where the head was. If only Kitty Hawk had an opening ... if only Kitty Hawk had an opening ... if only Kitty Hawk had an opening.

Saying it three times didn't make it come true.

Then Sharky hit open water, throttled up the engine, and the boat began to skip across the swells like a stone on a lake. A very big lake with very big swells, and nowhere for Sean to plant his feet on solid ground.

"Green gills, Sean?" Emily positioned herself beside him, and with one hand, she held her slicker closed around her throat. When he shook his head yes, she said, "I'm a sand person, not fishing. I feel your pain."

"I don't think you do." He barely got the words out before belching bile and forcing it back down. Sharky set a white bucket with a metal handle on the deck just in front of him, tapped Sean's knee, and pointed into the bucket before walking away. Sean lifted it and hugged it to his chest, keeping his chin centered over it.

"Two points in your scorebook for riding along. The Banks is calling, so I'm off to enjoy the view." She stood, gave him Ricky's two-thumbs-up hand sign, smiled and—using various parts of the boat as handholds—found her way to the stern where the spray from the bow spattered her slicker with every hit and jolt on the waves.

Passing through the Inlet and rounding Portsmouth Island led them into deeper water on the Atlantic side of the Outer Banks, where the water had a thousand miles of unobstructed opportunity to build into heavy swells. Instead of hitting the small surges of the Sound like a jackhammer, the *Pamlico Queen* now crawled up the swells, the engine roared, and she slipped over each whitecapped crest into the next trough, opening up a fresh opportunity for yet another adventurous journey up the next wave.

Spray washed from the tops of the swells, sweeping out in long streamers, with the whitecaps along the crests frothing like powdered sugar frosting. The steel wool sky weighed down the sea, scrubbing it of color and compressing the trip down the eastern shore of Portsmouth Island and the Cape Lookout National Seashore into a crawling struggle with one wave after another until even Sharky called out, "How important is it for y'all to get down there to do this?"

"What, have a look-see? For our investigation, vital. What we find down yonder might say if we have an investigation to pursue or not." Diane held one fist clasped to a stainless-steel stanchion, and she wiped spray from her face. Even on the portions of the boat that offered some protection, the wind pummeled them, keeping anyone from staying dry. Only their slickers provided any barrier from the sea spray, and then only what they could keep sealed from the intrusion of the wind-driven fingers of salt water.

From his position on the boat, hunkered down and his arms wrapping his plastic bucket, Sean closed his eyes and tried to keep his stomach under control. *If we have an investigation.* They'd better, he thought, with what he was suffering.

"Buck up, Sean." Jason leaned in, having to almost yell to be heard. "You'll get yours. I want to check with Sharky and see if there's an update about the boat we're chasing down."

"Why?" Sean managed to ask. If it was stranded on the beach, it wasn't likely going anywhere in this weather, even if someone was aboard.

"Salvage hunters. If someone recovers that boat, say, returns it to a safe harbor, they can get a reward. Lots of people see salvaging boats as easy money."

"Not easy." Sean felt his stomach jump as the boat reared off the top of a swell and slammed into the lee side. "Where would they take it?"

"South. Or maybe back to Silver Lake if that's a closer option for them." Jason shrugged under his waterproof outer layer, and his bulky cable knit under the slicker shifted the slicker's hood around his face. "Who knows, maybe we can get back to shore all in one piece. First, I have to clear things with the sheriff and Diane."

Sean saw the grin on Jason's face as he turned to walk away, and somehow, he didn't find it funny at all.

Jason first stopped to talk to Sheriff Pafford. After several minutes of hand motions and pointing, the sheriff nodded, called to Diane, and conferenced before sending Jason off to the ladder leading up to the pilot house to confer with Sharky. Ricky was at the stern with Emily, both holding firmly to stainless steel chair backs, and their bodies rocking in unison with each hit of the boat into the swells.

In the pilot house, Sharky got on the radio, and after a time, Jason returned to stand beside Darlene and Diane. He headed towards Ricky and Emily, and for several minutes, his shoulders rocked with theirs, the three swaying bodies jarring and shifting as one person, before Jason waved to Sean and headed his way.

He sat beside Sean and pointed to the shore along their starboard side, where they could see sandy dunes just visible when the *Queen* topped the swells. "Look at all that. How long do you think a boat would last washed up on the shore?"

"Not long." The boat they were on shifted, the shore disappeared, and spray impacted the glass, obscuring even the roiling gray skies.

"Great Island Fishing Camp has offered to send a truck down to see if the sailboat is still on the sandbar where they saw it last. Even if it is, they said we might not be able to access it. Phillips Boat Salvage has also been searching for it. If they've claimed it—" Jason shrugged.

"That's what you expect, isn't it?" Sean felt hope. It might mean they could return to shore, and his stomach could return to a normal condition, meaning not wanting to throw up.

"Suspect not expect."

The boat shuddered, felt airborne, and then hit the bottom of a trough with bone-jarring intensity.

"Ouch," Sean let out involuntarily.

"Weather's picking up. Sailboat or no, Sharky may be heading in. Keep that bucket close. You may be needing it."

Jason tapped the bucket, stood, and holding on to whatever was at hand, he made his way towards the pilot house and the skipper manning the controls and the radio. Sean watched him go, and he wondered why anyone ever paid good money to come out on one of these.

Then his stomach turned loose, and the bucket in his lap became the best friend he could hope for, at least for the next five minutes.

Chapter 3

Finding the Lighthouse

HYDE COUNTY SHERIFF DARLENE PAFFORD held to a stainless pole on Sharky Jenkins' sport fishing boat, and her arm vibrated with each impact of the hull on the surface of the water. Her face was wet and cold, despite the protection of Sharky's slicker.

She thought of Michael, her son, in college in Omaha. Winter took your breath away there, even more so than in her hometown of Brunswick back in Ohio, but they never suffered with this. Miracle Whip or mayo … she shivered and let go of the thought and grinned. This or that, one or the other. Give up one thing, and something else takes its place.

She wouldn't mind giving up these barrier islands, though, the reason she was based on Swan Quarter and left Ocracoke to Suzanne DeSantis. Still, a measure of responsibility for Ocracoke came with the job she held, and she highly respected Deputy DeSantis—and Lieutenant Turnipseed even more.

Diane might be a fully-fledged Outer Banker, but she knew her stuff, and Darlene enjoyed working with her on the occasions that intercounty cooperation allowed it.

Sheriff Kringlebach from Manteo had shared his disappointment that the C-District lieutenant had allowed Deputy Taylor to waste so much of his time and the county's resources on pursing that recent hotel billing scam. *"I have a B-District team that can handle it perfectly well without that young whippersnapper up here bungling around in B-District affairs."* But Darlene discounted that as little more than jealously for the loyalty the lieutenant commanded from her C-District team.

It was more widely known that an explosion just north of Buxton on Hatteras Island had injured one of the state medical examiners from Raleigh, and when different county representatives met up, they often as not used the incident to tease and sometimes deride Dare County for letting that "slip through its fingers like sand in a sieve." The whole, murky affair embarrassed Sheriff Kringlebach, and he'd firmly put his thumb on the investigation and insisted that the C-District team file it away and move on.

Moving on made nothing disappear. The investigation was shelved and listed as unsolved, and with the current intercounty drug sting going down … well, to Darlene's way of thinking, it didn't do to discount anything that might tie in to locking up bad people who needed to be put away for a while.

She noted Jason Romney headed her direction. His slicker kept coming open at the waist, and when the wind blew it wide, a darkened band appeared down his sweater and his pants. He didn't seem aware of it, or he was and knew there was nothing to be done until they got ashore.

"Sheriff," he called to her when he was close enough for her to hear over the roar of the wind and the battering echo of the water smashing against the hull. "Some people might could get upset at this type of weather, but me, I appreciate you letting me tag along."

"It's a shame we're turning around," she yelled back. He was only feet from her, but the roaring of the wind and water was a freighter's foghorn, and cables and lines—basically anything loose on the boat—vibrated with foreboding intensity. "My appreciation to the fishing camp for saving us from a wasted trip. Well, from going further on a wasted trip, as we managed it halfway, didn't we?" She laughed.

"Yes, ma'am. I think Sharky was getting worried, and he doesn't worry about much, so he's happy we're heading in."

Darlene searched in the distance to her left. The shore was only visible part of the time with the boat climbing and cresting swells, but it hunkered on their port side, proof that they had turned, although with the direction of the wind, to avoid the worst of the buffeting, they weren't headed straight up the coast.

"There's a cut along here, isn't there?" Darlene pointed towards the shore, discovered it wasn't where she expected it to be, and changed the direction of her arm.

"Yes." Jason didn't elaborate, and he wiped windborne spray from his face with the flat of his palm.

"Wouldn't the water be calmer in the Sound? I've noticed the deputy over there. The ride's not agreeing with him."

"Yeah, I expected that when he set foot on board. He's a good man but not much of a water rat. Me? I love it out here, the wilder the better. That cut you're talking about? Can't trust it, not in this weather. It's the same with most of the passages through the Banks. Go out in the morning, and fishermen have to check the reports to know where to return in the evening. Sometimes the passage you used at dawn has shifted, and you'll beach your boat if you take the same way back. It's the sand. It moves underneath the water like a mess of schooling fish."

"So, we have to head back the way we came. The Inlet'll be

open, I presume."

"Yes, ma'am. Look there, that wide stretch of water, that's where we're headed." The water still churned, but just where Jason pointed—the Inlet—the massive swells they'd been fighting were smaller and hopefully less rough. "That's Portsmouth Island just to the left, and there, that smudge on the horizon, that's Ocracoke, but the oceanfront side. The village is on the opposite shore, and that's where Sharky's headed."

"To calmer water, right?"

"Miracle Whip, mayo?" Jason grinned at her. "Sorry, I overheard you earlier. In college, I dated a girl from Cleveland. She used to make that reference when I'd ask where she wanted to go for the weekend, telling me it didn't make any difference. She also liked chili on her spaghetti. You go for that, too?"

"And B-Dub's." She was enjoying this connection with her past life.

"Ah, Buffalo Wild Wings. See, even us Outer Bankers know a little bit about the wider world."

"So, I guess you know about that?" She motioned towards what was likely the Cedar Island ferry in the distance. Waves lashed the sides, and it didn't appear to be moving. The *Queen* was fighting its way through the islands and into the Inlet, with the engine straining on the steeper swells, and the ferry disappeared and reappeared as Sharky's boat danced the waves.

"I guess with this weather … sandbar, perhaps?" He shrugged.

"Remember, Miracle Whip, mayo. Tell an Ohioan what you mean," she chided him. "I don't know much about the state ferry system. I use it for what it is, transportation where there's no roads, and I let others take care of the operation and main-tenance, just as I do the highways that crisscross the North Carolina landscape."

"Right, right." The *Queen*'s hull hit hard against the water, and Jason's body jerked as he responded to the sudden change in motion. "Ouch, Sharky," he said with a smile. "Give us a break."

"About the sandbar," Darlene prompted.

"You know all this is really shallow. Up north in the Currituck Sound, you could walk from the Banks to the mainland."

"Walk across the Sound? Isn't that several miles? No deep spots?" She laughed. "I bet there's deep spots."

"I should have expected a joke from you, Sheriff. What you generally have up north is about five feet of depth all the way across. This—" and he pointed past the motionless ferry being buffeted by the waves, taking in the expanse of Pamlico Sound with the sweep of his arm, "—is deeper by only a margin. Even the marked channels can fill in without warning. The ferry beaching on a sandbar is more common than you know."

"So, is that ferry in any trouble?" What she wanted to ask was whether *they* were in any trouble. If that deputy didn't get off this boat pretty soon, she expected he'd be needing a freshly scrubbed spittoon. He was likely to have the one he was holding about filled by now.

"I can talk to Sharky. He might have heard something over the radio."

"He can contact them direct, can't he?" She was the sheriff of these parts. She should know these things, she supposed, yet … ferries … water things … the Outer Banks … were not things that especially interested her, and there were people who liked all this. She was content to leave it with them. They could claim the title of expert over all things Outer Banks, and she would gladly return to Swan Quarter where she belonged.

"I'll find out." Jason did snug up his slicker, pulling it tight around his waist, and he climbed the ship's ladder to the pilot house on the upper section of the boat. As he disappeared from

Darlene's view, she noted how wet his shoes were, but then, she felt the water filling hers, also.

"SHERIFF?"

Darlene was keeping Sean Taylor company, and she looked up to find Jason Romney holding to a pole and leaning her direction. She smiled. "Did Sharky say it'll come out in the warsh?"

"Not exactly." He laughed. "He did say we could expect rain before we reach Silver Lake, so we might get *warshed* before we get there. The ferry, too, I expect, if they can't get unstuck."

"So, Miracle Whip or mayo, the sandbar's a thing. I guess the vessel really is stuck."

"Yes, ma'am. You can say that. They have requested aid, if we are of a mind to offer it. Are we? Sharky wants to know."

"What sort of aid?" She looked to Diane Turnipseed, wondering how the lieutenant would handle such a request. If it was to deliver a message, then of course. However, if they needed to physically dock with the ferry, could this boat do that? The tossing sea didn't especially bother her, but ships did sink in rough weather. It was the reason the Outer Banks were known as the Graveyard of the Atlantic. Hatteras even had a museum by that name, making it a verifiable fact Darlene couldn't dispute.

Jason spelled out the request. "A pregnant woman heading over to Morehead City for a medical appointment. The pilot of the ferry thinks it's a possible panic attack, but she really wants off the ferry. He hinted they might work themselves off in a few minutes, but he also said it might be when the tide comes up."

"And that's when?"

"It's still on its way down, so several hours at least."

"I would like to discuss this with Diane—"

"I expected that, Sheriff, and I spoke with Emily, and she

conferred Sharky's message to the lieutenant. She says it's your island and your county, and she's behind you whatever you decide."

"She did, did she?" Darlene snorted a disbelieving laugh. "In those exact words?"

"Not exactly, Sheriff. Her actual words were that someone don't got the sense that God gave a minnow. For all sakes, of course we'll help, but this isn't my pot, so you go get Sheriff Pafford's take on it, then tell that pilot up there to hightail it over there."

"Then the lieutenant's already fixed this. Let's hightail it over there."

"Let me get Sharky's input, see if this can be done." He nodded and headed back up the steps.

Sean Taylor hugged his bucket and moaned, "Seriously? I thought we were heading back to Silver Lake."

"Soon. You let me know when you need that bucket warshed out. Until then, I'm headed over to talk to Ricky and Emily. You'll be okay here?" She asked it like a question, but she knew he would. Being polite was a part of being an Ohioan, and even out here on the edge of the world, there was no need to let that part of her ever get away.

She did note that the water was calmer and the boat was jarring her less, and yes, she could walk without holding on to keep her footing. Ricky and Emily were in a lull in their conversation, and she let them know she was there by asking, "You needing a bit of rain? I hear it's coming our direction."

"Welcome to our neck of the boat, Sheriff Pafford." Emily nodded to her. "That ferry. Are we headed that way? A pregnant woman in distress, who can resist that?"

"Your deputy, for one." She indicated Sean with a twist of her head. "All he wants is back to Silver Lake and, I suspect, his feet on solid ground."

"Some time on the sand … I wouldn't mind that either."
Emily smiled.

"Can we do this? I mean, dock with them?" Darlene nodded
toward the approaching ferry.

"Come along side? Oh, yeah," Ricky assured her. "I'll drop
some bumpers over the side, and Sharky will use the engine to
hold us in place while the woman transfers over. No problem,
that is if she is brave enough to climb over."

"But matching speeds—" Darlene took a deep breath. "Two
eye will tell you that's not a joke."

"Think like a Banker." Ricky grinned. "That ferry's not
moing, so there's no speed to match, just the push of the waves.
Trust me in this." He glanced at the dark, brillo pad sky overhead as fresh, evenly spaced dark spots began to scatter across
their slickers and the boat deck. "Nah, not rain, too. I guess I
was making a good choice to stay in town and work on that
house. I've given Mick the job now, so nothing I can do for that
except enjoy the ride. Or maybe I'm a pariah. Jason and Sharky
got the good weather this morning, and I ushered in all this."

"Who dey!" Darlene pumped her arm in a cheer-like motion.
"You now control the weather?"

"You're a hoot, did you know that, Sheriff?"

"Darlene, please." She smiled. "It's all in the sandwich.
Gotta find the good in life. Thirty minutes the other side of that
ferry, I've got another two-hour ferry ride home. Throwing it all
in the warsh sometimes fixes a situation to where it doesn't
seem so bad after all."

"You think our pregnant woman will agree with you?"

"It's all in the warsh." She was having fun with this man,
playing up her Ohio background, like he was at a farmer's
market with her.

One thing Darlene was reminded of was that being on the
water was a time-consuming affair. On paper, the distances

between the islands making up the Banks were little more than a move of the mouse on her computer. In a car, that meant hours of driving. Today she was learning she had to double that time in a boat. Eventually, though, the ferry grew out of the waves, and they could recognize individual automobiles, then people on the deck, mostly ferry employees, and Darlene wondered that more people weren't out and about and marveling at the silly sport fishing boat ripping across the brutal Sound water when they were trapped by an errant sandbar.

When Sharky maneuvered them alongside, and she stepped onboard and introduced herself as the county sheriff, she learned why. The cars were strapped down, their wheels lashed to the deck, and no one was allowed outside their vehicle due to the rough seas. She followed the ferry workers to a silver Nissan Murano where they tapped on a window and watched it slip into the door.

"Sheriff Darlene Pafford." Darlene introduced herself to the pale, nauseous-looking woman in the passenger's seat. Her husband, beside her and wearing a beard, reached across and offered his hand.

"Nathan Preston from west of Fort Worth. This is my wife, Paytyne."

"That's Texas." Darlene grinned. She had a sister who'd married a man from Springtown, also in Texas, not far from Fort Worth. These people were a long way from home. "Your wife is the pregnant one, right?" Two people in the car. Miracle Whip, mayo, except she hoped not this time. If he was the pregnant one, then they had a whole different corn hole game in play, one she didn't want to delve into.

"Well," and he glanced at his wife's stomach and said, "Likely you could call it that."

"And she wants to head into town ... I'll warn you, we're glad to offer her a ride, but it'll be back to Ocracoke. We're on official county business and headed that way."

"Paytyne, honey?" He took his wife's hand. "You sure about this?"

"That doctor's *appoinment* is gonna have to wai'. I just wan' off this boat." Her words were blurred. She grimaced, placed her hand over her mouth, and paused for half a minute before continuing. "Please, Sheriff?"

"Road trip time, then. Come on, honey. Let's get you out of here and onto our boat. You may not be dodging this deer by much, though. We've got a sick'un on board ourselves, and he's hoping he makes it back to dry ground before he pukes again." Darlene motioned to the men at her side, and when she stepped away, they moved forward, opened the SUV's door, and helped the sick woman climb from the car.

The rain that had begun as large whelps of water was now sharp and biting, and Nathan offered an umbrella to Darlene. She took it, thanked him, and opened it to hold it over Paytyne as much as possible.

Jason and Ricky waited on the *Pamlico Queen*, riding the fishing boat up and down as the smaller craft wrestled with the waves. They could have been undersea divers in their slickers, barely discernible one from another in the murky, moisture-infused air. The scent of salt, fish, and diesel fumes was a blanket across the scene, and Paytyne accepted their hands, but she coughed when an oily diesel fog wrapped them for a moment before being blasted away by the gods of the wind and the sea.

Emily moved forward to help, and when she recognized the pregnant woman, she took her hand. "Paytyne? I thought you were having your baby back in Texas. Fort Worth, right?"

"Aw, man, you know each other?" Jason looked from Emily to Paytyne and said, "How is it that women from halfway across the country can meet on a stranded ferry and still know one another? That should be illegal."

"Because we're women, so you hush up," Emily cheerfully reprimanded him. "Come with me, Paytyne. You can tell me about it when we get you seated."

Diane Turnipseed directed Sean Taylor to allow room for their new guest. Sean moved down the bench, crablike with his shell of a bucket, his eyes on the roundly swollen pregnant woman joining him.

"You can borrow my bucket if you want." Sean tapped the side of it.

"Thank you," Paytyne said.

"Sean," he offered, holding out his hand.

"Paytyne," she returned, but she didn't shake. Instead, she covered her mouth with her hand as her face turned green.

"Paytyne Preston?" He perked up when she nodded.

Then the skies vomited a torrent of cold and wet, the engine of the *Pamlico Queen* roared, and as Ricky yanked the bumpers aboard, they pulled into the Sound with their destination obscured by the onslaught pummeling the waves into liquid submission all around them.

"I EXPECTED we'd be there in under thirty minutes." Darlene apologized as she consoled the green-gilled woman seated next to Sean Taylor. "But this weather … well, it's like they say down south in Kentucky, if the good Lord's willing and the creek don't rise. It seems like the creek's already flooded every-thing, so all that's left is for us to get on board. Our skipper says we might be another hour or two at this."

"Kentucky isn't south, ma'am. It's west of here." Paytyne dabbed her mouth with a cloth and studied her bucket. Sharky had rummaged up one for her, also. Her eyes were red, and she had the bucket on her knees, where it fought for a place on her lap with her baby bump. "This smells, and I am so sorry."

"Never you mind the smell. A good sweeper will take care of that when we get back, that or a warsh down. And Kentucky?" Darlene laughed. "I'm sure two eyes on a map will tell you Kentucky is west from here, but I always want it to be south. That's the Ohio in me. It's like that place named Michi— " She hesitated as the word caught in her throat. "Naw, I can't even say the name of the place, but you know where I mean. It's always north, cause my brain is always in the Buckeye."

"Buckeye. You get that name from the nut, right?" Jason Romney. Everyone's eyes turned to him, and he shrugged. "I told the sheriff I have a connection to Ohio. I know a few things."

Ricky Johnson laughed. "A side of you I didn't know about. I want to learn more later." He grinned at Jason, who had joined them to stand by Diane Turnipseed, close enough to offer her protection on the rough passage but not close enough to touch.

Darlene studied the two Dare County employees, taking in the emotional dynamics bubbling between them. It was like an electrified rubber band. Anytime Diane looked at the man, sparks flew from her eyes, as though there was a connection but not one that the lieutenant necessarily approved of or wanted to pursue. She pushed him away, and he was back at her side as soon as the sparks quit flashing. Darlene found the man engaging in a professional way, and she decided that Emily would be the one to feed her the scoop on the flash of lightning that seemed to fire between them each time they were a cornhole board's length from one another.

Emily climbed down the ship's ladder from the pilot house, calling out, "Excuse me, but Sharky wants to know if y'all have watched the clock."

"Y'all?" Jason teased her. "Since when do you say y'all?"

"Since I was a baby with my feet on the sand. I grew up here, be reminded. Just because I learned to talk in New York doesn't make me one of them. Us Downeasters can talk island talk anytime we want to. Now, for your clocks. All this dark isn't just the storm."

The rain still pummeled the waves, but when they looked past the bow of the *Queen* toward their destination, it had disappeared. In the distance, occasional lightning illuminated sections of the cloud cover, visible as ghostly afterimages through the rain-shrouded haze.

"Look towards the starboard side." Emily motioned with her hand. "Our charted course is a big horseshoe, first west, then follow the channel, and east back to Silver Lake. It looks to be the clouds are insisting on an early evening. We're effectively losing about two hours of daylight."

"We won't get stuck, will we?" Paytyne held her bucket like a lifejacket aboard a sinking ship. "I mean, the driver can find his way even if it gets dark, right?"

"Yes." Emily motioned for Sean to do his crab walk once again, and she wedged in between the two seasick landlubbers. "First, Paytyne, why is this baby not happening back in Texas? It seems you and your husband were headed back when I saw you last."

"It's Nathan's cousin. He lives in Goldsboro, and he's getting married next week. Nate lived with his family just outside Fort Worth while growing up, and they are more brothers than cousins." She smiled wearily as she brushed damp hair back from one side of her face and hooked it over one ear.

"So you drove out in this condition, or did you fly?" Emily took Paytyne's free hand, moved the bucket to the deck, and patted her arm.

"Drove—"

"You didn't." Emily laughed. "You are a braver woman than I knew. It's twenty hours or more by car."

"Farther than from Brunswick, even," Darlene chimed in.

She liked this brave little woman. Her son Michael might be in college now, but she remembered how difficult it was when he came, and in the early months of his life they had only struggled more. And to travel, too? It was nearly beyond imagining.

"I have another month, and my doctor back home said that's plenty of time, and that there's doctors and hospitals all over around here. Even if something happened, the baby would be fine. We came a week early to spend time with Nate's cousin at his beach house, then the baby started feeling funny. I had to go to Morehead City to stay in my hospital plan. Nate and I had no idea the ferry would do that to me. We had so much fun out here on our last visit."

"Insurance," Diane Turnipseed muttered. "Insurance companies don't got the sense God gave—"

"We know how you feel, Diane," Darlene said, stopping her tirade. To Paytyne, she said, "The baby is likely making the difference."

"It gets dark fast out here, doesn't it?" Paytyne looked around, just then really taking in the curtain of darkness enveloping them. The lights onboard the boat glowed, creating a miniature lighthouse crawling over the swells, but beyond the gunwales, she was correct. The waves were barely visible. Occasionally a whitecap crested the side of the boat and caught in the onboard lights, but the storm-thrashed North Carolina night was catching up with them, a tightening noose of black velvet soaked with cold and damp.

A buoy came up beside the boat, and Jason called out, "Channel marker!" as he noted the green light peering back at them from the starboard side of the boat. A wave crested just at that time, riding up the side of the boat, and momentarily eclipsing the channel marker. When the boat settled down, the marker was behind them at a slightly different angle, and the boat's engine roared as Sharky adjusted his direction to keep them on the correct course.

Darlene Pafford's radio squawked, one more layer of sound against the jangle of fishing equipment, people's voices, and the staccato battering of the rain, and it took her a moment to reach to her belt and respond.

"Sheriff Pafford here. Over." She released the talk button and held up her free hand. Like a series of windvanes atop a string of Ohio country schoolhouses, the people onboard with her turned her way, waiting like open books to be filled with information.

The radio squawked back, loudly enough for everyone to hear, "Sheriff, don't you worry none, but this is Brandon. You catch that? Come back at me if you do. Over."

Darlene frowned. Brandon Scarbrough played the role of Ocracoke Island Liaison, a position created by Hyde County to alleviate residents' travel to Swan Quarter to take care of county business. He worked out of the community center but only two days a week, then only half days at that. The man had a side gig taking care of summer homes on the island, although in summer, it sometimes seemed his job as liaison fell prey to being his side gig. Certainly, with this weather, he wasn't likely out with his trailer mowing lawns, but it also wasn't either Monday or Wednesday, and they were long past noon when the liaison's office shut down.

"Yes, Brandon. Surprised to hear from you."

"Like I said, Sheriff, don't you worry none, but Deputy DeSantis asked me to come in and man the radio for a bit. She suggested I might earn a few dollars overtime if you catch my drift."

"I catch your drift. I suppose that can be done. Where's the deputy off to that she called on you to help her out?"

Before Brandon could answer, the radio crackled with static then screamed with feedback, and towards their island destination, the sky lit up with lightning like a series of electric dominoes, one knocking over the next as they tumbled across the rain-infused and cloud-choked horizon.

"Brandon?" Darlene pushed the talk button as she called his name, then released it for his response. In the radio's silence, she tried again. "Brandon, this is Sheriff Pafford. Are you reading me? Over."

"Ma'am, yes." Brandon's voice crackled with static. "I'm guessing you're barely in range. I've been trying you for an hour. Now, the roads up to the Hatteras ferry might be awash, but we survived the last storm and—"

About then, rolling thunder from the lightning created a drumline of ominous suggestions. The roads awash? Surviving the last storm? If it was this bad where they were, what were conditions on the island?

"Brandon!" She tried to interrupt him but with no success.

"—we can get 'er done. Now, the deputy says that boat you're chasing's already moored in Silver Lake, so your trip's of no account any longer. The last she heard, so she said, is that Phillips Salvage is trying to file on it for salvage reimbursement. They don't want to give it over to the county, so she's run on up there. She needs you to get back soon's possible so you can deal with Phillips. You've got more clout, she says. Come back?"

"Yes, Brandon. Can you hear me now? Over." Darlene released the talk button and waited, still holding up a hand to ask the people on the *Queen* to give her some time.

"Yes, ma'am, Sheriff. I hear you just fine. The radio's cleared right up."

"Thirty minutes, maybe an hour. This isn't a Sunday road trip. The weather here's pretty rough, and we're making slow progress right now." Since the bout of lightning and the ensuing drumline concert, the wind had picked up, and the boat was being battered. She could hear the engine struggling at each swell. The radio squealed, spoke to her in full static overload, and she tried to reconnect with the county liaison. "Brandon? You there? Darlene over."

His voice finally came through. "We lost power for a bit there. Sorry, Sheriff. You were saying? Brandon over."

"How bad is it? Over."

"Like I said, we survived the last 'un, and I guess we'll survive—"

Darlene let him play out his story, and she asked Ricky and Jason, "Can Sharky make faster progress? It seems the whole village of Ocracoke is about to sink under the waves. This is the county liaison, and Deputy DeSantis needs us back urgently."

"I can head up and ask, but in this?" Jason shrugged. "If we are of a mind to rush, we might be of a mind to run aground on a sandbar. Your call, Sheriff."

"Lieutenant Turnipseed?" Darlene held the mike away from her, with Brandon Scarbrough still reciting his version of events back on the island.

"To tell the story honest, Jason's right. We might oughta let the skipper drive the boat as he sees fit."

"Then let's get on board." She turned her attention back to the radio and Brandon's rendition of the storm's potential aftermath.

"—and there's three cows out near Springer's Point, just wandering in the preserve like they know where they're going, so soon's you get here, Sheriff, the better we'll be. It's a boon you'll be on the island to help the deputy out. Brandon over."

"That's good to hear, Brandon. Looks like we might dodge the deer this time, you think?" She laughed, even if it sounded forced. Lights that could be Ocracoke Village had appeared through the rain, and she assured him, "Thirty minutes. Can you contact the deputy and let her know?"

"Yes, ma'am. Don't you worry none. We can get 'er done.

Brandon out."

Beyond the lighted interior of the *Pamlico Queen*, across the shining and wet gunwales, and past the white-capped swells picked out and as quickly tossed aside by the *Queen*'s forward spotlights, the opening to the Ditch was marked by pinpoints of light that could only be the windows of residential and business structures hunkered down against the storm.

"Hear that, everyone?" Darlene dropped her "hold-up-for-a-moment" hand. "We got three cows out near Springer's Point, but they act like they know where they're going."

"They do, huh?" Emily laughed. "I know where I'm going when we get back, and that's to get a good cup of coffee. Do cows like coffee? I'll be glad to treat."

"If they share a little milk with you? Perhaps heavy on the cream?" Jason Romney grinned.

Diane Turnipseed shook her head and said, "You two, you might be above your knees, but that's a good one." She smiled at the joke.

"Diane?" Jason analyzed her as if discovering a rare and never-before-seen species of extraordinary and exotic life. "You *are* in there. I hoped you'd come out and say hello before this investigation was over."

"Don't start with me, Jason Romney. You work for the county full time now—"

"I will as soon as Sheriff Kringlebach approves my paper-work." He was in full happy mode with Diane's relaxed attitude, as anyone could tell by his posture and grin.

"Don't give me that. The man can put you off, but you're already approved by both departments. Just his signature is all you need. He's just keeping you on your toes."

"Keeping the lieutenant on her toes," Emily substituted.

"What does that mean?" Ricky shifted a glance from Diane to Jason, then turned to Emily. "I mean, I'm not part of the sheriff's posse, so to speak, so it's none of my business, except that Jason rents a room in my house, but how does putting pressure on Jason keep the lieutenant on her toes?"

"Steven Hill," Sean Taylor called from his bench of woes, out of the rain and marginally protected from the repeated curtains of stinging rain still blasting the *Queen*.

"He's the, um—" Ricky searched then snapped his fingers, "—medical examiner, right?" Then his eyes opened wide. "Ooh, that explosion in the dunes near Avon. The county covered the repairs to his motorcycle, didn't it?"

"Insurance covered the repairs. The county only provided a rental car for Steven until his bike was repaired, but yes, that seems to be the sand bar Jason's on." Emily squeezed through the group to tap on Sean's knee for a place to sit. When she was comfortable, she said, "He's embarrassed we haven't resolved that one. Being as the medical examiner was involved, the whole state knows Dare County hasn't resolved the case, and that rankles."

"Who's embarrassed?" Ricky frowned. "Not me, and I don't think Jason. Steven?"

"Morton," Diane said, meaning Morton Kringlebach. "And Darlene, you don't need to go telling Morton we're talking about him. He's a good sheriff, and I'm embarrassed, too, but I'm still dogging the case. If you want the story honest, I'd put some of my people on it full time, but Manteo says no, so we're working it in our spare time."

"What spare time?" Sean called. "No one gives me spare time—" Then his face contorted, and he interrupted himself by grabbing his bucket and pulling it tight. However, nothing happened, and he relaxed. "That was a bad one. Please, shore, get here!"

Paytyne Preston smiled, then the boat twisted on an especially large swell, and she scrambled for her bucket, also.

DARLENE CLIMBED the ship's ladder to the pilot house to check in with Sharky Jenkins about how their journey was progressing. She found him one hand on the wheel and the other on the throttle control. Each time the boat was slammed by a wave, he jerked with it, then pulled himself together and revved the engine or backed it off a bit. His torso rotated and twisted as he worked the wheel, revealing the effort it was taking to keep the craft on course. After a short time admiring his masterful control of his boat, she called, "Might get a trifle damp, you say?"

He saw who it was and called, "Hey, y'all. Sheriff Pafford, right?"

"Darlene'll do. I think we're more than a trifle damp." In the distance, in addition to the channel markers, the rain caused the lights on the shore to twinkle.

"Yes, ma'am. Like wrestling a shark in a hurricane, but we're not underwater yet, so's I think we got a good chance to make it in before the real bad weather hits."

"Real bad weather?" She laughed. "A stranded ferry, two sick passengers below, and a time or two, I thought we'd be swamped. That is the right word, swamped?"

"Water aboard?" Sharky grinned. "If so, swamped is as good a word as any, I'll give you that. The tricky part's just out there." He pointed through the windshield, where the wipers cleared away thick waterdrops—which were as quickly redeposited by the angry clouds overhead—and the spotlights lighting their way revealed quick glimpses of churning, turbulent waves that bucked and flung water at the sky as if in retribution for being pounded by the incessant rain.

It was a battle of sky and sea, and only a fool would venture to call the outcome and hope to be proved correct in the dangerous gamble. Darlene remembered Diane saying that she'd bet tomorrow's breakfast … well, not Darlene, 'cause this storm could go either way.

"Why tricky?" Darlene asked.

"The Ditch. You hit it right, or it puts a fist through the side of your boat. The dark—" He panned the sky with one hand and said, "Don't mind the dark. Got instruments, and by golly, they serve me well, but the dark with this weather, that's a real field party, ain't it, now?"

Over the island, lightning continued to strip the darkness from the horizon in jagged javelin thrusts of white-hot liquid anger, with the island flinging its own electric javelins back into the sky. It was a battle of light that only gave way to darkness under the assault of the driving winds and rain.

"I suppose so. Thank God for shore power—" Then a white-hot light exploded somewhere deep on the island, flared up, and brilliantly illuminated the bottom of the cloud layer. The lights on the shore blinked once as if winking at the *Pamlico Queen*, teasing her seductively, only to go black and remain that way. Darlene suspected she had spoken too soon.

"Nah, that's not what I wanted to see," Sharky said, as he fought the wheel against an especially large swell. "Only one thing to do now." He reached under a shelf and pulled out a leather case.

"Turn around?" Darlene's heart pounded. The man had already revealed how dangerous it was to enter Silver Lake under the cover of darkness, and he said the storm only made it worse. What other option was there?

"No, ma'am. Can't turn around now. Just need to find the lighthouse." He pushed the leather case her direction. "You take those, and we'll make it through the Ditch and tie up just fine, safe in the harbor."

She opened it and pulled out a pair of binoculars.

"There's the next channel marker." Sharky pointed, and it

appeared to their right. "So's the lighthouse should be about there." He motioned off into the darkness.

"The power onshore is out. How will I find it?" It was white, she remembered, but not very tall. She lifted the glasses to her face, focused past the boat's lights on the water, and only found darkness.

"The light's got a battery backup. I'll watch for the channel markers, and you find me that lighthouse. You ever had Cheerwine and Krispy Kremes?"

"Together?" She didn't have the slightest idea what he was talking about, but one thing was for certain. She still didn't see the lighthouse.

"Yes, ma'am. This is even better. I'll show you what this old boat can do." Sharky slammed the throttle as if he wanted it to jump forward, an impressive move designed to show the engine's power, but instead, it began a shuddering climb up the next swell, and when it crested the wave, there, just ahead, just for a moment, a flash of light appeared in the darkness. "There, catch that, Sheriff. We follow that in, and we'll find ourselves snug as sardines in a tin."

As the boat tipped forward, heading down the backside of the wave, Darlene's sense of up and down slipped along the deck, and she dropped the glasses to her side and grabbed for a handhold. She laughed and said, "Too much chili on my spaghetti, I suppose. Down south in Kentucky, they call that walking crooked."

"Still gettin' your sea legs." Sharky leaned into the wheel, putting most of his weight on the port side, as he fought the boat shuddering down the lateral wall of the swell and trying to skitter to the side and out of the channel. "Hold the rail with one hand and use the other to steady the glasses. You'll get it."

She did as he recommended, and she realized her brain had been empty as a freshly scrubbed spittoon. She'd turned completely loose of any handholds to affix the binoculars to her eyes. She was a verified Ohio landlubber, and even she knew better than that.

Her best views came just after the wipers cleared the glass. Patches of lightning were enough to orient herself between soil and sea, and she ran the binoculars along the shoreline, back and forth.

"Not the way to do it," Sharky said.

"Oh?" Did he want a turn, then? She'd be glad to man the wheel if he intended to criticize her like a dingbatter out to embarrass herself and everyone with her.

"Too low. You're watching the shore. The lighthouse is inland. The tops of the trees are where you want to be. That's where you'll find it. Channel buoy! Quick, red or green?"

"Green, um, no, a red triangle."

"On starboard?" He didn't turn her direction but watched the water just in front of the boat. "Quicky, missy."

"Starboard? That's on the right, right? Yes, red triangle on the right."

"Said it before. This is like wrestling a shark during a hurricane. We're headed off course." He spun the wheel as hard and fast as he could, and the boat heeled to the side and smashed into a brick wall of wet on the port side. The items in the pilot house rattled as the boat seemed to shiver down a solid embankment of concrete water before being released to leap ahead into an open trough of inky black. Then the floodlights dipped inside the trough, and the bottom seemed endless.

"Sharky?" Darlene held her breath and couldn't feel her heart. She also couldn't see the bottom of that wet hole in the sea. The heavy wave action seemed to have sucked the very water from the ocean floor, leaving nothing to cushion their fall except the sandy bottom.

"Channel marker," Sharky called out. "Color?"

"Green circle, yes, green."

"Whoa!" Sharky seemed to relax. "Now, treeline. You find me that lighthouse, and you be sure to hold on with one hand. You can never tell when another whopper of a wave will reach up a fist to try to drag us down to dance with Poseidon at the bottom of the Sound."

"Thought Poseidon lived in the sea." Darlene was pretty sure she had located the lighthouse, and she described to Sharky the scene in the binoculars. A long series of lightning flashes revealed several coastal buildings and multiple windows with faint lights inside. "Candles in some of the windows. The lighthouse must be the bright one."

"The tall one. Lights being out should make the lighthouse easier to find. Up, missy. Over the trees."

"I'm fixed on it, or I would be if you kept this boat stable." She dropped the glasses from her face to hold on as she was jounced violently around.

"It's the pilot house. Up here, the motion's more. Likely your friends feel safe and grounded."

"Like a beanbag into a cornhole game. How long do the backup lights in the lighthouse last?" She had it in her sights once again and hoped it didn't go out before they reached the harbor.

"Likely all night, even if the electricity stays out. Which way is it? I need to feel my way in."

She braced herself and kept a running description of where the light was, like the hands on a clock, as often as she could see it. Occasionally it was obscured, and several times, the boat twisted left or right, and she lost it.

Then, as quickly as they had gone out, the lights along the shore flickered on, blinked out once more, and after several tense moments, blazed at full brightness, offering the struggling vessel an inviting welcome home. A cheer from the main deck told them that the passengers below had noticed.

"Who dey! Dodged that disaster," Darlene breathed out, barely whispering. She held the binoculars tightly in one hand as she let them fall from her face. The boat still bucked and struggled with the weather and the waves, but somehow, the lights on the shore now seemed as comforting as Miracle Whip on a sandwich. "Like a game of cornhole," she joked to Sharky. "Right through the Ditch, right?"

"Mebbe, mebbe not." The man's focus on piloting his boat intensified as he revved the engine for a bit before backing it off when it began to whine. "Lookit right 'chere. Salvage. Some people abandoning their boats, likely."

A large vessel, more workhorse than beautiful, appeared out of the darkness, just visible in the shine on the hull from the *Pamlico Queen's* floodlights. A crane bled seawater and rain, and behind it, highlighted by a massive floodlight, a sailing vessel with ragged sails thrashed like a sailfish behind a sport boat.

"That can't be our boat," Darlene exclaimed as she lifted the binoculars for a closer examination. "Brandon said it's already in the harbor."

"Can't say I have an opinion there, Sheriff. That though's the Phillips' people in the *Go for Broke*. They're all over out here during storms, making a haul, near as I can tell." Sharky broke into raspy laughter.

"That's a joke, right?" Darlene slipped the binoculars back in their case and slipped it into the compartment Sharky had retrieved it from.

"Yes, ma'am, Sheriff. That's a joke." He glanced at her and grinned.

"My two eyes tell me you have this under control, so I'm headed back downstairs."

"I got it like a shark in a hurricane." He laughed again, likely releasing tension built up from the prospect of entering Silver Lake under the cover of darkness. The lights back on seemed to relax something in the man.

Down the ladder, the first thing Darlene noticed connected with something Sharky had said. It was calmer, though the water still resembled a mixing bowl churning at high speed. Also, she no longer had trouble finding the lighthouse. Once you knew, she figured, then you knew just where to look.

Sean Taylor was no longer hugging his plastic bucket, although Paytyne still claimed ownership of hers. Sean called to her, "Sheriff, you missed it. The whole island went dark. You should have been down here."

"Sharky and I didn't notice. When was this, Deputy?" She smiled, and she said to Lieutenant Turnipseed, "Diane, is he always that, um—"

"Overexcited?"

"I was going to say dense, but overexcited sounds better."

"I like dense better. You might oughta know, I don't always see eye-to-eye with the deputy. We have our differences."

"I'm pretty sure I noticed. How about you and Jason? I've seen a few sparks there, also."

"That man is not fit for discussion."

Several feet away, Jason was laughing at something Emily was saying, and Ricky slapped him on the back like he was in on whatever they were discussing.

"Then let's dodge that pothole. You see that ship?" The rain had let up, and the vessel Sharky had identified as the *Go for Broke* obscured a portion of the lights on the shore. The spot-light on the sailing vessel was more prominent.

"And the sailboat. Not ours, though."

"Salvage. Someone else overboard?" Darlene grinned. When Diane didn't respond, Darlene prodded the hornet's nest with, "It got abandoned somehow."

"For all sakes, Sheriff, boats do come loose from their moorings. Who's to say—" The lieutenant stopped mid-question and frowned, thinking about what she had been about to ask.

"My thoughts, too. We both saw that boat last night, well, not this one, but ours; and it *was* windy last night."

"Nothing moors on the ocean side, though," Diane said, though it sounded less a correction than a thoughtful observation. "We might oughta look into that before deciding something that might be nothing more than our imagination."

The very pregnant Paytyne stood, pushing her plastic bucket aside with her feet, and called, "Is there a restroom on this boat?"

"For all sakes," Diane said, and she looked towards Darlene, "As if they would make a boat without a head. I've got this." Diane called to the younger woman, "This way. I'll show you."

Ricky, Emily, and Jason moved out of Paytyne and Diane's way as they slipped belowdecks and disappeared, but what caught Darlene's attention was how steadily they managed their way belowdecks.

Not holding on to every handhold in sight.

She realized the water might still be kicking up like a pond at a fish hatchery on feeding day, but the swells had died back to nearly nothing. What was the word for it? *Slickcam* as the natives liked to say. Except that on this trip, *slickcam* was only in comparison to what they'd experienced for the last couple of hours. Even the rain was reduced to fine needles rather than fat pebbles of molten fury. Off the bow, the harbor lights and the buildings along the Ditch were in sharp focus, as they were no longer obscured by driving rain. Ahead of them, the *Go for Broke* was fully visible now, with the reflections of the buildings and shoreside lighting painting in the ship between the gunwales and the waterline, and the floodlight aimed at the ragged sailboat trailing at her stern winked off.

"Sheriff?"

She disconnected from watching Sharky navigate the Ditch to discover Sean Taylor hovering over her shoulder. She nodded at him and offered him a smile. "Yes?"

"You know I'm here to serve, no matter what, but I've never been so sick before. I've got no regrets for being on board with y'all, and I want to reassure you I'm a hundred percent here a hundred percent of the time. So, about me being sick over there, can we not talk about it much?"

"I already fixed it. You don't worry about a little seasickness." She hadn't but she understood, and she'd mention to the lieutenant that she thought the deputy might feel embarrassed if Diane brought it up; and while she didn't have any say over Dare County matters, she knew Diane might appreciate a heads up.

"I was glad the lights came back on." Sean's face relaxed with her assurance, and he began to bubble. "I bet these people along here—" he pointed to the residential buildings alongside the Ditch, "—never get tired of the boats going in and out. I like boats, well, not riding on them, but to watch them, sure. Do you like boats, Sheriff? You must since you're sheriff here."

"They're useful, so I guess I have to if I'm sheriff in Hyde County." She didn't, however, and didn't particularly care for the string of barrier islands known as the Banks. She was anxious to get back to her home in Swan Quarter.

Then the water truly became *slickcam* as they glided through the Ditch, left the narrow channel behind, and found their way into Silver Lake and protection from the storm.

THE *GO FOR BROKE* passed the *Queen*, motoring back towards the Sound, navigating the Ditch to seek out additional castoff ships for salvage by the time Sharky had the *Pamlico Queen* reversing into her mooring site. A set of shoreside hands was already at work on the tattered sailboat the *Queen* had trailed through the Ditch. Most wore yellow slickers, shiny with swirling mist under the overhead lights lining the wharf, the dissipating remnants of the storm the *Queen* had fought out on Pamlico Sound. With the back of the boat visible under the lights for the first time, the name *Money Pit* with *Swan Quarter* just under it in smaller script told a bigger tale than the owner, whoever that was, could have anticipated.

"T'weren't that right," Diane Turnipseed snorted when she read the name aloud. "Don't see how vessels like that are a good investment, not when left to litter up the Sound on a windy night."

"I suppose some people find them worth the money," Sheriff Pafford observed. She ran her eyes around the moorings along the shores of Silver Lake. "If that one's not ours—"

There were several boats in the harbor, many of them motor yachts, but with sailing a popular option for summer people, there was no shortage of vessels with masts. Most had the sails furled and covers snapped firmly in place over the cockpits, but one stood out. The sails, although fully intact, flapped loosely, suggesting the vessel had escaped the worst of the storm god's fists that had battered the *Pamlico Queen* just beyond the Ditch. The one they'd followed in? The *Money Pit* bled with the scars of the storm's fury in her tattered sails and the disarray vomited over her deck. If she hadn't been salvaged, likely she would be underwater by now. In the Sound, it might not have been far under, but sunk was sunk, and the damage from ten feet of water was as disastrous to electronics and wooden boat interiors as a hundred feet.

Their boat had police tape along the wharf, evidence of Suzanne DeSantis ensuring county access for what might soon be an investigation, that was if they uncovered evidence that someone had gone overboard and not that the boat had blown loose from its moorings. If it was tied to the drug bust from the previous night, evidence for that would be especially helpful, whether cash, stashed contraband, or drug residue. K9 Handler Zack Halsey would be the one to determine that, along with Goldie, his trained golden receiver. He wasn't on Ocracoke, not that Darlene knew, though with their hair-raising trip through the Ocracoke Inlet, the man's location on the Banks hadn't been foremost in anyone's mind. To get him there was an hour at minimum, and that was just ferry time. The drive down the island added thirty minutes. If overwash blocked the roads … and Darlene sighed. Maybe tomorrow, which meant a night on the island. She wondered what acceptable accommodations Officer DeSantis could put together for them … and whether she should bring it up now or later.

Islands.

This was why the Banks held so little appeal to her. Nothing was convenient on an island. Absolutely nothing. No farmer's market. No opportunities for road trips. And on this island, she could never say, "Oh, it's thirty minutes down this road," because she would be sending people into the ocean, for Pete's sake!

Sharky completed his maneuvers to nestle gently against the dock, and Ricky and Jason leaped ashore to affix the lines firmly to the cleats. Darlene assured him he could bill the county for his time and expenses, for which the man seemed grateful. Paytyne Preston was first off the boat, and Darlene joined her.

"Paytyne, honey, we're here. Do you know someone who can meet you?"

"Nate's cousin. Nate's my husband. You met him on the ferry." Paytyne seemed distracted, and she found a bench and sat on it heavily. "The ground seems shaky. It's never done that for me before. Do you think I'm sick?"

"No, honey, you just need your land legs back. Your brain

was already learning that the ground under your feet wasn't stable, and now, it's got to relearn that it is. Resting is the best thing for now."

Emily joined Paytyne on the bench. "How's that baby doing?" She smiled as she studied Paytyne's face. "No green gills, I hope."

Diane Turnipseed called, "Darlene, if you want to look over that boat, I see Deputy DeSantis over yonder. We might oughta head that direction."

"Go," Emily assured Darlene. "I can watch the young lady, and you go help the lieutenant out. Get the deputy to help you. Sean loves to spend time on boats." She grinned impishly.

"Who dey, done deal." Darlene turned to locate Deputy Taylor, and she called, "Deputy Taylor, I need you with me. The lieutenant and I are headed over to inspect that sailboat, and you're part of the team. I want you along."

Sean was in a threesome with Jason and Ricky, with Jason washing down the deck of Sharky's boat, and Sean playing out the hose and controlling the waterflow from the stability of the shore. Ricky held a push broom in one hand and a long squeegee tool in the other, and he followed along after Jason. Sharky was up top inspecting the outside area around the pilot house, likely for possible wind damage due to the brunt of the storm that had tried to take them down.

"I'm—" Sean started to lay down his water hose, looked at the spigot alongside the dock, and at Jason and Ricky. "Jason," he called, "the sheriff says she needs me. What do you want me, um, to do?"

"Me?" Jason backed off the water and took in Diane, Darlene, and the two women on the bench. He glanced at Ricky, pushing water along the deck with the long-handled squeegee, and he said, "Right now, I need you to do what the sheriff wants. I expect that boat we've been chasing might could be a lot more interesting than cleaning on this one, as fascinating as it is. You let me know what you find when you get back."

"Of course." Sean's shoulders sagged, and he called to Darlene, "On the double, Boss. You can count on me."

The women were already heading toward the salvage company's boats. Silver Lake was good-sized, and Sharky's berth was a decent distance from DeSantis' location. By the time Sean caught up with them, they were speaking with Deputy DeSantis, and she was giving them the scoop.

"You see that boat over there." Suzanne pointed, indicating the men scrambling over the *Money Pit*. "That's what I found when I got here. I told that company manager to get it together. This isn't shoofly pie. Last I heard the county gets first crack when there might be a crime involved—"

"Hold your taters for a second," Diane said. "Do we know there's a crime been committed?"

"They don't know that one's not been committed," Suzanne said. "When they tried to argue, I pulled out my badge and said they could talk to the badge, 'cause I was taking this boat over as evidence. Sheesh, I got me a college degree. What do you think all those men have? A fistful of calluses and absolutely nothing else."

"Shush that," Diane said, grinning. "You done been aboard for a look-see?"

"Yes, ma'am," Suzanne volunteered. "Sometimes I don't get the island thing, but I do get what's not right aboard a boat. That lifejacket from last night—"

"The one the boys found—" Diane started to say.

"No, ma'am." Suzanne ducked her head. "My apologies, Lieutenant, no disrespect intended, but not that one. Last I heard, it didn't match up with those on the dopeheads' boat." She raised her head, fighting a grin, explaining that she had received an updated report that they might have missed.

"You found something important onboard." Darlene stated it as a known fact. The expression on her deputy's face was cornhole certain.

"We're not missing a lifejacket any longer. Only thing is, it doesn't match this boat. And one other thing."

Deputy DeSantis led them onto the boat and to the stern. The boat, despite having been adrift in heavy seas, was orderly, new, and well-maintained. The sails, consisting of one large mainsail and a smaller jib sail, loosely flopping even now, and wet with the mist that refused to leave them alone, were pristine with no visible wear. Yet, roughly tied to a cleat on at the back, a ragged, dirty hemp rope, unlike the white nylon elsewhere on the boat, ran alongside the hull and disappeared into the water.

"Salvage line?" Diane knelt and placed her hand around it.

"Pull it up, ma'am," Suzanne suggested. "You'll see."

She did and found the end tattered and frayed, but unlike the rest of the weathered hemp, the tears on each strand of severed hemp were fresh and bright.

Darlene noticed something else. Black marks up the side of the hull from the waterline to the gunwale, as though someone had scrambled aboard in a hurry, leaving evidence of their shoe soles during the middle of the night.

She pictured the five men marched up from underneath the Avon pier. Black-soled boots on each man. Now, if this wasn't evidence for a missing sixth man, what was?

And yet, if so, where was he? The rope Diane held, not cut, but rather forcefully ripped apart as evidenced by the tattered and frayed ends. She suspected some sort of craft, roughly tied to the larger sailboat with shoddy rope, then jerked hard in a rough swell, and the weathered hemp line suddenly giving way.

That left one answer still out to sea. Who had been on this boat originally? And how was it connected to their drug bust?

And if it was, where were they now? God help them if dead

bodies started washing up on the shore. They had started out hoping someone hadn't fallen overboard during a storm. Now, they might have to begin a search for someone who had. Someones, she should say, as this rope indicated both people aboard and people who wanted to be aboard, and likely for ominously different reasons.

"Deputy DeSantis," Darlene called, "we're needing Zack and Goldie here quick as they can catch the ferry. Diane, can I get you belowdecks with me to look over things? And you, Deputy Taylor, road trip over to the rest of our team and see who can join us. I'm calling a team meeting in fifteen minutes."

She was satisfied to see Sean Taylor grin like a puppy on a play date as he shifted his stance and took off running.

Sharks in the collards. She'd heard Diane say that, and being aboard this boat, it fit the situation perfectly.

Sharks in the collards indeed.

Chapter 4

A Rash of Deputies

METALLURGIST JASON ROMNEY, former Carteret County deputy and hopefully soon-to-be a fully approved Dare County employee, held the water hose and let it run across the deck of the *Pamlico Queen* as he studied the Hyde County sheriff and Diane Turnipseed at the rear of the sailboat tied up partway around the harbor in Silver Lake.

For a moment, he cut his eyes to forensic investigator Emily Bryant sitting with their rescued pregnant woman, Paytyne Preston, and observed Emily patting the young woman's hand and giving her the emotional support the younger woman obviously needed. Emily had taken to the rough seas like an otter in a trough, as unperturbed by the crazy swells and caterwauling wind as a seasoned seaman. She was a good one to have on their team, as she never seemed flustered no matter the situation.

"Ricky," he called. "Look at those women down there. What do you suppose they're discussing?"

He felt his friend step to his side, and he nodded towards the sailboat. Across the back, he could just make out the name, *Dutchman,* out of Newport News. That would make its home port in Virgina, he considered. Not a far sail for someone who knows what they're doing and are enjoying themselves. Might could get to the southern Banks in a day and back again, if they were of a mind to do so ... and perhaps get caught up in a sudden squall they hadn't seen coming.

Was yesterday's heavy weather a sudden squall, or had it come through on the weather forecast, plain and out there for the boat's pilot to plan around?

"You thinking something, Jason?" Ricky held his squeegee over the side and let the water drip from its smooth, sharp edge.

"Yes. Deputy DeSantis is full time on the island, right?"

"I suppose. I'm not privy to Hyde County's personnel assignments, but that was the impression I got."

"She's pretty smart, I suppose." She would have to be to be trusted with the entire island of Ocracoke in her back pocket.

"I heard her tell it that way more than once. She has a college degree, and she doesn't take guff from anyone." Ricky grinned.

"Okay, let's leave it at that." Jason laughed. "But, yeah, I heard that from her too. My point, I think the woman found something important. You see what they're doing?"

"Playing in the water?"

His comment was justifiable. Diane stood on a step at the waterline just at the back of the boat, and she knelt and inspected a line that trailed from a cleat on the stern and down into the water. Suzanne DeSantis stood on the deck and beamed with satisfied self-confidence, telling Jason she had something, she knew it was good, and she was waiting for everyone else to catch up.

"The way I see it," Ricky observed, pointing with the squeegee, "that looks like a case needing solved."

Diane had pulled the line from the water, and the ragged ends were apparent even from a distance. Then she called Deputy Taylor, spoke to him for a moment, and he took off running their direction.

"I guess she wants one or more of us down there." Jason grinned.

"You, I reckon." Ricky chuckled.

"I should be so lucky. That woman's a hard nut to crack. Every time I think she's about to throw me a chance, she pulls in the line again."

Sean Taylor had reached Emily Bryant, and he stopped, spoke to her, and pointed towards the three women aboard the *Dutchman.* Emily took a moment to speak with Paytyne, patted her hand once more, then stood and started that direction. Sean looked straight at Jason, grinned like a lighthouse beacon, and headed their direction.

"Lucky you, it seems," Ricky teased. "Trust me in this, the messenger boy is on his way to you."

"Let it alone, Ricky, on both accounts. I'll work on the lieutenant at my own speed, and Taylor?" He paused and shook his head. "You can hardly fault a man for giving his job everything he can. You good on taking care of the rest of this?"

"I've washed down a deck before."

"This'n, likely." Jason grinned and offered him the hose.

"That's pretty close to right."

"Talk to Sharky, too. If I get a chance and he's still about, I'll stop by. There's fish in the hold, and I want my share in your freezer."

"You're a hoot. A salvaged boat, an outing across the Inlet, and likely a drowned body, and you can't stop thinking of what you caught out there. A true fisherman at heart."

"A hungry one, anyway." He greeted Sean. "Hey, my man. Y'all down there got the situation under control? I think I might have seen some solving going on."

"Likely, but I'm not in the loop, not fully, anyway, so I can't be for sure. Still, I'm here to serve no matter what. I always say that, and I mean it." He shrugged and tapped his temple. "A good mindset is what you need to be a good law enforcement officer. What you think is who you are, so be positive for a positive life. That's what I say."

"And not a bad thing to say, don't you think, Ricky?" Jason laughed. "You're here for a reason, Deputy, and Emily done disappeared down there, so, what is it?"

Sean looked confused for a moment, glanced at the bench Paytyne now commanded alone, and back to the *Dutchman* and the women on the stern, gently bobbing up and down as the sailboat lifted and fell in the protected swells moving across the inland harbor.

"Deputy?" Jason prompted.

"Oh … oh, yes. A meeting. The sheriff is calling a meeting in, um—" and he looked at his watch, "—nine minutes. She wants you there." Sean grasped his equipment belt, one hand on each side of his waist, and adjusted it by shifting it left. His cuffs rattled, which was of no account, but his flashlight was a bigger deal. He bumped it with his wrist, it fell to the decking just alongside the shore, and Sean watched with a horrified look on his face as it began to roll towards the water's edge.

"Whoops-a-daisy," Ricky called out, and he flicked his long-handled squeegee effortlessly onto the shore and stopped the flashlight's progress. He slowly worked it back Sean's direction.

"Oh, man, that was close," Sean said, and he knelt to retrieve it.

"Lucky you," Ricky quipped with a laugh.

"I know," Sean said. "Thanks."

"Okay, Ricky, this is yours to finish up," Jason called. "If I get a break, I'll hit you up for dinner back at the house. What time are you expecting to catch the ferry up island?"

"In this?" He looked out over Silver Lake where the mist still fell, creating a haze around the lights lining the harbor. He pulled up a sleeve to study his watch. "Long as the ferry's running, hmm, a couple hours at the latest. Otherwise, I'll have to overnight here."

"Yah, a bad situation, to be forced to overnight on the best island of the Banks." Jason grinned. "Deputy? You ready to head on down?"

Once on the shore, they walked Garrish toward the rest of the combined counties' team. On the way Jason questioned if Sean knew where the rest of the deputies from the previous evening were, principally Calvin Dingman. He half expected to see Zack Halsey, as he was Goldie's handler, although he didn't know if his presence had been requested by Sheriff Pafford yet. It would be, he was certain, because that's what he would do. After all, a drug bust, an abandoned boat, and now, the ladies clearly finding something on said boat. The team meeting had cinched it for Jason. The sailboat was definitely suspect at this point, and Goldie would be the one to determine if drugs were part of the picture.

The reason for Calvin? He was Jason's man-of-the-hour, someone who often came across as a country bumpkin but who knew his stuff. His backcountry mannerisms were what broke the ice with the backcountry Downeasters inhabiting the lowlands of the North Carolina shorefront.

How did people say it? It takes one to know one. Jason considered that it took one to create trust with one. That was the magic in Calvin Dingman and the reason he hoped he was either on the island or headed their direction.

"Any news on who else might be joining us?" Jason casually probed the deputy for information as they walked.

"Pretty sure Deputy Dingman was coming on the next ferry this morning."

"That's good news," Jason said, with a satisfied nod. He noted Sean checking the flashlight on his belt, and the young deputy's boot caught on a crack in the asphalt. He tripped and nearly tumbled, and the flashlight came loose in his hand.

"Shoot, another near disaster."

"Deputy." Jason stopped him. The lights along the street cast long shadows, and the deputy's face was mostly hidden. "Take time and fix that tool. Why's it coming loose so often?"

"Don't know." Sean shrugged. "Emily says I'm not careful, but I try to be. Things just happen when I'm not expecting it, and—" he sighed, "—anyway, I'm here to serve, so no regrets, right?"

"You are gung-ho, my man." Jason approved of the man's attitude if not his struggle with professional behavior.

"Is that bad?" Sean studied the boat they could just see through the buildings along the waterfront before looking back at Jason. "I try to do my best, that's all."

"No, it's not bad. It's what I like about you."

A set of headlights pulled in just where Sheriff Pafford, Diane Turnipseed, and Suzanne DeSantis had been surveying the boat. They could see Emily Bryant and Deputy DeSantis, but the others weren't in their view. The vehicle, a truck by the headlights, turned under a light, and mint green paint flashed before disappearing into the evening.

"That," Jason said, "I believe is Calvin."

"You can tell that from just his headlights?" Sean sounded impressed.

"Yes, all metallurgists can." At Sean's amazed *whoa,* Jason grinned. "That and the green paint. No one else I know has a truck that color. Let's get on down. The man's brilliant, and I bet he has something to say."

It might not be something Diane would appreciate, as she thought the arriving deputy was a swamp hick with no learning, but Jason knew differently. Calvin was respected in Hyde County. It was time Diane learned to respect him, also.

"CALVIN!" JASON called to the Hyde County deputy. The man was out of his truck and wearing a black cap with Sheriff Hyde County in gold and orange with black shoes finishing out his feet. In the dim light, the stitching on his cap popped, while his khaki shirt swelled around his fleshy midsection.

"That you, Jason Romney?" Calvin spat, the tobacco juice invisible in the darkness, and he worked his mouth before going on. "Shucks, bub, what'cha got going on here? It's like we done had a drug bust, 'cept it didn't get busted all the way."

"I might could ask you the same question, my man. I expected you would show up. Then I saw that mint green Ram you drive, and I knew there would be something interesting happening around here."

"T'wouldn't be surprised, myself. That Deputy Taylor along at your side?"

"Yes, sir," Sean piped in loudly and proudly.

"What do you know?" Jason asked. He hadn't been at the drug bust the night before, and he wasn't sure how much he would be allowed to participate in what was happening now. However, the sheriff had requested him to join them, so he had high hopes that he could jump in the pool, if he wasn't already swimming with the school of deputies on Sheriff Pafford's multi-county team.

"About last night or today?" Calvin was still working with his equipment belt, and he finished up and slapped the buckle with the flat of his hand.

"Either. My knowledge is as scant as cod in the Sound, so anything you can tell me is more than I know."

"Which is normal as cod on a plate." Calvin laughed. "We got five booked and locked last night. You hear that?"

"Okay, I overheard a little bit, but not much more. Deputy Taylor here is more in the know that I am."

"Oh? I'll be ding-danged." Calvin chuckled. "Never expected Jason Romney to admit there's something he don't know. Maybe the deputy needs to take your place—"

"Let the teasing alone, Calvin. Just tell me the latest. You're here, so you must know something."

"Shucks, Jason, teasing between friends isn't anything a taco won't solve. I'm doing what most of us from Swan's doing, trying to get back up to the Quarter. I didn't want to drive all the way round, and Ocracoke's the quickest way, even if it does mean two-and-a-half hours on the ferry home. Then Suzanne rings me and says this boat's been lodged here, and she needs help with securing it for the county." He shrugged, as though he was following directions, even if they made no sense to him, before finishing with, "That's why I'm here."

"You have a clue where Zack is?"

"Halsey?" Calvin shook his head no. "Goldie, though, she's got it going on. There ain't nothing she can't find when she gets her nose into the right spot, that's for certain."

Diane called from the boat, "Jason? You still jawing with Calvin? You ever heard of time on the clock? Y'all are using up county time, and we don't got enough of it as it is. Get your-selves on down here."

"Yes, ma'am," Jason called out. He leaned toward Calvin, "I think she wants us to join her. I don't know, though. Should I tell her to leave it alone and let us talk out what we need to talk out?"

"She's your boss, so if you want to eat another layer of spicy—" Calvin broke off his cautionary warning and grinned. "Anyways, you get my meaning, bub. And remember, I work for the sheriff. I get to ride on up to Swan Corner. You shoal your boat with the lieutenant, and your ride back up to Hatteras might be an overdone pot of baked bean, more spicy than you want."

"Hit me with it next time right between the eyes, Calvin." Jason laughed and called to Sean Taylor, "Deputy, us two are heading out to the boat. You coming?"

"Can I hang out up here and wait for Zack and Goldie?" Sean shifted his weight nervously from one leg to the other, and his equipment on his belt jostled audibly.

"Has Zack been contacted yet?" Jason didn't have his radio with him, as his department gear was at Ricky's house.

"Deputy DeSantis called him over the radio while you and Deputy Dingman were talking. The ferry lodged on a sandbar on the way over, and it's arriving late, but yes, he knows."

"And you don't think he might can find us? C'mon, Deputy. Notice I don't have any gear. Remember, I was off for the day and out fishing with Ricky when I was hauled in to chase after that missing sailboat. I'm depending on you to be my ears when that radio on your belt calls in."

Calvin nudged Jason to get his attention and asked, "Has Manteo approved your transfer from Carteret yet? I heard Kringlebach was dragging his feet."

"Not yet, but I'm being assured he will. I'm like Deputy Taylor, just wanting to serve—"

"And get a paycheck?" Calvin grinned.

"Well, that never hurts, does it? Right now, waiting to serve might be more accurate."

They were at the boat, and Jason pulled himself aboard and stood aside to make room for Calvin. Before Sean could board, Diane called to him, "Deputy Taylor—"

"Sean, ma'am, please. You did promise—"

"For all sakes," and she stopped herself. After a moment,

she began again, "Sean, Sheriff Pafford's done called the Hyde County K9 handler, and he's on his way. That right, Darlene?" She shifted her attention to the sheriff for confirmation.

"Suzanne made the call," Darlene corrected, "but yes, we fixed that and he's meeting us here, right, Suzanne?" She threw the question DeSantis' direction.

"Absolutely, Sheriff. Some people don't get the island thing, but I do. We don't have maids and butlers down here to tidy up the loose ends, so when something needs done, I get to it and get it done."

"That's for certain," Calvin commented. "There ain't nothing that DeSantis can't handle."

"Likely better'n you," she shot back at him.

"Hold your taters, deputies," Diane interrupted. "The point is the man knows we're waiting on him. Sean, you get on back to the road and wait on the K9 handler and his dog. I bet tomorrow's breakfast he'll appreciate someone pointin' him our way when he shows up."

"Of course, ma'am." The relief in Sean's voice crackled. "I'm here to serve. Whatever you need me to do." Even in the fractured darkness and layered shadows from the various lights along the street and fronting the harbor, he could be seen standing taller as he disappeared into the deeper ink along the road, hidden to the law enforcement officers gathered on the stern of the recently adrift sailboat.

THE VESSEL, whether abandoned by accident or design in the Atlantic waters just off the coast of the Outer Banks, was now moored as salvage on Ocracoke Island. Down the shore, Ricky Johnson could be seen with Sharky Jenkins, working to make one of the remaining ferries that evening back to Hatteras Island.

With Zack Halsey yet to arrive, Jason's hope of joining

Ricky in Avon for a late supper was growing dimmer by the minute, just like the sky overhead. The charcoal horizon left from the storm would become a black velvet canvas, a mocha blanket snugly draped across the island, punctuated by the electric jewels of occasional streetlights along the road … as long as the power didn't go out again. It was unlikely the sky would clear, Jason reminded himself, although it couldn't stay stormy forever.

At least the wind had died down.

Sheriff Pafford was talking, bringing everyone up to speed on what they knew and suggesting it was less than she wanted to know. *Like chili on spaghetti*, she was saying, *we sometimes need to try something unfamiliar to solve the crime.*

"It's a crime now?" Jason whispered to Calvin.

"Booked and locked, if the sheriff says it that way."

It was the tattered hemp rope that convinced Jason she might be right, that and the black marks up the hull suggesting someone climbing aboard without a formal invitation.

Likely without *any* invitation. The boat had a swim step and a ladder. Wouldn't that be a better way aboard if you were invited?

He was beginning to wish and wish hard that he had been allowed to participate in the drug bust the night before. He might have seen clues, information to feed his need to bring about closure to this and any set of unresolved events, like the relationship between him and Diane. Manteo and Sheriff Kringlebach were cramping his style. This, what they were doing right now, gathering clues and solving crimes, was what he was made for. And to do it on Diane's C-District Dare County team? If he could get Morton Kringlebach to see that, to look through Jason Romney's eyes …

Then Sean Taylor yelled from the road, "Hey, everyone, I see Deputy Halsey coming this way."

"K9 handler," Jason muttered to himself. "Deputy is the tag I want to carry, and in C-District, Morton Kringlebach."

The barking of a dog and the sound of tires crunching gravel overrode the repetitive slap of water against the hull of the *Dutchman*. A door slammed and Zack called out, "Sean, you got an itch in your shorts to take Goldie for a walk? She's been in the back for a long time."

"Sure," Sean returned. "I'm here to serve."

"Where's the sheriff? Lay it on me."

"Right through there." Sean, little more than a shadow in the darkness, pointed their direction.

"If you please, walk Goldie down when you're finished."

"Yessir," Sean said, then whistled and began talking to the dog as his voice faded into the island's ambient background noises.

Then a light flickered, and stick-thin Zack Halsey appeared carrying an oversized flashlight, with a brightly colored bandana in his hand, and a cowboy hat with a feather on his head.

"Zack, finally," Sheriff Pafford called out. "Put that light up and come on aboard."

The K9 handler stopped, flicked his light off, peered at the group on the sailboat, and said, "Sheriff, you know I don't much like boats. Please don't do this to me tonight."

"I love you, too, Zack. Join us, please."

"I prefer keeping my feet on the sand," the man muttered, but he did climb aboard just as Sean and Goldie appeared out of the darkness to join the best of the two counties now gathered on the *Dutchman*.

"DEPUTY DESANTIS?" Jason approached the jeans-wearing Hyde County deputy. He knew her from his days in Carteret. The two counties abutted one another, and when based in Morehead City, he often skipped from one county to the other as he headed up to Kill Devil Hills via the Cedar Island ferry and the Outer Banks chain of barrier islands. Overland, however, the counties were miles apart, and to get from one to the other, he was forced to meander north to New Bern and bushwack for a couple hours across Craven County to reach Hyde.

There was nothing wrong with New Bern, and in fact, he found it ideally beautiful, snuggled at what he considered the real mouth of the Neuse River where it truly opened into the Pamlico Sound, but the Craven County route from New Bern to Swan Corner was filled with nothing much of interest to him.

Meaning, no Diane Turnipseed.

Then, after several hours driving shoreside through Craven, the Swan Quarter ferry to Ocracoke managed to squander even more time than the sometimes tedious ferry from Cedar Island to Ocracoke. With Deputy DeSantis permanently assigned to the island section of Hyde County … and well, that was the blackbird in the pie. Since he didn't want to squander his hours driving overland, she was the deputy he regularly interacted with when Carteret had business with Hyde.

Yeah, they knew one another. He also knew her husband, Teague, on the Beaufort County payroll. The man often described his wife as a whippersnapper, and Jason agreed. He liked working with her for that reason. He supposed she reminded him of Diane in the way that she was quick, efficient, and businesslike.

"Deputy Romney?" Suzanne turned to him with a teasing smirk. "Oh, not yet, huh? It's just what? Metallurgist? Is that what I heard?"

"Leave it alone, Suzanne—"

She held up her hand, her palm facing him. "Talk to the hand, Jason not-yet-deputy Romney. When you get your badge from up in Dare, you can tell me to leave it alone, and I will. Until then, let's just say that fish in a skillet all cook up the same, but some don't get done as fast as others." She grinned.

"Okay, Deputy. I admit defeat." Yes, he truly enjoyed DeSantis and her bantering wit. "I understand you're setting up accommodations for some of your Swan Quarter brethren."

"I am, am I?" Her eyes twinkled. "Last I heard, you and Ricky had a dinner date back in Avon. How's that working out for you?"

Jason glanced at his watch, let his mind run through the ferry options from Ocracoke to Hatteras, factored in the time it would take to drive to the north end of the narrow barrier island—

"Answers. I need answers." Suzanne snickered. "That watch isn't slowing down just because you look at it longer. Last I heard, you can still catch the ferry up to near midnight. Is that your plan? You borrow Halsey's hat, and you can play the part of midnight cowboy."

"You really need to let that one alone." The K9 handler and Goldie had disappeared into the belly of the sailboat along with Sheriff Pafford and Diane. Sean Taylor remained on shore, hovering nervously while attempting to look vital to monitoring anything land-based, and Emily and Calvin Dingman were using a bright flashlight to inspect the rigging on the boat's mast and boom.

"Sure, sir cowboy. Here's where we stand: Sheriff Pafford has suggested she doesn't want to spend two-and-a-half hours on the ferry tonight just to turn around and come back, so I've got a friend here on the island that runs an inn. She's shut down for the season, but she said that since it's the sheriff and maybe a few deputies, and if they didn't expect too much in the way of service, she'd see about outfitting the beds with linens for the night. You wanting to stay too?"

"My ferry's only an hour. I think I can safely head home and still be back bright and early."

"You can, can you?" She chuckled.

Goldie appeared out of the companionway and leaped onto the deck of the boat, and Zack Halsey's feather-topped hat emerged. Standing beside the mast, Calvin Dingman called out, "I'll be ding-danged. Zack's come back to life. How was it down there, bub?"

"Not a minnow in the water." Zack knelt, called the dog to him, leashed her, and handed her off to Sean. "Another walk? I think Goldies likes you."

"I aim to please," Sean bubbled, sounding relieved at not being asked to climb aboard the boat. He waited as the dog jumped over the gunwale onto the pier then disappeared with her into the shadowy island landscape.

Darlene and Diane were next to surface. Darlene seemed pleasantly surprised, but Diane's face was a dark cloud.

"What?" Jason called out. "Good news or bad?"

"Depends," Sheriff Pafford offered. She glanced at Lieutenant Turnipseed, raised her eyebrows, and when Diane motioned for her to continue, the sheriff said, "No drugs. Not a sniff. If there were any down there, it's like someone took a sweeper and sucked it all away. Even pristine, for a boat that was found abandoned down to Lookout and towed in as salvage."

"Good news, right, Sheriff?" Suzanne smiled, as though maybe the sheriff would call it that way.

"Maybe not," she answered. "Diane, you want to give your view?"

"Thanks, Darlene. What I seen down there, well, some things are not ours to wish away. It weren't as if someone were forced to abandon this boat, now was it? Full stocked pantry, fridge still packed, even the beds made—"

"Cept that one," Zack called out.

"For all sakes, Halsey, I saw it," Diane snapped. "If I tell the story honest, something's not righter with this boat clean of drugs than if it were packed like a tin of sardines."

"Would you like me to take a look?" Emily remained beside Calvin, and Diane turned to her as if noticing her for the first time. Emily offered, "I might see something other eyes are missing."

"Nothing for you to see, but sure. Gets me, though. Somebody's gone somewhere, whether in a dinghy, just plain overboard, or—" She didn't finish her thought, but she had wandered to the rear of the boat just to where she could see the tattered hemp rope and the black marks clambering up the side of the hull.

"Don't forget the missing man from last night," Sean called from the shore. He was back with Goldie. He touched her backside, and she heeled at his feet.

"For all sakes, Deputy," Diane called, then muttered, "Some people don't got the sense—"

Jason heard the rest of it, even though she didn't complete her sentence. *Some people don't got the sense that God gave a minnow.* If someone on this boat did fall overboard, they certainly didn't have the sense that God gave a minnow. However, if they were thrown overboard, either alive or—God forbid— dead, that was a whole different skillet of fish. He glanced at Suzanne DeSantis to find her looking back at him. He knew exactly what she was thinking because it was churning in his head, too.

If there was a man overboard, was he alive or was he dead? In either case, how soon until he showed up, and would he be found washed ashore on the beach … or staging another drug incident that might impact innocent island residents?

A clean sweep on this boat wasn't good news at all, not from Diane's point of view, and likely, not from anyone else's, either. It opened too many crab pots for them to search through without additional help.

Lucky for this investigation, Jason knew right were to find the people they needed.

JASON STROLLED northwest along 12 towards the ferry landing and his truck. Named the Irvin Garrish Highway where it wound through Ocracoke Village and wrapped the eastern shore of Silver Lake, he enjoyed the village's post-storm, leaf-littered atmosphere in the muted evening light. With the remnants of the storm now moved onshore, this was all that was left to say, "We survived once again!"

He was parked at the Visitor's Center near the ferry landing, though not the ferry to Hatteras. That was on the north end of the island a half hour up the narrow sand spit where the island became a slender finger that served as a corridor to locals and visitors alike. When traveling the Banks from Morehead City in the south, the Cedar Island ferry gave passage to Ocracoke, then it was on to the Hatteras Island ferry northwards towards Hatteras Village, Buxton, and Manto miles up-island.

No roads led to or from Ocracoke. None. Not a one, and that was much of the appeal to those who called the overgrown sandbar home. Only the North Carolina ferry system kept the residents tied to Hatteras, Cedar Island, and of course Swan Quarter on the mainland.

The islands along the Outer Banks were a series of fish on a stringer … separate but always swimming in the same order, stacked one after the other. His destination along the stringer of barrier islands was north, past the twelve miles of sandy shoreline and looping for an hour around the Hatteras Inlet crab spawning sanctuary.

Suzanne DeSantis had sorted out the members of the Hyde County team overnighting on the island, including the sheriff, Calvin Dingman, and Zack Halsey. Goldie, of course would be with the K9 handler, but that was expected. The dog was considered a full Hyde County officer and received respect as such.

Emily lived two hours up, an hour the other side of Hatteras on Bodie Island, so her travel time wasn't much better than the Swan Quarter folks, and Diane? She was a hard nut to pack in a fish crate. It made sense for her to stay but it was likely she wouldn't. Home was her aunt's old beach house, although she also had a place in Elizabeth City that Jason was familiar with.

Sean Taylor was likely to go one way or the other, especially if Clifton Magruder showed up. Taylor was besotted by the Carteret County deputy's drone-operating skills, and Jason didn't know of anyone up north that expected the young deputy to show up for dinner, breakfast, or any other meal.

Headlights behind Jason created long shadows that danced in front of him as he walked. He expected the vehicle to drive on by and was surprised when it slowed and became Sean's lifted Jeep. The passenger window rolled down, and Deputy Magruder leaned out, revealing a tattooed arm under his rolled-up sleeve, laughed, and called, "Down in Morehead, we know how to hitch a ride. You need one of these, Jason."

"Is that so, Clifton? Up in Avon, we know how feet work, and we put 'em to use," Jason teased back. "You hit it off with Sean now?"

"The kid offered me a ride. How could I refuse in a vehicle like this?" The man's sun-bleached hair caught in the dull light that dotted the highway, although darker roots revealed his true hair color, giving the man a Japanese anime-character vibe.

"You didn't bring your truck over, did you?"

"Why, when I can leave it over on Cedar?" Clifton normally liked to catch a ride with one of the other deputies in the department when he could. Down in Carteret, it was expected, and his coworkers accommodated the man. Up here, it was everyone to himself, though it seemed Clifton was yet to figure that out.

"Sean, good for you for picking up the slack and accommodating Clifton's needs. We wouldn't want him to have to walk now, would we?"

Clifton snorted and shook his head.

"Hey," Sean called from the driver's seat, "you can ride, too. I've got plenty of room."

"My feet work fine, so thanks but no thanks. I'm parked up to the Visitor's Center. If I have time, I might stop for a coffee at the Anchorage."

"Harborside might be open." Clifton turned to Sean. "I gotcha covered for coffee if you wanna stop with Jason. I can show y'all the footage I got today."

"From the drone?" In the glow of the dash lights, Sean's face lit up. "Of course."

"We'll catch you there," Clifton called to Jason.

"Looking forward to it, Jason," Sean called from his place behind the wheel of the lifted SUV.

As Clifton rolled up his window, the Jeep stumbled in first gear, and Jason overheard Clifton tease, "Oop, oop, not that way …" Jason smiled, thinking of the man's wife, Sara Lee, and his two children, Wayne and Twila. At eight and six respectively, they had a good father, one who loved to talk about them and who seemed to enjoy being a parent about as much as he enjoyed his job as drone pilot for the county.

When Jason walked past Harborside, Sean's Jeep was there already, and he stepped off the highway, across the darkened parking lot, and through the doors leading into the building. He checked his watch as he walked under the overhead light, calculated the drive time to the ferry, and decided he'd miss one ferry no matter what he did, and that would give him about thirty minutes of conversation with the two deputies before he needed to head out, maybe forty if Sean would drive him the rest of the way to the Visitor Center.

Then Clifton called to him, Jason waved, and he moved forward.

CLIFTON HAD out his video unit and was demonstrating to Sean how to replay the shots he'd gotten earlier, telling him he'd only been able to video back on Hatteras, as the weather was too rough by the time the ferry crossed the Ocracoke Inlet.

"Still, this is great stuff," Sean said. He was enamored, and his eyes remained glued to the screen until the recording played out. He glanced up, "You are staying over? Deputy DeSantis has arranged rooms for everyone. Sheriff Pafford's covering the cost."

"I hadn't planned to—"

"The weather's clearing. You could send up your drone tomorrow, and I could help—" Sean caught himself, and he backpaddled. "—that is, if you need my help. I'm, um, I mean, I could stay here on the island. Suzanne asked me if I was, and I didn't exactly say no. Please?"

"Hey, sure, no problem, kiddo. If the sheriff's covering, then I'm good." Clifton glanced at Jason and laughed. "The boy's got some enthusiasm, huh?"

"More than you know, my man. Enough for all of us."

"You staying, Jason?" Clifton's coffee appeared, and a second one for Jason.

"Not if I can help it. Out on that boat all day, I need clean clothes before I start another morning. You don't want to be around me if I'm in these duds come noon tomorrow."

The conversation continued, with talk of how many days Sheriff Pafford would fund Clifton being "on loan" from Carteret, what the drone operator might find on a flyover the next day, and where the accommodations were that Deputy DeSantis had set up. Jason ventured that things had been slow up towards C-District in Dare County, and did Clifton have a problem with inviting some of the deputies from up that-a-ways down to Ocracoke if Diane approved it?

"I should have a problem with that? I'm not from Hyde." Clifton popped a stick of gum in his mouth before offering the pack to the other two men. Sean accepted and pulled a stick free, but Jason waved it off, saying thanks but not for him.

"What I'm asking," Jason said, "is if you'd have a problem, that is, if you were in Hyde County and this was your investigation."

"Well, I'm not and it's not. I'll tell you, Jason, back home, we accept all the help we can get. You know that from the years you were there." He glanced at Sean to find him struggling with unwrapping the gum, and he asked, "You need help with that?" He held out a hand, palm up, to take it.

"I can do this." Sean yanked the edge of the paper and tore it free, leaving a silvered slip of foil down the stick; and he shrugged and grinned before slipping it in his mouth. "Tastes the same. I can't tell any difference."

"It's your boat to float," Calvin said with a shrug. He turned to Jason. "I've been keeping track of the time. To miss another ferry means an extra hour before making it back to Ricky's. You about done with that coffee?"

Calvin claimed the tab, the three men made their way outside, and they headed towards the ferry landing, the Visitor's Center, and Jason's truck.

Jason figured Ricky was home already, or at least he would be by the time he arrived. He had at least two hours to go before calling it quits for the day. Catching the ferry was only the first step along the way.

"DIANE, JASON here." Jason had his phone beside him and connected to his truck. His voice through the cabin speakers was a warning that he had no idea how the woman would respond to his phone call. Somehow, he'd never learned to read her well enough to avoid the trenches she seemed to dig around herself.

"I weren't born yesterday, Jason. I can read my phone the same as anyone. You on the ferry?"

"Yes, ma'am." It was going to be one of those conversations, but at least she hadn't snapped at him. "I decided to head back to Avon and come back tomorrow, if you think you need me to."

"Jason!" She said his name hard. "You asking that? It wasn't like I weren't listening, now, was it? I was there the same as you, and it's plain as taters on a plate that Darlene was including you in everything we did. It don't matter to her that Morton can't get his underpants sorted out. Was there any metal on that boat?"

"I suppose so, ma'am. The mast, for one, and the cleats. Lots of it, in fact." He was getting her gist, and he was liking where she was going. Terse, businesslike, and to the point, the very things he liked best about her.

"And you still our metallurgist? Morton's not pulled that from you, has he?"

"I've not seen the notice in my mailbox." Well, Ricky's mailbox, but it was all the same as long as Jason was paying rent.

"Then you be here in the morning. And you stop by Kat's and bring me coffee. I need a cuppa blackie I can actually down without choking on it."

"So, you're staying overnight." That surprised him. "The coffee'll be an hour old when I pull up."

"I bet tomorrow's breakfast I can microwave it fine. Anything else?'

"Yes." This might be the sticking point that sent their conversation into the watery depths. "I listened to the sheriff, also, and I'm seeing a situation that might get beyond what we can handle. Do we need more people down here?"

"Dump it on me, Jason. Who are these more people?"

"Oh, some deputies you might know, maybe a K9 handler that wouldn't mind providing us a mess of cinnamon buns come breakfast—"

"And has a daughter living on the island." Cynthia Ellison was the Dare County K9 handler for C-District. Her daughter, Shelby, might be a wild tear, but she lived on Ocracoke and often had a finger in every crime pie that was going on. Sometimes she knew things, if she chose to share them with her mother.

"That's the one I was picturing, that is if the collaboration between our respective counties allows for that."

"It might oughta need to." Diane seemed to be thinking, and the phone was quiet for a time. She broke the silence with, "I want Toby here. We'd be above our knees to break up a good team."

"That'll leave Mary." *Alone and on patrol*, but Jason didn't need to say that. He did want it out there for Diane's acknowledgement and approval. Seargeant Mary Wilson lived up in Manteo on Roanoke Island with her husband, Tony. Jason had no idea if Tony was home or at work in the Gulf of Mexico on the oil rig that employed him. She and Ashley Dixon, who manned the lobby desk at the Buxton sub-station, would be holding the southern end of Dare County together by themselves.

"Deputy Hall?" Diane put the name out as a teaser.

"Might work, if the man's got some time he can give from B-District." Robert Hall was the B-District deputy on loan from B-District to C-District during the investigation during which Steven Hill, the medical examiner from Raleigh, was injured by an unexplained explosion in the dunes, one that was still unsolved and that rankled with Morton Kringlebach, the Dare

County Sheriff. "Should I check on that?"

"My aunt Lucille used to say, might could, might oughta don't get it done."

"I take that for a yes." He wanted verbal confirmation that couldn't come back and haunt him.

"For all sakes, yes. I'm hanging up now." And the phone went dead.

It was about as well. The ferry was pulling into the Hatteras ferry landing, and it was about time for Jason to start up his truck and head on into Avon where he hoped Ricky had fired up the grill and had some grub on.

THE NEXT morning, Jason hit his blinker at the Buxton C-District sub-station, and he slowed his maroon Ford FTX as he waited on an older minivan in silver to trundle by, likely heading north up the island into Buxton, Avon, or even farther up the string of living sand structures, each one breathing in sand on one side and expelling it on the other. It was the way of barrier islands, always on the move, although the people who inhabited them didn't always appreciate the islands moving from under their roads and houses and depositing the precious sand they called home somewhere else up and down the island chain.

With the road clear, he touched his accelerator and let the burble of the big powerplant under the hood ease him across the lane of oncoming traffic and into the parking lot. He'd arrived too late to contact Cynthia Ellison the night before, and this morning, he hadn't been able to reach her by phone, so Ashley at the sub-station was his next line of defense. Or offense, as he might need to chase down a few of the people he hoped to help with the investigation. This whole deal had turned from a simple operation involving multiple counties to missing drug smugglers, a pilotless sailboat, and unknown people who must have been planning to pick up the drugs from underneath the pier at

Avon. He was certain of one thing. No way were those dope runners about to drop off millions in drugs and not have someone show up to retrieve them.

Was that where the sailboat came in?

He shook his head and pulled into a parking space. He guessed he'd have to let that alone, leastways until Morton got his shoulders unhinged from the chips he seemed to be carrying on them and gave him full entry into Dare County's data trove of interesting and insightful information.

A steady wind pulled at his clothes as he walked toward the building, bringing with it salt and fish and just a hint of diesel. When he tried the glass door that fronted the lobby, he was surprised to find it didn't open. He leaned closer to the glass, noticed adhesive residue, peered around it, and didn't see anyone at Ashley's desk. The overhead lights were off, also, suggesting what, a holiday? He wasn't aware of a holiday that would require shutting down the sub-station. Then, Morton seemed fixated on keeping him at arm's length, so that meant there could be several things he was unaware of.

Glancing towards the parking lot, he located the district's covered trailer, a metal unit in white that rested at the back of the lot in exactly the same place as every time he was here. The only powered vehicle around was his truck, but this was only the front lot, and he considered walking around to see if Ashley's car could be behind the building when he remembered Diane's words from the night before. *Might could, might oughta don't get it done.* He grinned, walked determinedly down the covered porch that ran partially along the length of the building and around the end. He frowned. Sean Taylor's department-issued patrol car was in the lot, but he knew the deputy was in his lifted Jeep over on Ocracoke. There were other county offices in the building, but no one was home.

He pulled his phone from his pocket and searched to see if

he had Ashley's personal number and didn't find it. He had Diane's, but he didn't want to go there over something so trivial as an unmanned sub-station. Cynthia Ellison? Mary Wilson? He hadn't been able to reach Cynthia, and he didn't have Mary's. He hadn't been involved with C-District long enough to create personal contacts with all the deputies and staff. Emily, sure, and he likely had Sean Taylor's, but they were both on another island, one that didn't help him out here.

Robert Hall popped into his head. He was with B-District, and they'd worked together recently, but only because Steven Hill from Raleigh was serving as the county's medical examiner and had gotten injured, requiring the loan of Detective Hall as a stand-in for the medical examiner until he could resume his duties. Jason had his number, but being up in B-District, it was unlikely that he would be of any help.

Okay, he decided, and he began briskly walking toward his truck. He knew where Cynthia Ellison lived in Salvo, just up from Avon where he was renting a room from Ricky Johnson. She wouldn't mind if he stopped in to see if she could join them on the next island down, and if she wasn't there, Jason knew her husband Richie could likely point him the right direction. When he climbed in and shut the door, on the porch and wedged between two floorboards, yellow paper fluttered.

"Oh, yeah, that's got to be important." Jason climbed back out, took several loping steps forward, and retrieved the paper. Clear tape decorated the top and the bottom, and it matched the adhesive residue on the glass door. The message said, "In Case of an Emergency, call ..." and it provided a number with an island area code.

"I don't know that I expected that," Jason said aloud as he glanced back at his truck with its open door. "Might could be an emergency, if I want to call it that way. Might could, might oughta don't get things done, so emergency it is."

He tapped in the number on his phone, hit call, put it to his ear, let his eyes rove the parking lot as the line began to ring, and he waited for someone to pick up and answer.

"BY MY good graces!" C-District Sergeant Mary Wilson's familiar voice came over the line. "Jason Romney, am I glad to hear from you."

"You are, huh?" He chuckled. "Mary, I'm down here at the Buxton sub-station—"

"And you saw Ashley's note on the door to give me a call."

"Not exactly on the door but close enough. I tried calling Cynthia and got no answer; I didn't have your number; and with the offices here locked up—"

"That's right, you've been off the island, what, down fishing? I hear the lieutenant's got you on her investigation down to Hyde County. Did she come up with you?"

"Should she have?" Jason found Mary's question interesting. Normally, everyone had a hand in everyone else's tackle pouch. Something big must have washed in on the high tide. Not a dead body, he hoped.

"It would be nice if she did. Things been a bit whopperjawed since that storm yesterday."

"The reason the sub-station is closed, I guess."

"That's the way I call it. Some of us can't get there. Some kook went cattywampus driving over the Bonner, shut down the bridge completely. I offered to haul out the *Lightin' Bug* to get on down to the sub-station, but Tony's coming in from the Gulf tonight, and well, he doesn't cotton to me sailing that far on my own this time of the year. I was supposed to meet him at Danny's down in Vidalia, but likely that's not happening. Don't know how that's going to turn out."

"I'm not following, Mary. Vidalia, Georgia, all that, yes, but how could the bridge be shut down?" The Bonner, as Mary

— 135 —

referenced, was now no more than a pier, as the state had constructed a new and better bridge to replace it and only a portion of the old bridge was still standing. However, he recalled, people who'd lived on the Banks and driven Highway 12 for years still sometimes called it that, and he pictured the small boat Mary kept moored in Shallowbag Bay Marina on Scarboro Creek. Using it to bypass the location of the old Bonner Bridge made a kind of obvious sense, but the bigger question was how the newer—and vastly expensive—bridge could be out of commission in the first place.

"You didn't get wind down there on Ocracoke yesterday? I understood that's where you were having your little fishing expedition."

"Yeah, we got wind, and we hightailed it back into the harbor, too."

"Silver Lake." She sounded wistful. "The *Lightin' Bug* has fond memories of Silver Lake. Anyways, that big rig driver yesterday didn't heed the wind warning, and he went right over the railing of the Bonner."

"Into the Sound?" Jason knew it was bad if that was the case.

"Into the Inlet. Like clams and red sauce," Mary said, as if that summed it up. "Likely the reason you didn't reach Cynthia. She's there on the southern end, and well, I'm about to be on the northern end. I had some things in the boot of the Tacoma for my drive to Georgia, and I needed a bit of time to unload, you understand, but Deputy Hall volunteered to step in for a bit … though it is his district, so I'm not so sure it was all volunteer." She sounded pleased at that.

"Sheriff Kringlebach likely volunteered for him."

"By my good graces, did I just hear Jason Romney say that?" She truly laughed. "About time someone said some sense about that man. He's a fine sheriff, but good decisions come in threes, and the sheriff sometimes reels in his line on number four. He's not always the fastest cod on the coast."

"We might should let that alone and move back to the bridge before you get yourself in trouble, Mary. How's it shut down?"

"Somebody weren't listening."

"Over the side. I heard you fine. That doesn't block the bridge. Hit me with it. What's the rest of the story?"

"A crane. Will that do the job good?"

"I see." He did, too. "They setting up to fish that big rig out of the channel?"

"Clams and red sauce. Nothing else is getting through, either atop the bridge or under it, and likely for the rest of the day. Don't expect the sub-station down Buxton ways to be opened up except for an emergency till this afternoon or tonight, and likely then, Cynthia'll be on her own, that's if she can break free at all."

"Sure. I don't guess Diane knows about this? I haven't spoken with her since last night."

"I suppose Karen in Manteo might could have contacted her, but there's nothing the lieutenant can do from down there. It's been busy this morning, and our radios up here work as well from the lieutenant's end as it does ours. Sometimes things come in threes, and we got to spend our time readying ourselves for the next big one. I see the crane up ahead. Look at that, taking up the whole bridge. No wonder no one's getting through. I'm hanging up now."

"Thank you, Mary," but he wasn't sure she was still on the line. Practical, thoughtful, a bit brisk. Mary was a good officer, and Jason looked forward to spending more time with her when Morton Kringlebach signed his transfer to Dare County and C-District.

He debated on what to do with the emergency number notice, and he touched the tape on the backside to check the adhesive. If the wind had blown it off once, it likely wouldn't adhere to the glass a second time. Tires crunched in the drive and rolled into the lot. Ashley Dixon climbed out.

"You found my sign," Ashley called out. "You could have left it on the door."

"The wind beat me to it. I'll let you put it back."

"Don't need to now. I'm here." Ashley smiled. As she stepped up on the covered porch, she took the emergency number from him and quipped, "That's better, I know. Do you need inside?"

"Nah. I need to get back on the ferry. Diane wants coffee from Kat's, and I'm the delivery boy."

"Then I've got something for you." She unlocked the door and headed to the break room without turning on the lights. He followed her as far as the lobby, and she talked as she disappeared. "Todd had a flat this morning, and I had to run him to the shop. That's where I've been."

"Okay." Todd was her husband. They'd met once or twice. She returned with a reusable, foldable tote with a flat bottom. She offered it to him.

"This is for you."

"And?" He took it without looking inside.

"Buns, cinnamon, I think. Cynthia brought them in early, thinking y'all would be back today. If they stay here, I'll likely have to notch another hole in my belt. Besides, buns and coffee. What better way for the lieutenant to start her morning?"

"And Sean's? Doesn't Cynthia do him a special one?" The K9 handler liked to prepare a special bun for the deputy with extra icing.

"He's still there, too?" Ashley shook her head as if in disbelief. "We might as well all pick up our hems and move on down that way. One island closer to the big city, huh? It's at his desk. I'll get it."

"If you want to call Morehead City big," he called after her.

Then, compared to Buxton, Frisco, or Hatteras Village, it was a metropolis.

With the extra cinnamon bun in the bag, Jason made his way to his truck, to Kat's for coffee, and to the ferry line to await yet another hour-long journey from the island of Hatteras, across the Hatteras Inlet, and into the village of Ocracoke where Diane was likely waiting impatiently beside her microwave for her morning supply of Kat's fresh "cuppa blackie."

After he sorted himself into the ferry line, he killed the engine on his truck, pulled the cup he'd ordered for himself from the Kat's bag on the seat, and flipped back the small plastic edge of the lid. He took a sip and closed his eyes to enjoy the heady steaminess of some of the best coffee on the East Coast.

My apologies, Diane, he thought to himself. *You can microwave yours as much as you want, but it won't be as fine as this.*

And he had no regrets as he finished the entire cup.

EMILY BRYANT stood beside her basic, unmarked white sedan and waved Jason down as he rolled off the ferry on the Ocracoke side of the Inlet. He hit his blinker, pulled to the side, and rolled down his window to see what she needed.

"No Sean?" He grinned at her.

"Oh, he would likely be here, but his current infatuation isn't with me. He and Deputy Magruder are out on an early date with the deputy's drone." She crossed her arms to hug herself and said, "It's chilly this close to the beach."

"That is the Atlantic Ocean out there. You expected something different?" He nodded his head to his empty front seat. "You can join me inside if you want."

"I smell coffee. I'm thinking about it. And, could it be that you have cinnamon buns in there?"

"Straight from Cynthia's oven."

"So, where is she? I'm here for Toby. I miss the rowdy

goof."

"You still haven't heard, then. Yesterday's storm blew a big rig off the Bonner straight into the Sound."

"What? Off the new bridge?" She laughed. "You can't make this stuff up, but why would that keep her from joining us? Mary can handle that fine."

"They have a crane blocking the bridge, and no one can get past until they fish it out of the channel. The truck went over in the only place deep enough for boats to get through. Cynthia's managing the south end of the bridge, and Mary was headed to the north end when I spoke with her."

"No Toby then. That's leaves us only one thing to do. I need your help to prank Sean. He could do with something to spice up his life."

"I see. That's all I'm good for, pranks."

"We'll see if you're even good for that. At, I suppose I mean. That was to be Cynthia's job, but since she's still over there—" she pointed towards Hatteras, "—she's of no use to me. If you prove yourself, maybe you'll get a second chance …"

He chuckled. "All right, what do I have to do?"

"Are those cinnamon buns in a box?"

"A bag, anyway." He showed her. "Inside, I'm not sure."

"Let me see." She took the bag, lifted two paper bowls, one upside down on the other and wrapped with cling wrap. A note on it said *Sean*. Underneath was a larger box. She handed him the smaller container. "Put this under your feet. I'm replacing it with something from my car."

She carried the bag to her car, set it on the trunk, and lifted a food box from her back seat and set it on top of the larger one already in the bag. She returned the bag to Jason with a grin.

"So, the prank? Can I know my part?"

"Just make sure Sean gets that top box. Tell him it's special from Cynthia." Emily could hardly keep the grin of anticipation off her face.

Jason had no clue what it was that Sean would find in the box, but he expected it to be very, very good.

AT THE OCRACOKE sheriff's office, Jason offered the coffees to Diane, and he greeted Darlene. Suzanne DeSantis appeared from a back room, saying, "I smell coffee. Last I heard, someone brings coffee, there ought to be enough to go around."

"Hey, Suzanne. There's enough." He'd made sure to order up eight cups, and they were double stacked in his Kat's sack, four on bottom and the remaining three on top. Diane had them unloaded, and she was setting them out for everyone to take. Even after an hour, the ones from the bottom stack still steamed. He was surprised to see her pull out a heat pack from the bottom of the bag and toss it in the trash. He frowned at Emily and asked, "Are the two deputies joining us?"

"Soon," Emily said. She stepped to the dispatch radio and lifted the mike. "Calling all officers. Calling all officers. Taylor and Magruder, are you out there? Come back at me."

"Zip that lip and hand that mike to me," DeSantis said with a shake of her head. "This isn't shoofly pie we're making here. Here's how you do it." She clicked the mike and said, "Deputies Taylor and Magruder, this is Suzanne DeSantis at the Ocracoke station. We need you to return ASAP. Copy, over."

"Copy. Deputy Taylor here. Clifton's bringing in the drone. Over." Sean sounded out of breath.

"You tired, Deputy Taylor? Didn't think we had a big enough island to wear out you city folks." She grinned at Emily.

"She's in on it," Emily confided to Jason, but she put her finger over her lips to indicate that Sean wasn't to overhear.

The radio returned, "I heard the radio and had to run to the Jeep. Clifton's packing the drone and I need to help. We'll be right there. Sean out."

Sheriff Pafford pulled her cup of coffee from the microwave, and she waved them into the inner sanctum, which was little more than a room with a table against one wall and a set of folding chairs leaned against another wall. The rest of the items in the room were organized as well as could be asked of a building that did too many duties in too little space, but they were able to each open a chair and be seated. Cinnamon buns from the bottom box in Ashley's bag multiplied around the table. The sheriff and Deputy DeSantis moved a coat tree to reveal an old-fashioned chalkboard on the wall. Suzanne found a box of chalk in the front room, and the tray along the bottom held an eraser.

Sheriff Pafford offered the chalk and eraser to Diane and asked, "Diane, you want the duty?"

"You might could do as good as me, so you have at it, unless one of the deputies wants to do the honor."

Darlene held the items around to no takers, and she studied the chalk and said, "Down south in Kentucky, they call this field marking powder. But when it's all you've got, you get on board." She took a stick of chalk, turned to the board, and wrote, *Man Overboard on Ocracoke Island.*

"We're sure about that?" Emily said with a tease in her voice. "We haven't found anyone who went overboard. Maybe they went swimming."

"For all sakes, Emily," Diane said with a smirk. "Jumping or falling, it don't matter. Overboard is overboard."

"Just stating the obvious, Lieutenant. They might still show up."

"As did I," Diane retorted, but it sounded friendly. "And yes, we hope they show up and soon. Our crab pot's way too light, and we want to haul it in soon."

The door in the front room opened, and Sean's voice called,

"Do I smell cinnamon buns?"

"In that bag on the front desk," Emily called out. She leaned to where she had a good view into the room.

Jason shifted his position to see also, and when the deputy lifted Emily's box out of the bag, he looked at Deputy Magruder and grinned. When he began to open it, it started to vibrate, and when the lid came off, twenty mechanical, windup butterflies came whizzing out and headed all over the room. Clifton laughed, Emily smiled with satisfaction, and Sean was so startled that he dropped the box and stumbled back into a filing cabinet, creating more ruckus than the small office had heard all morning.

Jason smiled. Sean's cinnamon bun was in his truck, and he'd send the kid out to retrieve it as soon as he was back on his feet.

Diane, who apparently didn't know the prank was about to play out, called, "For all sakes, Deputy Taylor. We're having a meeting in here. If you had the sense that God gave a minnow …" before she let her reprimand die away.

Suzanne DeSantis was in full laugh mode. It was her first time to experience one of Emily's pranks, and she rescued one of the butterflies from atop a cabinet, causing it to flap three more times before dying all the way.

"That was a good start to the meeting," Darlene quipped.

Jason threw Sean his keys and told him his breakfast bun was in his truck. The younger deputy glared at Emily as he passed, but on the way back in, the bun was nearly half gone.

Jason laughed. Despite himself, he liked Deputy Taylor and wished him the best in everything he did.

OVER THE course of the morning, the team made another visit to the boat pulled in by the salvage team. In the light of day, the marks on the stern were more apparent, and it was decided that someone definitely had tried to board the vessel secretly. Why it was abandoned or whether something else could have taken place became the big question. It was too early to determine whether a crime had been committed or whether the entire event was simply an accident or something weather related. The weather had been bad, both the night they had first sighted the vessel and the day it was pulled in by the salvage crew.

Research on the boat's owner didn't help much. Paperwork uncovered in the navigation station inside the vessel matched the registration number, but that took them to a fractional boat ownership syndication called ShareBoating of Newport News. Suzanne had left them a message that they had one of their boats tied up in Silver Lake, and they were waiting on a callback to find out more. Emily went online to find out about ShareBoating only to learn that the boats in the syndication's fleet weren't owned by individuals. Interested parties purchased guaranteed time with the vessels, one or two weeks, or as much as a month a year, but there was no guarantee which boat any particular owner would be on when claiming their time.

That meant the people aboard, well, those who had once been aboard, since obviously no one was aboard right now, could be anyone participating in the timeshare. And since the program allowed owners to lease out their owned time ... the pool of prospective missing people was like sand dollars on the ocean floor. Reach down and grab a handful, and you were as like as right to have pulled up the ones you searched for.

The mood of everyone on the team shifted when Detective Robert Hall of B-District up in Dare County stepped through the door at the Ocracoke office.

"Robert, good to see you." Jason was first to greet him.

"Bit out of your jurisdiction, aren't you, Jason?" Robert offered his hand and winked.

"Same as about half of us here. Don't know if you've met

Clifton from Carteret, and Sheriff Pafford—"

"I'm pretty familiar." Robert cleared his throat, shifting to a more serious expression. "Is the lieutenant home?"

"Here? On the island?" Robert nodded, and Jason said, "Sure, in the next room. You need her?"

"I'm afraid I do." Robert pulled an envelope from his pocket and offered Jason an apologetic shrug. "Tell her I've got something for her from Sheriff Kringlebach."

"Not good news, I guess."

"Hand delivered? Not likely. You know about the wreck up on the Bonner? Or I should say the Basnight, but that'd likely confuse you. It does everyone else."

"I know the bridge. I've heard about the wreck. What about it?" Jason didn't see the need to reveal his recent trip to the neighboring island. The incident as described by Mary Wilson had seemed completely under control, if a nuisance for Dare County residents.

"That's what's set this off. Can you get her for me?"

"Certainly." He knocked on the door to their small incident room, and when it opened, he requested to speak with Diane.

When she opened the envelope and read what was inside, she spat, "So, that's how it is? Morton's above his knees this time. I'll tell you this—" at which point she stopped herself, looked around, and noticed everyone watching her.

"Tell us what?" Sheriff Pafford asked innocently.

"Morton's trying to shut us down." Diane held up the papers from inside the envelope. "That man sent a deputy to personally deliver this to me. I'm to report to Manteo immediately."

"I don't know that this falls under his—" Darlene began.

"*I* fall under his jurisdiction," Diane barked. She took a deep breath and apologized. "I'm a big girl, and I should say sorry. So, sorry. I need to get up to Manteo. Deputy Hall, were you given any further instructions?"

"No, ma'am. Just to deliver this to you."

"What are your duties for the rest of the day?"

"You mean patrol assignments? None. With the drive and the ferry schedules, Sheriff Kringlebach cleared me until I got back."

"You think you can delay that for a few hours? Deputy Romney needs assistance, and he could use your help."

"Jason's a deputy now?" Robert looked at Jason and grinned.

"You heard me. Now, you staying or not?"

"You're the lieutenant. You outrank me, ma'am. I'm here as long as you request my help."

"Emily? Whatever Jason asks, you have my permission. Deputy Taylor, where are you? You, too, you answer to Jason. The rest of you I don't have any power over, so whatever Darlene asks of you. I'll try to be in contact, but don't expect anything soon. The longer until you hear from me, the more time you have to find out whose spoon is in what pot and work out what might coulda happened to get us to the bottom of this fish ladder we are about to have to climb." She yanked her jacket from the coat tree, and as she pulled it on, she muttered, "That Morton Kringlebach don't have the sense that God gave a minnow."

She made her way outside, and the wheels on her Explorer spun as she pulled away. Jason asked Robert, "What was that about? Hit me with what you know."

"The Bonner wreck and you people from C-District all down here." He seemed to want to say more but couldn't manage to commit.

"Out with it, Robert. I know about the big rig and the crane. There's more by the look on your face."

"The driver was still inside, and in the back ... there's no consensus, but it may have been involved with that drug bust from the other night."

"The pickup vehicle." That's why the rig had ignored the wind warnings during the storm. They were late for the heist, either that or they'd been told to hold off because of the police activity. That meant the missing cache of drugs was still out there. And now, by order of the lieutenant, a large portion of the C-District team was stranded on Ocracoke.

Sheesh, Diane, he thought. *I might could have solved this back on Hatteras. And now, you've stranded me here.* He definitely hadn't expected this, not by a ferry ride across the Hatteras Inlet. Well, he could only do what he could do. He called to the sheriff, "With your permission, Sheriff Pafford, if I could speak to my people?"

With her nod, he motioned for them to follow him into the next room.

Chapter 5

The Ferry Turns Around

LIEUTENANT DIANE TURNIPSEED snapped her truck door closed, threw the envelope and letter from Robert Hall into the seat next to her, and started the engine. Fury vibrated her arms, and she could barely think for the words on the paper.

Manteo. Now. Immediately. *And amid one of the least opportune situations her C-District team had ever found themselves in*, Diane groused to herself.

She stared for a moment at the small law enforcement station, the sign identifying it as the sheriff's office on Ocracoke Island, trying to keep her thoughts under control, when her head erupted again. *Unmanned boats, Morton. Drug smugglers missing and possibly running loose on the Banks. For all sakes, there might be someone dead out there, and you need me to spend the entire day driving up to Manteo so you can salve your wounded pride all because you haven't wiped every crime slate clean with your brilliance and skill.*

It takes more than brilliance and skill, Morton Kringlebach. It takes legwork, people you can trust, and time. Sometimes lots of time. Something she didn't have enough of, especially not today and on this island.

It seemed she sat there far too long, her anger radiating from her, and when she slammed the vehicle into reverse and felt the wheels spin as she pressed the accelerator, the world outside caught up with her. The jumble of thoughts in her head … they had tumbled around her like a school of frightened minnows with Morton Kringlebach a circling killer whale, on the hunt and driving them forward. Diane refused to be hunted, not in that way. Morton was above his knees if he thought he could squelch her investigation. There were ways … there were ways.

In the twenty minutes it took to reach the ferry landing, she realized what she had done back at the sheriff's office, and she could berate herself and laugh about it at the same time. She muttered, "I'll bet tomorrow's breakfast Jason Romney is happy as a crab in a mud bath about now." She pulled into the priority lane at the ferry landing to head up towards Hatteras and noted Charlie Bronson, a security guard with the Department of Transportation and assigned to screen passengers and vehicles boarding the ferry, walking her way. She rolled down her window.

"Mornin', Miz Turnipseed. Don't see official Dare County folks down this way much. How you doin'?" He took off his cap, likely to show respect, but that's how Charlie was, respectful of the female gender and law enforcement in general.

"A bit of intercounty cooperation, Charlie. And how do you know this is a county vehicle? Not marked, not at all."

"Don't have to be, Miz Turnipseed. Everybody knows you." He nodded and smiled. "You and Miz Ellison. Her daughter Shelby's got a place down by the village. We see her about once and agin. And it's not like Buxton's not easier to reach than places the likes of Cedar Island ways. We get by the sheriff's office up to your end of the Banks time and again."

"I'm sure you do, Charlie. How long?" She gestured toward the landing. It was devoid of any ferries, and she'd driven in with her thoughts thrashing like a sea bass in a bucket and not watching her clock. Yet, she could be polite when it came to it, and Charlie deserved that from her, and likely that's why the question had fallen out of her mouth.

"Fifteen minutes maybe. Hey, did you survive yesterday's weather okay? Some of the island roads round abouts was awash when the worst of it came through. I guess you missed that, you being from up in Dare."

"Reckon I did, Charlie." Diane pictured the boat ferrying them down to Cape Lookout and barely making it back in. To tell the story honest, she'd rather have been on the island. She would have enjoyed missing Deputy Taylor's very public show of weakness.

A ferry horn drew their attention to the water.

"There you go, ma'am." Charlie pointed loosely with one arm. "The boat looks to be in a few minutes early. Course, that don't mean we'll be leavin' any early. You understand that, of course." He nodded at her and glanced at cars filling the ferry lines. "I best be off, Miz Turnipseed. You have a safe trip across the Inlet."

"Shush that," she called with a grin. "I always do."

As he walked into the sea of cars, pausing to look at license plates and anything that might be of interest to the security guard in him, she considered his remark about Shelby Ellison. She'd already been a point of discussion in their investigation, which according to what the team on Ocracoke had decided this morning, was what it had become. Whoever was missing was intentionally missing, and she didn't think they were missing because they wanted to be. More likely, because someone else wanted them to be, and that created cause in her book, an investigation-worthy cause.

Aboard the ferry gave her time to process. Jason now in charge, by her authority, too, even though Manteo was still dragging its feet on approving his transfer. She hadn't wanted Jason in Dare County originally, and certainly not in her C-District Patrol Area, but when Robert delivered that letter … her gut feelings didn't often mislead her. She'd cottoned to Jason as the most capable person she was leaving behind.

What did that say about how she really felt about him? She wasn't one to give in easily, and she'd fought his shenanigans to woo her, but there was no doubt she trusted his skills at his job. Her gut feelings to put the throttle in his hands said something even she couldn't argue about, not to herself.

She shook her head and focused on her meeting with Morton. Through Buxton, then the highway up the island was likely an hour, if she pushed herself, more likely an hour and a half with real people out on the road, and there were always real people out on the road.

And what had Emily Bryant said about the Bonner? She guessed she needed to find out about that. She pulled her radio mike from under the dash, and she keyed it on.

"Lieutenant Turnipseed calling Karen Midgett. Checking on the status of the Bonner. You there, Karen? Over."

If the Bonner was out, she likely wasn't getting to Manteo, that was unless they had the emergency ferry running. Inside, she wilted at the thought of that. She should've inquired from Robert back on Ocracoke. Her fury had robbed her of that option, and she let it go, with, "I'm a big girl. My fault. Some things we can't wish away—"

"Karen here. I'm your Outer Banks source of information for Dare County." Karen chuckled. "My apologies. We just turned Crabs loose onto an unwitting and unwary local population. The man's a mess, but he had us in stitches this morning.

What can I do for you, Lieutenant?"

"Crabs" Hardy was a rough-living character with hair down his back like a possum's tail. He was essentially harmless but did get arrested occasionally for inebriation and weed consumption. Consuming, that wasn't too bad. Sharing with the island youth usually got him a night or two in the slammer. Some people enjoyed his humor when he was coming down from a high, but Diane had little patience for the man, especially after a previous experience with him sharing his "stash" with the granddaughter of one of her coworkers.

"The Bonner, Karen," Diane began, but the mention of Crabs Hardy had thrown her mind into a salt pond, and the mud was sucking at her knees. She released the talk button on her radio. It was likely she'd stumble over her words before she said two more things. Mammucked was what she was, tired and messed up, and well, not wanting this meeting with Kringlebach to happen. She could hear Cynthia Ellison, the C-District K9 handler, muttering, *Sand dunes don't get taller just because we want it to be so.* This one Diane would like to wash out to sea, and she would be doing her share of pushing if she thought it would do any good.

"Yes," Karen replied tentatively. "What about it, Lieutenant?"

Diane realized she hadn't really asked a question, and she said, "I can get through?"

"Not on the Bonner. It's not there anymore. There's a new bridge. Those of us who come north from time to time know about it." Karen could be heard laughing over the connection.

"You know where I mean. I need access to your location."

"You not coming all the way here, are you, Lieutenant? Might be in for a leisurely outing between Pea Island and Bodie. I understand they're using the backup ferry, and not the big one, either. They've got that one up north. Don't know what they want with it up there, unless they're outfitting it with fancy urinals, though I wouldn't mind a better women's room. Why do men always think they deserve the big toys, and us women, well, we get the little ones. Some sort of compensation factor for something they don't have, don't you think, Lieutenant? I'm just rambling on, and I didn't think, Lieutenant. I suppose you want to talk for a minute, and here I am with my finger on the talk button and not letting you get in a word edgewise. Here's edgewise, Lieutenant. Over."

"Likely I am heading up your way, Karen. The sheriff has requested my presence in Manteo. I'm on the ferry from Ocracoke, so it'll be a couple hours."

"More than a couple, Lieutenant. Everybody and their uncle want through, and even priority people like you, well, there's only so much room on a tiny ferry. You getting the picture?"

"I'm seeing it pretty well, Karen. I don't suppose Morton noted the distance in travel time from Ocracoke Village all the way to Roanoke."

"So that's where the deputy lit out to. By the look on his face, it wasn't a good place he was going. He said he'd likely not be back before sundown, so as not to expect him in the office before tomorrow morning. Oh, hold, Lieutenant. We've got a visitor."

Diane would have preferred to sign off the radio, as she now had the information she needed. Karen, as the county dispatch officer, was outstanding at her job and liked about as well as a fried hushpuppy on a plate of fishcakes, and that was saying something. However, she liked joking over the airwaves, a trait even her husband, Jake, a teacher at a middle school up that direction, tried to rein in. Karen wouldn't be reined in, and maybe that was a good thing. Over the live connection, Morton Kringlebach's voice caught Diane's attention.

"Karen, that deputy I sent down called in? I can't have him

bungling around when we got a bridge out of commission, not enough operators for the temporary ferry, and a patrol district lieutenant chasing after ghosts in the sand dunes. I'm getting ribbed every time I head up to Raleigh. I won't be embarrassed by that woman any longer, you hear that? Not with a county performance review bigger than an East Carolina stuffed pepper about to fire up. I may be close to retirement, but I'm not so slickcalm that people no longer respect the gray in my beard ..."

He blustered on, a nor'easter battering anyone in earshot, and quietly Karen whispered over the radio, "Sorry, Lieutenant. I didn't intend you to hear that. I'm signing out."

The radio went silent. *So,* Diane thought, *that's what's got Kringlebach's underwear twisted in his trousers.* Some of it she had surmised, but the man was above his knees if he wanted the investigations in her district neatly gutted and hung out to dry. They weren't quite dead yet.

The ferry was fully underway at that point. She had a window cracked, and the smell of diesel filtered through the opening like marsh gas under your feet when you headed out crabbing after a big storm. It stank about as bad as Morton's tirade, but like swamp gas, keep far enough away, and it don't bother you none.

The problem was, Diane would be strolling right into the marsh without knowing all the firm places to walk. She was likely to stir up some nasties no matter where she stepped, and like marsh gas, she would likely stink to all heavens for a long time to come no matter how quick she skedaddled away.

DIANE PULLED up to the grandiose building that formed the Dare County complex in Manteo, and she shook her head. Their little Buxton sub-station down in C-District was filled with island charm, from its clapboard siding to the welcoming porch roof that shaded visitors who came to call.

She narrowed her eyes at the marble-like columns fronting the main county complex's red brick façade … more Southern belle than island idyll. *Welcome to Tara*, she thought with a grin. Despite her deriding analogy to the fictional Tara plantation, it wasn't the county buildings that had her mammucked. It was the man she wrestled with that had her attitude all churned up and ready to spit. She liked to give her district officers and deputies room for independent thought to chase down ideas and get the bad guys, and it seemed to work. Some bad guys took longer to bring in than others, but that was how being an islander worked. The biggest fish take the longest to work so's you can pull 'em into the boat.

Any sport fisherman worth his salt knew that.

Then she didn't suppose that Morton tossed his line all that far to sea. His world stopped at the borders of Roanoke Island. Cross east or west, and you were good as gone, of no mind, swallowed up in the distant borders of a sand no-man's land.

She opened her door, not surprised and yet surprised at the difference in being off the Banks. Manteo was only one island over, a quick trip over the causeway and the Baum … and yet, the salt in the air, the subtle beat of the water, the birds that hugged the shore … all of it was missing here. She could be in Washington or Raleigh or Fayetteville for all this felt like the Banks.

At the entrance to the building, she caught her reflection, paused, realized she was wearing yesterday's uniform, and decided, *For all sakes. It's not like I ain't been overnight on an island that's not my own. I shoulda taken a stop at the house*—and she let that go. She hadn't—didn't even think about it—and now she was here. Morton would have to deal with the reality that she had been working, which was what working people did. She didn't hole up in a fancy office and command her people to come to her each time a fish flopped away, leaving her basket was too empty to say she was doing a good job at what she did.

"Karen," Diane said in greeting as she approached the dispatcher's desk. She paused, undecided whether to ask if she needed to prepare herself for a nor'easter or if the winds had calmed down. The rant from earlier still rankled.

"Don't want to be you," Karen said with a look of sympathy.

"That answers what I wanted to ask. How you doing, Karen?"

"Better'n you will be in about five minutes," she said, this time offering up her words with a grin.

"Okay, I'm heading up yonder. I'll have a look-see at what the sheriff wants, and if I can get a word in, maybe tell him my side."

"And I got a bridge in Brooklyn I want to talk to you about."

"It's not like I'm not listening, Karen, but I'm gone."

"Yes, ma'am."

She turned away and began to fiddle with her console, suggesting they had company Diane was unaware of. Diane turned, recognized the gray in the beard, and she nodded.

"Morton."

"Diane." He looked surprised, as if he hadn't been sure she would make it. "Hortie's expecting you. You can head that way." He ambled on by, trying to be casual, but down the hall, he turned towards the restrooms.

"When you gotta go," Karen said, though she kept her eyes glued on her console.

"Shush that," Diane reprimanded her. "Make a change and be the dispatcher your people want you to be."

"Every day, Lieutenant. You better get on down. Hortense has you a chair waiting."

Diane shook her head as she walked away. Karen's spicy comments had eased her prickly attitude. She figured Morton would spike it back up soon's she had him face to face without anyone around for him to try to impress.

Around the corner and into the sheriff's suite of rooms, she opened the door to find Hortense Cumberbatch with a tube of whiteout dabbing at a document winding through an electric typewriter.

"Hortie," Diane said in greeting, only to see the short, round, gray-headed woman jump.

"Oh my, oh my!" Hortense pulled the small brush away from the paper, touched it again, and said, "That'll do." She turned to Diane, tilted her head up to peer through the bottoms of her thick glasses, and said, "It's you. Morton didn't expect to see you today."

"Immediately. That's what his missive to me said." Diane wanted to bark at the elderly woman. She also wanted to know why the sheriff had said his secretary was expecting her but his secretary now said the sheriff wasn't. Somebody's fishing line was all twisted, that was certain.

"Come now, that was me." Hortense smiled primly. "But I knew it was what the sheriff wanted. And you are here."

The door behind Diane opened, and the sheriff walked through, still drying his hands with two folded paper towels. He dropped them in Hortense's trash can, nodded to the elderly woman, and motioned Diane into his office. Once inside, he positioned himself behind his desk, pulled out a file folder, and opened it.

"Lieutenant Turnipseed," he began, his eyes glued to the file and barely acknowledging her across the desk from him, "you may be seated."

"Yes, sir." It rankled, elevating him with the term of respect, but there it was, out there, and she supposed she would survive it. She lowered herself into a chair, continued to sit tall, and waited on what he had to say. She had a few words of her own, cannon balls of fire to lob at the man if he even suggested that they shut down their investigation down the island chain. Her patience had evaporated with her entrance into this office. Speaking her mind might blow up in her face, but she intended to say what needed to be said, and tomorrow's breakfast or not, she was a big girl, and she'd take what she got.

It was her team members down on Ocracoke she fretted about. They didn't deserve what would likely be Morton's virulent wordstorm, and she was certain he was about to let it fly.

DIANE CLENCHED her jaw leaving Sheriff Kringlebach's office. In many ways, it was a simpler affair than arriving had been. One part of her mind was focused on what she wished she'd been able to say, and the other half sorted out possibilities to undo what that man thought he had the power to do.

She barely got out, "Afternoon, Hortie," before she was past the woman's desk and out the door. At Karen's desk, she paused, caught Karen's eye, and she felt the volcanic words of fury about to spew forth.

"Not here, Lieutenant," Karen cautioned her. "Ears be listening."

"Understood. I need a cuppa blackie." She nodded to the dispatcher and walked briskly out of the building, wondering why she hadn't set off the fire extinguishers. The steam coming out of her ears must be enough to bake a rasher of clams on a grill.

Standing under the trees of Roanoke Island, she paused, closed her eyes, and put her mind to formulating a plan to counter Morton Kringlebach's self-centered and self-serving designs on C-District's attempts to solve what had become a highly involved series of incidences. They had taken immediate action to interrupt the delivery of drugs at Avon Pier. Even Morton hadn't been able to argue with their success there. And their plans to pursue the unmanned sailboat? Data collection. No investigation went forward without that. The sheriff was above his knees if he expected her team to analyze information they weren't allowed to collect. For all sakes, data collection was at the core of good police work, and her people were the best. Only when the data was analyzed could they begin corrective actions, the reassessment of what they'd assumed or had to fill in with probable information, and the fine-tuning of their pursuit toward the end goal, that of bringing any miscreants to justice.

She pictured the Bonner, or as Karen had so kindly pointed out, the bridge that had replaced the Bonner, as she'd crossed the Oregon Inlet heading north. The path of the emergency ferry had allowed a view of the truck as it was lifted by the crane back onto the bridge. Diane hadn't identified any guard rail damage, a testament to the solid construction of the new bridge that had replaced the old one, but the large trucking rig entwined in the crane's cables and dangling over the side of the bridge hadn't fared so well. The trailer portion was skewed sideways on its frame and buckled in front of the wheels. She didn't see how it was still attached to the cab section. Another example of good engineering, she considered. Even so, the residue of its bath in the Inlet hadn't been kind to its appearance.

A dirty result of a dirty deed by dirty people. That's how Diane saw it, and she didn't think she was wrong. She hated that someone had died in the accident, but she considered it like this: It wasn't like they didn't know what they were doing, so what was done to them was about what they could have expected.

After her meeting with Morton, all two hours of it, she expected the obstruction on the bridge was cleared. Mary Wilson lived just down the road, and Diane didn't expect she would have headed down to Buxton immediately. She opened her eyes, pulled out her phone, and punched in Mary's number.

She held it to her ear as it began to ring.

"ABOUT TIME someone gave me a call. Yes, Lieutenant?"

"I'm a big girl, Mary—" Diane growled and couldn't continue.

"Yes, ma'am." Mary chuckled. "I'd be a wampus cat to argue with that."

"You free for coffee? I need a cuppa blackie to settle the sharks swimming in my waters."

"By my good graces, Lieutenant, coffee's just what I was thinking a few minutes ago. That dingbatter getting himself blown off the bridge … you did hear about that, am I right?"

"More than heard. I'll tell you about it over coffee. How about Dunkin's? I can be there in ten minutes."

"On 64? How about Taco Bell by Whalebone Park? I'm in the drive through and about to the window. I can order up two coffees and have 'em ready when you pull in."

"Whalebone." Diane considered the location and placed the eatery in her mind. It was east, over the causeway and on the actual Banks where she wanted to be, as not in Manteo and not on Roanoke Island with a sheriff that was circling like a barracuda around a sinking ship. "Don't mind me, Mary. It's not like I'm not listening. Fifteen minutes. You have that cuppa blackie waitin'. If I tell the story honest, I'm gonna need it."

Diane ended the call, moved toward her black Explorer, climbed inside, and started the engine. As she pulled away, she heard Morton Kringlebach's words thrashing in her head, like a carp on a fishing line whipping about just to see what damage it could do.

"All that's done down there, Lieutenant. Done, you hear me? That intercounty cooperation? It's good for our public image, but it's costing us time and manpower Dare County doesn't have to spare. Can you give me concrete evidence there

were six men on that boat? No? That's because there were only five. That sailboat you insist on chasing down? Let the salvage company deal with the insurance company. And one more thing. That incident with the medical examiner? I want your report closing that down. It's done. Over with. Explain it away however you want, but that case with that dead professor is closed, and I want all of it closed. Am I making myself plain?"

His words were pretty plain, but what she wanted to say was, "That's a big no, Morton. You don't got the sense that God gave a minnow, cause we've got cause. We just need time to collect the data. We close that case … well, we don't know that it's done, not unless everyone agrees that there's no more information to collect, and I, for one, don't agree."

She didn't say it, though. She acted like a big girl, took her lumps, nodded when the sheriff expected her to nod, and now, she needed to bounce her thoughts off someone who would tell her if she was whopperjawed or if there was a way to sideswipe the lobster cage the sheriff wanted to trap her and her team in.

She backed out and pulled away, daring anyone to get in her way. She needed to get to Taco Bell. And she needed to gather her team in Buxton. They had plans to assemble, ones that would ensure that their investigation was brought to its correct end.

"Like a flea collar on a ship's cat," she muttered. "Keep you occupied with something else, Morton, and you won't know what we get up to down island, will you?"

She wasn't exactly sure of her plan, but she had a team that might could come up with some really good ideas, and she would start with Mary. And a good cuppa blackie, of course.

"THAT MAN wants to do what? By my good graces, you did give him a piece of your mind? I know he's the sheriff, but it's like clams and red sauce." Mary nodded her head as if Diane would understand the undercurrents of her words. She chuckled. "It's like I hear you say, Lieutenant. Some people don't got—"

"—the sense of a minnow. I do say that." Diane took a sip of her coffee, inhaled the aroma, and smiled. They were sitting in Mary's C-District SUV in the Taco Bell parking lot and watching the traffic as it cruised up and down 12 heading deeper into the island. Diane's black Explorer was to the side and partially obstructed the view of a wall of trees to the northeast, but the southeast view of the highway was perfectly clear. A delivery truck pulled into the 7-Eleven at the corner of Gulf-stream and the Old Oregon Inlet Road, and they could hear the vehicle beep repeatedly as it backed up to unload.

"I suspect you got a plan, Lieutenant, otherwise we wouldn't be sitting here in my truck just now." Mary sipped her coffee. She also had a cinnamon bun half unwrapped and took a bite. "Nothing to compare to Cynthia's but filling nonetheless."

"Some ideas." Diane drummed her fingertips on the seat before she pulled a small spiral notebook from her breast pocket and flipped it open. "You're still on the clock for the day?"

"Yes, ma'am. After the bridge fiasco, this is my lunch. Thought I might patrol some, wander around the neighborhoods south of the lighthouse. Let the people know that we know what they're doing and when they're doing it. You needing me someplace special?"

"If you've got the time. Tony's still coming in tonight?"

"Far as I know." Mary waited to see where Diane was heading. She kept her eyes on the truck in the 7-Eleven lot.

"Vidalia, still?" Mary had planned the trip and been approved to head on down, but the drug bust had become a slippery eel, and Diane hoped her sergeant's spoon was still in the pot she intended to stir with her C-District personnel. She flipped through the spiral and stopped on the first blank page. She pulled a pen from inside the wire rings and wrote: TEAM

MEETING in all caps.

"I would be, 'cept as you know, things come in threes. I suspect you're about to give me number three."

"The first two?" Diane smiled but she didn't look up. Mary could read her like a fish market broker. One glance and she knew what was inside her head and whether she wanted aboard ship or not. It sounded like she was already aboard.

"One, you people going down to Ocracoke, and two, me being assigned to cover the Bonner accident."

"Not the Bonner," Diane prodded, although she called it that also.

"Close enough. Own to it, Lieutenant. How are you using up the rest of my day?" Mary crumbled the paper from her cinnamon bun and wiped her fingers. She pointed to the glove box. "I got me some wipes in there, if you don't mind, Lieutenant."

"I'm calling a team meeting down to the sub-station in Buxton. Everyone. You think you can do that?" She pulled the wipes from the glove box as she spoke and handed them to her sergeant before writing *6:00 – Buxton – Everyone* in the spiral. She slipped the small notebook back in her pocket.

"I can, and you can. I got me a radio right here, so I'm supposing that's not the way you want it done."

"I might oughta lay it out plain, Mary. I don't want nothin' that will get back to Morton just yet. I might have to do all he tells me to do, but I got my own way to do it. He wants to make himself look pretty—"

"Retire with a clean sheet, you mean. Something to boast about with his grandkids. He's catering to those kooks back in Raleigh that he likes to cozy up to—"

"You pulled in that mackerel and skinned and gutted him already." Diane laughed. She was glad she had contacted Mary and they were sharing a coffee in the woman's cruiser. The sergeant was fishing from the same dock as she was, and if Diane could work this out, the C-District Team might well pull in a mess of a catch. "You get on down yonder and get Ashley at the sub-station to get in touch with everyone. Stay off the radio. Use personal lines if you need. I'm making a few contacts of my own, hopefully to change the rudder on this investigation and keep us afloat a bit longer."

"What time?" Mary was already aboard.

"The meeting? About that—" Diane had written down 6:00, and she considered drive time, the ferry schedules, and how quickly she could jostle around and get her side of the sandcastle tamped into place. She decided it was workable. "Six. That's late, but this is vital. I don't mind if Sheriff Pafford or Braxton Sallinger's there, so long's they can keep mum until I arrive."

Pafford, of course, was from out of the county, and Sallinger was Coast Guard, and that was way out of the county. Still, they were the very ones that might help her pull this off.

"I'll lock 'em in the boot of my car if they so much as make a peep." Mary grinned.

"You do that. I've got my cell if you need me. Thanks, Mary."

Diane exited the sergeant's Explorer and caught the sun reflecting off the word Police scrawled down the side. A rainbow of color hit her, then the door latched shut, and it became just a decal. In her car, almost identical to Mary's but unmarked, she placed the remains of her coffee in the console, started the engine, and headed back over the causeway towards Roanoke Island and Manteo, but she had no plans to stop there.

There were bigger fish in the sea, and she intended to reel some of them in.

AFTER TWENTY minutes of hard-focused driving, Diane considered her choices and berated herself. "I might coulda seen this coming. Six this evening? And I'm winding the long way up yonder. Don't know that I'll make Buxton by midnight."

Up yonder was her home in Elizabeth City in Pasquotank County, the one she rarely visited, as she normally camped out in her aunt's old beach house out on the Banks. After all, the beach was on the Banks, and Elizabeth City, while charming in an inland way, wasn't even close to the beach.

There was one very important thing Elizabeth City did have: Governor Killian Ehringhaus.

The man had long since escaped the fish basket of government, but as a former Gales County sheriff, and even more importantly, as a charter founder and head of the North Carolina Retired Sheriff's Foundation, Killian Ehringhaus' voice carried weight with the elected sheriffs in the state. The Foundation worked for housing and other retirement benefits for those who had been elected as county sheriffs in the state, and it received strong support from most counties statewide.

That included Diane, who was a member and who paid voluntary dues; and Dare County, which supported the Retired Sheriff's Foundation through fund-raising initiatives and intercounty cooperation across the state.

Killian, as Diane had known him her entire life, now lived in Elizabeth City in Pasquotank County, and was personable, effusive, and a motivating force that was hard to ignore. He had also been her aunt's benefactor decades before when women attending college was a challenge. Diane had called him Uncle Killian until in her college years when she learned that he was much more than her aunt's good friend and one-time mentor. By then, of course, Killian's stint as governor was long past, and his time as the Gales County sheriff was even more distant.

Killian Ehringhaus was the primary reason Diane Turnipseed held the office of lieutenant in Dare County. He had become her mentor and a motivating influence in every decision she had made to get to where she was today.

Today's time on the road gave her the opportunity to think about what she would say to Uncle Killian. He would expect her to call him that, although if she didn't, he would likely do little more than reprimand her with a smile and a hug. At his age, he spent most of his days in a wheelchair, although he could traverse short distances when the need arose. For him to stand and offer her a hug each time she visited was a warm caress on her heart. He was the one man she considered worthy of love and respect, and she was certain he felt the same about her.

Today, she intended to rally his support in her cause to back down Morton Kringlebach in his determination to crush C-District's investigative efforts to uncover the whereabouts of two possible missing people—and the number could be much higher. There was no way to tell without gathering the evidence, which Morton wanted to refuse to allow her team to do.

Crossing the bridge over the Albemarle Sound and heading north, she worried about the time her route was wasting. The drive would have consumed an hour and a half up the banks on 158. She was spending nearly twice that taking 64 and cutting north through Edenton, but that was the pot she'd set herself in, so she let it go. Later, coming into Elizabeth City, she debated whether to head straight to Ellswood, Killian's plantation fronting the Pasquotank River, and decided that if she was boasting the lived-in look when she met with Morton in Manteo, she downright needed a change before heading to Ellswood. Killian would appreciate that from her, but more, he would expect it. He was a true Southern gentleman, and she had learned to respect that part of his character.

She turned off in town and wound down the leafy street leading toward her home. She'd chosen it because it was out of the way and offered her a level of privacy in what could be a very public profession. The real estate agent had also sold her on the garage apartment behind the old home. Diane hadn't cottoned to it at first and had left it unrented for several years, until after her aunt bequeathed her the old beach house on the Banks. Diane had rented the garage apartment at a greatly reduced rate to a professor at the state university on the south side of town. Her caveat was that he maintain the outside of the property to the standards of its idyllic southern locale.

She pulled in the drive, ran her eye critically over the front façade of her home, and nodded. Carroll Shelton was keeping up his end of their rental bargain. She killed the engine, made her way to the porch, and unlocked her green front door. Inside was as she expected: blinds closed, stale air, and a thin patina of dust. Then, if she spent more than a day or two a month here … but that was one more thing to let go. On the floor just inside the door, mail littered the floor. She scooped it up, flipped through it for anything of importance, and dropped it in a basket on a table. In her bedroom, she opened a large wardrobe and rifled through it for something appropriate, dressy but not formal, attractive but befitting an officer of the law.

And a shower. She headed to the bathroom, turned on the water, made sure the water heater was still heating, and she began her preparations to meet with Uncle Killian Ehringhaus.

She caught her image in the mirror as it began to steam, and she nodded at the fierce expression glaring back at her. *Morton Kringlebach, you want a powerplay? You might oughta consider who you're trying to hoggletie. There's bigger fish in the sea than you ever seen off the shores of Roanoke Island. Even Raleigh ain't seen the likes of the storm that's fixin' to roll over you.* Then the image disappeared into frosted moisture; and with a towel in her hand, Diane placed a fresh bottle of shampoo within easy reach, chose her favorite shower sponge, and gave in to the hot water for a time.

Freshened and looking forward to meeting her mentor; and

dressed in tan slacks, closed-toed shoes, and a navy blazer; Diane stood before a mirror and pushed her drying hair back from her face. Hair was always too much trouble for her, and she fished a wide, navy hair clip from inside a drawer. She sternly worked the mass of tresses to the back of her neck and captured them with the clip before taking a small detangling brush and pushing it through at her temples to smooth and flatten what didn't want to be smoothed and flattened and finally down the short tail hanging beneath the fat clip. Satisfied, she gathered her keys and phone and found herself at the front door. She looked around her, took unexpected solace in the room's clean lines, spare decorations, and unlived in ambiance. Her aunt's place on the beach? A tumble of beachside memories, mostly dusty, and too precious to declutter or disturb in any significant way. A flyer in the jumble of mail she had tossed into the basket on the table caught her eye, and she reached for it.

Have You Seen This Child?

The single-sheet insert was part of an advertisement packet and revealed images of four children, all under fifteen. Under the pictures, each child received a name: Saoirse Byrne; Connor Byrne; Sarah Garamata; and James Nwadike. Two were obviously siblings, with strawberry-blonde hair and lightly freckled faces; the third boasted dark, straight hair and creamy brown skin; and the last was a midnight storm with violent, twisted waves of hair whipped heavenward by his ethnic background.

In smaller print, the dates the children had gone missing told something about the criminal element—or perhaps bad parenting—that comprised the lives of many people. The last two, Sarah and James, had slightly ambiguous faces, reflecting their date of disappearance: ten years earlier for Sarah and three for James. The images had been age-adjusted to fifteen and thirteen, with the oddly blurry facial features that incurred. Not so with Saoirse and Conner. At seven and nine, their pics reflected a missing date mere days earlier.

Diane turned over the insert, noted the deliver-by date on the card, and realized it had arrived only that morning. She started to drop the insert back into the basket before tucking it in her blazer pocket. This wasn't her field, her county, or her case, and while it was sad, she had a possible drug smuggler running amok down in Buxton if he hadn't yet made it further south to Frisco or Hatteras Village; and evidence strongly suggested that the missing pilot and possible passengers of that sailboat now in Silver Lake were connected. One of K9 handler Cynthia Ellison's sometimes prescient quips stuck in her thoughts: *"You don't know what's coming down the road if you don't look in the rearview ..."*

She pulled the insert from her pocket, studied the images once again, and slipped it back inside. *Is this my rearview? The thing I should be baiting onto my line?* She didn't see how, but it took up little room in her pocket. She flipped out the lights, opened the door, stepped outside, and locked it behind her.

On the way to her SUV, she heard her name and looked towards the rear of the property. Professor Shelton had a hand in the air and was jogging her way. He wore a late-twenties face and an athlete's crisp way of moving.

"Professor, good afternoon."

"Carroll, please, though I answer to everything." He laughed and stopped just in front of her. He wore joggers and an elastic headband. A pronounced cowlick to the right of his forehead escaped and gave him a jaunty appearance. "I almost missed you."

"I'm heading to a meeting, Professor, er, Carroll." She smiled to take the tang off her slip. The Governor didn't know about the meeting yet, but they were having it, sure as hollandaise sauce on fish cakes.

"A minute, that's all I need. I noticed a spot the squirrels have been chewing your roof. I can see it from my front window upstairs, though not likely from down here. Would you like me to place a call to a roofer?"

"Yes, please. You can have them bill me or—"

"Send the receipt and deduct it from my rent?" He grinned. It was how they often worked out extra expenses. He covered the bill out of his pocket and paid it back through reduced rent, over several months, if necessary.

"Either. Is that all?"

"I see you found the insert from today's ad circular." He gestured to her pocket where the top of the insert showed. "Sad story about the two Byrne kids. The ad company only posts kids under fifteen, but as I hear it, their parents are missing, too. The whole family, just gone."

"Local people?" Meaning that he must know them to know the parents were missing. The dates on the insert were very recent, as in only days ago.

"Nah. One of my students at the university. Those are her little brother and sister. I'm just the one that turned in their names and photographs and pushed them to get those in today's delivery. There's a whole story there, but you've got a meeting, and I'm in training for a marathon. New York next year." He smiled, waved, and was off down the street, his legs pumping, and his arms over his head in a *Rocky* stance of victory.

People like the professor were the reason she liked this part of Elizabeth City. Too bad it wasn't nearer the beach. She might want to live here all the time. She shrugged, climbed in her vehicle, and began making her way to Ellswood. The Governor would be able to help her. And she was certain he'd be glad to do it.

"GOOD MORNING, Jerrold. Is the Governor available?" Diane stood on the colonnaded porch of Ellswood, a two-story expanse of potted shrubbery and Southern hospitality that overlooked the Pasquotank River in the distance. Jerrold Swainey was the Governor's private secretary, though he did much more for his aged employer than just secretarial work.

"My, my, Miss Diane, won't the Governor be so happy today. He's missed you stopping by for a regular visit."

"I've missed being here, too. Is he available?"

"Good lawd, yes, Miss Diane. You come right this ways. He's in his office like he is most every afternoon." Once she was inside, he closed the door after her and motioned down a hallway to the left. "Of course, I don't know how much work he gets done. Always complains that nobody has a job for him to do, but that's just the Governor, you see. He always feels the need to be busy, and it does seem to him that the world's moved right on by, him in his wheelchair and everything, though I guess that's as it should be."

They were at the Governor's office door by then, and Jerrold nodded to Diane, knocked on the door three times very lightly, placed his fingers into an ornate metal depression set into one side, and slid the elaborate wooden slab into a recess in the wall. He said softly, "Governor, you have a visitor," before stepping back and motioning that Diane had permission to enter the room.

TWO HOURS later, Diane was back on the front porch, and she turned to face the river as Jerrold Swainey gently latched the front door of ex-Governor Killian Elringhaus' luxurious estate, closing the two men inside and leaving Diane to tackle her investigation once more to *hopefully* reveal who the missing man was who *in theory* had gone overboard down yonder on Ocracoke Island.

Hopefully and *in theory* had been stressed to her by Gov. Elringhaus, as in any investigation, the outcome wasn't decided by the people collecting the evidence. That was up to a higher authority, whether the court system or some other agency. After a warm greeting, with a hug and a kiss to her cheek, her mentor and trusted confidant asked what brought her from the shores of the sea to his inland paradise. His eyes twinkled as he settled himself back into his wheelchair and adjusted the sleeves of his white suit.

Diane related her frustrations and learned that the Governor knew of Morton Kringlebach's impending retirement and understood his desire to leave office with a bit of flair and panache. He hadn't heard of the possibility of someone over-board or the intercounty cooperation over the drug smuggling sting, but he thoroughly approved. The elderly man's still-vibrant attention to detail revealed itself with the next thing he said.

"You have something in your pocket, I see." He motioned with his hand.

"It's nothing, Uncle Killian." The advertising insert with the images of the missing children still peeking out of her blazer pocket … it crinkled as she tried to slip it further inside, but no matter what she did, it didn't fit. She pulled it out to fold it when Elringhaus held out his hand.

"Hogwattle. That'll never come out in the wash. Let me see nothing. I'm an old man in this big old house, and nothing is what I have to pay attention to most days. This nothing is a better nothing that what I was doing before you arrived to brighten my afternoon." He smiled, and his halo of white hair gave him a prescient, all-knowing quality.

"You may be disappointed." She held it out. When he took it, she explained the connection to her renter. "Professor Shelton who rents my garage apartment here in town teaches the sister of two of the children—"

"At the university?" Elizabeth City State University was

located down the river from Ellswood, not far from the Elizabeth City Airport, although it wasn't visible from the estate. The Governor was a staunch supporter of the educational facility and often hosted university events on the grounds of his property.

"Yes. Have you heard of him?"

"Carroll, I believe. He rents from you?" He looked off to the side of the room as if pulling up an image of the man in his mind. "Yes, yes, an athletic type, likes to do marathons. I believe I've seen the man on the river. A rowing team? No, sailboats, that's his forte. Tell me more of his connection to these children."

"Just the two on the left, the Byrne siblings. I bumped into the professor in my driveway today, and he brought them up. I can find out more if you wish."

"I think these children might be the ticket to buy you time in your investigation down south." The Governor's mind took a leap Diane didn't follow, and he waved the insert in the air and winked conspiratorially. "The Albemarle Sound. Why, the professor could sail right down to Dare County. You do know that from Elizabeth City, we can see Roanoke, if we care to try hard enough."

Diane didn't think so. With a drone, perhaps, and a telescope … but she nodded and listened along. She encouraged him with, "And, Uncle? Sort the crabs into the correct pots for me."

"That's my island girl," he teased. "Our two counties, right next to each other, you say?"

"I don't say. I seem to recall a Camden County and even a Currituck County. What about those?"

"Now, now, girl, don't distract me." The Governor paused in thought. "You mentioned intercounty cooperation down south. If Morton's willing to swim with Hyde … Sheriff Pafford, am I correct?"

"You know you are." The man might be in a wheelchair, but

his memory was as sharp as shark's teeth on a surfboard.

"I've not seen a man that could stand against a strong-willed woman, and Sheriff Pafford is that. Let me contact our sheriff here in Pasquotank, get our two counties cooperating in a search for these two little children. I'll ask for Professor Shelton to request a meeting with Morton … maybe with the Governor, too, the current one, not me—" he chuckled, "—though if it eats a bit of Morton's time and attention, I can set that up, too." He shrugged as if he might do exactly that.

The man's suggestion was like reeling in the biggest Spanish mackerel ever seen on the Buxton shore. If Diane had suggested it, she'd have felt above her knees, likely swimming in the collards, and slippin' her spoon into a pot it had no business in; but when the words rolled out of the Governor's mouth, it sounded right as the sun peeking over the dunes on a crisp fall morning.

As Diane opened her vehicle's door and seated herself inside, she slipped on her sunglasses, started the engine, and let her mind ramble over the plan her aunt's friend, her mentor, and now her salvation was putting into motion to buy her C-District team the time to collect the evidence they needed to continue what would hopefully become a full-fledged investigation along with Hyde County, Carteret County, and likely Beaufort County.

She checked her dash clock. Nearly 4:00. She could make Buxton in less than two-and-a-half hours. She might be late for the meeting, but a phone call could take care of that. She put her truck into gear and headed down the estate's long, manicured drive towards the highway. This time, she would follow the shorter route through Camden, Point Harbor, and over into Kitty Hawk. She'd even sacrifice changing back into her uniform. She now had a plan in place to trap Morton Kringlebach in a fish weir of Uncle Killian's making, and she was certain as leaf peepers on a fall morning that Morton Kringlebach would no longer have the time to impede the investigative tsunami about to be unleashed by her C-District team that would inundate the southern half of the Outer Banks.

Especially with Hyde County at their side, and maybe even the Coast Guard if Diane could get Ashley to contact Braxton Sallinger and invite him aboard.

"THEY SAY saltwater cures all, but ooh, ooh, can this be the same Lieutenant Turnipseed we saw as recently as this morning?" Emily Bryant stood at the door to the incident room, and her question filled the lobby as Diane entered the Buxton C-District sub-station.

Jason Romney appeared behind her with a cup of coffee from Kat's in his hand, and he let out a low whistle.

Diane snorted, "You people are gonna see on my left a way out the door and on my right a way back to your seats. You might oughta keep that in mind before you get above your knees this evening."

She waved their comments away with her hand, but she could hardly keep a smile of warmth from her face. She suspected the warmth was spreading across the rest of her, too, and she turned her back to them to look at something— anything—on Ashley Dixon's desk.

"Yes, ma'am, Lieutenant," Ashley whispered to her. "I agree with them. And you're welcome to inspect my desk as long as it takes for that brilliant shade of red to fade from your face."

"Not you, too, Ashley." Diane flipped a sheet of paper to the back. There was nothing on either side, but the appearance of being occupied was the important thing in the moment.

"You sign them," Ashley called out loudly enough for even the people gathered for the meeting in the incident room to overhear, "but read the addendums at the end before you do. It might take a while, so I'm heading home. My shift ended twenty minutes ago."

Diane glanced at the clock. 6:20. She expected Ashley could tell her the seconds, also.

"Thank you, Ashley," Diane whispered.

"Yes, ma'am, but I'm really gone. You folks lock up after yourselves and don't forget to turn out the lights." Ashley pulled her keys from the top drawer in her desk, jangled them loudly, and called to the others, "Ashley has left the building. No cheers. Elvis was never here."

Diane smiled as Ashley snickered on her way out the door. Feeling braver but now wishing she had remembered to collect a fresh uniform on the way down—and then she kicked herself. She had a fresh uniform, or at least Ashley could have picked it up from the cleaners in Buxton. But that was a big no, as she still would have been caught out when she arrived. Emily as lookout would have caught her dead no matter how Diane tried to avoid it, and besides, she didn't have the conniving mindset to sidestep situations like this. She only figured out her plan after she tripped into the crab pot sitting beside her door. She squared her shoulders, firmed up her mouth, and turned to face her detractors and hoped they didn't compliment her aberrant clothing again.

Inside, she found Jason Romney sitting meekly on the back row with his coffee cup to his lips and intentionally looking anywhere but at her. She wanted to growl at his whistle from earlier, but his freshly slicked-back hair did look good on him. Next to him, Emily watched her, letting her eyes track Diane's every move, and the woman barely kept from smirking when she caught Diane looking at her.

She was surprised to see Coast Guard Ensign Courtney Cruickshank with her short, blonde hair in the room. The woman smiled brightly in a girly way when Diane's eyes stopped on her for a moment. Sheriff Pafford was nowhere to be seen, but Hyde County's Calvin Dingman, with his black sheriff's cap on even in the room sat one seat away from the ensign. That didn't surprise her, the part about the sheriff not being present, but she would have expected Darlene Pafford to send Zack Halsey or Suzanne DeSantis instead. Then she recalled that Suzanne was the lone deputy on Ocracoke and would likely choose to remain there. And Jason was in cahoots with Calvin, so that explained that, especially as Zack had Goldie to oversee, and the canine officer didn't need to be at this meeting. What input could a dog give, no matter how accomplished she was at ferreting out illicit drugs?

Sean Taylor stood by the window, clean and crisp in a freshly pressed uniform, and Mary Wilson, next to him, nodded towards Diane when their eyes met. She would have been surprised to find Clifton Magruder in the room, though she had hoped to share her news with someone from Carteret County, her way of keeping them swimming in the bait bucket and more importantly, *knowing* that they were in the bait bucket.

Before Diane could begin talking, Robert Hall walked in the room, seemingly comfortable with the people already present, and lifted a hand to Diane. He sat next to Jason. *Okay, Robert,* she thought. *I asked you to stick around. You can be my liaison back to Manteo. Let them deep dive for what I'm about to toss out tonight.*

She welcomed Ensign Cruickshank first. "Courtney, thank you for joining us—"

"Yes, ma'am. I'm having a happy moment being here. Lieutenant Sallinger tried to make it, he really did, ma'am, but he had a schedule conflict." Courtney tittered. "I didn't catch her name, but she was pretty as a lollipop."

Laughter punctuated the room, and Diane called, "Hold

your taters, deputies. Let the ensign finish. Anything else, Courtney?"

"Yes, ma'am. I was taught to introduce myself when I first meet someone, so everyone, I'm Courtney Cruickshank, and being here with you-all—" She scrunched her shoulders. "Why, ain't this the best day ever?"

"I expect it is," Diane agreed, taking a deep breath, and moving on to Emily. "Emily, have you heard more about our seasick passenger from the ferry?"

Sean brightened, as if his trial aboard the sport fishing vessel the day before was being recognized. His grin dimmed when Emily said, "I spoke with Paytyne Preston this afternoon, and she was able to reschedule her doctor's appointment in More-head and meet her husband there this morning. I believe they intend to be back this direction sometime this evening."

"Then she survived." Diane stated it as a fact, slotting it away like wrapping a tuna steak and placing it in the freezer, still there but stored away for later use.

"Yes, ma'am," Emily replied, her eyes playfully on Sean Taylor's wilted expression at realizing they weren't going to ask him about how he was doing after spending the day seasick during a nor'easter.

"No one from Carteret," Diane murmured, as she headed to the front of the room. "Shame—" Jason's hand in the air caught her eye, and at the lectern, she signaled him her permission to speak.

"Let's not say that." He didn't continue but tilted his head to look towards the ceiling, then cut his eyes back and forth as if to say, *What are you missing, Diane? Do you see it yet?*

"Say it, Jason," Diane said, harsher than she intended. The man had put his spoon into her pot, and she wanted to know what he was trying to stir up.

"Morton has yet to approve my transfer, so technically ..."

He let the last word fade away and grinned at her.

"You don't like me assigning you as deputy?" *Let that bite, Jason Romney. You want to cross my line when fishing with your smart cracks, I'll yank the line harder'n you.*

"Oh, I don't know. I 'spect I could get used to it." He tilted his chair back on two legs. Across the room, Sean grinned like a lighthouse at dusk, and Mary looked away like there was some undercurrent that had been stirred before Diane's arrival and was yet to surface. Emily nudged Jason's chair a bit further back, and he jerked as he caught himself before the chair tumbled backwards.

Already … Diane hadn't even brought up the news from Governor Elringhaus, and already, the entire meeting was hitting low tide. She rapped the lectern with her knuckles and said sharply, "Morton Kringlebach is being asked to aid Pasquotank County in a multi-county search for a missing family. I have every expectation that he will be asked to meet with the governor to coordinate the operation. I'm sure that Morton will be excited, especially as he sees his upcoming retirement already cresting the horizon, and this will be a way for him to prove his worth and dedication to the North Carolina voters who have kept him in office all these years."

More than one face was speechless at Diane's vote of approval for Morton Kringlebach. She hadn't meant to say all that, and she wasn't sure she would have if Jason Romney hadn't looked so charming as he nearly fell backwards in his chair.

"Intercounty cooperation," Ensign Cruickshank called out brightly into the shocked silence. "And you invited the Coast Guard to tag along. Ain't this the best day ever?"

The room broke apart, a scramble of mackerel in a net, with words thrown out like bait and astonished looks wetting people's faces. Calvin Dingman was the first to set his thoughts free.

"I'll be ding-danged. Like in my own backyard. Up to Swans' we got it going on but that ain't nothing compared to you folks." He shifted his heavy torso in his chair, the metal frame groaned, and he pulled a can of tobacco from a pocket, studied it as if considering whether it was appropriate, and put it away.

Sean let out, "Intercounty cooperation?" He looked around with a grin. "I'm a hundred percent in. Y'all can count on me."

Emily pulled a fart bladder out of her purse, set it in the seat next to her and called to Sean to come *sit himself down.*

Mary Wilson walked over to Robert Hall, and together they wound up in a back corner and began a discussion next to a storage cabinet that strangely enough stood partially open.

Jason Romney stopped by Sean and pointed out the fart bladder, causing Emily to return it to her purse with a pouty face, then he pulled Sean aside and looked to be giving him instructions.

Diane's head spun. Her announcement was intended to scoop up all the county minnows in the room and get them swimming the same direction … her direction … not scatter them about like startled bait fish. Her phone began to ring—the distinctive tone faint but one clearly hers and no one else's— but she couldn't locate it on her person. She searched and frowned before stepping into the reception area where it was in plain sight on Ashley Dixon's desk.

"Never did that before," she muttered, unable to remember having it out as she entered the building. She lifted it and saw Ashley's name and number on the face. She glanced at the incident room, which had gone strangely silent, and she clicked to answer.

"Yes, Ashley. Did you forget something?"

"You're at my desk?"

"I am, why? Might I oughta ask what's going on?"

"No ma'am, you cannot ask what's going on. Just stay there a minute, then be nice and act surprised."

The phone clicked off, and Diane looked at it suspiciously. At the bottom of the screen was a notification of a text from Karen in Manteo. She started to click it but the quiet in the incident room distracted her. She didn't like surprises … and she didn't especially want to walk back into that room. "If those people …" she began to herself, then straightened her back and decided to play this straight. Whatever they had planned, she would act like she knew they had baited her, and she was in on the game all along.

The real surprise was Ashley Dixon in the room holding a cake with lighted candles. Not even Diane was able to keep a puzzled expression from knotting her forehead.

"Ashley? For all sakes, you went home already, so you said."

"Maybe as far as my car. That's where the cake was. You know we have a back door." She shrugged and smiled.

"You people are way above your knees. A birthday cake? Whose? I know it's not mine, so?" She searched their faces for the guilty party.

"You might could know if you stepped closer, Diane," called a voice that could only be Jason's.

"You might could tell me if you'd only talk louder, Jason Romney," she retorted. Then she caught the number of candles, saw the sheriff's star in the icing, and realized the cake was in Dare County colors.

"Happy fifteenth anniversary, Diane." Emily took her arm and pulled her forward. "And you dressed up for your party. How thoughtful of you."

Like Emily thought she would do that, then she caught Emily's wink as the crowd began to sing the Happy Anniversary song. Diane smiled, and she lifted both her hands and called out over the voices of the singers, "To tell the story honest, I thought you dingbatters might forget, and after I dressed up and all. Am I above my knees if I ask for a knife? I'm hungry and ready to eat."

Mary held up a serving knife, and she offered it to Diane. It was when Sean took his slice of cake and found a seat that events ramped up a notch. It seemed that Emily's fart bladder didn't remain in her purse but instead found its way under him just as he sat down. Emily clapped and encouraged everyone to cheer. Even Sean found the composure to lean back, take a bite of cake, and ignore the red streaks of embarrassment crawling up his neck and into his face.

The party didn't stop Diane's mind from poking and prodding the events the day had lodged into her mind. The text from earlier kept intruding, and she opened it. *Sheriff Kringlebach is off to Raleigh. Says he needs to postpone reviewing your investigative reports. Will meet with you in a week. ??? Karen.* Gov. Elringhaus had kept his word. Missing children, a missing sheriff, and a missing man. The children, that was out of her jurisdiction, and she had no trouble letting that go. It was sad, but her plate was about full right then. The missing man? Like her aunt Lucille used to say, the bed you make is the one you wake up in, and Diane didn't think she was ready to lay down her head just yet. She also didn't know how long the sheriff would be missing, and she needed to get her team busy.

Then Jason appeared at her side, offered her a slice of cake, and remarked, "So, you got to ride the emergency ferry across the Inlet."

"What?" She frowned. "What's that got to do with anything?"

"It was how we had time to do all this." He grinned. "You called the meeting for six, and the rest, well, good opportunities aren't meant to be wasted. My idea, by the way."

"Hold your taters. You planned this?" She didn't know whether to fume or appreciate his efforts.

"Leave it alone, Diane. Enjoy your cake and have a good time. You can chew me out tomorrow. Happy fifteen years with the county." He nodded to her and walked away to stop by Calvin Dingman's side.

Fifteen years. It hardly seemed that long. The bigger issue in her mind was the missing people from that sailboat. Had someone gone overboard, or were other things about to wash up on the next tide? At least with Sheriff Kringlebach off to meet with the governor, they had a little more time to gather evidence and hopefully solve the mystery of just what was going on.

Chapter 6

Stranger at Silver Lake

DEPUTY SUZANNE DESANTIS of Hyde County and Ocracoke Island checked the thick, gold watch on her wrist. It was the least feminine thing about her, and that was saying something. Jeans and a black jacket, that was her way of expressing herself to the islanders she worked with.

Not for, not against, but with, a team, unlike with her husband up on the Beaufort County payroll. Teague liked being married, or so he liked to say, just didn't enjoy being partnered with a firecracker for a wife. The idea of being a firecracker brought a smile to Suzanne's face and she stood from her desk and lifted her black jacket from the coat tree near the door. Three black jackets remained behind, all hers, each for a different season. She had named the four of them: Thunderbasher, Stormroller, Heatstroke, and Winter Candy. Today she slipped her arms into Winter Candy. With the recent weather, frost crackled in the air. Jack had come to North Carolina to shake hands but he had yet to establish a firm foothold on the Outer Banks. On Ocracoke, the hardiest of the islands along the chain of barrier islands, the people were bluster-proof, hardened to the worst the sky gods could do to force them to hike up their waders and flee to the mainland each winter.

The kooks, the dingbatters, that's a different story. They ran at the first signs of overwash, and Suzanne laughed at the red of their taillights as they frantically drove onto the ferries, either north to Hatteras or south to Cedar Island. They only wanted the best of life on the tiny spit of land, not the real experience of living on the island. Ocracoke life was surviving winds that battered the island trees like it was the bottom of the ninth and the score was tied … then Suzanne let that metaphor go. That was Teague, baseball fan and always wanting to head inland to see his team play. She couldn't even tell you what team he worshipped. Nah. Like she used to say to him when he had his eyes glued to a game on the television, "Turn that off, open up your brain, and a little knowledge might seep in." Teague hadn't appreciated her advice, and that's why he was in Beaufort, and she wasn't.

She pulled the door open, stepped outside, and closed it. It never occurred to her to lock it, not on Ocracoke. Who was there to break in, and if someone did, where was there for them to go? No roads left the island, and she could stop either ferry with a call. Besides, she knew most everyone on the island. She lived with them day in and out. Her besties, or her worsties, if they challenged her or were so ingrained with independence that they were willing to risk arrest for speaking their mind.

Suzanne studied her car absently, a newish Dodge Charger in gray with lights but no markings. The newish was important, as the salt air even now washing over the island turned cars into Swiss cheese every few years. Overhead, the flag on the station's pole stirred, snapped once, then settled back to a gentle shake every now and then. She looked up, took in the sky, and worked her keys out of a pocket. She might know everyone, and this island might be a pimple on a fish's bladder, but the ferry was the other side of the village and too far to walk. She wanted to head to Silver Lake and ensure their crime exhibit moored in the harbor wasn't conveniently finding its way to the docks of Phillips Boat Salvage. If so, she might have to haul in and gut some slimy suckers who thought the law didn't apply to them.

She pulled out onto the Garrish Highway into town, still Highway 12 on all the state maps, but the Garrish nonetheless; and as she idled by Jason's Restaurant with its green-and-white sign that proclaimed STEAKS!, she realized she was about hungry enough to chase down a bluefin and slice off a steak before she let it go. She'd also be content with a slice of pizza, a sub, or any of Jason's seafood options.

"Get it together, Suzanne," she muttered, as she applied the gas and let the car slip past the familiar eatery. Hunger was one of the reasons she'd resisted the opportunity to head up to Buxton to meet with Diane Turnipseed's teammates. She enjoyed the Dare County officer, felt they made good casting partners aboard the good ship Law Enforcement. Sometimes she pulled the line from the reel, and other times Diane did, but they usually came to terms with each other's position in the hierarchy of their respective counties and got along well enough.

Around Silver Lake, she slowed her car, and the engine became a rumble through the accelerator, the muted sound of the tailpipe telling any eavesdroppers that its power was more than adequate to any demand she might place on it. At a break in the visual barriers offering views of the protected harbor, she found the boat was still fully intact with its crime tape shouting that no one was permitted aboard until the sheriff's office was finished with its investigation. Satisfied, she looked back to the street, waved at two teen boys on skateboards, and noted several unfamiliar cars tailing one another from the direction of the ferry.

"Some people don't get the island thing," she said to herself as the cars passed her by. "No place to go in such a hurry. Take your time, people. Heck," she chuckled, "sometimes I don't get the island thing, but I don't want to get run over by some dingbatter." She decided to follow the spawning trail upstream and make herself visible. Let the newly hatched dingbatters see the Law present and accounted for on their first foray into the island interior, and maybe the safety of the island's inhabitants would remain intact for yet another day.

Just shy of the ferry landing, she parked her car, and with her unmarked doors, triggered the lights atop the vehicle to flash but left the siren alone. No need to rile the hometown folks when all she wanted to do was make herself known to the kooks come to spend the afternoon on the best island on the Outer Banks. Of course, not all the arrivals were kooks. Many were familiar to her, some come to nest in their home pool after a day or a week down south or on the mainland, and others using the island as a causeway to their destination up to Buxton, Avon, or heading all the way to Kitty Hawk. Those people still had another ferry to go, but they accepted it as part of the process, or they would have chosen the long way round back on the mainland.

A lifted Jeep waiting to exit the ferry, wearing eyes mounted on its roof and peering over the top of a line of vehicles, caught her attention. She pictured Sean Taylor's massive off-roader but the sky eyes on this Jeep weren't of the county variety but of the wannabe off-road type. Meaning, they were more for show than for go. As the Jeep reached the ramp, she noticed a mature female in the passenger's seat, with striking auburn hair. Through the windshield, the woman's looks revealed her atten-tion to her appearance and a determination to retain her attrac-tiveness for as long as possible. The driver dropped the window on his side, and he thrust a freckled arm to cut into the thick sea air as he called, "Officer, over here."

He motioned with an open hand for her to step closer.

"Yessir, what can I do for you?" Suzanne took two steps his direction but didn't approach all the way. She took in his coarse blond hair, the face covered with pale freckles, and the physical frame that filled the Jeep's window, unlike the woman next to him. This man was a muscular beast, likely from haunting gyms to stave off the years she could see around his eyes. She tried to place his face, somehow familiar, yet his name was a slippery eel.

"You're DeSantis, right?" He turned to his wife and said, "Honey, this is the officer Carrot told us about."

As soon as she heard the name Carrot, Suzanne's memory opened the flood gate. The resemblance between this man and his son shot through her like a salmon up a fish ladder, and she smiled and said, "I think you got that right. That you, Coach Bertram? And you, Mrs. Bertram, how are you doing?" She moved closer to the open window and nodded at the buxom woman.

"Never better, dear. I'm Rebecca. You know my boy, Carrot?" Rebecca wobbled the fingers on one hand apologetically. "He's better known as Kerry, at least off the islands. Perhaps you're more familiar with that name."

"Yes, ma'am, I knew who you were talking about. We got a line behind you still, so we can't chat too long. I guess you're heading up to Hatteras. Manteo, right? You coach at the high school there, Mr. Bertram, am I right?"

"Hot dog," he chortled to his wife. "They even know me down here. How's that for you, Becca?" He turned to Suzanne and said, "You see my boy, you tell him to quit jawing with that Franklin boy. He needs to get on home and do his chores."

"Thank you, Mr. Bertram. I'll do just that." A horn honked

from the direction of the ferry, and Suzanne motioned them on with, "The ferry to Hatteras is that-a-way. Don't want you to miss it."

She smiled at the retreating brake lights as the couple slowed for a man who must be nearing ninety sporting cream slacks, a dark blazer, and a dapper fedora wrapped with a tweed band. If they only knew *why* she was familiar with their son … and she pictured a few beer-drinking sessions with the "Franklin boy" that she'd had to bust up in the past year, but maybe it was best not. The elderly man tipped his cane to the Bertrams in appreciation before making his way to the opposite side of the street and down the walk toward the Visitor's Center, before the Jeep moved past and out of sight.

Someone more familiar gunned her old truck engine and idled forward from the opposite side of the ferry. Minnie Shonda, who owned the Snappy Teapot up in Waves, had a truck with the bed piled as high as a mound of seaweed on the beach and covered with two tarps in two different colors and tied down and under the bed with long straps. Several chair legs poked out, and through one gap, a wooden rocking horse revealed its toothy face. She came through on a regular basis. Cedar Island and down to Morehead City was the best navigation route to the used goods auctions Minnie liked to peruse to top off the stock in her resale shop. She headed down to Jacksonville or west to New Bern weekly, or even into Raleigh occasionally, though she didn't hesitate to share that the real bargains weren't in Raleigh any longer. Too much money floating around to drive up the prices.

Suzanne called, "Hey, Minnie! Good shopping day?"

"Got me quite a haul, don't I?" Minnie cackled. "Bed's 'bout as full as a truck can get, don't'cha think? Don't wanna get run over, Suzanne. You have a good'un." She looked forward, her truck jerked ahead, and she swayed and bumped the direction the Bertrams had gone.

A motorcycle rumbled by, the familiar riders likely passing through, two teens by the name of Sibley Jenkins and Chad Lannigan. Chad was in front, and he had the visor on his helmet shoved up so that Suzanne could make out his face, and the girl on the back was bundled in a UN Chapel Hill hoodie, so that could only be Sibley. Both teens now attended the University of North Carolina at Chapel Hill. The two had worked full time for Lawson and Kitty Wells at Beach Burger in Waves during the past summer, and now that they were away at college, the Lawsons kept them on the weekend rotation as a way for them to earn a little pocket money when they were home. Lawson and Kitty said they were two of the best workers they'd ever had.

Sibley and Chad almost caused Suzanne to miss the vehicle coming up right behind them, a rusty minivan with one missing hubcap. The exhaust backfired, and she jerked her head around just in time for a suspicious face to duck below the window line as if attempting to hide.

"No, you don't," Suzanne spat, although her words were more to herself than to anyone around her. If they were doing anything suspicious and thought she was about to ignore it, they could talk to the hand, 'cause she was having none of it. "Hold up," she called, raising an arm into the air to catch the van driver's attention. She stepped forward to visually obstruct the vehicle's forward motion, though she wasn't stupid enough to actually get in its direct path. Deputies got killed through such nonsense, and she was having none of stupid on her island.

She was surprised when the rust bucket coughed, surged forward, then died; and the engine began to crank hard. Before she could react and think, *What? They're not actually driving away!,* it fired up. Billowing black smoke from the exhaust clouded the air, forming a smoke screen to disguise the van's identity from anyone off its stern. It began to lurch forward, hesitatingly at first, barely avoiding the skateboarding teens from earlier.

"Luka, Sam, get off the road," Suzanne yelled.

The boys lived north of the British Cemetery up past Teeter's Campground. They often skated to Silver Lake. They were usually well-behaved, but they had taken advantage of the van's hesitation and attempted to cross just as it surged ahead. Once she determined that they were in the clear, she lunged after the van, reaching the side in time to slap her hand against the up-rolled glass of the driver's door. She tried to catch a glimpse of the person inside, but in the aftermath of the boys; the coughing, surging lurch of the vehicle; and her amazement that someone was *trying to escape on an island with no roads that went anywhere*, she couldn't manage a good look as the van began to roll faster than she could run.

She stopped, shocked for a moment, with her palm against her forehead, before the awareness of people around her looking to her for guidance in this unusual display of defiance for island authority jerked her back into action.

"Get it together, DeSantis," she muttered. "This ain't shoo-fly pie. Last I heard, you were the law around these parts, and you got a car to carry it out. Move."

She cut back and fell into her gray Charger, wishing for once that she had *Hyde County* blazed across the doors with *Deputy* shouting for people to get out of the way. This was a chase, and she had people she needed to pursue. The practical side of Suzanne DeSantis flipped on her siren to go with her lights, and she threw the transmission into gear. With an eye on Luka and Sam, now on the sidewalk with their skateboards, ends up, with the pointy part on the ground and the backside balanced underneath a downturned palm, she searched for the elderly gentleman who had crossed earlier wearing the fedora. He was seasonal, she thought, as she'd seen him before, but his name didn't come to her, if she'd ever known it. The islanders, like Luka and Sam, yes, those names she had, but those who only fell onto the shores of the island for a week or two a year, well, those names sometimes slipped off her radar, and she had to be reminded.

No time for that today. The gentleman was likely still inside and watching the goings on from the safety of the Visitor's Center. The Visitor's Center alone was enough to brand him kook, though Suzanne didn't judge the yearly visitors for such, unless they proved they deserved it. That rusty van? They lived up to kook stigma, and she was determined to put them in their place. With her siren blaring, she hit the gas, felt the big car surge out onto Garrish, and she headed after the van, hoping to catch it before it disappeared onto one of the occluded and sometimes narrow island lanes.

THE PROBLEM, Suzanne decided, after stopping for a family group with three strollers and two pups on leashes, was that this was a family-friendly island, and the families that she was pledged to protect by their very nature had difficulty moving out of the way even when accosted by flashing lights and a siren. This group was crossing the street, had seen her coming, and as Suzanne slowed for them, they tried, oh but they tried to skedaddle out of the way; but one toddler started crying, her mother had to find someone to navigate her infant's stroller, then she had to encourage her daughter that the loud noise wouldn't hurt her, and that yes, it was okay to move to the side of the road, and no, the big gray car wasn't going to run over her or her brother or anyone else.

Suzanne sighed, turned off the siren to help them out, but by the time she eased past the group, waving to thank them for their cooperation, she had lost sight of the rusty van. She pulled over, jerked up her coat's black sleeve and studied her chunky gold watch and the hands showing the time ticking past. Three minutes, and now, no telling where the van might be. Behind a house, inside a garage, wandering a street that Suzanne was on the opposite end of? If so, by the time she got there, it would likely be somewhere else. She pulled her phone from her pocket and dialed the ferry landing up to Hatteras. With the Cedar Island ferry just in, the van wasn't heading out this way anytime soon, so if it was going off island, Hatteras was the only way.

"Ferry landing. Hold, please."

Suzanne waited as the person on the other end yelled out for someone to *tell that yellow car to wait right there. He has an expired tag.* She didn't know what that was about, but it was none of her business, at least for now.

"Okay, yes," the speaker on the other end of the line said, "how may I help you?"

"It's Suzanne DeSantis. Is this Somner?" Somner Trotter was Luka's father. He worked the Hatteras ferry dock on the Ocracoke side.

"What's Luka done now, Deputy?"

"Nothing." She laughed. "Riding his skateboard with Sam down to Silver Lake, that's all. I called about a minivan that might be heading that way. Rusty, missing a hubcap. If it shows up, pull it over and give me a call."

"Sure thing, though it sounds like half the vehicles I see. Anything else?"

"Just the van. I appreciate it, Somner."

"Then I'm off. I've a yellow car to inspect. Hope their boot's not full."

"Same," she quipped and disconnected the line. She drummed the steering wheel, thinking on what to do. How big was an island? Well, this one was very small, but that didn't mean she could be everywhere at once. She considered Clifton Magruder and his drone, and for a moment, she wished for one of her own, or at least for Clifton to be onsite to make his available to her. That wasn't happening, and with summer gone, much of the island had been vacated by those with better places to spend the winter. That was good and bad, in Suzanne's mind. There were fewer people to navigate among but also fewer eyes to aid in locating her rusty minivan. Across the street, with a small case over her shoulder, 26-year-old Kay-Kay Kopacz trundled down the steps from the Silver Lake Motel, tripping lightly on her feet as if today was the day her ship was coming in. She worked oversized, white-rimmed, rhinestone bedazzled sunglasses onto her face and looked up and down the street before heading the direction of the ferry. Multiple earrings in each ear caught in the light and vied for Suzanne's attention with the yellow tips on her green-tinted blonde hair. Suzanne rolled down her window.

"Kay-Kay, hey!" When Kay-Kay lifted her glasses and glanced around in confusion, Suzanne called louder and waved, "Over here, Kay-Kay."

"Officer 'Santis, yi-ya!" Kay-Kay released her glasses to her nose and waved vigorously. "Let me git over there."

"I'm waitin'." Suzanne glanced at her watch, thought of the minutes slipping away, and looked back at Kay-Kay and noted her sandals. The young woman worked at the motel during summer, but it wasn't summer any longer. She called as Kay-Kay approached, "The motel still open?" It was her way of inquiring without asking why Kay-Kay was there if she was no longer employed for the season.

"Yeah, maybe, I guess. Miss Judy—" Julia Jacobson, the manager and part-owner "—needed inventory, and I was work-ing when the last shipment of cleaning supplies arrived. She promised to pay me if I came in to help sort them. She can be a sweet thing. Wha'cha can I help you with, Officer?"

"A van just drove by, Kay-Kay. I thought maybe you might have seen it …"

"Ew, yucka-roo." Kay-Kay wrinkled her nose. "Did it have a missing hubcap?"

"It might." Suzanne smiled. "Did you see it?"

"Worse." Kay-Kay pursed her lips and looked down the road towards where Garrish cut left to the sheriff's office. She shivered. "It rolled down the window and whistled at me."

"It?" He or she, Suzanne wanted to know.

"I don't know what it was … not a woman, for certain. A grubby little person. And stinky."

"Stinky how?" *Details, details. Spit it out, Kay-Kay. I've got me a van to chase.*

"Drug stinky. You know, weed stuff."

"Marijuana?" Suzanne wanted to laugh. Kay-Kay looked and dressed like a vagrant hippie, but she didn't even know the name for an entry-level substance like marijuana. *Good for you, Kay-Kay.*

"Yeah, that. I said to them, Honeypot, you just drive on and leave me be. That's exactly what I said, Officer 'Santis."

"Good for you, Kay-Kay. Did you see where they went?"

"*It* went—" and she stressed her first word "—towards the ferry."

"Not around the lake." That cut off about half the island, and that was good.

"No, ma'am. They didn't go fast, not like I wanted them to, so's I could get on down where I'm going, so maybe they weren't going to the ferry. I just thought, yeah, git out of here, all the way to the ferry. Don't come back, and that's why I told you the ferry. I didn't see them actually go to the ferry."

"I understand. You did good, Kay-Kay. Never trust the no-goods." Suzanne smiled and reached for her window switch. The air outside was cool, too cool for Kay-Kay's sandals, and the thought of the young woman walking the island in them made Suzanne shiver even in her warm car.

"Glad to help. Yi-ya!" Kay-Kay waved once and turned her attention back to the road leading towards the ferry.

Suzanne glanced in her rearview as she pulled away, smiling at the made-up words of youth. She'd never understand island girls, even if most people now considered her one. She paused her car at Lighthouse Road ... and found herself unsure of how best to search. At least she knew, according to Kay-Kay, that the van had come this direction, and she felt the wheels of her Dodge Charger pulling her to the right as she turned towards the lighthouse, driving slowly to peer one direction and then the other into driveways and anywhere it might park to eliminate every possible nook or cranny it might be.

She felt she got a bit of a break as she approached the small parking area for the island's iconic lighthouse. A National Park Service truck suggested a trusted source that might have noticed whether the van had come this direction, if the ranger happened to be outside. As she pulled past the truck, her heart began to pound, and she checked her equipment to ensure she had what she needed at hand. Someone was slipping up, and it wasn't her. The rusty van was wedged in at the most obvious location on the island. Did they think she wouldn't drive down Lighthouse Road? Or that hunkering down behind an extended cab truck provided them anything other than cursory protection?

Pulling in tight and leaving her Charger blocking the van's exit route, so there was no possibility that it could work itself free, she took her keys with her, locked her car, and walked up to the old wreck of a van and peered in the windows. Window tint peeling, ripped seats, and junk everywhere, including two sleeping bags open and rumpled, which indicated someone possibly sleeping rough. She glanced over the site where the lighthouse perched searching for the ranger with the truck, expecting him to be managing the grounds, perhaps working on the wooden walk or the railing that stretched the hundred feet or so from the parking area to the lighthouse, and she frowned at the dark blot where the white door should be at the base of the white, stone lighthouse.

Inside ... *inside!* She looked back at the filthy van, to the ranger's Park Service truck, and back to the lighthouse. Why was no one outside? She tried to think who might be on duty today, as the lighthouse was rarely open, but sometimes it was. Rob-Roy Haupt? Vernon Heinrich ... or Rena Ward, a petite woman in her sixties ... oh, lord, she hoped something hadn't happened to Rena. Her heart began to pound, and with fear tracing her veins with fire and pummeling her leg muscles like pile drivers of urgency, she bolted for the open lighthouse door. Her heavy boots on the wooden walkway leading past the old keeper's quarters and towards the lighthouse drummed with the necessity of getting there fast, of finding out where the park ranger was, and whether the men from the van had instigated a situation that might become a tsunami of disastrous proportions. She ducked under one tree overhanging the walkway, perfectly aware it wasn't low enough to impact her passage, yet instinctively looking into the branching foliage for anything or *anyone* suspicious. At the end of the walkway where it turned towards the lighthouse, another tree drew her attention upward, yet she found nothing. As she drew close enough to see into the lighthouse, she was chilled to discover the stairwell—normally roped off when open to keep visitors from inadvertently wandering upwards—clear and no one monitoring it. Her eyes jumped up the exterior of the building ... what could she see ... nothing from this angle ... yet, up she looked, her heart still pounding, and she wanted to call out, but to warn someone when that might be the very thing that caused them to do something desperate?

Movement from behind the lighthouse caught her eye, and she was relieved to see Rena's white hair above her brown uniform. Rena was singing to herself, facing away from her, and so likely she thought she was alone.

"Rena," Suzanne called softly, just enough to get the petite woman's attention. She gave a quick glance back towards her car to ensure that the rusty van was still parked where she had trapped it, then inside the lighthouse—nothing different there—and back to Rena.

"Officer DeSantis!" Rena smiled as she turned. Her nametag touted her as Grace. She answered to Rena Grace, as Southern girls of her era often did, but Rena was fine, she often reassured friends and visitors. She held a potting spade in her hand and slipped off pale green gardening gloves.

"How are things?" Casually, as though Suzanne had just happened to dawdle by and hoped for some conversation.

"Oh, you know. No visitors today, so I'm doing a bit of tidying up."

"No one? The door's open …" She let the *open* statement hang, hoping to make her point without frightening anyone, least of all herself.

"Oh, yes." Rena smiled wider. "It's nice to give visitors the opportunity to see the inner workings of our park treasures, and this place is a treasure. Shame they're not showing up."

"You're letting them climb?" *Get my point, Rena. I'm making one.*

"Certainly not. Why do you say that?"

"It's not roped off today."

"It certainly is." Rena pressed her mouth tight as if insulted. Roping off the stairwell was not something she would let slip. "Let me come around."

The gate leading from the walkway to the grassy area was on the front side of the building as seen from the road, and Rena disappeared for a moment behind the lighthouse and reappeared on the opposite side. She opened the gate, took the steps purposefully, looked inside the lighthouse, and gave out a very Southern huff of amazement, and her fists went to her hips.

"Now that's not the way I left it. I've not seen anyone, not a soul, Officer. Who would do that, anyway, unhook the rope?"

"That van?" Suzanne pointed. "Did you see who got out of that?"

Rena looked toward the road, squinted, then back into the lighthouse. "No, I did not, but I'll be mighty unhappy if they snuck in without my knowing and are prowling around where they ought not to be. Shame that people do that. Nothing better be damaged."

"Do you might if I step in with you?" Suzanne now had her hand on the butt of her gun. Rena seemed to be taking this in stride, but Suzanne had seen the van and the people inside, she knew Kay-Kay's tale of what went down there, and she suspected these people would do whatever it took to keep from being fingered for whatever they were up to.

"Now, why would I mind that?" Rena pushed forward into the interior of the building.

There was just enough room for them to stand easily side by side, with a storage tank to the right, a little space around the circular stairwell in the middle, and a window at the back providing a little light. The red brick wall forming the interior contrasted with the painted stone exterior, giving the walls a heavy, sturdy feel, as though no storm that battered Ocracoke would ever be strong enough to defeat the mainstay of Ocracoke's historical legacy. Upwards, the red brick structure narrowed quickly, and the space around the stairs closed in like a grasping fist, squeezing tighter and tighter with every step towards the lantern room at the top. The flat bottoms of the metal treads obscured any views of who might be further up, giving the darker upper reaches of the thick-walled building a sense of dread, even of foreboding doom. What was waiting overhead, or should Suzanne be asking *who* was waiting overhead? It might make the difference between today and tomorrow in someone's story about their island experience.

"Rena, do you mind?" Suzanne touched her on the arm to get her attention, and she had out her gun. She put a finger to her lips and pointed outside.

"What? ... oh, oh! Of course." Rena's eyes went wide. She took in the barrier rope roughly cast to one side and tumbled in a careless heap, glanced at the darkened overhead space, and silently backed out the door to give Suzanne the room she needed.

"I'm climbing," Suzanne mouthed, keeping an eye on Rena until she acknowledged her words, and she pointed upwards. When Rena gave her a thumbs up, she grasped the rail with her free hand and began to work her way up one step at a time.

ABOUT HALFWAY up, just as Suzanne was getting over being creeped out with being in the lighthouse and thinking how easy it would be for someone to ambush her ... and the lack of escape options that didn't include falling forty feet onto a concrete floor, loud knocking on the metal door at the entrance to the lighthouse caused her to jump and nearly lose her gun.

"Rena?" Suzanne called down the steps, keeping her voice hushed, as she trained her eyes on the treads above her head and what she could see past each one, which wasn't much more than murky gloom.

"Nah, it's me, Shelby." The reply echoed up the towering structure.

"Shelby Ellison?" Suzanne relaxed. Anyway, she had about decided no one was in the lighthouse besides her. There had been no sounds, no motion or shadows, nothing to indicate the men from the van had come up the steps.

"You know another Shelby, Officer DeSantis?" Shelby

laughed. "I got some information for you if you want it."

"What's that?" Suzanne still had her gun out, but she leaned over the steps and looked down at the young woman centered in the light streaming in the open door. She glanced back up, too, just to be certain, although the lighthouse had remained eerily quiet during her entire time inside, except for the current conversation between her and the woman below.

"The people in that van out there. I saw something and thought you might be interested. By the way, they ain't up there. You can come down now."

"I can, can I?" Suzanne sighed. Shelby was Dare County Officer Cynthia Ellison's daughter, her wayward youngest now living on Ocracoke, likely from all accounts to hide from her mother. Shelby wasn't exactly the most upstanding member of Ocracoke society, and Suzanne had delt with her before, not always in a good way. Even so, she wasn't one to intentionally mislead law enforcement officers. She preferred to watch from the sidelines and not share helpful information even when she knew it might benefit an investigation. Suzanne trusted that if Shelby said they weren't in the lighthouse, likely they weren't. She holstered her gun and began making her way down the steps.

At the bottom, Shelby was outside with Rena in a puffy jacket punctuated with pockets of various sizes, and she held a cigarette to her lips, drawing on it. When Suzanne stepped outside, Shelby glared at her with a squint, dropped her arm with the cigarette, flicked ash with her little finger—a practiced and unconscious move—and worked her mouth while holding in the smoke. After a moment, she opened her lips, and as she began to speak, clouds of used up cigarette residue filtered out with her words.

"You don't need to tell my momma I'm telling you this, Officer, you understand me?" Shelby flicked the cigarette again, acted like she intended to put it to her mouth, then stopped and let it hang at her side.

"Suzanne, Shelby. We do know one another." *Keep it friendly*, Suzanne said to herself. *Get her to talk, or she's likely to scamper away like a skittish rabbit.*

"Yeah, we do. Not always a good thing, is it?"

"It can be. What am I not supposed to tell your momma?"

"That I'm helping out the police."

"Oh, that." Suzanne laughed. "She wouldn't believe me if I told her." Shelby grinned, and Suzanne knew she was playing the situation right. Rena stood to the side, and she looked like she was trying to stay out of it.

"Likely right, there." Shelby did take a quick puff on the cigarette before saying anything else, realized she'd let it burn nearly completely away, and she dropped it on the walk and ground her shoe on it. "Those guys—" jerking her head towards the rusty van "—are no good. When they seen your car coming, they cut through past my place, and I came to let you know."

"I thought you lived—" and Suzanne hesitated. Shelby didn't have what you might call a permanent address. She took shelter where she could find it, sometimes renting space from someone, often crashing in a back room, or completely rough, when the weather permitted. Suzanne realized she couldn't be certain exactly where Shelby's current address was. The last one she remembered was the other side of Garrish which wasn't the direction of the ferry, any docks, or where she had parked her car. The lighthouse was on one side of the island, and Shelby's last known address was on the far side. How, or why was what Suzanne wanted to ask, but skittish rabbits didn't like too much attention aimed their way. She waited instead to see if Shelby would continue to trust her with what she'd come to say.

"Yeah, I move around a lot." Shelby toyed the burned-out cigarette butt with her shoe. "And, well—" and she glanced at

Rena "—I was meeting someone, only I didn't know it was those guys, and I don't deal with them."

I knew it, Suzanne crowed to herself. *Druggies, perhaps connected to that thwarted heist over on Hatteras.*

Shelby continued, interrupting Suzanne's excitement. "Those guys tried to sell Jade some. You know Jade's my daughter, right, Officer, er, Suzanne? She lives with my momma up north past Buxton. I got no patience with people want to sell to kids. Anyway, if you promise not to tell my momma, I'll tell you where they might've gone."

"Last I heard, your momma's not on the Hyde County force, and up in Swan Quarter, they don't get this island thing. What gets done, out here we get to it and get it done. I got no reason to shout out your business to anyone up Dare County way without a formal request, and no one's requested I tell them anything you tell me. Does that do for you?"

"Okay, then. That car they came up in? You might do a search. I bet you might find something inside. Those men, well, they done gone overland back towards Silver Lake. Not sure exactly where, but all I know is that there's two places to get off this island, that way and that." She generally pointed west towards the Silver Lake ferry landing and north towards the one up to Hatteras, then absently worked a fresh cigarette out of a pocket on her sleeve. "A lot of good the Hatteras ferry does them without a car, and they came in on the one from Cedar Island. Makes me wonder where they might be going if they're going back into town."

"But you have a good idea." Suzanne did, too, that was if they were, indeed, going to try to escape the island. There was a ferry to Portsmouth, but that would do them no good. However, Swan Quarter? If they made that ferry, and there was no one on board to arrest them ... did she have cause to have them picked up on the other side?

Rena interrupted her thoughts with a soft, "Deputy, perhaps I should lock up, do you think?"

"Whew—" Suzanne let out a hard breath, puffing out her cheeks. "Likely, Rena. Sorry you didn't get more visitors—"

"Least the sort I wanted." Rena chuckled. "I was about to close up the lighthouse anyways, so it don't matter much. I'll get Rob-Roy or Vernon down to look around and see if any damage was done."

"Do that. Keep yourself safe." Suzanne nodded her approval at the park ranger's suggestion, and she turned to Shelby. "You need a ride anywhere? I got my car right down there."

"Um," and Shelby cut her eyes towards the parking area at the end of the wooden walkway. "I need me some milk if you got two dollars I can have." She refused to look at Suzanne and instead studied the unlighted cigarette in her hand.

"As long as you don't light up till after I drop you off." Suzanne held her breath for a moment to see if this was when the skittish rabbit took off.

"Fine. Okay, when you want to leave?" Shelby tucked the smoke into a crumpled pack and slipped it back into the pocket on the arm of her jacket.

"Soon's we can get there. Rena, you sure you feel safe?" No way did she want to leave her alone if those roustabouts might still be round about.

"Yes, but to make you feel better, I'll make my way out with you two. Let me lock the door." Rena jangled a set of keys at her waist and chuckled.

The three women exited the lighthouse grounds, and Suzanne and Shelby sat in Suzanne's car for several minutes after Rena drove off.

"They're not coming back," Shelby said, not exactly growling or complaining, but she was fiddling with the pocket holding the pack of cigarettes. It was clear she was ready to get moving. The quicker they got to the store to get her milk, the sooner she could light up her next smoke.

"Hrmp," Suzanne snorted, not too loudly, as she held up her *talk-to-the-hand* warning. "You got me thinking, Shelby, and I want to look at that van. You sit right here, and I'll be a minute."

"Okay. Not too long, okay? I'm needing to get back."

"Not too long, I promise."

Suzanne took her keys, climbed out of the car and walked the van's perimeter. At the driver's door, she tried the handle and was not surprised to find it locked. The others, too, until she got to the back liftgate. That one, when she lifted the handle, clicked open, and she looked at Shelby through the Charger's window with a mock surprised expression before lifting the gate all the way. A rank, stuffy, slept-in aroma tumbled out of the van. She stepped back to let as much of it as possible dissipate, only to find it still clung to the interior when she leaned inside to inspect the contents, meaning it had been this way for some time. How did people live like this? she wondered.

She opened Shelby's door and retrieved two rubber gloves and a clear evidence bag from the glove compartment. Her first find was the stem of a crack pipe, not even covered or disguised, which gave her probable cause. She dropped it in the evidence bag and tagged it with a marker before rolling it up and slipping it inside her pocket. Deeper in, other tidbits of possible drug use rose to the top of the murky cesspool, but in the well under the cargo area she hooked the catch of the day. It was mostly empty, even clean, except for two empty canvas backpacks roughly rolled and crushed against one side, as if the rest of the cargo area had been hurriedly emptied.

Of drugs, Suzanne was convinced.

She pulled out the backpacks, unzipped the pockets, and found the first backpack totally empty. It exuded a chemical odor, but that was for a drug testing kit to determine. The second one was more informative. Wedged into a twisted corner of the largest compartment, a small baggie with white power tumbled out when she held the bag upside down and shook it.

"Not shoofly pie last I heard," she said under her breath, as she lifted it from the floor of the van to inspect it. She peeled off one glove, pulled her phone from her pocket, and she tapped the number to the sheriff's office in Swan Quarter and waited as it began to ring.

"Sheriff's office, Dottie here. What can I do for you?" Dottie was Charlotte Widmer, the secretary at the Swan Quarter Sheriff's Office.

"Hey, Dottie. Suzanne here. Who's there today?"

"Me." Dottie laughed. "Then you know that. Who else, you mean. The sheriff's out up to Washington and oh, yes, Calvin is around somewhere. He got in from the ferry about thirty minutes ago. Two ferry rides in one day's tuckered the man out, though, so I warn you on that."

"Okay, then, Calvin."

"You want I should call him in? I think he's in the staff room eating." Dottie laughed like it was an old joke.

Suzanne considered the man. He came across as a swamp hick, but Suzanne knew him for a good fit with the country-type people in much of the county. And Jason Romney from down in Carteret and waiting on approval for his transfer to Dare, well, Calvin was Jason's man-of-the-hour when something needed done. In this, though?

She made the call and said, "Yes, Dottie. I think I do need to speak with him. If you don't mind—"

"Sweetheart, I never do. That's why I sit at this desk all day, to help out people like you. Hold on for a moment."

Calvin came on the line with, "What'cha got going on, Suzanne? I'll be ding-danged if I didn't see that boat still in the water there at Silver Lake when I came through. Thought you'd have that all wrapped up by now."

"Yeah, Calvin, last I heard, that's up to Diane Turnipseed. I've got something else going on here. Don't know if it's tied up with the same investigation but it might be. Dottie says you're tuckered but I need help from your end. You good with that?"

"Me tired? Nothin' a taco won't solve, that's for certain. Tell me what you've run upon."

"Drug dealers maybe on the ferry headed your direction. That interest you?" She kinda thought it would.

"Like a pot of baked beans and about as spicy." He chuckled.

"Then that's a yes, I take ..." *Say, it, man. Answers, Calvin. I need answers,* Suzanne groused to herself, not for the first time today.

"You're killing me, DeSantis. I was in Buxton last night. Remember that meeting you couldn't spare an hour on the ferry to attend? Yeah, t'wouldn't have hurt you, you know. It was Turnipseed's fifteenth anniversary celebration with the Dare sheriff's office. I know you two got a bit of a competition between you two—"

"Get it together, Dingman. You're tuckered, I need answers, and bringing up the lieutenant from Hatteras doesn't get us where we need to be. What do you need to arrest the dealers that might be on your way?"

"Okay, sure," he said, and in a whispered aside, "Normal as cod on a plate, that's for certain."

"What's that, Dingman?" Suzanne was about ready to bark at the man. She only held back as she knew it would tangle her chances of reeling him in.

"Yes, I'll help. You got ID on the men I'm supposed to retain? You said dealers, so I'm supposing more than one."

"I need to open my brain," she muttered as she thought for

a minute. "No, but I can send you the plate numbers on the van they were driving. Can you work with that? You've got a couple hours before they arrive." The ferry required over two-and-a-half hours to cross the Sound, and if there was anything to be found out, surely by then …

"On foot, then." Calvin seemed to be formulating a plan. "I'll need a visual description to know who to lock up. Please tell me you've got that." He ended his request with a hopeful twist in his voice.

"Um, let me think." She hadn't seen them, more the absence of them. Kay-Kay's description wasn't much better, calling the driver out as "a grubby little person" not even truly defined as male or female. The ferry attendants riding over from Cedar Island with the old van might be able to give her something, but they would be back on the water towards the mainland. Finding anything from them would be difficult at best.

"Not booked and locked, I take." Calvin snorted, and his amusement came through the line just fine. "Might need you over here if you want me to hold them. Otherwise—"

Suzanne knew the otherwise. Let them go. Sometimes living on an island with only two ways off seemed a good thing, and other times, she was a fish in a skillet, broiled up and about to be served for someone's dinner. Still, she had a couple hours before she could do anything, even if she was being backed into a trip to Swan Corner, something she absolutely didn't want to do.

"Let me work on it, Calvin." She looked at her chunky watch, worked out the ferry times in her head, and caught Shelby in her patrol car pointing to the spot on her wrist where a watch would go if she had one. Shelby opened the door and held up one arm with an unlighted cigarette between her fingers.

"I'm lightin' up if you don't get back here."

Suzanne groaned, and she said to Calvin, "Here's the tag

number on the van. See what you can find out. I've got someone to deliver before she lights up a cigarette in my car. You ready to write it down?"

"Shucks, you're killing me, DeSantis. I was ready to write it down the first time you said it."

"Here it is …" She stepped back, read out the number on the plates, then walked to the windshield and gave him the VIN in case the tags were fake. When she disconnected, she climbed back in her car and caught a whiff of cigarette smoke. "Aw, Shelby, I asked you not to."

"What? You're the one out there on your phone. Besides, I only took two puffs and put it out. No big deal." She held up a partially burned cigarette. The end still glowed on one side, and as she lifted it, it went dark.

"You got a way about you, Shelby." Suzanne started the car, shifted into reverse, and drove away from the lighthouse back towards Garrish. She was leaving the van unlocked, but then there was only one of her. Besides, this was an island! Where could it go? In her head, she began to click off Hatteras, Cedar Island, Portsmouth Island, Swan Corner … then the residue of the cigarette smoke overwhelmed her, and she began to cough. She glared at Shelby, "Only two puffs?"

"Maybe three or four. I didn't count." Shelby shrugged as she looked out the passenger's window with a disconnected air.

Suzanne let it go. More vital was how to get out of that ferry trip to Swan Corner. As she swung her big car into The Community Store's parking lot, she was already evaluating where she would spend the night on the mainland. Shelby made it clear she could walk home as she took the milk money from Suzanne, and as she disappeared into the store, Suzanne muttered to herself, "I got me a college degree, and I'm still not smart enough to get out of this."

She put the car in reverse, headed back along Garrish

towards the ferry landing, and caught the sign for Rusty's Island Boat Tours and decided that might be a thing. If Rusty wasn't busy, and as this wasn't the busy season—

She tapped her blinker and pulled off the road, hoping that Rusty was available and willing to make an emergency run to the mainland. It would be even better if he was willing to wait on her and bring her back again, but one thing at a time.

That was the best that she could do, even with her much-lauded college degree.

SUZANNE STOOD behind Rusty Cashwell, who helmed the sportfisher *Lightning Strike,* and she held on for dear life.

"Yes, ma'am," Rusty had assured her when she pulled up at his boathouse. "I can get you there plenty fine, just not on one of my tour boats. Those old pontoons will cover the distance, but you might as well take the ferry. We won't go no faster than they do, but if you want to get there quicker …" He left that hanging, leaving her to think on it.

A quick call to the ferry terminal had suggested that yes, numerous people had boarded the ferry as walk-ons; and while any number of them might be the people Suzanne was looking for, without a clearer description, they couldn't be certain. A couple seemed like good matches if she could have someone there to catch them at the other end, meaning she needed to get there before the ferry arrived. She figured the cost of Rusty's boat was on the county tab, as Calvin had as much as said she was required on Swan Quarter quick as she could arrive. Finally, a call to Brandon Scarborough, the Ocracoke liaison for Hyde County, and she had someone to cover her duties while she was off island.

The ferry would be more comfortable, Rusty had cautioned. The *Lightning Strike* was Rusty's personal sport fishing boat; and yes, he could wait on her in Swan Quarter, so long's she didn't have to stay too long. How long? He had shrugged and looked up at the sun and asked her if she was certain when sundown came about for the day.

She understood. Twilight was the witching hour. If she had to be on Swan Quarter beyond that, he was leaving her stranded. And she would be stranded, as she was now halfway across the sound, and her car was still back on the island. She would be afoot if Calvin didn't pony up and be there when she arrived.

The best part was the speed at which the *Lightning Strike* traveled. It was also the worst part about their rush journey across the Sound, as thirty-five knots was brutal on her knees. Still, Rusty had promised forty-five minutes, barring rough water, and that knocked two hours off the ferry's travel time. The expedited transit came at a premium, though, as it emptied the boat's fuel tanks like a thirsty clamdigger onto a jug of ice water after a hot day in the mudflats.

The shore grew out of the wet air in the distance, little more than a green and brown smear on the horizon, then came into sharper focus as they entered Swanquarter Bay. The smell of the water and shore changed, became earthier—ranker, some people might say, the aroma of vegetation and soil and the life and existence of animals that populated the mostly deserted shoreline. Few people lived on the water in Swan Quarter. You wanted your home to still be there when the storms that thrashed the Bay from time to time moved on to other areas along the coast.

The *Lighting Strike* passed the cutoff to the ferry terminal, a safe haven carved out of the North Carolina soil and tucked neatly away so as to be nearly invisible, both from human eyes as well as from Mother Nature when she thrust her fist into the sea and stirred up the wind and the waves. Suzanne had let Calvin know she would be dropped off just past Newman Seafood on Landing Road, though she expected Rusty would head further in to dock at the pier, perhaps walk up to Hobo's for some fresh seafood to eat while he waited. If so, she chuckled and gave even odds he might have to cook it himself.

Then she saw it, a mint green Dodge Ram, and relief flooded her. As Rusty passed Newman's, Suzanne ran her eyes along the shore for any sign of Calvin. "Get it together, Calvin," she muttered.

"What's that?" Rusty had the boat barely moving, and he swept the moored vessels along the dock as he searched for a place to pull up.

"Never you mind. What needs to be done to get me off this boat?" She was getting antsy to find out if she'd beat the ferry over. By her watch, maybe, but they still had to drive back down to the ferry landing, and that could be fifteen minutes or more, depending on how ready Calvin was.

"Just let me find a berth. You say I can bill the county direct? I don't need a requisition or something like that?"

"Last I heard, the county pays its bills. You want something on paper, I'll write something out now." She thrust her hands into the pockets of her coat. She was cold, she didn't want to, and she wanted that clear.

"No, ma'am. I'm good. Besides, I know where the sheriff's office is." Rusty was backing in, and he grinned.

"I 'spect you do. Thank you, Rusty." Calvin appeared at the end of the dock with a large coffee in his hand, just what she wanted about then. "How long can you wait?"

"An hour, maybe?" He looked at the sun, squinted, and nodded. "Maybe a little less."

"Not too much less," she said, without a sliver of humor in her words. She wanted him here when she returned, as she wanted to sleep in her own bed when nighttime rolled around.

She didn't expect Calvin would care much, so she'd have to push him to get things done. Then it occurred to her, if he was here, who was at the ferry terminal looking out for her suspects? Or had they already arrived and vanished into the interior, never to be seen again?

"Talk to the hand, Calvin," she muttered, as she pulled herself off the boat and onto the dock. "Not one excuse better come out of your mouth if you've let my suspects escape. I better not've endured that nightmare trip across the Sound for nothing."

She marched up to him as he lifted his coffee to his lips and pulled her sleeve up to glare at her gold watch to make it clear that time was of the essence. She barked, "The ferry, Calvin. Who's covering that?"

"The ferry?" He lowered his coffee and blinked. "I'll be ding-danged. Did I forget about that?"

"Calvin!"

"Shucks, Suzanne." He broke into a grin. "I got Zack watching the whole ferry landing. Goldie's with him. Ain't no one getting past with Goldie there."

"Let's go then. And coffee, you got some of that for me?" He'd better. Maids and butlers. They had everything in Swan Quarter. Surely they had coffee, too, cause she could use some, and sooner was better than later.

"In the truck, ma'am."

Finally, she thought. *Something's going the way I need it to go.*

Chapter 7

Lost in Swan Quarter

HYDE COUNTY DEPUTY CALVIN DINGMAN pulled the door to his mint green Dodge gently closed, and when it clicked, he gave it a firm tug to finish the job. The interior was clean and neatly organized, and that meant it smelled good. Right then, *smelled good* meant like roast coffee. He did keep a lidded cup for his spitting tobacco, but the lid was for the smell, as it offended most people, and even Calvin agreed it was a nasty habit, just one he'd never managed to break.

Once Suzanne DeSantis was satisfied with her seatbelt and situated in her seat, he lifted a cup of joe from the right-side cup holder and held it out for her to take.

"Ma'am, plain black, but I got some of those little cream cups in a sack behind the seat if you'd like that."

"You couldn't do cinnamon roast?" Suzanne took the cup, flipped up the drinking flap, and inhaled the aroma before cutting her eyes his direction. Her expression said she didn't expect an answer.

"In the glove box is a fresh shaker of cinnamon, if you think that will do."

"You're serious?" She reached for the latch, paused, and chuckled. "Last I heard, that's not how it works."

"T'wouldn't expect it would, even for a shaker full. So, what'cha got here with this ferry thing? That trip over on Rusty's boat'll shoal your day if the weather picks up while you're out in the middle of the Sound. You musta considered this real important."

"It gets worse when the weather picks up?" Suzanne drew a large hit of coffee from the cup and let it swirl in her mouth for a bit before swallowing it. "Worse than this coffee? Where's those creamers?"

Calvin had the engine running and the transmission in gear, and he held his foot on the brake as he reached over the seat and pulled out a brown paper bag with a coffee logo on the front. He handed it to her. When she took it, he eased onto Landing Road, which was little more than a wide track, and asked, "Rusty waiting?"

"Yes. As long as this doesn't take too long."

"It ain't like we got a pot of beans over here ready to dish out. Before we get things booked and locked, likely we'll need a little simmering time to bring things to a boil."

He stopped talking for a spell as they approached town. The track had become tarmac and developed a stripe in the center, and he slowed as he flipped on his blinker to take a right on Oyster Creek towards the ferry landing. After the turn, he shifted his bulk in the seat, checked his rearview mirror, and increased his speed. The county courthouse slipped by on the right, a big brick building with a massive, covered portico, the entire place so substantial that it felt like it had been thrust from the soil a millennium before rather than having been assembled by human hands. Then several houses crawled past before he hit his blinker again, once more aiming to the right.

"Okay," Suzanne said. She'd had a few minutes to process, and her face reflected her opinion of his slower-than-desired timeframe for her Swan Quarter business. "I'll need a place to overnight, if it comes to that."

"Likely it will, but that can be sorted out. Anyways, that's nothing that a plate of good, old-fashioned Southern cookin' won't solve. Are you hungry?" She was so thin, he wouldn't be surprised if she was hungry all the time, and he considered that she might smile more with a plate of oysters in front of her.

"What I need is answers." As Calvin approached the parking lot, she pointed to a white Hyde County Dodge SUV with a green and orange stripe and Sheriff emblazoned on the side. It held down the parking area net to the ferry landing. "Don't see Zack. That's his car. What's going on here?"

"Shucks, Deputy, likely giving Goldie a break out back. This is normal as cod on a plate. Ain't no rough water coming up for us to navigate just yet. Let's let things settle in the water a bit before we worry about whether to pull in the net. Once I stop, we can check and see."

"Didn't say anything about pulling in a net." The truck came to a standstill, and she released her seatbelt and tripped the door latch. "I don't want my two suspects to bail and disappear. Not like this is an island and they've got nowhere to run."

"Don't suppose it is," Calvin agreed. As she climbed out and marched towards Zack's car, he took a long drink of his coffee until the final residue took on the taste of unmixed creamer, and he put it back into the cup holder in the console. He watched her peer in the windows, then begin scanning for the missing K9 handler. He let his thoughts ramble a bit as he unhitched his seat belt and opened the door. *Your island didn't keep 'em penned all that well, now did it? You might have a college degree, deputy, but this is my own backyard. I'll be ding-danged if I let you island people show up those of us in Swan Quarter.*

She was heading back, and halfway to his truck, she stopped and patted a pocket. She pulled a clear bag from the pocket with a pipe inside.

"Startin' up, Suzanne?" Calvin grinned, hoping to break the ice between them.

"I forgot I had this. It was in the van with my two suspects. With Zack and Goldie here, perhaps this will help her identify them."

"So's, two scallions, that's how many we're looking for. You couldn't describe them earlier. You sure about there being two?" Calvin took the bag from her, noted the marks on the outside, and nodded. This could be a clue if Zack thought Goldie might agree.

"Yes, I think so. Just two. Pretty sure, at least, with nothing to make me think there's more. There's Zack." She pulled the bag from Calvin's hand and called to him, "Zack, take a look at this."

Zack had Goldie on a leash, and he rubbed her head and nodded as the deputy described what she proposed.

Here's what Calvin knew: when Suzanne's suspects saw three lawmen, two patrol cars, and a drug-sniffing dog, they would light out like landlubbers with a mess of alligators on their heels, meaning, Calvin expected a chase, one he firmly intended to wrestle down and hogtie before the pig could begin to squeal.

And squeal it would. He had that down booked and locked, normal as cod on a plate. Or oysters, maybe with cornbread … even a pot of beans would hit the spot. He smiled, paused, and spat a wad of tobacco off to the side, before walking Zack's direction to see what plans were being diced up to throw into the mix.

K9 HANDLER Zack Halsey, with his stick-thin limbs barely fleshing out his county-issue clothing, touted his trusty feather-festooned cowboy hat, and as Calvin approached, he tipped it up, pulled a bandana from his back pocket, and wiped his forehead before dropping his hat back down and tucking the cloth back into his pocket. Today he boasted black pants with a khaki shirt, finished off with heavy black shoes. They would have steel toes, to Calvin's best guess, much like the ones on his own feet. He didn't see Zack's oversized flashlight, then it wasn't dark, and he'd likely left it in his vehicle, if he had any sense.

Calvin caught the end of a sentence, with Zack sharing that Rusty Cashwell was a good man, and he'd appreciate the county's check for transporting Suzanne over, as the low season for tourists sometimes made money tight. Only thing, Calvin noted, was that he referenced the tour operator as Ryan and not Rusty; then he remembered they were linked from way back, grade school, Calvin recalled.

"Zack," Calvin said, as a way of inserting himself into the conversation, "you got the deputy here up to speed?"

"What speed?" Zack chuckled. "We're having a little porch time here, nothing to see or do until that ferry arrives. I was telling the lady that not a minnow in the water's gonna get by me and Goldie here. Whatever you need done, get Goldie on it, and there's not anything anyone can do 'cept put their feet on the sand and let her at it. Isn't that right, Goldie?" He knelt, his legs little more than hinged chopsticks, and gave her a quick hug and neck rub before standing again.

Faintly, the throbbing of an engine across the water caught their attention, and Calvin glanced to the landing. Two men wearing similar clothing were at the ferry landing talking, and one laughed and threw his hands apart while spreading his fingers wide to indicate an explosion. A third man walked up, seemed to catch what they were laughing about and shook his head before calling to them that they wore watches for a reason. The ferry was about there, and were they planning on the people onboard offloading themselves? Only one vehicle was in line to return to Ocracoke, a utility service truck with Cape Hatteras Electric Cooperative on the door, indicated by the letters CHEC in capital letters alongside a stylized image of the Cape Hatteras lighthouse. The pilothouse of the ferry appeared first, as the massive boat motored along the channel from the Bay into the protected ferry harbor. Richard Flythe, the man who'd spoken with Deputy DeSantis earlier, stood at the bow ready to lower the ramp and lock the ferry onto the landing. Calvin walked his way, and when the ship was close enough for his voice to carry, lifted an arm to get his attention.

"Calvin," Richard called in recognition. "Be with you in a bit."

"You know what I want?" He wanted the man to keep everyone on the ferry until Zack and Goldie were ready.

"Don't worry. The woodpile ain't chopped yet." He grinned and turned his attention to the ferry as it approached the landing.

Calvin cut his attention to the two deputies with him and noted Zack kneeling once more with Goldie, this time with the pipe outside the plastic bag for her to sniff. DeSantis stood beside them, her arms crossed, watching critically. Calvin appreciated the woman's policing skills, but she was a spitfire when things didn't go the way she wanted. Those jeans with that black jacket, well, no one could say her husband Teague didn't have good taste in women, even if he found it impossible to live with her, as evidenced by his job in Beaufort County. Calvin had spent a weekend hunting trip with Teague after he left Hyde and figured he'd likely do the same if he was married to the woman.

As the ferry docked, Zack and Suzanne joined Calvin, and

the three of them scanned the ferry. There were cars, but it was far from full. People too, though they were just lining up to exit. They would come off first, giving them the chance for Goldie to assess each one.

"Two rough and readies," Calvin said to Suzanne, hoping she had something more to identify them with than something so vague.

"In a crack cloud, if that pipe I found is any indication," she confirmed.

"Got that, Zack? Don't want to run upon some shingles in this. Two rough and readies in a crack cloud. You and Goldie got it going on, I hope."

"Yessir." Zack held his hand on Goldie's neck with the leash firmly wrapped around his wrist. When the ramp locked in and the passengers began to walk across, he said, "Search, Goldie."

As it turned out, Goldie's presence wasn't entirely necessary, except as a backup option. Two faces appeared, and Calvin blew out his cheeks and exclaimed, "Jack and Thomas. I'll be ding-danged. I shoulda known."

"Someone you know?" Suzanne.

"Likely your suspects, so long's Goldie confirms it. Jack Sellew and Thomas Conner. Coupla lubbers been picked up by us before—" About then, Jack and Thomas caught sight of Calvin, Zack, and Suzanne, and they darted around the people waiting in line and took off fleet-footed through the parking lot.

"Somebody needs lunch," Zack said in amazement. "Goldie's not even sniffed 'em out yet."

"Calvin?" Suzanne's voice was a hardtack biscuit ready to crack someone's head. "You doing something or what?"

The two men were now heading towards Oyster Creek full tilt, with puffs of Swan Quarter billowing into the air with each footstep. Calvin closed his eyes for a brief moment before announcing his plan.

"Deputy DeSantis, looks like you're making your way back with Rusty tonight. In the office, they can call over to Newman's, Hobo's, wherever and get him to pick you up here. Zack and me, we got a chase on our hands. Zack, you head to your truck and get Goldie set up. I'll meet you on Oyster."

The look of relief on Suzanne DeSantis' face was sharp as cracked glass as Calvin called towards the ferry, "Got what we need, Richard. Thank ya', sir, for your help."

"Anytime you ask," Richard called back, but by then, Zack was loading Goldie, and Calvin had left Suzanne standing alone at the ferry landing to find her own way home.

Inside his green Dodge truck, Calvin lifted his radio mike and keyed it for Zack, informing him, "Zack, I'm moving out. You got that dog hogtied and ready to move? Over."

"Hold up there … 'bout got it—" the sound of a clicking safety belt punctuated the background "—and now I'm ready to get my feet on the sand—"

"More like your tires on the tarmac, but I get'cha. Now let's make sure those lubbers don't get farther away than they can spit."

Calvin's tires spun before he could back off his foot, evidence that his truck was powerful enough to get any job done. His radio crackled, and he took his eyes from searching for the men to glance at it for a second, muttering, "Not a good time, Zack." He determined to ignore it, as it would come back at him if it was really important, and he felt himself become the eagle-eyed spotter from his teen hunting days … able to see a deer at a mile away and tag one at half that.

Movement north alongside the road, more rustling grass than anything, yanked his eyes sideways. "Jack, Thomas," he muttered. "I'm coming for you boys."

It didn't make sense to him that these two yokels had anything to do with the sailboat they had seen the night of the raid at the Avon pier. They were small time, but small-time finks were sometimes the very link that connected them to the real lubbers that were into the big time. He slowed, checked his rearview to ensure that Zack was just behind him, and lifted his mic.

"Zack, come back at me. Over."

"Yeah," the man replied. "Having a bit of porch time?"

"Yeah, porch time. Look into the grass. See if it feels suspicious to you. And what did you need a bit ago?"

"Um, coffee?" It sounded like he chuckled.

"You hit my radio—"

"Uh, uh. Not me. And yeah, I see the grass. You thinking that's our men?"

"Jack and Thomas, yeah. Check it out."

He watched in his rearview as Zack unfolded himself from his SUV, now in his official county cap, with his massive flashlight in his hand, *the better to bash you with, my dear.* Calvin pictured Little Red Riding Hood, only this was Zack the Scarecrow Man. Still, he was the best K9 handler on the Hyde County roll, and Calvin liked and appreciated him and enjoyed working with him. Zack tromped around a bit, turned to face Calvin's truck and shrugged, and high-stepped back to the road and walked up to Calvin's truck. Calvin dropped the window on the passenger's side.

"Not them." He leaned on the door with one arm on the sill, and he shook his head.

"Got that." Calvin pursed his lips, thinking.

"Seems they got a cousin up towards the lake. They hid out there once before." The lake was Lake Mattamuskeet, encircled by a ring of roads, some houses, a church, a couple of schools, and several small communities. A right nice place but spread out and sparse, too, meaning lots of places to tuck away and hide.

"Seems I remember that." Calvin's radio crackled again, and he looked at Zack and picked it up. "Deputy Dingman here. You're barely coming through. Say again. Over." He frowned when he saw Zack grin, and the K9 handler put his hands in the air as if to say, "Don't want to get zapped with lighting, so don't blame me for the screw up."

Then Calvin's phone began to ring. He frowned harder, put the radio mike into its clip, and pulled out his phone to study the screen. *Charlotte Widmer.* "It's Dottie," he said to Zack. He touched the screen and said, "Hello, Dottie. Calvin here. Zack and I are running down Jack and Thomas. They seem to want to disappear—" He paused, then answered, "Yeah, Sellew and Conner, the same—" He paused again, looked at Zack, then said, "Sure, I can take a call from Charlie. Have him ring me." He wondered what Charlie had to tell him. This was getting weirder by the moment, and he still had those two lubbers to track down, ones he seemed to have misplaced for the moment. He clicked off the call to Dottie and waited for his phone to ring.

"Charlie Bronson?" Zack asked. Charlie was the security guard on the Ocracoke side of the Hatteras ferry. He wasn't on the mainland, but he *was* in Hyde County, and that meant, of course, that he was familiar as beans in a pot. And a good man, too, occasionally calling Swan Quarter for support when he ran up against a situation that needed more than Suzanne DeSantis could provide in her pretty pair of jeans.

"The same," Calvin said absently. He pondered, then asked, "You know where this cousin lives? It's been a few years—"

"Oh, yeah. Used to be one of them upper bankers and moved down here after a storm damaged his place, maybe Fran in '10?" He shrugged. "Can't tell you the address, but find it? Sure."

The phone rang, and Calvin tapped it to answer. "Yeah, Charlie. What'cha got for me?"

It seemed that Brandon Scarborough, the Ocracoke liaison,

left in charge for the day by Suzanne DeSantis, had received a message from Deputy Sean Taylor of the Dare County Sheriff's Office. He hadn't been able to contact Suzanne, and his next option had been Sheriff Pafford, only she was unavailable, too. Would it be possible for Calvin to talk to the deputy, since they had worked together on the Avon incident several days back? Charlie was out of the loop, and he hadn't been able to answer any of the deputy's questions.

"Yeah, Charlie. Seems like everyone's running upon some shingles today, but I got this booked and locked. He expectin' me to wait for him to call, or do I need his number?"

"I think this phone will allow me … let me look … here. I can transfer you. I was talking to the man, and he's on another line. If this disconnects, once and agin, you can drop him a call. His number is …" and he rattled over a series of digits. Calvin pulled a pen from the overhead visor and scribbled the numbers on the palm of his hand. When Charlie tried the transfer, instead of connecting with Sean Taylor, the phone blipped and went dead.

"Them upper bankers," Zack commented, shaking his head.

"Charlie's Ocracoke. Not an upper banker." Calvin returned the pen to the visor and looked at the K9 handler with a raised eyebrow and a reprimanding nod.

"All islanders." Zack grinned. "What about the two we're chasing? We get close, I bet Goldie's got their number. Let her on it, and lightnin's gonna zap them from behind. Zap, zap!" He held out an arm and jabbed his hand toward the ground two times in quick succession, a lightning strike of slightly less deadly proportions.

"Let me contact this deputy over in Dare County. There's nothing going on with Jack and Thomas that a bit of patience won't solve." He was clicking the numbers as he talked, and in speaker mode, the phone began to ring audibly. It picked up almost immediately.

"Sean here. Is this Deputy Dingman?"

"That's for certain. What'cha got going on, Sean?"

"Thanks for calling me back. I think the call dropped—"

"That's a good one." Calvin laughed. "Pardon for interrupting, but likely Charlie didn't know what he was doing. Go on, bub."

"I tell everyone I choose to serve no matter what, and I have no regrets about my job and the commitment I've made, but—" Sean's voice fell off, and his exasperation hissed over the connection like unreeling line from a casting rod.

"Sure, sure, even in my own backyard. It's nothing a taco won't solve, however bad it is. Give it to me and we'll see what needs to happen." *Uh-oh,* Calvin thought. *What now?* He glanced towards Zack who was hearing everything to see the man shrug his bony shoulders. Zack pointed back to his truck and made walking motions with his fingers, and Calvin understood that he needed to give his K9 officer a break. He motioned for him to get to it and turned his attention back to his phone.

"See, Calvin, um, can I call you that?"

"Shucks, bub, that ain't nothing I mind. Been calling you Sean."

"Good." Sean laughed nervously, like he was about to broach something he wasn't sure he should jump over. "You heard about the lieutenant's party the other day, right?"

"Which lieutenant and what party?" *You're killing me,* he thought. *I was there, Sean.* Likely it was nerves on the other end of the line. Calvin had picked that up from the man that night under the Avon pier, skittish as a lobster about to go in a pot.

"Oh, sorry." Sean backtracked. "Lieutenant Turnipseed, we had her fifteen-year celebration in Buxton."

"The party I attended." Calvin almost chuckled but didn't want to distract the younger man.

"You were … oh." Sean's embarrassment soaked the line. "I remember. I don't think we talked, and, well, sorry."

"Ain't nothing. You were chumming up with the fart bladder, and Jason and I were in our own backyard—"

"Is that all anyone remembers about me?" Sean wailed. "I'm gonna get Emily back for that."

"I bet you do, that's for certain. Now, back to your call. What'cha got?" Outside in the grass, Goldie was squatting and taking care of her business. Zack was at her side, although she wasn't on a leash. Calvin needed to get Sean wrapped up by the time the dog was back in Zack's SUV.

"See, our counties are teamed up for an investigation, or we were. Do you know Sheriff Kringlebach?"

"Not personally but who he is, sure. We've spoken though not much more than that." *Were?* That caught Calvin's attention. He thought the cooperative effort was still on the burner and simmering nicely.

"The sheriff doesn't think there's anything to that sailboat we found. You remember, the one with no people on board?"

"Yes, I was there."

"Okay, right. I'm sorry, but I'm nervous asking this."

"Normal as cod on a plate—"

"What?"

"It means I could tell. Continue."

"Oh, sure. See, the thing is, I like being on this case. I don't always get that, to be on a real case, and the sheriff wants us to wrap it up. Except he's away for a couple weeks, and that means we don't have to. You know, wrap it up."

"That's good, right?" Calvin wasn't sure what the man was telling him, or at least trying to tell him.

"I want to help, to prove to the lieutenant that I can do this. Only I don't have the authority to do what I want."

"Oh—" Calvin was seeing the picture. The man was hoping

to sidestep his lieutenant by asking someone from the other half of the shared investigative team to intercede and toss the snapper on the grill. "Likely I won't have the authority, either, bub."

"Hear me out," Sean pleaded. "I'm about commitment and respect, and I won't do anything that disrespects the lieutenant, but you know Jason Romney."

"That's been made clear." They were talking to each other at Turnipseed's get-together. He had just mentioned that. What was the man getting at?

"Jason asked me to contact Hyde County for him. His transfer to Dare County hasn't been approved by Sheriff Kringlebach, so he doesn't have the authority either. He needs your help."

"For?" Why hadn't Jason just called direct? Calvin was further afield with everything Sean said.

"To contact the Coast Guard. Courtney's on board, but she said we need Lieutenant Sallinger's signature before they will step in."

"Ensign Cruickshank?" Ensign Courtney Cruickshank had represented the Coast Guard at the sub-station in Buxton the night of Lieutenant Turnipseed's celebration.

"Yes, the sailboat's gone missing—"

"From Silver Lake?" Calvin was fully attentive now. "Your lieutenant knows, right?"

"I want to say yes," Sean took a deep breath over the phone, "but no, she doesn't, and she can't find out."

During the conversation, Zack Halsey had walked Goldie back to his county-issue SUV and gotten her aboard, and the stick-thin man appeared once more at Calvin's window on the passenger side. He pulled his black cap off before placing his hands on the windowsill and ducking his head to peer inside. The crumpled cap revealed a portion of the orange stitching announcing him as a member of the Hyde County Sheriff's

Office.

Calvin considered Sean's words. *She can't find out.* Yet, if this request came from Jason Romney, there wasn't anyone Calvin trusted more than Jason. And Cruickshank was correct, being an ensign, she was outranked by Sallinger. It all lined up, except for *she can't find out.* He held up a finger for Zack to give him a moment and tossed the shrimp in the oil to sizzle.

"Deputy, I got what's going on mostly, but about not telling your lieutenant, that might be what shoals this boat. Give it to me straight. My K9 handler and me are chasing down some suspects, and we need to get them booked and locked. Be concise."

"See, um, okay—" Sean paused, audibly took a deep breath, and jumped in. "—not *can't* find out, just that she doesn't think I can do anything right, and I want to prove I can. If I can locate the boat on my own, then, well, you get what I mean."

"And she won't know about this how?"

"Lieutenant Turnipseed is looking into the overturned truck at the north end of Pea Island ..."

Calvin relaxed and let out a laugh. The man wanted respect. His boss was conveniently occupied, and he thought he could bake up a meritorious badge of accomplishment before she got back if he hustled and squeezed it in the oven. He would normally say no to any unofficial request like this, but if Jason had suggested it ... well, his trust in Jason was solid as the soil under Swan Quarter and even deeper than the dirt his truck was parked on.

"And you say Courtney suggested this, huh?" Calvin needed the deputy to commit, not just suggest.

"Sort of. She said she just can't do anything without higher approval."

"And how can the Coast Guard aid in finding this boat?"

"Um, it's a boat?" Sean's tone questioned that he even had

to explain. "And it's evidence for a crime. Everyone thinks so. Nobody can be allowed to steal it, or whatever happened to it. The Coast Guard, well, they have lots of boats. They can search everywhere."

"They might help search for missing crime scene evidence, that's for certain."

"You'll help, then? You can count on me to do whatever you need me to. I'm a hundred percent there a hundred percent of the time."

"I'll be ding-danged if I'm not saying yes. No promises, Deputy. One thing, I want to talk to Jason before I bite into another layer of spicy guacamole. You get my point?'

"Maybe. You don't mean food, right?"

"You're killing me. No, I don't mean food. Let me talk to Jason and we'll see what needs to happen then."

"You can't." Sean cleared his throat and clarified his retreat. "Sharky volunteered to take him out to look for the sailboat. They left earlier. Jason said he would be out of touch, and I was in charge of this."

And they would have a radio on the boat and likely cell service, even if it was spotty, but Calvin knew Jason well enough to understand. The man was forcing the deputy to "man up," as people liked to say … to step up and own the respect he wanted to earn. He reached up, lifted his cap, and ran a thick hand over his balding scalp before tugging the cap back down to cover his forehead. He was aware of Zack listening in, and he committed.

"I'll contact Lieutenant Sallinger, but this isn't baked beans yet, Deputy. I don't make commitments for the Coast Guard. You good on that?" After enduring more enthusiastic excitement from Sean over the line, he disconnected and glared at Zack Halsey. "Don't know if I'm the fool or he is."

"Braxton, huh? You got an itch in your shorts to get your ears pinched?" Zack laughed.

"The lieutenant likes to challenge people." Calvin took a deep breath and thought of the extra weight he carried in comparison to Braxton Sallinger's tight, fighting form and of the times he'd overheard the man say, *I don't get tired. I get fit.* Still, the man lived up to the high standards he staked for himself, and he had gotten along with Calvin well enough when they'd had the opportunity to work together. "I need to give the man a call. Looks like the county's cooperative effort in that drug bust is going back on the cooker."

"Goldie'll like that. Get Goldie on it—" Zack grinned.

"I know, Goldie will solve the crime."

"Maybe. If you please, I'm heading to my truck. I got coffee that's getting cold. Buzz my radio when you decide what we're doing next." Zack waved and stepped away from the window.

Calvin considered contacting Station Ocracoke directly. Yet, that was only the first step in running down Sallinger, who likely wasn't there. As he recalled, the small Coast Guard subordinate station on the island only kept a couple of crew on site. His better choice was to contact the Hatteras Inlet station, perhaps speak with the master chief boatswain mate, the man who served as the officer in charge. Should he reference Jason Romney? How about Courtney Cruickshank? Or Lieutenant Turnipseed, whose C-District Dare County jurisdiction covered the area where Station Hatteras was located? No, not Turnipseed, as they might decide to contact her, and that would defeat Deputy Taylor's efforts to earn respect from his boss.

He lifted his mike and clicked the talk switch, saying, "Deputy Calvin Dingman calling Dispatcher Barbara Bowles. Over." He glanced out into the field of grass while he waited to see if the Hyde County dispatcher was available.

"Barbara here, Calvin. What'cha need?"

"I need to contact Station Hatteras with the Coast Guard. Can you find me that number?"

"Most likely I can. Give me a sec ... here. Ready to write it down?"

Calvin looked at his palm and decided he had room. He pulled his pen from the overhead visor and said, "Give it to me, Barbara," and he began to write as she called out the series of numbers.

CALVIN DINGMAN recognized the Hatteras Inlet station's 41-foot utility boat by the spray it kicked up as it churned the waters of the Pamlico Sound. As it grew closer, the white hull with its red diagonal stripe was confirmation that Lieutenant Braxton Sallinger had come through as promised.

When Calvin had managed to navigate the various phone channels to reach the lieutenant, Sallinger had laughed. "Send out someone? What'cha need, a teddy bear? I'm about to put you suckers to shame."

"You got a teddy bear to send?"

"That's a good one, Deputy. I tell you what, I'm on the other line with Bollinger. We've got a new boat coming in hopefully next year, one of those 47-foot models. A real beaut, and I'm helping them clear a few hurdles in the approval process. The faster the approvals go, the quicker we get our boat. You understand, you put your money where your mouth is, and things get done, so we're ensuring that our new boat is right on time. Doing this right is what it's about. When I'm through here, I'll meet you where, at the ferry landing?"

"You mean tonight? I was thinking in the morning."

"Tide's rolling in on this one. Sorry, Deputy. I've gottta head to Bollinger's in the A.M. early, and I also want to be there looking for this boat. That's a slice of my pride in losing that vessel."

Calvin winced. *A slice of his pride.* He hadn't expected the man to take the theft of the sailboat personally. He prodded his options. Bollinger Shipyards was in Louisiana, and he glanced at his watch, taking away an hour for Central Time. The shipyards in Louisiana might have a kettle full of daylight left, but here on the Sound, they would likely be slicing the bean paste thin to get Sallinger here and do any real searching by dark.

"How about the Bell Island Pier."

"Rose Bay, right? Expect us quick as I can get off this call."

Us? Calvin hadn't asked who might be with him, though he didn't expect it mattered. Instead, he focused on the time of day and the men he and Zack had temporarily lost track of. He got Zack on the radio and suggested that he and Goldie head on up to the cousin's place and see if anything suspicious showed up. Calvin wanted him to pin down their location but hold off on going in after them. They had tomorrow for that, as right then, backup might be in short supply, and besides, Calvin wanted to be there when they picked them up. He let his eyes follow Zack's taillights as he pulled away, and then he sorted out what needed to happen before he met with Lieutenant Sallinger. It was a short drive to the pier, and with the day getting away, he wanted something to eat before heading out on the water.

Now, he rolled the top to his Quarter Deli takeaway sack and set it behind his seat. He climbed out of his truck, closed and locked the door, and headed out onto the pier. The boat screamed in the distance, the sound of the engines coming through over the slap of the hull on the water as it hit each small swell with a pop that reverberated against the boards making up the walkway along the pier. The croaking, singing voices of the wildlife just coming out for the early evening faded into the hiss of the water along the side of the arriving boat, and as it pulled up to the pier, the sudden silence and the slap of the bow wave as it reached the shoreline and bounced back on itself defined the moment.

"Deputy Dingman," Sallinger called. He was standing, and

a young ensign was at the steering wheel of the boat. The ensign was short in comparison to the lieutenant but dressed meticulously as if he wished to make a good impression on someone he was meeting for the first time.

Or perhaps that was why he was with Sallinger, because he presented a high level of skill in everything he did, and the lieutenant trusted him. Calvin hoped he felt the same if they had to search in the dark. The shore of the Sound could be treacherous if a neophyte was at the wheel.

"Lieutenant Sallinger," Calvin responded. He noted the lieutenant's full camo pants and shirt, including his cap, in contrast to the younger man's spiffy appearance. Sallinger's boots were matte black against the lighter color of the deck.

"Ensign Christian Branch, our pilot and navigator. Ensign, meet Calvin Dingman, our guest for tonight." He turned to Calvin with a grin and lifted his chin as he chided him, "Hope you don't got a case of the shakes with searching in the dark."

"Your boat, your life." Calvin noted the ensign glanced his direction with a big smile.

"It's in the instrumentation. Show him, Branch."

"Yes, sir!"

The ensign's excitement with the navigation aids took several minutes to wring itself out, by which time Calvin was less worried about being out on the Sound after sundown and more worried about whether he should have brought the second half of his sandwich from his truck. If they were heading into the marshes, they were likely not making it home before morning, and he didn't see any hope of a good, home-cooked Mexican meal coming his way anytime soon.

An hour in, what Ensign Branch and Lieutenant Sallinger were doing didn't make any sense to Calvin. Lights, yes, they were on, bright enough to slice through the darkness like a spoon through chocolate pudding, but he'd expected they'd be running the shoreline, working the edges of the marshes, anyplace that might catch a sailboat blown across the Pamlico Sound. Offshore breezes could be strong enough. The process Calvin had pictured was marking Ocracoke Village on a map, noting the direction of the offshore wind currents, and tracing that line to the shore. That's where they would find the *Dutchman*, pushed into one of the shoreside marshes on the mainland side and hunkered down waiting to be retrieved, if it was anywhere.

Instead, the ensign was running a program on a computer with the logo SAROPS on the screen and looking up weather reports, currents, and distress signals for the past three days. He'd search another screen, note his own navigation information, input the information, and wait for the program to update before telling the lieutenant the next location they needed to search.

"So, you guys got something going on." Calvin took advantage of a lull in interactions between Sallinger and Branch. "What'cha got in that there computer?"

"The ensign is plotting leeway drift for a large sailboat. We don't know the exact length, so there's some fuzzy calculation going on. I put my money on a 40-footer, but a few feet difference can put the boat in a whole new location."

"Leeway drift?" Calvin wasn't a water person, particularly. He'd never heard of it.

"You know Austin Artenbury?" Chance's hand called for his attention, and Sallinger shifted his focus to the ensign, shooting Calvin an offhand, "Hold just a minute, Deputy. We'll get back to that."

The boat's engine slowed to a gurgling rumble as it paused in the darkness and the two Coast Guard men huddled over one of several screens, their faces glowing blue with the light, and Ensign Chance occasionally tapping at his keyboard. After a few minutes, Sallinger stepped back to Calvin's side.

"About Artenbury," Sallinger suggested, "any clue?"

"You're killing me with the question. It's a brand-new name to me."

"Lives up in Connecticut, so that's fair. Okay. He's the lone oceanographer in the Coast Guard Search and Rescue Division. You'd not forget him if you'd seen him. Snow white Hemingway beard, always wears a Coast Guard Search and Rescue polo." Sallinger laughed and pointed to the images of the Sound on Chance's screen and said, "He based that program on Art Allen's 1999 *Review of Leeway*. Best thing ever for finding lost ships at sea."

"SAROPS?" The letters on the logo.

"Search and Rescue Optimal Planning System. Just plug in your known facts, and it gives us a good idea where to look."

"I thought ships floated downwind."

"Nah, that's a misconception. That's what leeway is about. Even people who fall off cruise ships don't float with the current. That's based on a 1960 report in the *Coast Guard Alumni Association Bulletin* titled 'Estimating the Drift of Distressed Craft.' You think this boat we're looking for is distressed?"

"Like my own backyard."

"Here's the one variable the program doesn't account for, Dingman, and that's the big thing the ensign is trying to work out. Several years back, a diver fell off a boat, and the SAROPS program couldn't find him. It wasn't until they called in old Art Allen and he said, 'The man's swimming for shore.' The shore, Dingman, was eighteen miles away. We factored that in, and we found him. He was using a scuba mask to catch rainwater to drink."

"That sailboat's not swimming to shore."

"Unless someone's put up a sail and is navigating it—" He cut off as Ensign Chance called him over. After Sallinger listened to what the ensign had to say, Sallinger nodded, and the ensign hit the throttle, the engine began to thrum, and the utility craft leaped forward into the water sending spray to either side to disappear into the blackness. The scream of the props cutting through the water reached epic levels.

"Why the sudden urgency?" Calvin nearly yelled to be heard.

"Our search just ended." Sallinger's shirt underneath his waterproof jacket was buffeted by the damp night air, revealing that his frequent boast that he didn't get tired, he got fit, wasn't just a boast.

"What does that mean? Give it to me straight, Sallinger."

"There's been a near drowning up towards the Wysocking Wildlife Sanctuary. Some teens out in their grandfather's boat. The grandfather says they left out this morning to check some traps, and their possible location matches with a distress call we just received. That takes priority over your search for your missing sailboat."

So, Calvin said to himself. *I see how it is. It's mine now that you can no longer look for it.* He said, "This happen often?"

"More than we like. The Coast Guard pulls in ten people a day on average, and we lose three more. I intend for this to be one of the ones we save."

Calvin stepped away and stared into the darkness. He held on with one hand as the floor under his feet vibrated and occasionally jerked upward and slammed back down on a particularly large swell. He was perfectly dry, but even so, he felt the spray peeling from the side of the boat dampening any chance of him finding a meal any time before the next morning.

His sandwich in his truck, so lonely. He imagined eating it up, but that didn't make his stomach feel any fuller. He hoped they rescued the teens. At least there would be some good to come from this wasted night on the water.

WITHOUT A LOCATOR beacon broadcasting the position of the teens' boat, the darkness challenged the Coast Guard vessel as they approached the area near the wildlife sanctuary. When the boat slowed, the choppy water threw their lights this way and that. When they opened the throttle, they were bounced and jarred until they couldn't think. To make matters even more complicated, numerous other small craft had come out despite the late hour to join the search, and not all of them had spotlights to warn other boaters to beware. The smaller boats with their bow and stern lights easily vanished when the swells lifted them up and dropped them down the back side.

Lieutenant Sallinger directed Ensign Chance to approach likely looking vessels to speak to them about where they'd searched and what they might have located. Sounds? Debris? Even possible sightings might provide clues that would enable the Coast Guard vessel to narrow their search parameters.

Calvin noted the difference in how the professionals worked compared to the locals. The smaller vessels, while important in maintaining extra eyes on the water, couldn't provide precise location markers when they offered information to the lieutenant. They answered, "North a bit," or, "Back the way we came," or some such. Ensign Chance, however, continually added information to his computer, which then translated onto his screen. He could tell where their vessel was, as well as the shore, every vessel they had interacted with, and possible guesses where the teens might be. Three vessels in, their link to the lost boys swelled in importance.

"Ahoy, there," Sallinger called over the loudspeaker as Chance slowed the Coast Guard vessel to come alongside a smaller, boxy cabin cruiser. Under the Coast Guard's lights, the side of the cruiser read *Mary Ann*. "Coast Guard, Lieutenant Sallinger here. *Mary Ann*, may we come aside?"

"Coast Guard? Thank God you've come." A strong-jawed man, exhausted-looking and wearing a seaworthy coat that was only partially buttoned, stepped into the light. "Pat McNair here. My son, Hanson, piloting the boat. It's my grandchildren who are lost. Have you heard anything?" Even as he spoke, the man's eyes searched the darkness.

"I wish I had, Mr. McNair," Sallinger said very professionally with more empathy than Calvin expected. Sallinger went on, "I'm sorry for your distress, and you, too, Hanson. Both of you must be devastated. The report we received didn't have much information, so meeting you out here is a best-case scenario. What can you tell us about the boat and who might have been aboard?"

"It's my boat," Hanson volunteered. "The boys, my sons Riley and Benson, know how to pilot it. Life jackets, everything. They were out looking for clams to sell locally. They know what they're doing, and that's why we didn't worry until it started getting late, and then the distress call came in. We don't know why the locator beacon didn't kick in."

"Sure," Sallinger said. He glanced at Ensign Chance, nodded to tell him something that was just between them, and turned back to the men in the cabin cruiser. "What are they in?"

"A fourteen-foot whaler, white with a black Bimini top. Outboard, of course," Hanson answered, with the grandfather readily stepping back and giving over to his son.

"Radio?"

"Of course. It's fully equipped and legal. The boys have—"

"Never mind that. That's not why we're here. Frequency? Name of the boat? Does it have a transponder?"

"Class B but it's not transmitting, not that we can tell. We've tried tracking their phones, but—" The man shrugged.

"Ensign Chance, anything you can do about that?"

The exchange continued, but Calvin recused himself. He

had no skills in this area, and he would only get in the way. One thing haunted his thoughts. If a fourteen-foot Boston Whaler came with a transponder, even if it wasn't transmitting, what was the likelihood that a large sailboat would have one? Like tacos on Mexican night. And phones … he knew phones emitted a signal the police could track … their missing boat, the one from the drug bust, shouldn't there be some way to track it other than guesswork in the dark?

Calvin felt the moist blanket of darkness, the earthy aroma of the Sound, and the water against the hull envelope him. On this night, in this location, and for someone from Swan Quarter, he was lost as an alligator in a field of corn. He had no way to get back to his truck, unless he wanted to dive in and swim, which would only give Sallinger and the ensign another missing person to locate. Nor would he be able to swim far enough to get to shore, but even if he could, he had never transversed the wildlife sanctuary on foot, and certainly not in the dark.

The radio squawked into life, and Ensign Chance slipped on his headphones and answered. After a few moments of conversation and several glances at his superior officer, he disconnected from the radio and removed his headphones. He turned in his seat, took a deep breath, and held it.

"Okay, Ensign. Speak up." Sallinger.

"Yes, sir. Can I say it to you privately, sir?"

"C'mon, man, shape up. What'cha need, a teddy bear? Spit it out."

"Yes, sir." Chance glanced at the men in the boat next to theirs and back to Sallinger. "One of the boats has found someone."

"My god, they've located them," Pat said, his voice ragged with emotion. "About time. Did the boys say why they didn't bring the boat in before dark?"

"Hold on, Dad," his son, Hanson, cautioned him, with a

hand on his arm. "I'm not sure that's what the man means."

"Ensign?" Sallinger's face was neutral as if he already guessed. "If there's more, might as well get it out."

"They were still pulling the body from the water—"

"Noo!" Pat let out a painful moan that attested to his complete and utter despair.

Another person gone overboard. Calvin closed his eyes as he tried to imagine losing a son or grandson to the sea. He couldn't do it. All he could do was ask, *When does it end? Sallinger, I wish you could have saved this one for all our sakes.*

Calvin was jerked from his despair as Sallinger instructed Ensign Chance to get a location for the "situation" and stepped onto the McNair's boat to console and discuss options with them, wrapping a line from their boat around a cleat on the Coast Guard vessel before transferring from one vessel to the other. He knew this was hard, and they had his apologies for having to ask, but were they prepared to identify the person being pulled from the water? If there was identifying clothing, they might postpone the viewing until morning, but if not, would they be willing to view the body before returning to shore? His associate was locating where the person had been found. Of course, both men said, though the grandfather was sunken into himself, and the father was hardly better.

Sallinger called across the two boats to Chance, "Tide's rolling in, Ensign. What do you have for me?"

"Yes, sir! Coordinates ready. One thing, sir. They must have drifted quite a ways. This is off from what we expected."

"Excuse me, Mr. McNair." Sallinger looked from one man to the next, and for the first time, he paused before continuing. He shook off his momentary hesitation and said, "I need to discuss our next move with my associate."

"Of course," the younger of the two said. By now, the two boats were lashed together with an additional line from the *Mary*

Ann knotted around a second cleat on the Coast Guard vessel, and Sallinger leaped across the narrow, watery gap back onto his boat.

"Ensign?" Sallinger stood over the younger man, clearly expecting answers that were less vague.

"Sir," the ensign started, pulling his headphones off and turning in his chair, "even with time on the clock, currents in the Sound, and leeway drift, there's a limit how far a body would drift. The one they've located is outside the range I would expect."

"Swimming," Calvin inserted, remembering the lieutenant's informative speech from earlier. "I mean, if the boy went over-board or the boat capsized, he would have tried to swim for shore, right?"

"True." Sallinger's expression seemed to offer a new measure of respect to the Hyde County deputy. "Ensign, did you factor that in?"

"Um," and Chance hesitated, looking at his boss then to Calvin apologetically, "yes, sir, of course I did. It's still too far."

"But they have something to identify the body with, right? It must be on board by now."

"Yes, sir, but no, sir." Chance referenced one of his screens, and the information he'd loaded earlier was there plus an identifier for the location of the "incident" where the drowned person was located. The incident identifier was nowhere near the other information on the screen. "The body is on board but with no identity. No jewelry, wallet, or anything specific. Late teens, maybe twenty. No shirt and just wearing pants. They said he looks like he had been living rough."

"Two teens out for the day hunting clams. It could be one of them. Perhaps," Sallinger mused.

"Should we head that way, sir?"

Sallinger looked the direction of the relatives of the missing boys, gave Calvin a thoughtful look, and nodded at Ensign Chance. "I'll have the men follow. Let me untie the lines, tell them what we're doing, and we'll get started."

The smaller craft didn't have the engine size or navigation aids of the more advanced Coast Guard watercraft, so their speed was reduced as they moved through the darkness. That gave Calvin the opportunity to scan the blackness for anything out of place that might be out there. Secondly, the reduced speed kept the noise of the engines to little more than a burble, and the water slicing along the sides of the boat was the gentle brush of a cook's hand marinating the black, watery sauce all around them, painting it up and over the sides of the craft.

Calvin caught the echo of something out of place from across the water as they worked their way across the Sound.

"Braxton," he called, allowing the familiarity to escape his lips before he could pull it back in. "I'll be ding-danged. Did you hear that?"

"What'cha got, Dingman?" The fit, super-manly lieutenant moved to Calvin's side and peered into the darkness.

"There, again." It could be birdcalls, or voices ... but the sound chilled Calvin ... or filled him with hope. He wasn't sure which.

"Ensign," Sallinger called, "cut the engine."

"Yes, sir! Absolutely, sir!"

"The boy has enthusiasm," Sallinger murmured as the silence of the engines enveloped them. The sound of the cabin cruiser's inboards burbled, a muted throb, and an echoey, "Hey, hey," floated over the grainy surface of the water. A pair of binoculars found their way to Sallinger's face, and he handed them to Calvin and pointed.

In the distance, something white, and it was almost possible to imagine something on top moving. Arms? The voices were now perfectly clear, calling, "Over here!"

"Ensign, you get that?"

"Yes, sir! I'm on it." Ensign Chance restarted the boat, and with a broad sweep, began the turn towards another scene of potential disaster on the Pamlico Sound.

CLOSER IN, the ship's spotlight identified the bottom of an upturned craft being overwashed by swells. The imagined movement on top became two boys, and the voices turned ragged with relief. Sallinger hit the loudspeakers and called, "Riley? Benson? Wave if that's you."

The two boys thrashed their arms enthusiastically. Arriving at the upturned craft, the two teens wore jeans, although the younger of the two was missing a shoe, but they did have their life vests securely strapped around their torsos. Their faces were sunburned, and they looked exhausted. Sallinger pulled them aboard the Coast Guard vessel to ensure they weren't injured or in need of further assistance before releasing them to their family's arms.

"Disaster averted, that's for certain," Calvin remarked, as the cabin cruiser pulled away, barely creating a wake, with the upturned Boston Whaler tied to her stern and creating her own set of ripples. "T'wouldn't be surprised to see them right that boat and have it back on the water tomorrow."

The boys appeared as proficient as their father had suggested. They might have been exhausted, but as soon as they were aboard an upright vessel, they began to relate their story as though it was the best adventure ever, with the only complaint being from the younger one that they had lost their catch when they were capsized by a larger boat.

"A sailboat?" Calvin asked before considering whether he should let the lieutenant ask the questions.

"Maybe," the older boy said. "We yelled and yelled, but it was like no one was there. We never saw anyone, and Riley made me drop the key to start the motor—"

"Did not," the younger boy said. "You fumbled it—"

"Anyway," and his brother glared at him, "it just hit us and we rolled over—"

"But we were wearing our life vests. Did you see, Grandpa?"

The boys had wanted to inspect everything on the Coast Guard vessel before returning to their boat, tying off the upturned vessel, and heading to shore. Ensign Chance once again pulled up the location of the drowned man, and being on their own once again, hit the throttle at a harder pace until their vessel cut through the water like slicing a cake.

Calvin watched the spray as it caught in the lights, and he recalled Zack Halsey's words from the night of the drug bust ... *"with space for six preservers and only five still hanging there."*

They'd found the sixth preserver on the sailboat, and now the sailboat was missing. Was there a connection between the drowned man and that sixth preserver?

And if it was a sailboat—their sailboat—that had rolled the boys' Boston Whaler, how did the body they were heading to slot into that recipe?

Calvin approached Braxton Sallinger, and he offered him his hand and said, "You people got it going on, Lieutenant."

"There's three types of men on the water. I always aim to be the best." Sallinger took the hand and laughed. "I caught you used my name earlier. You have my permission to do it anytime. And thanks. Ten vs. three. I'll take the ten any day, and you can put your money on that."

"This body we're going to see?" Calvin offered the question casually.

"My daddy didn't raise no fool, and I bet yours didn't either. We'll work this out and put somebody to shame, Calvin," shifting to the more casual term of address, "'cause the tide's rolling in, and we're riding the leading wave."

Calvin laughed. Even without his half sandwich back in his truck, it was turning out to be a good night after all.

—————— Chapter 8 ——————

Clue at British Cemetery

COAST GUARD LIEUTENANT BRAXTON SALLINGER glared the direction of the sun rising across Ocracoke Island as he stepped off the 41-foot utility boat now docked in Silver Lake. He took in the clouds to the east of the island, now burning with reds and yellows, a perfect sunrise for any tourist visiting this late in the season, but he should be on an airplane headed to Bollinger Shipyards in Louisiana, not tied up at a dock in Ocracoke Village, North Carolina.

His first order of duty was to contact Bollinger. They had to hear from him that their meeting was cancelled. He didn't want them to think there was even a lick of lazy about him, and they would if he didn't shape up and do this right. He removed his waterproof jacket, knelt, wrapped a line from the bow around a dock cleat and without thinking or considering what he was doing, expertly knotted it. At the stern, Ensign Chance repeated the motion from onboard the vessel.

"Lieutenant Sallinger, sir?"

Braxton shifted his eyes to focus on the ensign, and they burned as he squinted against the glare of the morning sun. Tired, that's all it was. They'd pulled an all-nighter for something that should have taken no more than an evening. Finding the boys? A piece of cake especially with the observant Deputy Dingman riding along. That had felt good, to save two of the ten that were plucked from the water each day by the country's foremost water rescue service, the nation's best, the Coast Guard.

The deceased man felt less good, and still, they had no idea who he was, where he'd come from, or how he'd managed to get himself drowned in the Sound or in such a state. He hadn't been out long, as bodies tended to trend to fish food when they were submerged for extended periods. This one likely wouldn't have been pulled from the water at all except he was lodged on a sandbar. The shallow waters of the Pamlico Sound could be treacherous for boats of all sizes and drafts, but it was what would likely enable this man to be buried in a grave of soil and sod rather than enduring a watery demise being nibbled for dinner by the undersea denizens that prowled the Sound.

"Yes, Ensign?" Braxton heard his thick voice, and the only cure for that would be sleep.

"Should I head up to the station? If we're here any length of time, we'll need land-based transportation."

Station Ocracoke, the ensign implied, the large white building just on the shore at the end of the dock they were tied to. Manned by one boat crew with a single first-class boatswain mate as supervisor, it abutted the ferry landing. Transportation provided by the station was likely their only option for food this early, as their best bet would be just this side of the sheriff's department building close to Jerniman's Campground and the Variety Store. A sandwich shop down from the Variety Store was usually open early, and something to eat had been a topic of discussion since dropping Deputy Calvin Dingman back at the dock in Swan Quarter.

"Thanks, Ensign. I can walk up." They were on the dock attached to the station. From the looks of the building, no one was home. "It doesn't look alive. I suspect we're out of luck with a ride if no one's here."

"Sir, no one?" Chance stood straighter, peered at the building, and climbed from the boat. "The whole boat crew away? We didn't catch anything on the radio."

"For that reason, I suspect they are doing maintenance at the British Cemetery. You've been assigned here. Were you that fortunate?" Braxton managed a grin.

"Yes, sir, I was. Lawnmower duty. It wasn't bad. It shows a lot of respect, the Coast Guard still taking care of the cemetery after all these years. I was proud to help, sir."

"I'm sure you were, Ensign."

The British Cemetery was a throwback to WWII, when the British ship HMT *Bedfordshire* came to North Carolina's aid in '42 against German U-boats patrolling and sinking vessels in the shipping lanes along the Outer Banks. The *Bedfordshire* was sunk, and 37 Royal Navy sailors died. Four of those men washed ashore on Ocracoke Island and were buried by the locals. The site of their burial was maintained by the Coast Guard members who rotated to Station Ocracoke from Station Hatteras Inlet.

Braxton let his eyes climb from the broad, covered veranda encircling the ground floor of the white building, with its tall, retractable doors for the two boats assigned to the station, a 44-foot motor lifeboat and a 21-foot motor life inflatable, to the four-story tower topped by a glass lookout station. He felt of the phone in his pocket, unbuttoned the flap, and slipped it out.

"Let me try this first, Ensign. Maybe I can catch someone." He located the number for the station and pressed the icon to engage the call. After a moment, they could hear it ringing inside the building. After numerous rings, it switched to an automated information system, and he clicked to cancel the call. He turned to Chance, "You recall who's on duty? I might can get a personal phone call to go through."

"Ray Murray, perhaps, sir. He said something to me about it the other night but didn't give me any specifics."

"Ray's not the supervisor, though."

"No, sir. He might know who is. Should I give him a call? My phone's in the boat and fully charged."

"If they are at the cemetery—" Braxton cut himself off, thinking, and decided. "I won't disturb anything the men might be involved with at the cemetery. I have too much respect for that place and the men buried there. We can walk into town."

"Yes, sir!" Ensign Chance's face burst into an excited grin as they headed up the dock. "I enjoyed being stationed here. Pirate lore and all that. Have you heard about the smugglers' code?"

"Smugglers' code. Where did you hear that?"

"From Courtney, sir."

"Yes, Courtney." Courtney was Ensign Courtney Cruick-shank, and the lieutenant didn't need that explained. The term smugglers' code? He cut his eyes appraisingly to the ensign, aware just how touristy the term sounded, and wondered if the younger man truly believed in such nonsense. Heck, yeah, he'd heard of it, but his daddy didn't raise no fool, and he'd never put any stock into it. It was the kids, the new recruits, the *ensigns* that kept it floating in on every spring tide.

"Yes, sir," Chance said as they set a pace along the Garrish Highway that wound past the ferry landing and wrapped Silver Lake. "You know about Blackbeard, right, Lieutenant?" The man smiled brightly, as if revealing something that wasn't common knowledge.

"Clearly you know. Enlighten me, man." In the sun, walking would soon warm them up, and Braxton rolled up the sleeves on his camo shirt as far as was reasonable. His matte-finish boots weighed heavily on his feet after a night on the water, and he knew what it was. He didn't have his land legs, yet, and he was forced to focus on taking strides across soil that didn't move up and down, in and out, without regards to the people on top of it.

"C'mon, Lieutenant, you have to know about Blackbeard."

"That's good, man. I have to know about Blackbeard." Braxton let out a laugh, as much a challenge as that he found the ensign amusing. "Crack any history book, and there he is, so yeah. Tell me what you know about the smugglers' code."

"Maybe I said that wrong. Not smugglers but the code the pirates followed, yes, that's it, sir. See, when sailors turned pirate, they had to make rules to protect themselves. Like in the Guard, there were some things we must do, and others that are forbidden."

"Such as?" meaning with the pirates. Braxton adjusted his cap and raised an eyebrow at the ensign before pulling it back down on his forehead.

"First, no boys or women." He beamed brightly as if that was a revelation.

"Which meant no intimacy." The lieutenant fought a grin and wondered if the ensign got his meaning.

"What?" Chance frowned, putting it together. "Why would they forbid boys …" He paused and grimaced. "They wouldn't!"

"They did." Braxton laughed. "What else?"

"No gambling, no fighting with each other, how to split the treasure."

"Here's another for you. The pirate's code set their bed-time."

"What?" Chance laughed before spitting out, "Sorry, what, *sir*."

"Forgiven."

"What time, sir? Midnight?" The lure of late-night rum-drinking sessions and counting golden loot twinkled in the younger man's eyes.

"Round about eight, I believe. I think I could use some of that after last night. All-nighters aren't my thing any longer."

"No, sir, mine either," Chance agreed. "But eight, that seems early."

"Likely they picked sunset, which comes about eight most of the year. Anyway, I see food coming up." In the distance, the sign for the sandwich shop was just visible. They hadn't seen many other people in the village, and Braxton asked, "You have any money, Ensign?"

"A credit card, sir, if you think that'll do."

"If they're open. We'll get you reimbursed when we get back to Hatteras."

"Thank you, sir. It won't draft my bank for a few weeks, so I'm good."

By then, they could see the OPEN sign at the entrance. Braxton waited on the ensign to open the door, and they made their way inside.

COFFEE AND breakfast sandwiches hit the spot. Braxton had hoped for something more substantial, like ham and eggs, but what was available would have to do. Sitting at the small table, he watched the ensign wolf down double what he'd eaten and use a scrap of his sandwich to scrape the last of the mayo out of a single-serve container before pressing it into his mouth and chewing as if it was the last bite he would ever consume.

"So, Ensign, you brought up the smugglers' code—"

"The pirates' code, sir." Chance paused from licking his

fingers, then wiped the remaining ones with a paper napkin.

"Incidental." Braxton shrugged. "Why bring it up out on the road?"

"Not sure, sir." Chance shrugged. "Just, you being up on Hatteras with that drug bust, then those two kids telling about that boat that swamped theirs. I've been trying to connect that body we pulled in with everything going on. Drug bust, smugglers." He shrugged again.

"Pirates?" Braxton felt a smile at the corners of his mouth.

"If you want, sir." Chance broke into a toothy smile. "I like pirates, especially Blackbeard. Can you tell?"

"I'm not blind, Ensign."

"No, sir!" Chance sat up straighter. "Never, sir. I would never say that."

"That's a good man. What did you come up with, anything to connect the dots? I noticed how good you are with that computer on the boat. How about that computer in your head?"

"The cemetery here, sir, the one with the men from the *Bedfordshire*. I think that might be important in this case."

"Explain." Braxton didn't see the connection. It was a cemetery from the last century, a time nearly a hundred years gone. Certainly, it had a connection with today's Coast Guard, as the men who rotated to Station Ocracoke from Station Hatteras Inlet regularly maintained it; and the Coast Guard had a connection with the missing boat, as he had been there when the sailboat was originally sighted; and both he and Chance had been at the site where the dead man was pulled from the Sound the previous night; but to weave a needle through all of that and come up with a viable theory that explained things in a reasonable manner? And one that factored in a century-old cemetery that wasn't in use anymore except as a memorial? That was something not even he found plausible.

"Sir, you come here, well, people from not around here, and

what's the one place people would know, a place that's not messed with, you know, renovated, stuff like that, and is always open to the public?"

"Clearly you want me to say the British Cemetery."

"Sir, what else can it be? Those smugglers, if they wanted to leave someone a message, why not? When I first brought up the smugglers' code, I was really thinking of code words, like the Navajo code talkers back in the last world war. It didn't matter who heard the message, if they didn't know Navajo, the message was locked up tight."

"And the cemetery. Tell me, Ensign, what's the Navajo there?"

"The commemorative plaques, of course, sir. They're all over the internet. Everyone knows what they say, and no one's ever going to change them. Use them for code messages, and any smuggler can visit and read the code." Chance grinned like a kid sharing the secret word to enter a forbidden clubhouse he'd heard about, seen from a distance, and was only now standing at the door.

"This means you've got a plan. Is that how I should read this?"

"Yes, sir!"

"And?" *Spit it out, man.* He'd been awake all night, and his coffee wanted him to be up and busy. And now.

"We need to go there, sir. Look for clues."

Braxton looked out the window and rubbed his hand across the side of his face. He glanced at the ensign and came to a decision.

"Blackbeard, here we come. Police the table, Ensign, and I'll meet you outside."

"Yes, sir!" Chance stood, and he said, "You know, sir, Blackbeard doesn't have a grave. Legend is his body was thrown into the Sound."

Braxton shook his head, refused to reply, and exited into the morning sun. Yes, ensign, he knew that. It had been a joke, man. When the ensign joined him, he nodded down the road. "That way?"

"Of course, sir. I know exactly where it is."

"Then lead on, man. I'm with you."

THE WALK to the British Cemetery was direct and easy. The two men cut off Garrish at the Anchorage Inn and turned inland on the obviously named British Cemetery Road. Enough of the morning had slipped away that three adolescent teens in a golf cart trundled by, giving Ensign Chance an opportunity to speak up.

"School, sir? I hadn't thought of that."

"People still send their kids, Ensign. Yours will attend once you get married." Braxton had barely noted the teens. He was attempting to recall the wordage on the commemorative plaques at the cemetery but was coming up blank. The content, yes, describing the Bedfordshire as a converted Arctic trawler, but if what Chance was saying held any water, the exact phrasing of each sentence would likely carry weight.

"No, sir, Lieutenant." Chance grinned, showing more teeth than a sample set of dental implants. "Well, yes, sir, but I don't have any plans to marry anytime soon."

"That's a good one, Ensign. Your plans in the matter … let me say it this way. You won't get any say when a pretty girl gets her designs on you. She'll have you a bug in a rug, and you'll have a ring on her finger quick as the tide rolls in."

"Yes, sir, if you say so, sir." Chance's attention was on a gray-headed woman already out and working in a flowerbed. A spread of bare bulbs lay on a sheet at her side, and he watched as she selected one, put it back, and selected another to cover with soil. He called to her, "That'll be pretty come spring, ma'am."

She sat up and waved. "Thank you, young man. I expect so." She pushed her hair back over one ear and turned back to her flowerbed.

Past a slight bend in the road, the front grille of a Coast Guard vehicle just visible through the trees revealed that the lieutenant's prediction was correct. An orange cone marked the front bumper of the truck, which was parked on the side street and out of the way. Two men in long sleeves and blue pants, one with a grass rake and another with a wide sweeper broom, moved into the sun. A leaf blower whined, and as Sallinger and Chance approached, a third person appeared in protective eye-wear. An orange extension cord trailed from the leaf blower, and with a final whine, the handheld machine sent a cloud of debris into the air.

Surfman Ray Murry was working the rake, and Ensign Chance called and waved, with a congenial, "Good morning, Ray." The other two were Engineer Logan Radisson with the broom and Boat Crew Member Clary Cartier behind the leaf blower. When Braxton Sallinger stepped forward, Cartier killed the blower and pulled the eyewear from her face, revealing large eyes in a deep green color.

"Nice to see," Braxton complimented, "that there's not a lick of lazy around here. The ensign and I wish to look around when you're finished."

"Thank you, sir," the three returned in a ripple of respectful responses. "Right now, sir. We're wrapping up." The final words came from Radisson, and he flipped his broom to stand the tip of the handle on the ground at his feet.

"The rest of the boat crew?" Braxton glanced at Chance and back to the three working on the cemetery.

"Readying for the celebration, sir." Clary Cartier. She held the blower in one hand but had grasped the orange cord with the other. It ran up and into the truck, which had the back open, suggesting a power source for the electric blower.

"Celebration, Ensign?" Braxton raised an eyebrow at Chance.

"I don't know, sir." Chance shrugged.

"Then I suggest you find out." *Heck, yeah*, he thought. *It's been a long night, and while I normally say I get fit, today I am really, really tired.*

"Yes, sir! I will, sir. Thank you, sir. Ray?" Chance quizzed.

"Sorry, sir." Murray aimed his apology at Braxton. "We thought you were here to join in."

"The lieutenant and I have been on the Sound all night." Ensign Chance pulled Murray's attention back his direction. "I don't suppose you three know about the body pulled from the water, but you likely will. Anyway, the celebration. What about it?"

A relative of one of the sailors buried in the cemetery was visiting from the U.K. and the boatswain mate supervising the boat crew had decided to spiff up the cemetery for the occasion, to best reflect the care the Coast Guard provided the memorial while hopefully polishing the Coast Guard's image "across the pond."

"You say you're about finished?" At their assent, Braxton asked, "You're sure there's nothing the ensign can help you with?"

"Sir?" Chance's face twisted in dismay. "The code, sir? Don't forget that."

"Right. My apologies. The ensign has a plan for this morning, and we'll be out of your way."

"We'd be honored if you stayed for the ceremony, sir." Crew Member Cartier still held the blower, and she smiled.

"It's a ceremony, now?" Braxton turned his eyebrow her direction. "It was a celebration a few moments ago."

"Only a few words, sir. If you wanted to say something, I'm sure you could. The family would appreciate it." Engineer Radisson, the first time he'd spoken up.

"Who's your supervisor?" Braxton might agree but didn't intend to commit on the suggestion of a boat crew member. He needed to talk to the boatswain mate before deciding.

"Rodney Keith," Cartier shared.

"Rodney." Braxton pictured the man, wide shoulders and tree trunk legs. He was a take-no-prisoners sort of leader, yet he was well-liked by those who worked with him. "I'll have a word with Rodney and see what I can do. For now, though, this looks good. I'll let him know I found you at it and working hard."

"Thank you, sir," the three chimed in.

"Where will I find him?"

"Here, sir, in about fifteen minutes."

"Thank you." Braxton turned to Chance and asked, "Is fifteen minutes enough for what you need to do?"

"Yes, sir! Plenty of time, sir."

"Let's get to it."

In minutes, the cone was in the truck, the tools stored away, and the three crewmen were headed back to the station. The trees, the freshly trimmed shrubbery, and the silence that blanketed the area gave the cemetery a secluded feel, although it was nothing of the sort. British Cemetery Road was a thoroughfare, by Ocracoke standards anyway, slicing into the island's interior and often bombarded with humming golf carts, curious children, and cars transporting parents and grandparents to island eateries and shopping locations along Irvin Garrish.

The inspection of the inscriptions at the British Cemetery was interrupted by the lieutenant's phone.

"Braxton here," he answered. The lieutenant motioned for the ensign to move ahead without him, and he pulled the phone from his ear and tapped the speaker mode icon and waited.

"Jackie at Station Hatteras, Lieutenant. How about that flight to Louisiana? We got a call this morning about a missing lieutenant, and we were wondering what's up." Jackie was Jacqueline Powers from the Coast Guard station at Hatteras Inlet, a civilian administrative specialist who kept the place humming when the military-minded enlistees were preoccupied with rescuing rather than participating in receptionist-type duties.

"Yeah, that," Braxton said. He rubbed one eye, thinking, *This is a good one. I forgot to call in and cancel.* He also hadn't contacted Bollinger, but he could shift that to Jackie's plate. "Ensign Chance and I got a report of a drowned man in the Sound last night. We're on Ocracoke still pursuing the fallout."

"Another all-nighter? I declare, you might earn a gold star if you keep this up. I heard something about a missing sailboat?"

"Still missing. Let's not dwell on that. The ensign helped rescue two boys in an overturned Boston Whaler."

"And you sat by and did nothing. That's not the Lieutenant Sallinger I know." Jackie teased, her way of pulling information from people. She wanted to know more.

"Not so fast, Jackie. You'll see it all in my report. Can I get you to do something for me?"

"That's why I called you. What else have you let fall through the cracks?" She was laughing at him.

"My missed flight was to Bollinger to inspect the new build and pull the delivery date forward. Can you reschedule that for me?"

"What delivery date would you like? I'm sure they won't mind having that new boat here tomorrow."

"Not what I meant."

"Oh, you want a new appointment down *there*. What about sending Walter? He would love a couple days down south. That's his stomping grounds—" She referred to Walter

Schmidt, a rival lieutenant also stationed at Hatteras.

"Nah, we're doing this Bollinger thing right. Walter's a, well, he's not the man for the job, but you don't need to tell him that." Walter wouldn't push as hard as Braxton, and he wanted to shave some time off the build, not give Bollinger an excuse to use up all the time in their contract.

"Not me. Not a word escapes these lips. When do you want to miss your next meeting?" Said in a light-hearted, teasing way.

"Not sure." Music from towards Garrish reminded him that a celebration was about to begin, and he said, "I'm at the British Cemetery, and—"

"Love that place!" Jackie gushed. "I took my mother last year to the memorial service. So nice."

"We're having another one today. A relative is in from the U.K., and I've been asked to speak in about five minutes." Perhaps suggested, not asked, but he needed to wrap this up, and that gave him cause.

"La-di-da, respect to you. So, I can reschedule your appointment whenever I want?"

"Check my calendar. Thanks." He clicked to close the connection, and he called for the ensign to join him.

"This is exciting, sir," Chance remarked, as he brushed the toes of his shoes on the backs of his pant legs to remove the dust.

"Anything on the plaques?"

"Lots of possibilities, sir—"

A shiny, black car with tinted windows appeared, interrupting the conversation, and the tires crunched as they moved from American tarmac to British soil. The grounds were leased to the British Commonwealth so the men buried there could rest forever on home soil. Behind them, the boat crew led by Rodney Keith in formal dress blues and a white-and-blue hat gathered as a very old woman exited the car, helped by a younger man who looked enough like her to be a grandson. Two other cars joined them, one with the logo for the *Ocracoke Observer* on the side.

Three members of the boat crew pulled out instruments, including a trumpet and flute, and they began to play *God Save the King* as Keith stepped forward to welcome their visitor and show her around the small cemetery. Braxton glanced beyond the poignant scene and took in a number of townspeople in the background, many dressed for the event in their best, with a few more casually dressed observers likely happening on the morning's activities unawares and stopping to take in the music and the visiting foreign nationals.

Crew Member Clary Cartier, freshened in dressier digs, broke from the crew to step forward and speak to Lieutenant Sallinger.

"Sir, did you have a chance to think about speaking this morning? I feel it would be a great honor to have someone from Station Hatteras Inlet add their words to what our supervisor has planned."

"I haven't spoken with Rodney—"

"No need, sir. I mentioned to him that you were here, and he seemed pleased. He said he would leave it up to you, but if you could say a few words, he thought our visitors would appreciate your time. Her first name is Ruby. "

"He did, did he? Okay, let's do this for Ruby. I'll be watching you for my go-ahead." And in his fatigues with bloodshot eyes and his brain about to crash. Heck, yeah, he could do this and make it sound good. *Not a lick of lazy in you, Braxton. No teddy bears needed. You always get the job done.*

He felt a yawn coming on, and he suppressed it. That would never do. Cartier returned to her position with the crew, and as Rodney Keith and the U.K. visitors took up their positions alongside the memorial plaques and the graves, a photographer from the *Observer* snapped several photos. Keith took the hand of the elderly woman and spoke to her privately, then he saluted her and turned to voice his next words to the crowd.

"Today, we honor the younger sister of …" and he continued for a minute or so, before he paused and turned slightly toward Braxton. Braxton glanced toward Cartier, and she motioned that it was time. Braxton cleared his throat and began to speak.

"Partners in leadership, brothers in war, and forever linked through the sacrifice of the men we honor today. Ruby, I am honored to represent the U.S. Coast Guard Station Hatteras Inlet and wish to express my sincere appreciation and gratitude for the lives lost with the *Bedfordshire* and especially for …"

MORE MUSIC from the boat crew, some minor socializing, and the crowd evaporated, like a mist dissipating into the nooks and crannies of island life, island homes, and island backstreets once opened for the summer and now preparing to batten down the hatches for a winter blow.

Crew Member Clary Cartier located the lieutenant after the visitors from the U.K. were bundled up and shipped off to wherever they would spend the afternoon, asking, "Sir, would you like a ride to your car?"

Braxton turned to Ensign Chance and asked, "Ensign, how about a ride back to our car?"

"Sure, um," and Chance grinned, getting the lieutenant's question for what it was. "That'd be great, Clary, except our car's about one island away."

"Silly me," Cartier ducked her head and turned red. "You said you were out all night, and I saw your boat at the pier. Anywhere else I can take you while you're on the island? I will have to return to the station for transportation. Everyone walked here, so we're having to walk back."

"Sir?" Chance gave the lieutenant the choice.

"If I had a lick of lazy in me, I'd take you up on that offer, but I don't, and the ensign has more energy than two men know what to do with, so we'll be fine. We need to enjoy the weather while it's being friendly, anyway. Our feet will be satisfactory."

Braxton nodded his appreciation to Cartier, but what he needed was walking time to discuss the ensign's assessment of any possible clues he might have unearthed from the inscriptions sprinkled throughout the cemetery. She saluted him before joining her team heading to the station, and he noted the sun even now crawling higher into the sky. He had unrolled his sleeves before speaking at the ceremony, and he took the time to reroll each one a matching number of times. Satisfied, they moved down British Cemetery Road toward Garrish; and as they traveled, he quizzed Chance, "The plaques, Ensign, anything I need to be aware of?"

"To read, sir? Not unless you feel so inclined. I'm wondering if it's less about what they say than how they are arranged. Look at this." Chance pulled a folded sheet of paper from his pocket, and he opened it to a sketch of how the cemetery was laid out, along with the plaques and each marker. He had included the cardinal directions, north, south, east, and west, and the names of the two streets bordering the location of the cemetery.

"Explain." Braxton took the paper, studied it, and handed it back to the ensign. The cemetery area was tightly contained, with a sign identifying it as the British Cemetery, some stonework, and a white, picket fence delineating the actual graves. The fence was likely to keep people from trampling over the burial plots. People were curious, after all. They would walk wherever they were given access. A crushed stone pathway within the picket fence provided a walkway. A large granite monument told much of the story of the cemetery, with smaller metal plaques on wooden posts within the fenced off area, each one providing additional information about the long-ago incident.

"See here, sir." Chance pulled a pen from his pocket and clicked it to expose the ballpoint head. On an open area of the paper, he replicated the position of the plaques giving the historical aspects of the area with quick strokes, and then he connected each one with a firm slash. "There's a pattern, sir. Match it up with the island, and it might tell us something."

"Match it with what?" It didn't resemble Ocracoke that Braxton could tell.

"I don't know that yet, sir. The streets, perhaps, or different boats moored at Silver Lake. Maybe it's tied in with shops that are still open this time of the year." Chance was motioning around them at the things they could see. "Perhaps they left things scattered throughout town, a certain type of shell, or it could be the way the street signs are angled—"

"The angle of the street signs, a clue towards solving our crime with the missing sailboat." Braxton chuckled. "My daddy didn't raise me to be no fool, but if I'd suggested that to him when I was your age …"

"Maybe not the street signs, sir, but you've got to consider all the possibilities, or you'll never get the right answer. Like last night, you were telling the deputy about leeway drift. Nobody even guessed that was a thing before Allen and Artenbury. Now we know to look in places that suggest where something *might* have gone, not where we *expect* it to have gone." Chance grinned, as if he had made the announcement of a lifetime.

"And how do we do that on an island? There's no leeway drift on land." Braxton pictured the missing person from the sailboat tumbling down an island road end over end, tossed about by the wind. *That's a tumbleweed, Ensign, and the Outer Banks doesn't have tumbleweeds.*

"The way I see it, sir, there is."

"Oh?" Braxton paused. They were back at Garrish, and on the right was the Anchorage Inn. To the left, trees blocked the view, but directly ahead was Silver Lake. A recreational area with a waterfront pool likely belonged to the inn. Left would allow them more varied options if they wished to find lunch, but right would carry them back to the Coast Guard station.

"Yes, sir. On the sea, leeway drift is pressure, both from the wind and water, forcing an object this way or that. The same happens on land." He shrugged as if anyone could have figured out that.

"Go on, Ensign. Enlighten me with more of your theory." Braxton pointed right. They would head towards the station. Food would likely be available there. If not, they could take up the young crew member on her offer of a ride.

"All this, sir." Chance waved his hand at the crowded shores of Silver Lake. "Smugglers, would they choose this place to stash their loot? No, sir. Why? Pressure. Well, not exactly pressure like from the wind or water, but still. There are people, lots of infrastructure, and likely security cameras all around here. Leeway drift will force them out. They'll want a place where they can be unobserved."

"And your map of the cemetery tells us where that might be."

"I don't know, sir, but it might be a clue. Anyway, that's what I've got so far, and hopefully, it's something."

"Our only clue, and it's from the British Cemetery. Leeway drift, huh?" They were approaching the ferry landing, and they could see their boat bobbing at the pier. Braxton gave the ensign a sideways glance.

"Yes, sir. Leeway drift." Chance grinned.

"Then it's time we learned where our boat drifted to, and maybe we'll find the man that went overboard the night of our drug bust."

"Yes, sir. That's what I'm good at."

Braxton nodded. *It's why I brought you along, Ensign. It's time to earn your paycheck. Tonight, I want to sleep in my own bed, not spend it on a boat in the Sound searching for a sailboat that doesn't want to be found.*

He smiled at his turn of words. It was about time to put all those county people to shame and show them how good the Coast Guard really was.

LUNCH FOR the day was courtesy of Station Ocracoke at the invitation of Supervisor Rodney Keith.

Lieutenant Braxton Sallinger and Ensign Christian Chance passed the landing as the ferry was arriving, and they took the time to observe the massive boat as it navigated Silver Lake and lowered its ramp to allow the cars onboard to disembark the water-borne taxi service.

"That's two-and-a-half hours they'll never get back." Braxton's fog from his night on the water had lifted during the ceremony back at the British Cemetery, but with the morning nearing lunch, and no obvious opportunities for food within view, the murky side of life on a small island lapped at his doorstep.

"Yes, sir," Chance agreed. Then he grinned. "They likely think it's the best wasted hours of the day."

"C'mon, man, you really think so?" Then, they hadn't been up all night, either. Braxton would concede that.

"Of course, sir. We live here. Many of these people see this as something new and novel. See the different states?"

Sure enough, the cars had begun to exit the ferry, and while many of them wore local North Carolina plates, others revealed travelers from Florida, Virginia, and Texas.

Before long, the ferry was emptied, and the line waiting for access to Cedar Island moved toward the ferry to "load 'er up" for the return trip. Two trucks with long travel trailers followed one another on board, and one panel truck with FISH on the back and a refrigerated unit humming away over the cab caused the ferry to list to one side until the additional weight of the final vehicles leveled it out. As the final SUV drove onboard, a truck approached, proving that Rodney Keith, at least, hadn't walked to the cemetery. He rolled his window down to speak to the two men.

"Lieutenant Sallinger!" Rodney waved them over.

"Rodney," Braxton called, and he returned the wave and grinned, despite his clouded brain.

"You two, thank you for showing up this morning. Ruby shared that she appreciated your words. So did I. I don't have the eloquence you do, Braxton."

"Nah, it's nothing. You know why we're here, don't you?"

"Clary mentioned something about that missing boat." Rodney motioned towards the harbor. The dock it had been tied up at was visible but bare as a stringer of fish on a day without a catch.

"And a dead body out in the Sound. Hey, the ensign and I got breakfast at the deli down on Garrish—"

"Breakfast?" Rodney laughed. "Man, it's time for lunch. You two, my treat. Especially if you're willing to cook. How about it, Ensign?" He called his comment to Chance.

"Yes, sir. I can cook, and for lunch, I can cook up a storm."

"I haven't told you what we're having."

"Yes, sir. No matter, I can cook up whatever's in your pantry."

"He's always this chipper?" Rodney directed his question to Braxton but pointed towards Chance.

"Pretty much. I heard you say lunch. How soon?"

"Soon's your ensign gets it done up. I suspect my people

— 266 —

will be glad for someone else to do the cooking for a change. We don't have a CS, and our current AUXCA is on leave. We've been filling in, some meals more successfully than others."

"Ah," Braxton commented. By CS, he knew the station supervisor meant the culinary specialist, or chef, in other words. For a sub-station like Ocracoke, an auxiliary culinary assistance worker would fill in the gap if the station chef was away. If their AUXCA was also out, he bet they would indeed be glad for a break from cooking for themselves. "We're in. We'll meet you there."

Ensign Chance was good to his word, and he had a hearty meal of meat and pasta set out for each member of the boat crew by the time everyone returned and had changed into more casual clothing. Chance joined the crew round the table, and he regaled them with descriptive renditions of the events that had kept them out all night.

His drawing of the British Cemetery turned into a discussion of his theory of drug smugglers using the cemetery as a type of "smugglers' code." Ray Murray listened to the different views espoused by various discussion participants before inserting his observations into a lull in the conversation.

"Let me see that, Christian." Ray pulled the paper to him, held out his hand for the ensign's pen, and on the back of the paper, drew a simple sketch of the streets around the cemetery and wrote in *cemetery* on the wedge of land at the corner of Cemetery Road and Boos Lane. Then, to the side, he sketched what was clearly Silver Lake and continued down the western border of the island to the south past the village. Then he turned the paper around to show his friend. "What do you see in that?"

Ensign Chance touched the paper where Ray had drawn the cemetery, then ran his finger down the shore of the island before looking up at Ray with a grin.

"They match."

Braxton pulled the paper from the man, looked at it, and nodded to Ray Murray. They were right. The shape of the plot the cemetery claimed and where one section along the shore jutted into the Sound matched near enough to be exact, both pointing due west.

"What's this point called?" He laid the paper on the table in front of Ray and tapped the location.

"Springer's Point," Ray said, with several other crew nodding or saying they had been there.

"Populated?" Meaning, would leeward drift push drug smugglers toward Springer's Point or away from it?

Rodney answered, "It's a nature preserve. No one lives there. The Coastal Land Trust maintains it for hiking and such, fully accessible to the public."

"Leeward drift, Ensign?" Braxton nodded at Chance, lifting an eyebrow to make his point.

"Yes, sir, leeward drift." Chance grinned. He stood, retrieved a large bowl of banana pudding, handed out dessert plates, and began to fill each one and pass them out.

"Leeward drift?" Rodney twisted his face in puzzlement. "I don't get it."

"Ask the ensign to explain. It's pudding time for me." Braxton took the bowl of pudding offered to him, made his way to a window, and looked toward his craft floating in the harbor as he stood and enjoyed the last of his meal.

Leeward drift, indeed. That would be too easy. Braxton hoped the ensign didn't get a case of the shakes when they had to head back out to have another gander in the Sound. The next high tide was likely to roll over them before that boat made itself known. His phone buzzed, and he worked it out of a pocket. Without much of a glance, he put it to his ear and answered.

"Braxton."

"Is that all you have to say for yourself, Lieutenant Sallinger?" It was Jackie Powers.

"You have my new appointment with Bollinger?" He chuckled. "I say I want a day off first, if you do. Last night on the water's about done me in."

"About that, they say they'll try to work you in. I'm expecting a call back towards the end of the week. I called about a report I received. It's not *your* report, which it should be *eventually*, but it's *someone's* report, and I'm handing it off to you."

"That didn't make a lick of sense to me, Jackie. You caught what I said about last night about doing me in. Say it differently so I can follow you."

"The man you sent us from last night, well, it seems we need a medical examiner to determine the cause of death—"

"Wha—?! I mean, you're kidding me, right? Does some-body need a teddy bear for a good time or something? The man was face down in the water. He looked like he had been living rough at the end, but even I could see—"

"Hold on, cowboy," Jackie interrupted, crashing his tirade. "I'm the messenger, so don't string me on the trotline for just relaying the message."

"I'm sorry, Jackie. With last night … I need sleep. I'll try to contain my frustration."

"That's better, and I accept your apology. Now, the county says to call Raleigh, and they'll send someone out, hopefully today. They want to get this wrapped up."

"Dare County?"

"Well, sir, we are in Dare County. At least I am. You? Don't tell them you're in Hyde County, and they might hurry on out." She snickered, showing she wasn't especially irritated.

"And why is this my job and not Dare County's?" He wasn't sure that it was the Coast Guard's responsibility, and in his sleep-deprived state, he wanted badly to give it to someone else.

"Buck up, Buckaroo. I may work for the Coast Guard, but I'm only a civilian administrative assistant. I don't make the rules. I just disseminate them. The county did make one request, and that's for you to ask for Steven Hill, if he's available."

"So, this directive is from the county."

"Oh, did I say that?" Jackie chuckled. "You can forget you heard whatever you think I said. Do you need the number?"

"Text it to me."

The ensign had approached to collect the lieutenant's empty dessert dish, and he glanced at the phone. "Sir, anything I can help with?"

"Yes." Another reason to appreciate a gung-ho, enthusiastic subordinate. "Here's the number of the medical examiner's office. Request Steven Hill to come explain why our dead man died."

"Yes, sir." Ensign Chance took the phone and reached for the dessert dish.

"Not so fast. I'm still eating."

"Yessir, right, sir. You finish eating, and I'll take care of Steven Hill. I trust you're enjoying that pudding. It's my grand-mother's recipe."

"I watched you prepare it, Ensign. Your grandmother used a package mix?"

"Yes, sir, she did. Just like I prepared it today, and it was just this good, too."

"Right, Ensign." Braxton laughed. "You go make that call, and I might have seconds."

"Yes, sir. My grandmother would be pleased to hear you say that."

Braxton turned back to the window and noted a few clouds filling in on the horizon. He thought of that old saying, red sky at night, sailor's delight. Red sky in the morning, sailor's warning … or was it the other way around? Behind him, he heard Chance say, "Good afternoon, this is Ensign Christian Chance with the Coast Guard, Station Hatteras Inlet. I'm calling from Station Ocracoke on Lieutenant Braxton Sallinger's phone. We picked up a dead man in Pamlico Sound last night. Is Steven Hill available to serve as the acting medical examiner?"

Braxton scraped his dish as the ensign's side of the conversation continued, with a "Yes, ma'am," and an "I don't know, ma'am," and a couple instances of "I'm not sure, ma'am" in there. Braxton turned to look at him to have the ensign shrug back at him. The ensign finally lowered the phone, covered it with a hand and asked, "Where will Mr. Hill find the body, sir?"

Braxton almost said Swan Quarter, which would mean the Hyde County courthouse, but that was only because Deputy Dingman had been with them out on the Sound. His presence was incidental to the drowning, and the body had been released into Dare County's custody. Three organizational groups were tangled up in this, four if he counted Deputy Magruder with his drone-on-loan from Carteret County, all linked in the drug bust and maybe in the effort to match up a man found floating in the Pamlico Sound with the possible sixth man from the drug runner's boat or from the sailboat which was now definitely and conveniently missing.

"Sir? What would you like me to tell the lady?" Chance requested.

"Dare County. I'll call back and let them know where."

"Yes, sir." Chance put the phone back to his ear and relayed the lieutenant's instructions. Finished, he returned the phone to his superior.

"Thank you, Ensign." Braxton tapped his contacts, and without hesitation, he clicked on Lieutenant Diane Turnipseed's name. She had been their go-to person in Dare County during the drug bust. Surely she would know where the body had gone. When it picked up, he said, "Braxton Sallinger here. Diane? I need to see if you can give me some help here."

When he mentioned Steven Hill's name, Braxton knew he had made the right call. Diane assured him she knew Steven, he had worked with them many times, and she would make all the arrangements. Would Braxton like to be kept in the loop?

Heck, yeah, he thought. *Someone channeled this through me, and the Coast Guard never shirks its duty. We get tough, and we get going, 'cause there's not a lick of lazy where the Coast Guard's concerned.*

AFTER HIS all-nighter and two bowls of Ensign Chance's banana pudding—*made from his grandmother's recipe*—Braxton awoke to find himself in the Ocracoke Station's lounge with both feet propped on an ottoman and a blanket woven with images of the island roughly tossed across his torso and legs.

"Wha—!?!" He jerked his head forward, brushed away the burn in his eyes, and pulled himself to a seated position. A quick movement brought his feet to the floor, and he lifted the blanket with him as he stood. Three quick folds, and he draped it across the back of the chair, unsure what else to do with it. He checked his phone … an hour and a half. Heck, yeah, he had needed that. No, he didn't have the time to spare. He had to admit he felt better, but where the heck was his ensign?

He found the answer when cheering pulled him to the windows. Towards the boat ramp, the six duty watchstanders currently assigned to Station Ocracoke from Station Hatteras Inlet were divided into two teams in a race to see who could wrestle a lifeboat from the bays attached to the building to the water and launch them without overturning or someone getting submerged in the lagoon.

The station supervisor, Rodney Keith, and Ensign Chance

were to the side and cheering them on. Chance had an arm pumping the air as if he could inject enthusiasm into his team, but Braxton wasn't entirely convinced either boat crew was committed to winning. It seemed the fun was in finding ways to sabotage the other team, even if it meant abandoning their own efforts and leaving their team short-handed.

Boat Crew Clary Cartier from the ceremony at the British Cemetery darted to the opposing team to give Ray Murray a push on the shoulder, sending his team's boat askew. Ray raised a fist to yell at her, but his laughter meant he had enjoyed the roughhousing as much as Clary seemed to.

Boat Crew Joan Buckner, a tall redhead Braxton knew from Hatteras, was on Ray's team, likely to balance the male vs. female ratio between the teams, although she made two of Clary with her broad shoulders. She had a wrestling background, if Braxton remembered correctly, as evidenced in her wide stance and muscled legs.

Two others Braxton knew but hadn't spoken with since arriving on the island that morning were James Gaskill, boat crew, and Harry Farrow, serving in the same capacity. He recalled that James and Joan Buckner hoped for a future ship assignment, with James as an engineer in training and Joan as a deck watch officer. Both positions were entry level assignments on a ship, but if that was their dream … Braxton enjoyed the shore. Too much time at sea gave him a case of the shakes.

His phone vibrated, and he pulled it from his pocket. In one motion, he clicked to answer and put it to his ear.

"Braxton."

"Thank you, Lieutenant."

"Jackie?" Of course, it was. He still wasn't fully awake, but he was getting there, and he chuckled. "You're welcome. For what?"

"For taking care of the medical examiner, of course."

"It wasn't me. I contacted the county, and not Hyde—"

"I would think not." Jackie laughed.

"Oh, Hyde's all right. I've nothing against them, but then I'm not assigned to a county, because I'm—"

"Coast Guard! I've heard it all, Lieutenant. The best of the best and all that. However, we've got a hitch in our plans to get Steven Hill here."

"Diane Turnipseed with C-District said she was taking care of that." He shrugged it off. The contest outdoors was more interesting, and the watchstanders on Rodney Keith's side were carrying him over their shoulders and toward the water as if they intended to toss him in when they got there. One man underneath the struggling boatswain mate, Logan Radisson, Braxton thought, was dripping as though he had already gone in.

"I talked with Diane. She found Mr. Hill. He's perfectly willing to join us in the capacity of medical examiner, but the hitch is that he's on vacation."

"Does he want a hankie with that? It means he has the time."

"No hankies needed, Lieutenant. Hear me out. He's on vacation in Wilmington." Jackie paused, giving Braxton time to work it out.

Braxton painted the picture immediately. The drive from Wilmington to Morehead City was two hours on an easy day. The ferry terminal on Cedar Island was half an hour or more past that. And the last ferry of the day departed around four-thirty or thereabouts.

"A bug in a rug," Braxton said, not especially to Jackie, but as a stopgap in his thinking process. "He's on his way, then?"

"Yessir, coming up 17 as I speak to you."

"Through Jacksonville." If the man caught the last ferry, it would be nearly seven before he arrived, too late to seriously consider getting across Ocracoke to grab the free ferry to Hatteras. If he did, he'd be arriving in Hatteras Village about nine or ten, with another half an hour to get to Buxton and the sheriff's sub-station there. Who knew where the body had gone, likely to the main facilities in Manteo, another hour north. He thought, *Why Wilmington, man? Vacation in Dare County. Then you're where we need you.* If they needed him, and that was never a certainty. This wasn't Steven Hill's fault, but it was dang sure inconvenient.

"You coming up with a plan, Lieutenant?" Jackie, putting all the responsibility on Braxton, which he had to admit was right where it belonged, as she was a civilian employee of the Guard and not an enlisted member.

"What did Diane say?"

"Oh, lots." She laughed. "You know Diane. If it's in her head, it comes out. She said to see if he makes it. If not, she wanted me to ask if you still have your boat there on the island. That's your island, not our island, Lieutenant. I hope I got that sorted out for you."

"Yes, I'm with you. My daddy didn't raise—"

"—no fool. You keep saying that, mister, and one day you'll convince me."

"Why did she want to know about my boat?" He suspected he knew. He could make the trip from Silver Lake to Cedar Island and back again in less time than the ferry took one way. If Steven Hill missed the ferry, Diane had a backup plan, and it was him.

"As if you have to ask that." Jackie snorted at his question, and she said, "Contact her direct if you want. You need the lieutenant's phone number?"

"I called her first. She's in my phone."

"Silly me! Of course, she is. Well, Lieutenant, I'll let you get to it. I've got other things to do besides chat with you. Don't leave the medical examiner stranded. Now that he's on county time …"

"Thank you, Jackie, for the reminder. We're not county, remember," even though Station Hatteras Inlet *was* in Dare County, and a good working relationship between the two entities was vital to good law enforcement across the Dare County and Pamlico Sound region. "I might need Steven Hill's personal number."

"Diane thought you might. She's texting it direct to your phone."

His phone dinged, perfectly timed, and after he disengaged from Jackie, he studied the time displayed on his phone before mentally sorting the roads and travel time from Wilmington to Ocracoke. The man had to come through Jacksonville, a time-consuming jog away from the coast and always a bottleneck from the southern shores of North Carolina. He googled the last ferry from Cedar Island to Ocracoke, and it pulled up as 4:13 in his search results. He frowned, then noted that the actual departure time was 4:30. Confusing, that's what that was. He was certain Steven Hill *would* miss the departure, and now, he had to decide whether to wait to head out, considering that he might be wasting his time to Cedar Island and back, or if he was better to save a couple hours by heading out now and being there when Hill arrived.

Either way, it looked like Steven Hill was staying the night on the island, whether Ocracoke or Hatteras. He needed to make sure that Dare County had a plan to cover the man's accommodations. He opened his Contacts and tapped Diane Turnipseed's number.

"Turnipseed, here." She sounded preoccupied.

"Braxton, Diane. I'm calling about Steven Hill."

"Oh, yes. Hold your taters for a moment. I'm on another line." The phone went silent for a minute or two, and she came back on the line. "There, I'm free. About Steven, yes. We've worked out most of that for you. Did you hear from Jackie?"

"More than I wanted." He chuckled to ensure she caught that his comment was intended as a joke. "You don't expect him on the ferry, do you?"

"I'll bet tomorrow's breakfast on it. How's your afternoon playing out?" The question was clear. Can you pick up the slack?

"Right into your hands, the way I see it. I only have one question, head out now or wait to see if he's a faster driver than either you or I think he is."

"Ahh, some things are not ours to wish away. My watch is still ticking, so now is better, I reckon."

"I expected you to say that. Accommodations for the man? It'll be late when he gets up to your neck of the woods."

"Yeah, that's something else. When Steven and I talked, he was hesitant to bring his bike, not knowing if he would have to leave it somewhere—"

Meaning, Braxton thought, *that the good lieutenant was planning for him to ferry the medical examiner from Cedar Island all along.*

"—and he requested one of my officers to meet him in Ocracoke. She's to be his transportation while he's here."

"Sure. Why tell me?"

"She's already on the ferry your direction. With her car, of course, and she has requested to ride with you to Cedar Island."

"Fine." He considered that. He had planned on returning from retrieving the medical examiner and heading directly to Hatteras and bypassing Ocracoke entirely. If he needed to return for someone's car, then that was out. "Who am I meeting?"

"Emily Bryant. She's not with C-District specifically, but she *is* the county forensic investigator. It's why I'm sending her. She's sharp, and she might be of assistance to you."

"She will need to meet me here at the station next to the ferry landing." He glanced at a clock on the wall, calculated, then asked, "Two hours for her to get here, leaving her time to transfer her things from her car to my boat. I've got Steven's number. I'll coordinate with him for pickup on Cedar Island. Accommodations? It'll be late if they are heading back to Buxton tonight." And an hour later if they planned to drive into Kill Devil Hills or further north.

"If I tell the story honest, Buxton was my first choice, but there's likely better options in the village there. I'll have Ashley here at the sub-station call around and see what's available."

Braxton recognized the name. Ashley Dixon manned the front desk at the Buxton sub-station and took care of administrative details such as this. Braxton had spoken to her husband, Todd, on occasion.

"Anything else?" Diane seemed to consider the matter settled and likely had other things on her mind.

"You've connected the dots for me, Lieutenant. I appreciate your time and your help filling things in."

"For all sakes, Lieutenant, I'm not a coloring book. It's not like this isn't my job. I'm expecting you to hoggletie all this and get the county some results. You keep saying all that about your Coast Guard. It's about time to make a choice and be the man your superiors want you to be."

"Yes, ma'am." Braxton laughed. "I'm letting you go. I've got an ensign to coordinate with before I head to Cedar Island."

"You do that." The phone went dead without a salutation, and Braxton grinned. What a woman! He wouldn't want to work for her, though. He stepped to the door, opened it, and called, "Ensign Chance. You through playing out there? Cedar Island calls, and you're expected to be there with me."

"Cedar Island, sir?" Chance's pant legs were damp around the cuffs. He looked dismayed for a moment, then he pulled out his best Coast Guard self and snapped out, "Yes, sir. Of course, sir!"

Braxton closed the door. They had two hours, but it never hurt to keep ensigns on their toes. He found his chair again, pulled the blanket over him and planned to let the ensign ready the boat. He wanted more time with his eyes closed before they headed off with the Dare County forensic investigator in their care.

Chapter 9

Trouble on Cedar Island

FORENSIC INVESTIGATOR EMILY BRYANT adjusted the seat in her car. She was on the Hatteras to Ocracoke free ferry, and the cushion repeatedly vibrated under her with the thrumming of the ferry's engine. She drummed her fingers on her steering wheel. She had chosen to remain in her car, as opposed to heading topside to the small lounge, as the public areas on this ferry offered little to no appeal, and besides, the trip was only an hour one way.

An hour to plan a prank on Steven Hill.

She grinned and reached to stop her new Tarheel mirror trinket from spinning, turning it one way then another to allow the sun to catch in the crystal center portion embedded with the blue NC from the Tarheel logo. Around the outside, holding the crystal portion in place and allowing it to spin freely, the metal band was stamped in embossed black letters with Tar Heels.

"Tarheels," she said to the trinket. "One word, though I

guess they should know. Still—"

Behind her, in the seat, a package with the logo of a Kill Devil Hills bakery waited patiently. When Steven got in her car, she intended to offer him a brownie, only she'd eaten the original brownie and replaced it with a brown "E" cut from cardboard and painted to look like a real brownie. As a backup, she had a can of silly string in the console rigged to fire when it was opened. She intended for Steven to be the one to enjoy opening her console.

This off-island excursion would be one she enjoyed to its fullest. She said it all the time: *saltwater cures all.* You couldn't get much more "saltwater" than on a Coast Guard boat with a Coast Guard lieutenant and an ensign to pilot them across the Pamlico Sound.

One thing had surprised her on her drive down: the change in the weather. Certainly, summer had slipped into fall, and even on the Outer Banks, winter was winter, although it wasn't winter yet. However, it had been cool, even coat weather in the Hills, and she had brought a heavy jacket … the boat and being on the water … that always made it colder, didn't it? And still, she'd watched the temperature on her car's outdoor sensor climb up over ten degrees on her drive down. If she kept heading south, it was likely to become summer again, and who wouldn't like that?

Bare feet and salty hair were worth two points in her score-book any day.

Her phone rang, and she glanced at it to see it was Ashley Dixon at the Buxton sub-station. She tapped the phone, and when Ashley's face appeared, she teased, "So, Ashley, the lieutenant has you doing the dirty work, I see." She smiled, and the little image of her face in one corner of the screen repeated the expression just a second after she did. "What'cha need?"

"A day off work and a big box of Krispy Kremes. Are you

offering?"

"If you're willing to share." Thinking about it, she had forgotten to catch lunch before boarding the ferry. The prospect of being on the Coast Guard boat in an official, county capacity had distracted her, and her only thought had been getting on the ferry as quickly as possible. Now, she wished the brown "E" in the bag was a real brownie, because she would eat it up, if it were.

"Well, we'd have to discuss that. So, on to number two. The lieutenant would like me to relay a message to you. I'm reading this, so pardon me if I can't decipher her handwriting. If I get something wrong, blame the author, not the reader. Here goes: Past the ferry landing. Braxton Sallinger. Unknown ensign. Have plenty of Dramamine. Still working on your accommodations."

"Did I hear you say accommodations? Don't tell me you said accommodations, Ashley Dixon."

"I'm not telling you I said anything, Emily Bryant." In the phone's image, Ashley gave Emily an innocent look. "But you heard what you heard, so if you think you heard the 'A' word, well, you do with that what you want."

"What I wanted was to be back home tonight." Emily tightened her jaw, then she gave in and smiled. "Free night on the county. Do you at least have an island name?"

"I read what I said. You told me not to say it again. I'll call you when I know more, that is if anyone thinks to tell me what's going on. I'm the one always left out of the loop."

"I try to keep you in the loop, girl. Don't go leaving me out of the loop."

Both ladies laughed before the phones disconnected, and Emily was once more alone in her car. Up ahead, she could see the ferry landing, just a small space on the tip of a sandy comma separating the Atlantic Ocean from the Pamlico Sound. It didn't look like much, did it, but indeed, it was what kept the North Carolina mainland protected from the raging waters of the open seas … as long as they didn't rage while she was here, and she laughed as she imagined the storm as a giant angry man shaking his black storm fist at the island to threaten it and all the people who lived on its sandy shores.

The car in front of her flashed its brake lights, and she started her engine, released the parking brake and pulled forward. When her tires hit the tarmac, it felt almost as good as driving onto sand. *Ocracoke,* she thought. *Except for no roads to and from anywhere, I'd love to live here.* She did like her feet on the sand, although New York was sometimes fun, as was Manteo, New Bern, even Goldsboro … although for her money, Wilson was a better fit. Better shopping opportunities.

On the way into the village at the opposite end of the island, she allowed her mind to wander as she passed dune after dune, with only occasional glimpses of water. Mostly her mind wandered onto Steven's reaction when he opened his bag of brownies to find a single brown "E" inside. How much fun was that going to be?

Driving through the village, she noticed a shiny, black car with deeply tinted windows. It passed her heading east towards the ferry she'd just vacated. As she reached the ferry landing, she recognized a familiar face and rolled down her window and waved.

"Lieutenant Sallinger, hello."

"Emily?" Sallinger shaded his eyes and walked her direction. "I expected a county car. Why are you in this?"

"I don't have one assigned to me. This is my personal transport." She laughed. "I like the stipend more than the prestige. Where should I park?"

Sallinger motioned to an empty area, and she pulled up and cut her engine. She climbed out, gazed longingly at the brown bag from her back seat, and closed the door. She turned, smiled, and said, "I saw a fancy black car down the road. Any ideas what that's about?"

"Tinted windows?"

"Enough to look well-heeled. I assume you know the one?"

"We had a ceremony at the British Cemetery today. Someone named Ruby from the U.K. I said a few words."

"Oh, if I'd known, I'd have come earlier."

"You wouldn't."

"Likely you're right. Still, I'd have thought about it. How soon are we leaving out?"

"When you're ready. You have anything else you need to take with you?"

"A coat, perhaps. It was cold up north, but here ... what do you think? And my forensic bag possibly. Anytime the medical examiner is called in, that seems a likely tool to have handy."

"Your coat might not survive. I'll have a slicker for you onboard. The forensic bag, that's your call. We're going there and back with no side trips, unless you know something I don't."

"I know a lot you don't, but I'm here for the ride. You're in control. Just tell me where the coffee is, and I'll prop my feet up and let you get at it."

"Wrong ship, ma'am. That one docks in Miami and has stops in Nassau and Port-au-Prince, only I don't recommend you disembark there."

"Then I'm stuck with you. Do I have time to get some food?" She had out her key, and she released the deck lid and pulled out her forensic bag, with her camera and some additional materials inside. *Just in case, mind you*, she thought.

"Inside the station. My ensign prepared extra at lunch, and I can request him to warm something up. And yes, we have time."

His ensign prepared lunch? She was certain that Lieutenant

Sallinger was assigned to Station Hatteras Inlet. She wanted to ask why "his" ensign was cooking at Station Ocracoke, but the thought of food distracted her, and she filed the question away for another time.

EMILY ENJOYED Ensign Chance's meat and pasta, even reheated, but she swooned over the banana pudding, even as she declined an offer of a large serving or a second helping. She laughed and said, "I'll need two Dramamines if you keep plying me with good food."

She enjoyed greeting several members of the boat crew. The supervisor for the station, Rodney Keith, was off on a grocery run with Clary Cartier and James Gaskill. The hole in the attendance roster became Christian Chance's opportunity to introduce Ray Murray as a close friend from Hatteras. Emily picked up that both Christian and Ray liked to have a good time, and if they made it back this way, she planned to get with Christian to prank Ray. She had several good ideas in her bag of tricks that she could spring on the man. Lieutenant Sallinger finally pointed them toward the boat, telling the group that they had a guest to retrieve, and they would be back later.

"C'mon. This way, people. Not a lick of lazy in me, but you people I don't know about. Tide's rolling in, and I got me a medical examiner that wants to come this way."

"Yes, sir," Ensign Chance snapped, pulling himself tall and boarding the vessel. He mentioned Calvin's name as he instructed Emily to where she might be most comfortable. "The trip might get rough, and you'll want to be able to hang on."

Emily paused and asked, "Calvin Dingman? From Swan Quarter?"

"Yes, ma'am. He was out with us all last night."

"Calvin was with you when you found the body?" Why hadn't she been told? He might be a source of information that she needed to interview. The more she knew for forensics, the better judgement she could make.

"Well, yes and no, ma'am." The ensign was focused on readying the boat to leave. Ray Murray and Logan Radisson were prepared to release the lines as soon as the engines fired up. Before hitting the start switch, he looked at her and grinned. "He was with us, but we didn't find the body. We rescued the two kids from drowning."

"Lieutenant Sallinger?" She laughed. "Did you people also discover the cure for cancer, maybe revolutionize interplanetary travel to eliminate the space-time paradox?"

"That's good." Chance laughed. "Did you hear that, sir? Did we revolutionize whatever she said?"

Sallinger laughed, assured the ensign that they did not, and motioned for him to fire up the engine. As the boat trembled with rough power before settling into a throaty rumble, Sallinger opened a locker and selected a slicker for their guest. Emily donned the offered slicker and settled in for the ride across the Sound. As they exited the lagoon and entered the Sound, Ensign Chance upped the speed of the vessel until it felt like they were skimming across a bathtub, a very rough bathtub, with the bottom of the craft jittering and occasionally slamming into larger swells.

"How long does this last?" Emily asked.

"All the way," Sallinger assured her. "That's why the ensign chose your seating position so carefully."

"Time, I mean. Thirty minutes, an hour?" When she'd asked to join the ride, well, this wasn't at all like the sport fishing boat they'd taken on their failed mission to Cape Lookout. The weather might be better, but she couldn't say that for the ride.

"We travel at twice the speed of the ferry, and it takes two-and-a-half hours. So figure an hour-and-a-quarter," the ensign called to her. He had to yell with the sound of the wind whipping over the top of the boat.

The ride killed most conversation, except for occasional questions or pointers for various scenic views. They encountered the Cedar Island-Ocracoke ferry chugging along towards Ocracoke, but at twice the speed, it was soon lost to view. When Cedar Island topped the horizon, Emily was surprised at how beautiful it looked.

But beautiful was not the point, and she didn't know that it could claim that, but it was certainly welcome. It was land, and it was a chance for the ensign to slow the boat and give her body time to recover. When they neared the pier, Steven Hill was waiting with the man who had given him a ride, and he had a small leather case and a larger suitcase at his side. As they slowed, the man with him shook hands, gave him a one-armed hug, then waved as he walked back to shore.

"My brother-in-law," Steven shared as he handed his bags onboard and jumped in. He noticed the extra person on the deck. He put one hand on his hip and gave her a mock look of surprise. "Emily, is this a joke? I mean, hello. I didn't expect to see you. Do I get one of those?" He flipped the collar of her slicker and let it fall back into place.

"You, letting your beard grow." She laughed. The last time she had seen him, it had been tightly painted across his face. Now, he was a beach bum, or perhaps a mountain man, except there were no mountains anywhere near any beach that fronted the North Carolina shore.

"Vacation." He rubbed a hand across the beard. "Shelina is still in Antarctica, so there's no one to tell me otherwise. I like not trimming it."

"You poor thing." Emily seriously felt for the man, although she made it into a tease. Shelina, his wife, was a scientist and researcher now on the southern continent, and he likely missed her.

"Are we ready?" Sallinger interrupted the reunion. "We've still got light, and I hope to keep it that way until we get back. By the way, Hill, we passed your ferry on the way."

"My ferry? Seriously? Another joke? Is this woman rubbing off on you?" Steven shook his head and automatically found a place to position himself for the ride across the sound. As they idled away from the pier, he said, "I sure wanted to head down to Harker's Island. There's a ferry down there that goes to Cape Lookout. Have any of you ever been? My brother-in-law said it's beautiful on the point. It's like being all alone on a deserted island."

Emily raised her hand, and when Steven shot her a puzzled look, she yelled over the sound of the engine as the boat picked up speed.

"We were out towards the Cape a few days back looking for a missing sailboat. A storm blew up—"

"You were out in that? Even down south, we got slammed. You and who else?" Steven looked impressed.

"Let me see, um," and she counted off on her hands, "Sean. You remember him."

"Yes. Young, a bit cocky."

"Okay, you remember. Jason, me of course, Diane and the Hyde County sheriff. Plus a few others."

"Darlene Pafford? Why Darlene?"

"You do get around," she teased. Still, Hyde County called in medical examiners, also, so likely, he'd been there. "Hyde County and Dare County are in a joint investigation. Drugs, that type of stuff. Now, there's a dead body, and you're expected to tell us why he died."

"That's what Lieutenant Turnipseed said. I hear I might be staying on Ocracoke tonight. What do you know about that?"

"Well, I'm your wheels, so that means two of us. Ashley at the sub-station in Buxton is making arrangements, hopefully by the time we get back."

"Okay, but I'll need a good internet connection. I brought my work gear." He indicated one of his bags. "People hear we're going to an island, and they don't understand that we work real jobs, and that takes real work."

"Mine, too. Fully equipped for whatever we come across." Emily lifted the strap to her gear bag to show that she was equally ready for whatever they encountered.

"Sure," Steven nodded. "You understand. This is not a joke. None of this is a joke." He motioned around them.

They approached another ferry, this one heading toward Cedar Island. It wasn't packed, and it rode higher in the water and seemed to be making better speed than the previous one.

"Dead men usually aren't. This boat isn't either. This ride is beating me up." Emily was certain she would be sore tomorrow.

"Tell me why you came. You could have stayed in the village and waited."

"Sand, sea." She motioned around them. The sun was dropping closer to the Sound, and the sky was going red. In the distance, the shore of their destination was just visible. "I'm on the sand every day, but this, on a real Coast Guard boat? This rocks."

Steven nodded while keeping his eyes on the distant clouds just where the sun would soon be going down for the evening … before they reached the harbor, if Christian Chance didn't keep the pedal to the metal.

Then, if he did, she likely wouldn't be able to walk tomorrow, so they were in dire straits no matter which way it went. Truly, today, the Banks were calling, and they were saying, "Spend some time on the sand, Emily," and she was glad to agree.

"THE BLACK car and the British Cemetery. A ceremony?

What was that all about?" Emily leaned toward Ensign Chance. She had to be right next to him to carry on a decent conversation. Steven Hill had taken over Lieutenant Sallinger, and they were huddled over a screen looking at weather reports, depth charts, or other such boating stuff. She was a beach girl, and if it didn't impact her time on the sand, it wasn't of much interest to her.

"A fluke, that's all." Chance grinned, his ineffable cheerfulness refusing to be dampened even by the growing dusk and damp sea air.

"You must know more than that." The lack of information frustrated her. If she only had a fart bladder, she'd find a way to put it under the young man to get his attention, although how well anyone would be able to hear it was up for debate. Boating was proving to be a noisy activity.

"Sure, some lady named Ruby knew someone buried there." One of the ensign's screens revealed their course relative to the islands around them, and their little blip shifted position, distracting him while also revealing their progress. He adjusted course, and he continued, "She was British."

"With an accent British?" That would be interesting.

"I don't know." Chance shrugged. "I didn't talk with her. The lieutenant was asked to speak, and then everyone dispersed. One thing you might like. The crew at the station played live music."

"A party!" Emily laughed. "Now I wish I had come."

"Not that type of music. Monarchy music, the song that copies *America the Beautiful*."

"Ah, yes. *God Save the King*. Except it's the other way around. They had it first. She must have been someone important to get all that. Hey, I need to speak to the medical examiner, and I see he's free. We'll talk again later."

"Sure, anytime. I'm not going anywhere." He slapped his hand on the dashboard two times for emphasis.

Steven stood at the stern, his lanky body holding up a rigid support, and his legs absorbing the thudding impacts of the boat's hull effortlessly as it slapped each wave it crossed. He had pulled a pocket New Testament from his breast pocket and was reading it.

"Anything good in there?" Emily grasped a handhold, and she positioned herself next to him.

"Oh, lots." He touched the page to hold his place and looked up at her. "This is the story of Jesus turning the water into wine."

"Tell me, do you think that really happened?" The Bible wasn't her first choice in reading material, but she was casually familiar with many of the stories. This was one of her favorites.

"The wine?" He looked off across the water before turning back to her. "Many people do. They were at a wedding, according to the text. If you study the customs of the day, likely the wedding party was inebriated at that point."

"So, they might have been susceptible to suggestion?"

"No, that's not what I mean." He seemed to consider his words before continuing. "Really, I don't think it matters. The story might be about the miracle, but it's mostly revealing how much Jesus cared about the people he spent his days with. Whether the water became true wine or not is irrelevant."

Emily laughed. "Not to Southern Baptists. Or maybe I should say to the Methodists. To them, that wine is important. The Baptists wouldn't touch it, even if it was from Jesus."

"I heard you asking about the British Cemetery." He had closed the small book, and it disappeared back into his pocket. "Does the history of the place interest you?"

"Some." Then she chuckled. "Really, not much. It's like the wine story. It's more about the respect the Coast Guard exhibits by maintaining it than anything else. The history part was nearly a century ago. The world has moved on."

The radio signaled a call, and they turned to watch as the

ensign slipped on his headphones and Lieutenant Sallinger joined him. After a few moments, the lieutenant had a short conversation with the ensign, and he stepped their direction.

"Something we should know?" Steven posed the question.

"Yeah." Sallinger shook his head and searched the horizon. "I'm not looking forward to this, but at least I got a few hours rest this afternoon."

"That doesn't sound good." Emily pursed her lips, then asked, "What are you not looking forward to?"

"They've found the boat we spent last night looking for."

"I would think that's good news." Emily smiled.

"Not when it's on Cedar Island."

"We just came from there." She laughed. "You Coast Guard guys do get around. Anyway, ShareBoating will be pleased to know their sailboat wasn't lost by the Hyde County's sheriff's office."

"ShareBoating? The owners, I assume." When Emily nodded, he continued, "Maybe not so pleased. Someone reported the boat as capsized, so I suppose they only located pieces of it. Enough to identify it, apparently."

"Ouch," Emily said. "It was a nice one, too. Did anyone say what happened?"

"That's my job, and apparently, yours, too. They want you on the scene to evaluate everything."

"Tonight?" She laughed. "I hope not."

"Hm. Tomorrow would be nice. Sure, that will do. We would have to refuel in Ocracoke, anyway. We can stay for the night and head out in the morning. And you, medical examiner. She's your wheels. Will you be joining us?"

"Of course, he will!" Emily answered for him, giving Steven a mock cuff to the jaw. "Things blow up and our medical examiner's there. Isn't that right, Steven?"

"My body is somewhere north. You don't think I need to be

up there?"

"Your body?" She rolled her eyes. "He's dead, Steven. He'll keep. That's what the morgue's refrigeration units are for. It'll be fun. You'll see."

"Fun? The last time, things blew up," he said, puffing his cheeks out with the memory. An exploding sand dune had nearly decapitated him during a recent stint as medical examiner with the C-District of the Dare County Sheriff's Office.

"And that was so much fun. At least I had fun." Emily turned to the lieutenant. "When and where, Lieutenant? We'll be there."

Like she had said, she intended to enjoy her time on the islands to the fullest, no matter which one she was on.

EMILY STEPPED from her room at the Silver Lake Motel into the damp morning sun. Moisture hung in the air like a curtain, catching the sun's rays and giving everything on the island a feathery feel. The world was wet with jewels of glimmering fairy kisses. At least the moisture creating the heavy dew kept the "real-feel" temperatures tolerable, unlike in Kill Devil Hills where she'd been wearing a heavy jacket most mornings.

She stopped by her car and dropped off her purse, only to see the brown "E" bag still in the back seat. She smiled, opened the back door, and wrapped her hand around the top. At the door to Steven Hill's room, she knocked and called, "Room service. Fresh brownies. Want some?"

"Hold," his voice called from the other side of the door. After about a minute, the locking mechanism on the door tripped, and Steven pulled the door wide. "Thought that was your voice."

"I certainly hope you don't open the door like that for just anyone." She smiled and offered him the brown bag. He was barefoot, in pants and a white Tee, with a small towel in one hand rubbing his wet hair. Water spots speckled his shoulders, as if he had pulled on the shirt to answer the door. "Running late, are you?"

"I finally managed a connection to Shelina last night. Antarctica, you remember. Getting through is difficult at the best of times, so I have to take advantage when the opportunity presents itself. We had a nice chat."

"Just not the real thing, right?"

"Right. You brought this from up north?" He took the bag from her and sniffed it. "What's in it?"

"A brownie." She smiled transparently, and she stepped inside. His room was exactly the same as hers, except his bedding still reflected his shape in the linens. A damp, full-size bath towel draped the foot of the bed, and shoes filled with wadded socks rested under the edge of a desk chair. His laptop screen glowed, his point of contact with his wife the previous evening. "Go on. Open it."

"I'm slightly frightened. I've seen some of your gifts. They don't always go over well."

"You'll like this one." She pulled his curtain back, peered outside, then stepped to his bathroom to glance inside. The shower curtain was to the side, with water still coating both it and the tile tub surround. A wadded washcloth rested on the edge of the tub, with a small, open bottle of shampoo next to it.

"You looking for something?"

"Just verification. Typical man's room. I already stripped my bed this morning." She smiled brightly.

"For what reason?"

"It makes the maid's job easier. Now, to your brownie." She sat on the foot of the bed. Her leg brushed the towel, and she lifted it with two fingers and tossed it across the room to the floor. "Go ahead. Don't be chicken."

When he pulled out the brown "E" and gave it a puzzled

look, she laughed. He said, "I don't get it."

"Oh, you." She took it from him and turned it to where he could see that it was the letter E. "A brown E. I got you a brown E."

"Okay." He smiled. "That's actually very good. I would have enjoyed an edible one instead, but good prank, Missy. I was about to think I could trust you this time."

"Oh, never think that. Now, get dressed. We've got a sailboat to explore." She stood, moved back to the window, and opened the curtains to leave a section of the glass exposed. The wet light from outside formed a luminous puddle at her feet. "Sunshine later, perhaps."

"Hopefully. Out, now." He pointed to the door. "I'll be there in a minute. My shoes and my computer in the case, and I'm ready."

"Lieutenant Sallinger won't appreciate us being late." She pointed a finger his direction but softened it with a smile.

"I picked up on that. Thank you. Scoot so I can get dressed."

Emily laughed and moved outside, closing the door after her. Her phone rang, and she pulled it from a pocket. She didn't recognize the number.

"Emily. How may I help you?"

"Christian Chance. Good morning, Emily. I'm doing breakfast this morning at the station if you and Steven wish to join us."

"Any brownies?" She smiled, picturing her brown "E" prank.

"Um, perhaps. Would you like some? I might have a box in the pantry. I had planned on waffles with fresh fruit and yogurt."

"The brownies are an inside joke between Steven and me. I shouldn't have mentioned it. Waffles will be fine. Steven is headed to the car in a few minutes, and we'll be right there. Thank you, Christian."

"You're welcome."

She disengaged as Steven stepped through the door with his small bag in tow. His larger one had remained overnight in the trunk of her car. She released the deck lid for his convenience and climbed in the driver's seat. He placed his bag in the car and joined her. He set his brown E on the dash with his phone while he buckled up.

"Keeping your brownie?" She nodded at it as she started the car. "It might go stale up there."

"That's a good one. Any plans for a real breakfast?"

"The ensign called from the station, and we're invited. I obligated you to attend. I'm supposing I read that right since you're asking."

"If we're spending the morning searching for boat wreckage, let's get on with it. Who's cooking? Not me, I hope."

"The ensign, by his report."

"The young guy?" Steven drew in a deep breath. "I hope he knows what he's doing."

"I had his cooking for lunch yesterday, and I'd mark it as two points in any food scorebook out there. His banana pudding was heavenly."

"Okay, then." He took the brown E from the dash, and he grinned. "Any chance for real brownies from the ensign?"

"I did ask." She was pulling onto the road, and she chuckled. "He offered me the option of waffles and yogurt."

"Ouch." Steven tapped the side of the brown E against the dash. "Brownies would be better, but I can do waffles."

"You can?" Emily was reconnecting with how much she enjoyed the medical examiner's company. His dry humor clicked with her more rambunctious one.

"Seriously. But I will dream of brownies with each one I consume." He laughed and tossed the brown E onto the dash before taking his phone and beginning to scan for new messages.

Then they were there, and Emily slowed to not hit anyone at the ferry landing before pulling toward the station and breakfast by Christian. Her stomach growled, and she glanced at Steven and grinned. "That's me, by the way."

"I thought *I* was hungry." He swiped the screen on his phone, and it went dark. He held the door handle until she stopped, then he released it and his seat belt at the same time. In one fluid motion, he unraveled his lanky form into the clearing daylight. "The haze is less," he called to the inside of the car. "Might make for a good day on the water."

"Or at the breakfast table," she growled. That had to come first. She joined Steven, and stepping inside the station, she remarked, "I promise, the man said waffles." Yet, the aroma of fresh brownies invited their imaginations to run amok.

"Hm," Steven said, as he looked around the empty space. "Hello," he called. "Are we at the right place to order up?"

"In here," a youthful and enthusiastic voice called.

"When the sun shines," Emily said. She recognized the young ensign's over-eager zeal at everything he encountered.

"After you," Steven encouraged, and motioned her forward. "You know this place."

"Hardly. One meal, but sure. Ladies first."

"If you want. I'm hoping for brownies wherever we wind up." Steven grinned.

Emily headed through the door, calling out, "Do I smell brownies, Ensign Chance?"

When they stepped into the kitchen, the ensign was slicing peaches and adding them to a pile on a platter sectioned off into peaches, bananas, strawberries, and apples.

"I found that box I told you about." He wiped his hands on his apron, slipped on an oven mitt, and pulled out a pan of glistening brownies from the oven. A portion of the pan revealed nuts erupting from the surface. "Half with walnuts, half without. I didn't know your preference."

"Both," Steven said. "And better if you have ice cream."

"That I don't know," Chance admitted. "Feel free to check. Everyone will be down in ten minutes. I'm putting on the first waffles now."

To his word, he had two waffle irons heating on the massive range, and he opened them, spooned batter inside, and closed them. He tapped a timer to start a countdown, and he pulled a stack of plates from a shelf and set them alongside the flatware and napkins already on the counter. The timer dinged, and he flipped the waffle irons and reset the time.

"Can we help?" Emily offered, but the young man was a fish in its home waters. He seemed familiar with every rock and eddy in the stream.

"You can cut the brownies. The pan is hot. Don't burn yourself." Then the timer dinged again, and he released the waffle irons, used tongs to remove the waffles, and brushed the interior with butter before spooning in another helping of batter.

"I'm finding the freezer," Steven said, and he moved deeper into the kitchen.

"Leave me with the dirty work," Emily called after him, though, as she saw it, she could slice herself the largest piece.

That's exactly what she intended to do.

"DON'T WE have drones, maybe satellite images to tell us where to search?" Emily was again with Ensign Chance. Today, his screens made more sense to her. When they boarded the boat, she'd taken the opportunity to quiz him on some of what they showed. He was eager to answer questions, and she found him fun to talk with. She even knew the location they'd found the dead man Steven was here to see and that Ensign Chance had factored its location along with various tide charts into the reported sighting for the sailboat.

"Sure," he said, "but satellite images only happen when a satellite is overhead and aimed at just where you tell it to look. True, they are constantly updating the information on the ground, but in reality, it can take months before what's on the ground makes it into the pictures we see."

"A live feed, though. You have that available, right?" She imagined zooming in on one of the ensign's screens and finding the boat. They could nail its location without any trouble, "get 'er done," and be back on the sand in two shakes.

"Near-real time. Have you heard of SOAR?"

"Tell me about it."

"Not much to say. It's a satellite company that allows the public access to imagery that's very close to real time. For us? We're not going to get that today, even if we could access it. The satellites can't see through clouds. Even the haze this morning disrupts the clarity. Our best bet would be a drone if we had one, but they are limited by battery range, and the Pamlico Sound is huge."

"I thought we were headed to Cedar Island."

"Also huge. We are fully fueled, however. We can search all day, although that's not likely necessary. The report we have says the debris is in the National Wildlife Refuge."

"And we can just drive this boat in there? Won't we need a car?"

"That's exactly what we don't want. The refuge is coastal marsh, with boat ramps and everything. There are roads, sure, but the boat we're looking for will have gotten inside the refuge via the water. Hence, this." He slapped the dashboard of the boat and grinned.

Emily jumped when Steven touched her shoulder to let her know he was joining the conversation. She motioned toward the ensign and quizzed him, "Did you catch any of that?"

"The lieutenant and I were having a similar conversation. He hopes to have GPS coordinates for us soon. If so, we can motor right up to where the wreckage was discovered."

"What's the fun in that?" She teased as much as anything. "I hoped to hike in the swamps, maybe see bears and alligators and lions and such."

"Oh, no lions," the ensign called to her. "Black bears, maybe, although they are mostly concentrated north of here around the Alligator River—"

"But alligators," she teased. "If they have a river named after them? What say you, Ensign?"

The ensign laughed and turned his attention back to navigating the boat. Lieutenant Sallinger appeared with a sheet of paper in his hand partially filled with inked in words. They were in his personal script and difficult to read from Emily's angle, but he and the ensign soon fell into them, matching up facts on the paper with images on the ensign's screens. At one point, the ensign pulled up a map of Cedar Island, enlarged it to show a channel on the south side of the island, and traced a path with his finger through the Sound and into a wide cove that punched into the broad expanse of marsh. Emily noted the position where the ensign had marked the dead man's location. It has seemed a long way away before, but in this view, perhaps not so much. She didn't know that her observation meant anything, but she was along to observe, for whatever her opinion was worth. Sallinger indicated something on the paper, Chance readjusted the display on his screen, and they seemed to reach a conclusion. The young ensign tucked the paper under a keyboard and Sallinger left him to it and almost seemed surprised to see Steven Hill standing at the stern of the boat and searching for Cedar Island and Emily with her attention on the lieutenant's interaction with his ensign.

"Bears, Lieutenant?" She released her handhold and worked

her way towards him. She was having more difficulty than the medical examiner with the continual jarring motion of the boat skimming the waves at such a high speed.

"Bears?" He glanced off the side of the boat, and his eyes jumped across the scene as if searching the water. He turned back to her. "I'm not with you."

"Your ensign didn't exactly promise me bears, but he did say there's lots of them nearby. We are approaching a wildlife refuge. I'm expecting to see bears in your wildlife refuge."

"Oh, I see. The ensign likes to talk. Not a lick of lazy any- where in him, no matter what you ask him to do … or explain." He nudged his eyebrows up to make his point. "He's a good man but needs to be kept on track sometimes. I happen to know where there's a bear that's taken up residence in the refuge. We've made good time. The island's up ahead—" He indicated a green slash on the horizon. "—so we have time if you want me to have Chance swing by. Can't promise you'll see anything, but she had two cubs last time I was by. Maybe."

"Yes, I would like that. Riding over with you was fun yester- day, but we were in and out like hushpuppies in a frypan. Today, I expect a shore excursion. A real payback for riding over here twice in two days."

"You saw me talking to the ensign. I gave him the coor- dinates for the wreckage. I'll ask him how easily he can swing by the bear's territory. Bears do move in response to pressure from people or habitat, but the marsh has had a productive summer."

"Leeward drift?" She smiled.

"Now, that's interesting. What makes you mention that?"

"At breakfast some of the crew brought it up. I overheard and asked them to explain it to me. They sent me to your ensign, and I got an earful."

"Fair enough. How do you see it applying to our bear and

her cubs?"

"The same way it might apply to your drug smugglers. Leeward drift. Pressure from people or habitat, and the bear moves off to someplace less crowded."

"You did pay attention. The ensign would be pleased. Did he tell you what he surmised on Ocracoke?"

"That Springer's Point matches up nearly perfectly with the orientation and contours of the British Cemetery."

"What did you make of that?" He seemed to really want to know.

During their conversation, they passed an outgoing ferry mostly filled with cars, and their boat slowed as Chance navigated a route south of Cedar Island and to the west and north of Portsmouth Island, which diverted Emily's attention. "That's where we were before, but on the other side, right?" Emily nodded her head toward Portsmouth Island.

"We?"

"That's right. You had abandoned us. We looked for the boat down towards Lookout Lighthouse but had to turn back."

"The storm. I remember. It hit us hard up north. I wouldn't have wanted to ride it out in a boat."

"Well, we did rescue a pregnant woman from a stranded ferry."

"I read that report. Kudos. Cape Lookout is one island down, though. That's Portsmouth."

"I should remember that. Anyway, back to bears—"

"No, back to leeward drift and the British Cemetery. You're the forensic investigator, and I'm told you have a knack for seeing relationships between things and putting them together."

"I do need information to do that. We'll pass Springer's Point when we head back, correct?"

"With you two on board, yes. We have to drop you off at the station."

"That should help me out. Is there a place to land?" A dock or pier, she meant.

"Hm, no. Not at the Point. We can beach if the tide cooperates, or I can check on borrowing a private dock. It does get done."

"Why not stop off, then? Your ensign seems pretty bright to me."

Sallinger grinned. "I'll have him check into that side trip we discussed—"

Steven touched Emily's shoulder to get her attention and pointed toward the shore.

"What?"

"I was listening. Look, there." They were entering Cedar Island Bay, and on a small island on their starboard side, a female black bear stood on her haunches and watched them. Two cubs about half her size tumbled in the grass.

"Bears! I'm satisfied," Emily cooed. It was so perfect, a momma and her little ones out for a day on the water.

As they watched, the shore became trees, then a large house appeared right on the waterfront, with a long dock extending into the bay. Two people stood on the end waving and shouting as if they were trying to get their attention.

Lieutenant Sallinger accessed the PA system, identified himself and the craft, and requested them to indicate if they needed assistance. When they revealed that they did, he instructed Ensign Chance to maneuver the boat toward them. Once at the dock, the couple introduced themselves as Walter Schmidt and Lovie Cornette. Walter sported a top knot with his hair secured by a thick strand of twine, and Lovie's ebullient tresses leaped windward of her flowered, cherry-colored hat.

"Lovie, what a charming name! I'm Emily, and I adore your place. Is this your full-time home?"

Before they could reply, Sallinger interrupted and inserted a question of his own, "How may we assist you, Walter and Lovie?"

Lovie started a reply to Emily, "Of course not, my dear—" when her husband placed his hand on her arm.

"Now, Lovie, let's answer the man's question first."

"Oh?" She looked at Walter in surprise. "What question was that?"

"The boat, Lovie. Remember, we saw it yesterday, with that man on board?" Walter looked to Lieutenant Sallinger with a patient smile, and he nudged his wife's memory again. "Remember, just before we saw Shelby?"

"Shelby?" Her eyes glazed for a moment, then her expression cleared, and she was a different woman. "Mrs. Ellison's daughter. How could I forget that?"

Emily said, "Excuse me, Lieutenant." She turned to the woman on the dock. "Cynthia Ellison?"

"Oh, you know her?" Lovie smiled. "Such a lovely woman."

"You started to say this isn't your full-time home. Do you live up that direction?" Hatteras, she meant, but she had an idea they would know what "up that direction" meant when you were located on a North Carolina barrier island. If they were from up that direction, it would explain them mentioning Shelby, Cynthia Ellison's daughter. Cynthia was Emily's coworker and the K9 handler for the C-District section of the Dare County Sheriff's Office.

The biggest question in Emily's mind was what Shelby had to do with a missing boat from Hatteras Island that had gone missing from Silver Lake and wound up on Cedar Island. She knew Shelby could be a handful, but this was a bucket load of wet sand; and if this meant what she thought it did, it was about to be dumped all over them.

WALTER AND LOVIE'S story was a bit chaotic at best. They

hadn't intended to make this into a fish fry and invite the neighbors, they said, but the events had made an impact on them, and they had talked about it, unsure if they were responsible to say anything. Then, when a Coast Guard boat came patrolling right up Cedar Island Bay, well, it was the perfect, God-given opportunity, and they had run to the end of their dock to flag them down.

To answer Emily's question, their house had limited utilities and only motorboat access, and for the winter, they would be returning to their place in Buxton. For Braxton Sallinger, they described a sailboat fitting very much the description of the one that had recently gone missing from Silver Lake. No, they didn't catch the registration number or the name. It was far out in the bay. They only noticed it because the pilot didn't seem to be in full control—the sails were luffing one way, then the next—and he kept trying to start the engine to no success. He kept yelling at it, and that never works to start an engine. The yelling was what had gotten their attention in the first place.

"Yelling, how?" Emily glanced at the lieutenant for permission to take over, and Sallinger indicated for her to go ahead.

"Oh, mean, mean, mean." Walter nodded firmly, setting his top knot to bouncing.

"I felt so sorry for him at first," Lovie said, "but a man shouldn't be on a boat like that if he doesn't know how to operate it. It's shameful, that's what it is."

"Shameful," Walter confirmed.

"You mentioned Shelby. What part did she play in this?" Not something up to her usual rowdy behavior, Emily hoped. She didn't want to have to contact her coworker with news of her daughter's further descent into the cesspool of her crime-tainted life.

"Maybe no part," Walter assured her. "I only mentioned the young woman to bring Lovie's mind back to what we'd seen.

You remember, the sailboat. Sometimes Lovie needs reminding where she's been and what she's seen."

"Shelby?" Emily prompted the man to stay on the topic.

"The sailboat was already down there—" and Walter pointed north into the bay, "—and there comes Shelby in this little outboard." He indicated south and pantomimed her skimming past their dock in the same direction as the sailboat.

"She wasn't doing anything wrong, then." That was a relief to Emily. "Did you see her again or just that one time?"

"Oh, yes, we saw her again." He turned to Lovie who was enthusiastically approving everything he said.

"Can you describe that for us, Walter?"

"Same as before, except she started there and disappeared there." He pointed up into the bay and moved his hand towards its mouth where it widened and hit the western shore of Portsmouth Island.

After Lieutenant Sallinger assured the couple that they had done the right thing in waving them down, he asked if he could contact them if he had additional questions.

"Of course," Walter agreed. "We have good service at our place in Buxton, but here? We don't have a landline. If you see our boat here, you know we're home. Feel free to stop by anytime."

Lieutenant Sallinger instructed Ensign Chance to continue up the bay towards the location of the damaged sailboat. It was what they were here to see, and while the couple's story helped confirm the reports they had received and the location they were headed, it didn't seem to impact what they expected to find.

Emily wasn't so certain. Shelby Ellison didn't have her feet on the sand, especially in the area of personal ethics and the ability to make sound judgements. If Shelby had followed the sailboat in, and only Shelby had come out, there had to be a connection.

Emily just needed a little time to discover what it was.

WINDING INTO the ever-narrowing Cedar Island Bay, Ensign Chance slowed the big Coast Guard utility boat. Emily watched his screens revealing the lay of the land under the surface of the water. Even where there seemed plenty of room to maneuver on the surface, the depths indicated by the screens dictated a narrow channel they must follow, and at times, barely that. To their left, homes and businesses lined the distant shore. Often, the barrier between the water and land was a rickrack wall of tumbled and rough stone piled into makeshift seawalls. Occasional sandy beaches snuggled into breaks in the stone seawalls, and long piers shot fingers of wood over the vibrating eddies of water stirred at the utility boat's passing.

Finally, the narrow channel on the ensign's screen widened to take up more of the water that surrounded them. Low scrubland to the right was cut by channels of water, while on the left, swathes of trees cushioned the houses along the shore.

"Getting close," Ensign Chance announced.

"Where?" Emily stood looking for the wreck. They'd explored for hours, and she was ready to find it. The boat's slower speed gave her the freedom to move about without holding on, and she held a hand to shade her eyes as she scanned the water. "I don't see anything, and I'm pretty sure there's nowhere for a boat that size to hide."

"Maybe in those channels to the north?" Steven Hill hadn't seen the sailboat, other than to have a description of its size, but he was spot on. They had a fair view of the open water, and even the channels were hardly hidden, that was if something in them had a sailboat-size mast.

Ensign Chance throttled down the engine. Lieutenant Sallinger pressed binoculars to his face. Steven Hill studied the channels they could see into, and Emily made her way to the bow. She pulled out her phone, held it out over the water, and snapped several pictures of the surface.

"Seriously, Emily?" Steven began working his way her direction. "Water pictures?"

"Oh, much more than that." She had two fingers on the screen, and she expanded them. "Lieutenant, do you have the registration number of our sailboat?"

"Of course," he called. "It's how we know someone found the correct one."

"Can you locate it for me? I would like you to read it out."

"Chance," Sallinger said, "you hear that?"

"Yes, sir. Right here, sir." The ensign rustled some papers, and he handed one to Sallinger.

"Ready?" Sallinger called.

"While the sun still shines."

"I guess that means yes." Sallinger chuckled. He read the registration number for the boat aloud.

"Repeat the last three," Steven requested. He hovered over Emily's shoulder. When they were repeated, he stepped away, grinned, and said, "It's a match."

"For what?" Sallinger.

"The sailboat is there." Steven held an arm over the side of the boat and pointed down.

"This I need to see." Sallinger told his ensign to hold their position, and he pulled himself forward. Leaning over the bow, he located the white hull, now littered with silt, on her side in the shallow water. To the west, the mast disappeared into the murky depths, and the sails, one ripped, had begun to fill up with sediment and decaying plant material.

Emily moved back from the rail, and she held her phone over her head, then at an angle towards the stern. No matter what she did, she was unable to get a clear signal for cellular service.

"Does no one use phones out here?" She called to no one

and everyone. "I would like to speak to the lieutenant to update her."

"Her?" Steven looked towards Sallinger, who was paying Emily no mind. He knelt at the rail of his boat studying the craft just underneath them.

"Not Lieutenant Sallinger, silly," Emily said, snorting at Steven's question. "Diane, my boss. She wanted me here. I found it. Now, I want to see what she has for me next, well, other than babysitting you, Steven Hill."

"Thank you, Emily," he remarked with a dry twist in his voice.

"You're welcome. Besides, we've got a body for you to dissect. I might want to watch."

"You probably don't—"

"Hey, you two lovebirds, come look at this." Sallinger turned his attention to his ensign. "Chance, have you got this on your screens?"

"Yes, sir. I've recalibrated, and it's perfectly clear."

"Can you navigate keelside? There's something I want the investigator to give me an opinion on."

Emily studied the sunken boat as the ensign navigated around it. The "something" was located just below where the waterline on the sailboat would be if the entire craft wasn't already below the waterline.

"A hole, Lieutenant?" Emily hesitated to connect this new development with Shelby, but it seemed to fit too closely to ignore.

"Your opinion, Ensign?" Sallinger joined his ensign to peer into his screens.

"She was holed, sir."

"My opinion, too," Sallinger agreed. "We need to know if someone was aboard. Ensign, can we locate someone with diving gear?"

Emily sighed. She had thought she might be getting back to her home island. If they had to wait on a diver … she checked her cell phone once more. One bar disappeared before mysteriously appearing once again.

Not even a real phone signal. What a waste, and with sand just ten feet under the soles of her shoes. She wondered if the ensign would take her to shore to stretch her legs. She'd be glad to rejoin them when it was time to head back to her car. Until then, a game of conversation was in order to pass the time.

"Steven, I seem to remember you on a black motorcycle …"

AFTER AN INSPECTION, the big boat was devoid of people or their remains, but the divers located something the team hadn't back in Silver Lake. A waterlogged stash of drugs the size of Mt. Washington.

"What?" Emily could hardly stop the word when the diver came to the surface, set a sodden, plastic-wrapped package on the deck, and removed his mask to make the announcement. "We inspected this boat bow to stern back in Silver Lake. We had a drug dog cover the interior completely. Where were they hidden?"

"Not at all," the diver shared. "Scattered willy-nilly in the main cabin. They didn't make any attempt to disguise them." He was still in the water fully encased in a rubber suit, and he bobbed between his team's boat and theirs. He was able to rest his feet on the hull of the sunken boat and hold to a line off the side of the Coast Guard craft very easily.

"We suspected there was a haul stashed somewhere. Likely this is it." Sallinger dropped onto his haunches to inspect the dripping package.

"Oh?" Steven. He hadn't been there and was out of the loop about the drug bust.

"We received a tip and intercepted a major drug shipment

but were surprised not to locate any drugs when we busted the delivery team. Maybe they were a pickup team, instead."

"They were on the wrong island, if so. I need to call Diane." Emily shook her phone with no obvious change in connectivity. "Ooh, my phone."

"We can use my shortwave to call shore." The ensign flipped a switch on his dash, and a speaker squealed with feedback before settling down.

"The one is Buxton is out. It got dismantled a few months back, and it's still not repaired."

"Okay, that might be down, but our satellite phone's up and running. It will connect with every mobile or landline phone out there. You can borrow it if you wish." The ensign grinned.

The diver began bringing up additional drugs one packet at a time. Much of it was wrapped in waterproof containers or plastic, but other packages had taken on water, and they were sodden and needed to drain.

"Someone won't be happy that their drugs are ruined," Emily quipped. They'd be even unhappier that the drugs were now in the possession of the Coast Guard, but that wasn't her point. They'd tried to escape with them, only to lose them on a sinking ship.

"Wouldn't matter." The diver dropped a fresh haul onto the deck of the Coast Guard boat. "Likely why they scuttled it. It does seem strange that it looks to be scuttled from the outside, not the inside. Can't figure that one out. Be right back." He adjusted his face mask and dropped beneath the water.

That's when Emily could no longer sidestep the connection between Shelby and this boat. She knew there had to be a reason Shelby had followed the boat in but left the bay alone. She wanted to ensure it didn't make it back out. She wanted it to go down.

Still, by the account of Walter and Lovie, it didn't sound like the boat had been headed back out anytime soon. The man at the helm hadn't seemed to know what he was doing with the sails, and he hadn't been able to start the engines. If that was true, he was as good as stranded when he entered the bay and would likely have run aground eventually, forcing him to abandon his boat and likely the drugs he carried onboard. There was more to this, and she had to let Diane know.

"Ensign, I'll take you up on that offer of your satellite phone. You can charge the time to Dare County. I'm calling my boss up in C-District."

"I don't handle payments for its usage, but it will log the numbers if someone wants to know." He shrugged before explaining, "Here's how it works."

It seemed simple enough. She did have to look up the numbers on her phone and enter the one for the sub-station in Buxton. Ashley Dixon picked up.

"Ashley speaking. You have reached the Buxton sub-station for the Dare County Sheriff's Office. How may I direct your call?"

"Ashley, it's Emily. I need to speak with Diane. Is she around?"

"Oh, she's always around. Just not in the building. She went out a bit ago. You have her number, right?"

"Okay, yes. I'm on a Coast Guard satellite phone. Mine's not connecting. Is Cynthia Ellison there? No, wait. I need to talk to Diane first. Oh, sheesh. I get twenty feet off the beach, and I'm as lost as a starfish in a sandpile."

"I can have her call you. She shouldn't be long. Her exact words were, 'If I tell the story honest, I gotta see some sun or I'll be putting a spoon into the wrong pot and making a mess of things.' Then she disappeared out the door. I suspect she's on a coffee run."

"Thank you, Ashley. I'm off Cedar Island with the Coast

Guard, and it'll be a couple hours before I can get back, but I need to speak with her about Shelby Ellison. I think Shelby might be in real trouble this time, and I want to let Diane know before Cynthia finds out."

"Oh, that's good information. My lips are zipped. Can I unzip them for the lieutenant?"

"Yes, but no one else. Also, we've found the drugs from the bust the other day. Likely all of 'em. I'm looking at them."

"Oh, even better. The lieutenant will be glad to hear about this."

"The sailboat, too." Emily paused on that one, waiting to see how Ashley reacted.

"Sailboat, um, I should know what you're talking about?"

"From Silver Lake, the one that went missing."

"Oh, good. The owners were calling about when they could pick it up. That rental company, the one with the odd name?"

"Well, not soon. It's at the bottom of Cedar Island Bay."

"And I shouldn't tell them that."

"No." Steven got her attention, and she said, "Ashly, I have to go. I'll be there in a few hours. I'll speak to Diane then."

Steven said, "We apparently have it all. The divers are marking the wreck, and we're heading back. The ensign says about two hours back to Ocracoke. I'm ready for lunch."

"Or dinner." Emily looked at her watch. It was turning into a long day, and it wasn't over yet, not by a long shot. What was open on the island this time of year and at the time they'd likely return? Not much, but maybe something. If not, maybe the station would let them borrow the kitchen. Ensign Chance, tonight might be your night to shine.

Pasta again? Anything as long as it was hot and her feet were on the sand. That would sound about right to her.

Chapter 10

Discovery at Springer's Point

LIEUTENANT DIANE TURNIPSEED and K9 handler Cynthia Ellison, at the bow of the Hatteras to Ocracoke ferry, eyed the churning water, milk chocolate soup, with marshmallow seabirds testing the surface of the water before soaring aloft once more.

"Richie says weather like this skirts the edge of the devil's domain." Cynthia pulled her jacket tighter around her neck, and she shivered in the blustery wind. Toby, her K9 officer, was in the back of her green Jeep Cherokee. She'd driven her personal vehicle on this trip: out of the county ... meaning heading to Ocracoke ... and an attempt to stay low key for a visit neither woman wanted to make.

"Like as not Richie's right, though I think sharks in the collards would be my take on the devil's domain." Diane hesitated, then said, "Don't know what Shelby's thinking gettin' herself into something like this."

Diane badly wanted to commiserate with her K9 handler, but she was so angry at Shelby for getting above her knees in something that was none of her business that she could spit. And she was as much angry for the way Cynthia was being forced to deal with her daughter as she was with what Shelby had actually done. Exactly what, that was to be seen, but Diane trusted Emily's observations. That's how good police work got done. Let the people who knew how to do it right get on with it and trust their conclusions when they came up with them. Unlike Morton Kringlebach, who had been a fishhook in her little toe ever since deciding he was retiring.

She'd told Morton that the sailboat was likely a vital key to their investigation into that drug cartel, but he'd had them pull the investigative tape from it, and then it had gone missing. Except for the Coast Guard and Emily—and Steven Hill, she gave credit—they might could have lost it entirely. Now it lay at the bottom of Cedar Island Bay, though Braxton Sallinger had thankfully retrieved the drugs before someone had swept in and reclaimed the lot.

"*'O the bleeding drops of red, where on the deck my Captain lies, fallen cold and dead.'* Whitman, Lieutenant, from *O Captain! My Captain!.* You know we tried to raise Shelby right—"

"For all sakes, Cynthia, stop that." Diane didn't cotton self-pity nor trying to take up for someone who was tossing her net into murky water all on her own. "You and Richie raised Shelby right, and she ain't dead, least that I can tell. Some people just don't want to swim in the channel. You can say turn to the left or choose the thing on the right or just keep swimming, but that don't mean some people will bother to listen. You know that. Shelby put her spoon in a different pot than you or I might choose, and this is what she's stirred up. My aunt Lucille used to say that murky water don't get that way all on its own."

"I'm not sure I know what that means." Cynthia laughed, but her eyes were red, and she cushioned a sniffle with a wadded paper napkin from a coffee shop back in Buxton.

"Not sure my aunt Lucille did, either." Diane smiled. She pointed, "Dolphins. It's good to see dolphins in the Sound."

Several dorsal finds were breaking the water, then off to the side, a sleek body leaped from the water and splashed back down, leaving a trailing stream of whitewater icing zigzagging down a chocolate soup swell.

"It was warmer in my truck," Cynthia said. "We're up here where no one can overhear, so tell me the rest. The good Lord knows I've heard more than I might want, but there's bound to be more."

"You're a big girl—"

"That's a good one. That's what you say about yourself. Me? This is mess enough for two people, and I'm not sure I want to wade through it."

"To tell the story honest, I don't expect you would. That don't change that you're one of the toughest people I got working for me."

"Enough of that. We're where we are, so spit it out, Lieutenant. Tell me the rest of what Shelby's done."

The sighting at Cedar Island by Walter and Lovie; following the sailboat into the bay then exiting alone, as far as Walter and Lovie knew; the sailboat scuttled, with the damage going from outside in; the drug cache left undisturbed in the boat as it sank … Diane considered they might coulda said the same things and been more comfortable in one of the vehicles or in the ferry's compact passenger area up top, but up at the bow with the boat fighting the waves and the distant island for them to focus on was the best choice. Like throwing your line in a creek or in a pond. One's easy for catching fish, the other's better. This was the better option to give Cynthia the chance to deal with the news of her wayward daughter.

"This boat Shelby used." Cynthia took a deep breath, as though posing something that might make even more trouble for her daughter. "Shelby rides sidesaddle when she heads out on the water, and least that I can tell, no one's trusting her with a boat. How's she all the way to Cedar Island? That's a part of the story I want to dip my net into."

"It's not like I weren't listening when Emily told me that part of the story. If I tell the story honest, I wondered the same thing, but you're a big girl, and I guessed you'd reach the conclusion same as me. Seems we have the ferry landing coming up. How about we stop on the way in for a cuppa blackie? You head on out yonder to Shelby's, and I'll have a look-see for that boat she was in."

"You sure about that? You know how Shelby is. She won't see what's coming down the road, and she's likely to say things the way she wants me to think it—"

"Then she don't got the sense God gave a minnow, no disrespect intended, Cynthia. I want her noodling for catfish and the catfish to trip her up. Let her stick her hand all the way in. Likely, when I saunter up, she'll make a change and try to yank her hand right out of that hole."

The ferry had begun to slow, and an announcement started up to return to vehicles and such. The women headed to their respective automobiles and closed the doors just as the ferry nestled up to the ramp leading onto the sand-covered spit that was Ocracoke Island.

DIANE ADJUSTED the heat in her black Explorer to beat back the leading edge of the island's approaching winter. Ocracoke was only a few miles south of Hatteras, but being tiny, it seemed impossible for it to retain any of summer once the little tykes started back to school. She wrapped a hand around her Sweet

Tooth cuppa blackie and let the residual warmth soak in before flipping a new page over in her pocket notebook.

She pressed her pen to the paper. *1. How could Shelby recognize the boat? Ans. – She saw it from the pullout at the north end of the island the night of the raid; 2. Why would she chase it to Cedar Island Bay? Ans. – Perhaps she recognized the pilot; 3. Why would Shelby recognize the pilot? Ans. – ?*

Diane tapped her pen on the wire ring binding the pages together. She'd carried this small spiral for some time, and while it was filling up, there was plenty of room for more notes before she replaced it. The used section tended to be rumpled and refused to lay flat, with the unused portion still neatly ordered. The longer it remained in residence in her pocket, the bulkier it became, even with the same number of sheets inside.

She flattened the spiral and asked, why would Shelby have recognized the pilot of the boat … if that's what happened? The answer was tantalizingly easy but not one she wanted to consider. The two men Suzanne DeSantis had chased up into Swan Quarter? Shelby had known them because of a drug deal gone south, which she'd freely admitted to the deputy.

She revisited the third item on her list. *3. Why would Shelby recognize the pilot? Ans. – Likely a known drug contact.* Diane added the number four, and she took a sip of her coffee before writing her next question. *4. Why scuttle the boat? Ans. – Stop a drug deal? Stop the man? Murder?* She stared at the word for a time, then put a line under it. *Murder?*

Her alarm beeped, she closed the spiral and slipped it in her pocket, and she shifted the big, black beast into gear. Cynthia had warned her that Shelby wasn't living in the place Diane had visited when they were last here. Or in the last three places. She moved around frequently and slept rough when finances bested her and the weather tolerated her. Cynthia hadn't heard that her daughter had moved, but then she didn't usually hear, so that was that. She would text her boss the location when she knew. Diane checked her messages, read *Same as before*, and pulled into the street to head that way. Anyway, Cynthia was in her old Jeep Cherokee, long rusted from its life on the islands. Even if Diane didn't get the address exactly right from memory, the Jeep would be hard to miss. Find it, and she'd know she was in the right place.

A young mother in a stroller, bundled in a sweater and sweatpants and pushing a baby tented with blankets waved tentatively as Diane slowed to pull past. The Explorer's tires crunched gravel and last summer's leaves as they wound down the island's backroads until Diane saw the darkened taillights of Cynthia's Cherokee parked under a tree next to a tired rooming house. As she pulled up, she noted two people inside. Toby's shape shadowed the back glass, the taillights flashed, and Cynthia rolled down her window and motioned for Diane to come on up.

Diane parked, killed the engine, and considered the impact she wanted to make if the other person was Shelby, which seemed logical to her. She needed her utility belt and especially her cuffs. Have the cuffs out as though she intended to use them … sometimes they jostled people into rethinking their arrogance and bad manners.

Fully ready, and with the cuffs in hand, she opened her door and exited her vehicle. Cynthia called, "Passenger's side," and Diane understood. She crossed the back of the vehicle and approached the passenger's door. Shelby sat with her back to the glass, and Diane tapped it with the metal cuffs. Inside, Shelby hunkered down but otherwise didn't acknowledge Diane at the window. Diane saw Cynthia motion for her to hold up, then she hit the window switch and the glass retracted into the door.

"Hello, Shelby," Diane started, in an initial attempt to keep the interaction civil. She called across the interior, "Cynthia, hope you two have had a good visit." By good, she meant productive, as in, had the younger woman fessed up to why she was over at Cedar Island in the first place.

"Look at the lieutenant, Shelby," Cynthia coaxed. "You're not in trouble, not if you don't want to be."

"Right, Momma," Shelby said derisively. "You two here, that's trouble enough. People see the sheriff's office here, and they'll know it's me. I don't need kicked out of another place."

"Neither one of our cars is marked," Diane assured her.

"People know. They ain't as stupid as you think."

"Show the lieutenant, Shelby. She'll understand." Cynthia sounded more sympathetic than she had on the ferry.

"Yes, Momma."

Shelby shifted her position, at first glance revealing badly sunburned skin, with arms to match. Her hair was matted, and her skin hosted a mess of bug bites and scratches, but more notable were the black eye and bruises down one side of her face.

Diane returned the cuffs to her utility belt and said, "Dump it on me, Shelby. How'd this happen?" The sunburn, that was obvious, but the rest? The girl was usually a mess, but this was a mess of a different sort.

SHELBY, IT TURNED out, had been homeless and living rough for several weeks. The night of the sailboat sighting? It was no accident that she was sleeping on the beach. Her inter-action with Deputy DeSantis at the Ocracoke Lighthouse? She hadn't wanted to be taken home because she didn't have a home. She's taken to stashing a bedroll out on Springer's Point and making her way there most nights. It was when she stumbled on the drug stash that she knew something wasn't right.

"Drug stash," Diane repeated, thinking of Emily's report

from Cedar Island Bay. In Silver Lake, the sailboat had been explicitly devoid of any drugs, but the Coast Guard and their divers had retrieved a massive haul from off the underwater wreck.

"At first I was excited," Shelby confessed. "Maybe if I could trade some of the stash, I could get back into a place of my own. It's getting cold at night." She shrugged as if it was a valid way to score a place to sleep indoors, one likely with plumbing and heat.

"Sure," Diane said, not arguing, but she glanced at Cynthia with a puzzled look. There had to be more.

"The next part, Shelby. Say that, too."

"I hadn't taken any of it, well, nothing except some weed. That's how I got my room here. I traded Danni Jo, just something for her to smoke, you see, and she didn't pay me nothing, just let me have a bed for a coupla weeks. Honest, Lieutenant."

"You're staying yonder?" Diane pointed to the rooming house. Danni Jo was likely Danni Jo Lovelace, an older hippie-type who took in strays and down-on-their-luck singles. She'd rather hear about the marks on Shelby's face, but Shelby had thrown out the homeless line first, so she bit. "Sleeping rough this time of year is hard. I get that. I'm a big girl, so dump it on me, Shelby. Just say it all."

Shelby took a deep breath, tugged at her clothes, and looked at Cynthia, who nodded and said to *just say it.*

"Javier did this." Shelby touched her cheek. "He threatened to kill me if I took anything else of his. If I told, he'd do to me what he done to that family. I didn't know what he meant by that, Lieutenant. Honest. I don't know what family he meant, but that scared me."

"The kids, Shelby. You're leaving out that part."

"I know, Momma. I didn't get to it yet, that's all." Shelby had a disposable wipe in her hand, and she used it to smear dirt across her face, leaving it different but not cleaner. When Cynthia started to say something, Shelby held up her hand and jerked her head to stare into the floor of the Cherokee.

"Shelby," Diane said softly but sternly. "What kids?" The mention of children reminded her of the missing pair on the flyer back in Elizabeth City. Her brain was clicking, sorting what she remembered of the date of their disappearance, and whether it aligned with the events down here. It seemed a bit farfetched, but every morsel of information had to be factored in to ensure they left no stone unturned.

"He didn't really say anything, cept right when he hit me, he said, 'This is what I done to those kids.' I blacked out after, and he was gone when I came to."

"You knew this Javier already?"

"Momma—" Shelby pleaded. "I don't want to get hurt again."

"You have to tell what you know, Shelby. Answer the lieutenant's questions."

"All right." Her voice turned sulky. "Everybody knows Javier and that he escaped that raid you did up to Avon. I didn't know he was coming here, though. When I saw that sailboat and Javier was on it, I knew something was up—"

"And you stole a boat." Diane wanted that clarified.

"Borrowed, and I returned it. I'm not a thief." She spit out the denial hard, clearly hurt at the accusation.

"We've found the sailboat, Shelby. It's at the bottom of Cedar Island Bay."

"Oh." She sank into her seat and covered her face. "He was floundering but afloat when I motored away. I was angry that he'd hit me then got away with the stash. It wasn't right for him to have it all his way and not share a little bit with me. All I wanted was some weed, and he had plenty of that. Momma, what if he comes back to hurt me?"

"Lieutenant?" Cynthia shifted the question to Diane.

"To tell the story honest, we might have found Javier, that is if you can come look at the man we found."

"He's locked up?" Shelby seemed to brighten for the first time.

"If it's Javier, he's locked up forever. The man we found was floating face down in the Sound. The next question I have is where's the family he threatened? He didn't kill you, and if he let you live, they might still be out there, too. Are you willing to show us exactly where the drugs were stashed?"

"Momma? Should I?"

"Least that I can tell, you can't afford not to. Somebody might be out there, and if you don't help out the lieutenant, they might be dead as a dandelion before long. You don't want that on you, do you, Shelby?"

"No, Momma." She turned to Diane, with her bruised skin suggesting a relieved resignation at giving up control to someone other than herself. "I'll help. I'll show you where he left me."

"First," Diane said, looking directly at Cynthia, "take some time to get everyone cleaned up." Meaning Shelby. "I need to pull a team together and we'll go check this out. It might be a coupla hours. Can you work with that?"

Diane stepped back from the car as the window closed, and she pictured what she knew of Springer's Point. This wasn't her island, but she'd crossed it often enough to and from Morehead City to the south. She'd seen Springer's Point from the ferry, even if she rarely thought of it and had never visited. She did know that at over a hundred-twenty acres, it was a lot to search. And it would all have to be done by foot, as no vehicles were allowed.

Who could she pull in for the search from Dare County, Hyde County, or even Carteret? Would the Coast Guard commit manpower to the search? For once, she wished Sean Taylor and Jason Romney were present. How quickly could they get here … on the high-speed passenger ferry might be best if they could catch it.

Once inside her truck, as she started the engine, she lifted the mike to her radio and started to call Karen or Ashley or anyone, then remembered which island she was on. Sheesh, maybe Suzanne was at the Hyde County sheriff's office here on the island. Someone had to be around somewhere. If there was even a possibility that someone was alive in Springer's Point, they had to fix this. And now.

JASON'S RESTAURANT, just down from the Ocracoke sheriff's office, got wind and opened as a staging venue for the search, although at this point in the season, they were preparing to close until spring with shorter hours than normal. It was perfect in Diane's estimation as the building was devoid of diners; and with a large, open parking area, there was no lack of space.

"Jason," Diane said, offering her hand to greet one of the two owners of the eatery. "Much appreciation to you and James for allowing all us—" she glanced around her at the people already gathered, "—to make use of your place."

"Lieutenant," Jason nodded, taking her hand and giving it a shake before releasing it, "anytime Dare County gets with those of us in Hyde to find someone missing, that's island family pulling together. James is preparing coffee, so if anyone wants to park at the picnic tables inside, feel free."

"A cuppa blackie'll taste good. I'll let people know."

When Diane had contacted the Ocracoke sheriff's office, her call had forwarded to Brandon Scarborough, the Ocracoke liaison for Hyde County. He'd said, "Don't you worry none, Lieutenant. I may not be from around here, but I know exactly where Deputy DeSantis is holed up. She headed up to Swan Quarter but she's on the ferry back this direction. How soon you need her?"

It seemed that Brandon was a sieve, and as soon as Diane explained the situation, he said, "We can get 'er done, that's for certain," and by the time Diane had contacted Karen in Manteo and Ashley at the sub-station in C-District, she received a call from Brandon that Jason's was the staging venue for the manhunt, and when she was ready, she could join them.

Join them? At that point, she was waiting on her people to board the ferries to get to Ocracoke. She had no idea what to expect until she pulled her black Explorer into the parking lot. This might not be her island, but through Cynthia and Shelby and just living on the Banks and passing through regularly, she recognized the faces of many of those already present.

Somner Trotter, who worked the ferry landing on the Ocracoke side. His son, Luka, skated the island streets with his friend Sam, and if they were missing, he'd want others to join in the search. Of course, he wanted to help.

Kay-Kay Kopacz, only 26 and single, with her green-tinted blonde hair and multiple earrings, called out, "Hi-ya, Lieutenant Turnipseed. I got my case!" She pulled it from her shoulder and held it high. "What'cha can I help you with?"

Rob-Roy Haupt and Vernon Heinrich, both park rangers serving on Ocracoke, were in brown shirts and khaki pants. Vernon sported a darker brown coat. Rob-Roy raised an arm to wave and revealed a long-sleeve insulated shirt under his outer brown one.

Charlie Bronson, from the security detail at the ferry landing, must have been waiting for the lieutenant to show up. He was at her door when she opened it, and said, "Miz Turnipseed, how you doing? Once and agin, you Dare County folks doing us right here in Hyde. I knew I had to help soon's I got the call."

"Thank you, Charlie. What call?" Then it hit her. The sieve. Brandon Scarborough. Most times she didn't appreciate sieves, but today, she was fine with Brandon leaking all over the island. "Brandon, am I right?"

"Yes'm. He's a right good man, and he does us fine."

"I suppose so. Thank all y'all for showing up."

Emily Bryant and Steven Hill arrived in Emily's car, with Emily rolling down her window and asking, "What's the party?"

"For all sakes," Diane said, "you two the only ones not invited?"

"To what? This looks like a search getting ready to happen," Steven called from his side of the car.

"If I tell the story honest …" Diane didn't finish as the man would get her meaning, she was certain. "What do you know about Sallinger? He coming, too?"

"Not likely. He dropped us off and headed straight out with his ensign to the Hatteras station. We must have been disembarking when all this happened. We just happened by and saw the party."

Cynthia Ellison's Cherokee appeared, and it creaked as it pulled in and the brake lights flashed. Cynthia took time to release the back hatch, leash Toby, and let him jump down before joining Diane.

"The good Lord knows this is a day. Who are all these people?" Cynthia pressed on Toby's haunches, and he dropped at her side.

"Help. We might could use 'em, too, if they don't get too much in the way."

"You sure about that? Thought that was Toby's place to find our lost people, that is if they are out there." She scanned the crowd. "Deputy DeSantis. Wouldn't hurt to see her here, now would it?"

"Give it a break, Cynthia. Suzanne is on her way back from

Swan's, and the village wants to help. Did Ashley reach Jason and Sean?"

"Yes, ma'am. On the Express. I'm picking them up at the landing soon's it arrives." The Express was the high-speed passenger ferry that went directly from Hatteras into Ocracoke Village at Silver Lake. "Jason said Ensign Cruickshank will be with them."

"Courtney? For all sakes—" Diane cut off her comment. The Coast Guard ensign was too bright and chipper by far, but even a token Coast Guard participant meant they were still in the game. "I might need a cuppa. Jason said he was readying some. Do you mind? I'll watch Toby." She nodded the direction of the restaurant.

"He won't go nowhere." Cynthia told him, "Stay, Toby," dropped his leash by his side, and headed towards the building.

Diane's biggest surprise was seeing Coach Bertram's lifted Jeep drive up. Riley Bertram coached at Manteo High School, and his Jeep was bigger and flashier, if possible, than Deputy Sean Taylor's. He climbed down—literally—and closed his door before looking around to see who all was present. Then he knocked on the glass and motioned. From the far side of the Jeep, two sets of legs appeared, ones Diane recognized from the shoes, Nubbin Franklin and Carrot Bertram. The Jeep rocked, and eight furry legs hit the pavement, as the boys' dogs, Simba and Scar, joined them.

"Lieutenant Turnipseed," the tall man with his coarse blond hair and pale freckles called loudly. He loped her direction. "Hello. I know these boys give you people fits, but those dogs of theirs can track like no others, no offense to Toby there." He nodded to Toby. "You let me know what we can do. We're all in."

Diane wasn't an emotional sort of woman, but this, well, she felt supported by the people she tried to help every day, and she was glad they had showed up to try to noodle the catfish out of the pond. She hoped the catfish was still there ... and alive. Otherwise, there would be a lot of disappointed people out searching today, and she would be one of them.

TOBY, THE Dare County C-District's K9 officer, and Scar and Simba, the two hounds belonging to Coach Bertram's young accomplices, were on leash as the mob of village volunteers prepared to make their way to Springer's Point.

Deputy Suzanne DeSantis finally appeared, all business in her jeans and black jacket, with her chunky gold watch flashing from her wrist each time she raised an arm to direct someone where to go or where *not* to go, depending upon the disarray of the well-meaning but unfocused group. Before her arrival, several townsies had offered their vehicles to shuttle volunteers to the wildlife preserve, but Suzanne shut that down immediately.

"Get it together, people. This isn't shoofly pie. Last I heard, there's no parking down to Springer's Point, and I got me a college degree. I know how to walk a mile, so let's get this moving." Her gold watch flashed, and she pointed to Rob-Roy Haupt and Vernon Heinrich to split up, one to each end of the group for crowd control, otherwise they would become a crush of people, and "we don't got maids and butlers to tidy up loose ends, so men, it's up to you."

Diane Turnipseed thoroughly approved of Suzanne's technique in dealing with the people who had shown up to search for what might well be a missing family—if Shelby could be trusted, and the bruise on her face suggested she could.

"Jason, Sean," Diane called, motioning the two men to join her when they stepped from Cynthia's Cherokee. She was surprised but pleased to see Robert Hall from B-District in Dare County work his way out of the car along with Jason and Sean.

"Diane." Jason acknowledged Diane's cursory greeting as he approached.

"Dump it on me. How do you see it? These people, they mean good, but we're gonna have a mess of leafers wandering the Point. We've gotta keep 'em on their toes. Some of them will have a look-see and not know what they saw or get above their knees and distract others with nonsense. This may not be bushwhacker country, but for the Banks, it's the next best thing, and I'll be hoggletied if I intend to lose another person. We got one dead man already, and you heard about Shelby?"

"Yes," Jason let out, "and I hope the person who did that gets his. What he did should be illegal—"

"Should be?" Diane spat the response. "Is, was, and will be, Jason Romney. Nobody deserves—"

"Aw, Diane. I'm agreeing with you, not arguing. Let it rest for a change." Jason ran his palm across his face and looked toward the milling crowd and Suzanne DeSantis in conference with Courtney Cruickshank.

"Boss," Sean said tentatively, and when Diane cut her eyes to him hard, he stumbled, "I'm, well, I'm in this a hundred percent. You know you can count on me. Ms. Ellison picked up Shelby on the way from the landing, and she told us some of what happened. I say be positive for a positive result. We'll find 'em if they're out there. I'm certain of it."

"Thank you, Deputy—" and she caught herself, "—Sean. And Jason, I apologize. If the man that hit Cynthia's daughter is who we think he is, he got his already. We're pretty certain he's the person Lieutenant Sallinger and Deputy Dingman recovered from that sandbank in the Sound. Steven Hill hasn't had the chance to autopsy him, and we've yet for Shelby to confirm the identity, but yeah, the chances are good he got his."

"Okay, then, if you see it that way, what would you have Sean and me do?" The man looked at his younger compatriot as if to say, we're a team, so get with me, man.

"Kay-Kay, that's her with the green hair. She might need a bit of focus. She's all enthusiasm but little else. Still, her eyes are sharper than mine, so I bet tomorrow's breakfast she can see things I can't. You stick with her."

"Cynthia and Shelby, they'll be okay on their own?"

"Yes." Diane was certain of that. "Shelby's showing us our starting point, and we'll fan out from there."

Emily and Steven were handing out flashlights. The upcoming night hadn't stopped curling its fingers around the world, and they were gripping the island tighter and tighter. Darkness might well squeeze the daylight out of the sky before they were done as 120 acres would take time to search. Sections of this sandy spit of land that jutted into the Sound might reveal its treasures easily but much of the wildlife preserve consisted of up-and-down sand trails overshadowed by dense growth that could hide a lifesaving boat, and no one would know it was ten feet away.

Somner Trotter, a big man in a knit cap and a thick cable-knit sweater, his blond beard revealing his Nordic origins, had sidled up to Charlie, and they walked with Coach Bertram, Nubbin, and Carrot. Scar and Simba tugged at their leashes, and the teen boys seemed to find this a grand adventure. They waved at people in their yards, chatted with one woman working a flowerbed, and ran their dogs ahead and back again, burning off teenage energy.

A left at Lighthouse Road took the search party southwest, past the empty lighthouse parking area where three or four cars could have parked. At the Assembly of God Church, they gained another handful of people who wanted to join the search but lived closer to the trailhead into the preserve than to Jason's and knew where to find good parking. Another block, and Lighthouse Road ended, and the posse of people hooked left onto

Loop Road towards the trailhead.

Suzanne had worked her way to the front of the troop by then, and she held up the group before entering the preserve. She called, "Diane, if you could come on up here."

One of the new people from the church, a tall, thin man with a tasseled knit cap, called out, "Hey, Deputy. She's Dare County. You're ours. We're looking to Hyde County for instruction, not someone from Dare."

"Zip the lip, Jeremy Clabbins," Suzanne barked. "Fish in a skillet all cook up the same, or didn't your momma teach you that? We all want to find these people and alive, so I'll tell you what, you open your brain and some knowledge might slip in."

Several people around the tall man sniggered with amusement, and he seemed to shrink into himself.

Before Diane could reach the front of the massed mob of humanity, her phone began to ring. She considered whether to let it go when Courtney Cruickshank appeared at her side with a bright smile on her face.

"Lieutenant, I call that your phone ringing. You gonna get that? Somebody might wanna talk with you."

"Hello, Courtney. Thank you for showing up to represent the Coast Guard. I'm sorry Lieutenant Sallinger couldn't be here." There was more truth than the young lady knew in those words, but Diane smiled as she said them.

"Well, I'm having my happy moment helping all you people out." The phone rang again, and Courtney pointed to Diane's pocket. "My momma tells me to check my phone when it rings. She might be calling with something important. You want to get that?"

Your momma wouldn't be calling my phone, Diane said to herself, but the young woman was correct. She pulled out the device and was hit with a sick feeling when she saw the name on the screen. Morton Kringlebach had located her, and at the worst possible time. She motioned for Courtney to give her some space, held up the phone to show Suzanne she was taking a call, and she slipped it to her ear and clicked to answer.

"Hello, Sheriff Kringlebach. Lieutenant Turnipseed here. What can I do for you today?"

"How's that intercounty cooperation coming along down there, Lieutenant?" His voice was cool and restrained, and in the restraint, an explosive undertone simmered, a crab pot that had been on the bonfire too long and threatened to release the pressure inside. "I just returned from a fact-finding mission to Raleigh, by request of the governor, to be specific." He cleared his throat and said, "I expected to find a report on my desk wrapping up that explosion in the dunes involving the medical examiner. It seems someone bungled getting that to me ..." He let his words die away. When Diane didn't reply, he said, "Lieutenant, did you hear me?"

"Yessir, Sheriff." She didn't use his name, as she wanted this to be formal and quick. She had a search to lead, and the entire village was waiting on her.

"That explosion has embarrassed me, Lieutenant. I want you to know that, and the upcoming county performance review is important to me. To you, too, if you want that promotion to captain on your resume."

Diane breathed in deeply. Resume. That sounded like she might need one, and the only thing a resume was good for was job looking. She tried to deflect his question.

"Those children you went to Raleigh for, sir—"

"Ah, there we hit the thorn that's been in my shoe. Those children ... at the suggestion of ex-Governor Elringhaus, if I'm not mistaken. We discovered their location all right, Lieutenant. Vacationing with their parents on their family sailboat. Nothing out of order there. I don't suppose that side trip I was called away on had anything to do with you being out of county? I've spoken with Lieutenant Sallinger. The Coast Guard seems to think we're still pursuing, how did I say it, *intercounty coopera-tion.* Are we, Lieutenant?" The man's voice was still even, but the direction of his questioning said the lid to the pot was about to fly off, and with Diane's spoon inside, she was about to get splattered with the anger bubbling inside.

"Sir," Diane said, "with all due respect, I need to postpone this conversation. We've found a dead man in the Sound, a sailboat full of drugs is now in possession of the Coast Guard, and we have a possible hostage situation on Ocracoke at Springer's Point. I have a search party of about twenty officers and volunteers from four jurisdictions—" counting Jason as being from Carteret, seeing as Morton had yet to officially approve his transfer "—about to head into the wildlife preserve to begin a search. It's going to be dark soon, and we need to get started."

"I am not happy about this, Lieutenant. I had better not learn any of my B-District deputies are participating in whatever you have going on. When this is over, I want concrete evidence that the expenses you're incurring are justified."

"Yessir." She cut her eyes to Robert Hall, who by this time had a flashlight of his own and was paying particular attention to Toby as they readied to head into Springer's Point to search for the missing family reported by Shelby. "Thank you, sir. I'll be in contact."

"A full report on my desk. I'm not so slickcalm that you can pull this off a second time. Do you understand me, Lieutenant?"

"Absolutely. One hundred percent, sir." That was direct from Sean Taylor, and she hoped she said it believably and with sincerity. The line went dead. She looked at the screen, found the call disconnected, and slipped the device in her pocket.

Beside her, Courtney said, "I'm sorry, Lieutenant. My momma tells me I intrude sometimes. Maybe this was one time not to answer."

"You had good intentions—"

"That's paintin' the pig pink, don't'cha think?" Courtney giggled, her enthusiasm bubbling up once again. "If I got a lollipop ever time I had good intentions and messed up, well, I'd have more lollipops than I needed."

"I'm sure. Let's get over yonder and get this search under-way. I'm keeping you on your toes, Ensign. I expect you to find at least one of the people we're looking for."

Diane's bigger concern, if the children on the flyer were accounted for, who had Javier threatened and possibly beat up and left in the preserve? Had Shelby been truthful with them, or did she hope to divert attention from her own complicity in the botched drug-running scheme? Would they find anyone at all?

She hoped she didn't find herself without a job once this night was over. And captain? What had caused that to slip from Morton's mouth? Was a promotion something in the works, something she didn't know about?

"Shush that, Diane," she said quietly to herself as she walked Suzanne's direction. "You're a big girl, you've got a job to do, and you need to get to it." With new determination, she turned to the volunteers ready to head into the Point, and she called, "I'm Lieutenant Diane Turnipseed with Dare County. We'll follow Sergeant Ellison and her daughter to a starting location inside the preserve. Stay together. When we get there, we'll break apart and begin to search. Make sure at least one person in your group has a flashlight. It'll likely be dark by the time we're finished. Any questions?" She searched the crowd to find none, and she called to Cynthia, "Cynthia, Shelby, let's go."

Those at the front began to move, and within minutes, every-one was past the bike rack and the large sign that announced Springer's Point Nature Preserve, and they moved down the trailhead, with the end of the line hurried along by Vernon Heinrich in his dark brown coat with his flashlight already alight and visible for everyone to see.

THE HALF-MILE Jim Stephenson Nature Trail wound past small signs describing the various plants found in the preserve, including one with the image of the beautiful Georgia Primrose, and soon, the volunteers found themselves under a cavern of large live oaks with trunks twisting up from the sandy soil and offering a view that opened directly to the Sound. Diane located Cynthia and Shelby and made her way past Kay-Kay Kopacz, saying, "Pardon me, Kay-Kay," while nodding her thanks to Jason and Sean for sticking to the woman's side, before approaching the K9 handler and her daughter.

"Cynthia," she acknowledged, then turned to Shelby. "Living rough, Shelby. Where do we start? When you were hit, were you left close to where you were sleeping, or do we get to start someplace else?" *Meaning, did you really get beat up? Did Javier say all that you said? Or is this another of your shenanigans to embarrass your mother and likely me?* Morton Kringlebach flashed into Diane's mind, the man sitting in his office up in Manteo, arrogant and with the power to force her hand, if it came to it. She didn't want to have to admit defeat and give Morton ammunition to continue to badger her.

"This way, Ms. Turnipseed." Shelby pointed, looked to her mother, who nodded at her, and she started off down a narrow, sandy path, bordered by rail fencing and black needle rush, with the grass soon disappearing into yaupon and English ivy.

Diane called to those following them, "Keep on your toes and watch for poison ivy, people. I'm finding patches along the trails."

Somewhere behind her, she heard Jason Romney's voice, "Kay-Kay, yes, there's English ivy all out here. No, that's not it. Did you hear the lieutenant?"

Some people don't got the sense that God gave a minnow, Diane thought to herself. Then Shelby stopped, checked several trees, located a yaupon with a small string tied around one branch, and pushed her way past and disappeared into the undergrowth. She reappeared and said to Cynthia, "This is where I was staying, Momma."

"You catch that, Lieutenant?" Cynthia's attention was on her daughter, but she called the question to Diane. To Shelby, she said, "Sweetheart, we're where we are. The good Lord knows that life happens, and sometimes we don't know what's coming down the road. We do the best we can with what we know. Where did you locate the drug cache? Is it far from here?"

"Um, I think …" and Shelby looked both ways, the one the searchers had just covered and the other way, and turned away from the Sound, saying, "That way."

"Can you take us there, Shelby?" Cynthia, with the patience of a saint … or a law-enforcement officer with very good skills.

"I can find it again without too much trouble."

Shelby wandered through the undergrowth, went off trail once before backtracking as if confused, then seemed to decide she had found the location. There was nothing special about the place, other than some trampled needle rush grass and a few broken yaupon branches.

"This is the place? You're certain?" Diane wanted to hear her say it.

"Yes, ma'am."

"Okay, y'all," she called to the people along the trail. "We're fanning out from here. Suzanne, if you'll take Kay-Kay and go due east—" she knew Jason and Sean would stick with Kay-Kay "—and Courtney, I want you with me."

"Oh, I'm so pleased you asked. Thank you, Lieutenant."

Diane would have rolled her eyes, except that she was

fighting with keeping them from rolling up in her head. Courtney was *so sweet*. Coach Bertram pointed back the way they had come, indicating that he intended to head that direction with the boys and their dogs, and Diane waved her acknowledgment.

"Flashlights, people," Diane called, to remind everyone that the evening was creeping up on them. "Stay in small groups, especially as it gets darker. Stay on your toes and yell if you find something." *Radios*, she thought. *They should have those, or at least a common phone number so we could keep in contact with our phones* … but the crowd was doing what they had come to do, vanishing into the preserve to look for Shelby's missing family, and the time for better organization had come and gone.

"Diane," Cynthia said, "Toby's about ready. You riding sidesaddle with us?"

"Yes. What are you thinking we'll find?" That was as far as Diane dared express her doubts that Shelby had been on the up-and-up with them.

"I understand your question. You don't prove someone's guilty until you've got enough detail to prove they did the deed. That's what we're doing out here tonight, gathering detail."

"I stand reproved." Diane had to smile. "I'll make a change and be the boss my people need me to be. After you, Cynthia."

"Toby, search," Cynthia instructed in a firm, no-nonsense voice as she unleashed him. The German shepherd seemed to catch the change in tone from conversational exchange to business instruction, and his stance tensed as he froze and began to absorb the aromas and hints that surrounded him. He let out a short bark, and he dropped his head and moved forward, intent on doing exactly what was expected of him.

They were just making progress when Somner Trotter's voice echoed through the heavy growth blocking the view of most anything not within twenty feet. Courtney Cruickshank was the first to respond with, "Now that's the right way to get everyone's attention." She smiled as she listened to the words.

"For all sakes," Diane said to her. "Did you catch what the man said?" Somner yelling, yes, that she had heard, but to understand him, that was another mess of fish.

"Let me listen." Courtney, her expression as bright as ever, held one hear pointed the direction of Somner's yell. Other voices were starting up, and she frowned for a moment before announcing, "He's found something. A cabin or a hut … everyone's yelling now, so I didn't get it clear, but it's definitely something. Isn't this a happy thing?" She was smiling again.

"That can't be right," Cynthia muttered. "Last I heard, only things out here are the cemetery and an old cistern." Then Toby yelped, began to bark, and when Cynthia gave him the go-ahead, he surged into the brush, and the three women took off after him.

THE UNDERSTORY saturating the 120-acre preserve was a tangled barrier of dense shrubbery and vines, and the three women fought their way to the "cabin" located by Somner's group. Their appearance was a little worse for wear with scratches and leaves in their hair, but determination flooded their faces. By the time of their arrival, Scar and Simba were tearing about, barking uncontrollably, and Coach Bertram was yelling at Nubbin and Carrot to GET THOSE DOGS UNDER CONTROL. Jason and Sean appeared at the same time as Diane and her small group, with Emily and Steven Hill showing their faces on Suzanne DeSantis' heels.

Even Jeremy Clabbins, despite his aversion to Dare County authority, towed his group in, and he seemed attuned to whatever directions the Dare County lieutenant might provide.

Deputy Robert Hall of the Dare County B-District, who had at one time been on loan to C-District and now felt a part of the team, walked firmly up to Scar and Simba, grabbed their collars one at a time, and had the dogs quiet and settled without a word spoken to either one.

"Somner," Diane called. "What did you find yonder? Dump it on us quick. We've still got some light, so let's not waste it unless this is good."

"Yes, ma'am," he called. "This here looks to be some sort of shelter. Inside, well, someone's been staying here, though just who I can't make out."

"Shelby?" Diane pointedly looked at her.

"Not me, Ms. Turnipseed. I always slept in the wood. I ain't never seen this before."

"Suzanne, if you'll join us, and Ensign Cruickshank, you represent the Coast Guard. All of us together." She motioned them forward. Inside what was little more than a lean-to with a rough front wall were several blankets, all wadded and dirty, and other miscellaneous items. One appeared to be a towel with stitching on one end, and Diane knelt and straightened it. When she read the words, she stood, called Emily to her, and asked her to come take a look.

Although filthy, the name was clear. *Dutchman*, and just below it, the words in smaller text, *Newport News*.

"Well, I think that's pretty clear," Emily said. "A connection not even the sheriff can deny." She was aware of the conflict between the lieutenant and the sheriff, as was just about everyone else connected to the sheriff's office in Dare County.

"No evidence of people, though," inserted Steven Hill. "That's definitely not funny. If they're not here—" He didn't finish, and the implication was out there for anyone to see. The story was that when Blackbeard the pirate was using Springer's Point as his hideaway in the 1700s, and he was killed at Teach's Hole not far from where they stood, his body was tossed into the Sound to sleep with the fishes, so to speak. Had whoever was here, as indicated by the stitching on the towel, faced the same fate? Would they eventually wash up on a sandbar, as the man located by Sallinger and Dingman had done?

Were there more dead people in the Sound even as the search party stood in the preserve and hoped they were alive?

Toby, still unleashed, had joined those at the lean-to cabin, sniffing and inspecting the fabrics and other detritus strewn about, and he began to display agitated behavior. Cynthia shared, "Lieutenant, we should pay attention to the dog. Toby seems to think he's got something. Sand dunes don't get taller just cause we want 'em to, but that dog's smart enough to dig where he ought, and that's what he's wantin' to do about now."

"We might oughta let him dig, then. The sooner the better." The sky was fading, and flashlights were now beacons identifying where the groups of searchers were gathered.

"Toby, find," Cynthia instructed, and the German shepherd shifted position, dropped his head, and began tracking along the ground as if he recognized a smell he had picked up from the small lean-to.

Diane wasn't beyond crossing her fingers. She thought of the spiral in her pocket, the word she had underlined. Murder. She didn't think so now. This was bigger than anything that Shelby could have pulled off, at least by herself. She might not be innocent, but someone had been living here, or imprisoned here. Had they been tied up, starved, perhaps beaten or tortured? She shivered to think what the people staying in that lean-to had endured.

Then Toby began to bark excitedly, and Cynthia called, "Lieutenant, you need to get here now."

Diane followed Cynthia's flashlight and let it draw her deeper into the shadowy North Carolina bush. In her mind, the days when pirates roamed the island and many met their end seemed eerily real, as if she might stumble upon one of their unmarked graves at any point. When she reached Cynthia, the red-headed K9 handler was on her knees removing a gag from a slight, blonde-headed woman. The captive, filthy and with a busted lip, burst out in a ragged voice, "I'm Raina Byrne. My husband and my children. I know right where they are."

RAINA BYRNE'S hands were tied to a tree with rope that looked suspiciously like the rotten line found aboard the sailboat now at the bottom of Cedar Island Bay, and Cynthia was cutting it loose as soon as she had the gag removed from Raina's face. The woman's clothes looked like someone who had been living rough, even with their good cut and trendy, casual style.

"I'm Lieutenant Turnipseed with the Dare County Sheriff's office," Diane started, and the woman's last name hit her. "Byrne? Are your children Saoirse and Conner?"

"Oh!" Raina seemed to melt. "Don't tell me something's happened to them."

"There's a flyer out for two missing children up in Elizabeth City by the names of Saoirse and Conner. I was told they'd been located, that they were vacationing with their parents."

"That's us." She was barely holding together. "Our boat was hijacked in a storm, and we were forced into a smaller boat. Then the rope broke before the hijacker could cast us off and reboard our boat. I don't know what happened to it, but we ended up here and have been kept tied up and gagged." Cynthia had the rope free, and the woman tried to stand but couldn't.

"Did the hijacker attack you?" At the look in the woman's eyes, Diane knew why she had been separated from her family. "I am so sorry for what you've endured, but you're safe now. Where is your family? We'll bring them to you."

"My husband, Tom—" She pointed, and Emily and Steven tore that direction to locate them.

A tall man with dried blood in his hair, and the two children from the flyer, their eyes filled with shock, were released from their rope-bound solitude, and when they appeared, he held the little girl in his arms. When he saw his wife, he gave his daughter to Cynthia, and he dropped to his knees to hold his wife as tears soaked his face.

After a few moments, Diane interrupted with, "Tom, I'm Lieutenant Turnipseed with the Dare County Sheriff's Office, and this is Deputy Suzanne DeSantis with Hyde County. We need to get your wife care. Here's what will happen now …"

He listened as she explained, and as she talked, she waved Sean over.

"Yes, ma'am," Sean said. "I'm here to help, Lieutenant. What can I do you help you out?"

"Tom," she said, "this is Deputy Sean Taylor, one of my esteemed Dare County deputies, and I need to ask him to do something for me that's essential. Pardon me a moment."

"Of course, Lieutenant," Tom agreed, as he lifted a shoulder to press a dirty white tee shirt to his face and wipe away moisture pooling in his eyes. "Anything, just thank you for making the effort to find us."

"Of course," she said, and turned to her deputy. "Sean, I need you to find a radio or phone, or use mine if you don't have one. Call emergency services and request an ambulance, if they have one, and a stretcher. This woman can't walk out of here."

"Yes, ma'am," he said, and pulled his phone from his pocket. "I've got this, ma'am. I'm with you. We're a team, and I won't let you down."

"For all sakes, just do it, Deputy." She gave him a look that said to get with it, and she turned to Tom and Raina and shared with them that they had found a boat that was likely theirs, and it had been sunk.

"It was all about drugs. That's what we got caught up in. He had a stash here that he was supposed to transport out, but I don't know if he was successful. He wanted our boat for that, and then the rope he'd tied to our boat separated during the storm, and we didn't know if we'd survive. Have you found him?" The dread and fear in both their eyes told the truth of how they'd suffered at Javier's cruelty.

"A body," she said quietly, but also shared that they weren't certain it was the man who had tied them up. If they could provide identification, well, she knew how hard that would be. When anger creased Tom's face at the mention of any association with the man who had stolen their boat and tied them up, even to identify him, Diane assured him that any identification could happen tomorrow. Right now was for ensuring that he, his wife, and his children were okay.

"We're not okay," he said. "My children, and especially not my wife. If you knew what he did—" His voice wrenched, and he grabbed his wife and buried his face in her hair.

"I'm pretty sure we have a good idea," Diane said quietly. The sound of a siren in the distance drew her attention and filled her with relief, and she watched for the emergency medical technicians. She breathed easier when they appeared with a stretcher to carry Raina out of the preserve.

As the EMTs moved down the trail towards their emergency vehicle carrying Raina between them, and Tom with his daughter in his arms and holding his son's hand, Diane watched them walk away with a sense of relief. She turned to find Cynthia clipping on Toby's leash and Shelby watching her. Diane stepped to Shelby and said, "Shelby, thank you. You saved that family tonight. You've made your momma proud."

"I … um, well, okay, Ms. Turnipseed. If you say so. Momma, is she right? Did I really do that?"

"Sweetheart, of course." Cynthia stood and wrapped her daughter in her arms and said, "I love you, pumpkin. I should show it more. Like your daddy says, we're where we are, and right now's what we've got." She gave her a kiss on the fore-head and stepped back. "Now, let's get back to the car. It's time we got on home. You want me to drop you at the boarding house, or do you want to come back home with me for the night?"

"With you, Momma, please."

"Your daddy will be so happy."

Diane pulled out her flashlight and she clicked it on. The pool of light at her feet contrasted with the gloom of the centuries that weighed on Springer's Point. She was glad for one thing. Blackbeard might have died on this isolated spit of sand and scrub, but one family had been saved. They would get the care they needed, and their lives would go on. Likely in Newport News, far away from Ocracoke, but that was a very good thing, as she would certain this place would be a source of nightmares for them for a very long time.

Chapter 11

Loose Ends

"KAREN." Diane greeted the Manteo dispatcher for the Dare County sheriff's office as she entered the building on her way to Sheriff Kringlebach's office.

"Well, look who's here." Karen placed her elbow on her desk and rested her chin in her hand. "I dare say, Hortie better be nice to you today. You're the hero of the county."

"I wouldn't say that." Diane's stomach was twisted by her command performance in Manteo. She had been called in by Morton *immediately* after hearing of the results of their "mutual Ocracoke investigation" and she kept hearing the words *resume* and *captain* in her head. It wasn't a good feeling.

"*The Coastline Times* says so." Karen flipped a folded newspaper open to reveal the front page. There was Diane's picture with the title "Local Hero …"

"We'll see what Morton has to say."

"Oh, him. His retirement is all he talks about. And you, of

course." Karen giggled and motioned Diane on towards Hortie Cumberbatch and Sheriff Kringlebach's office.

Hortie stood as Diane approached, and she stepped from around her desk and took one of Diane's hands in hers. "Oh my, oh my, who do we have here? A hero amongst us. Welcome, Lieutenant Turnipseed. My, you have made us proud. Morton will see you immediately. Just go on in, dear."

"Thank you, Hortie," Diane said, as she pulled her hand away and moved towards the sheriff's door. She hadn't expected that from the sheriff's personal assistant. Inside, Morton looked up when she entered, and he set down his pen and indicated she should pull up a chair and be seated.

"So, Lieutenant. Success." He nodded and perhaps smiled, if the slight movement across his tight lips could be called that.

"Yessir." Diane waited on him to make the next move. She wasn't certain why she was here, and she didn't want to make the situation any worse than whatever was about to tumble out of the bait basket.

"I see you made a connection between your case and that truck that went off the Bonner."

"Yessir," though it hadn't made any difference since the driver didn't survive. With no survivors, there was no one to prosecute for blame or damages. The man had been a link in the drug runners' scheme but only at the lowest level.

"One more part of the investigation cleared and closed out. I appreciate that. Jack Sellew and Thomas Conner. You know those names?"

"Yessir." She had seen the report. It was called intercounty cooperation. She also knew they had been cleared—not of all wrongdoing, but of involvement in their intercounty cooperative investigation.

"Off our books. That's a relief." The sheriff leaned forward and pulled a file folder from beneath his keyboard. "Javier

Castella. The dead man. The M.E.'s report says drug toxicity was off the charts with a likely heart attack before he went in the water. He was identified by Shelby Ellison and the Byrne couple. It's a shame he couldn't be brought to justice for what he did to Mrs. Byrne."

"Justice was served, sir."

"Yes, after a fashion. It's a bit of a mystery how he got so far from Cedar Island. Any ideas there?"

"No, sir, but the tides are fickle along the Banks." She shrugged. That was something she didn't feel the need to pursue.

"Okay, then." He looked at her for a moment, then said, "Lieutenant Sallinger hasn't located who hit the boat those two boys were in—"

"Sir? I'm not familiar with that."

"Right, that's Hyde County business. Castella was already dead when that happened. Deputy Dingman had suggested a connection, but it was later dismissed when the M.E. determined the time of death. Anyway, to the point of this meeting. The county performance review is in process, and your handling of the incident down on Springer's Point is making me look good. I appreciate that, Lieutenant. Go out with a bang on my retirement, heh?" He actually smiled this time. "Gov. Elringhaus called to congratulate me, and Raleigh wants to do a write up on Dare County's retiring sheriff and note our accomplishments while I've been in office. I mentioned the position of captain in an earlier conversation. It still stands, that is if you'll consider it."

"Yessir. Thank you, sir. I'll keep that in mind."

"Are we good, Lieutenant?"

Diane studied his face for a moment before she found the words to reply, and she said, "Yes, sir. We're good."

She hoped she sounded sincere. Like Deputy Sean Taylor

liked to say, respect and commitment. That's what it's all about.

"Then, that's that. Thank you for coming up, Lieutenant." Kringlebach stood and offered her his hand.

Diane shook and exited. Captain? She didn't know. Her home was C-District and the outstanding team she had cobbled together out of the Dare County officers up and down the Outer Banks. She challenged anyone to try and take that away from her.

Inside her black Explorer, she started the engine and began the long drive back to Buxton and the C-District sub-station. She looked forward to getting home and back to work once again.

A Note from the Author

Ocracoke Island is much as I've described it, and Springer's Point and its connection with the pirate Blackbeard is part of the history of the island. He was killed at Teach's Hole, and by some accounts, he was beheaded and his body cast into the Sound. There is no gravesite for Blackbeard on Ocracoke Island, so if you visit, don't go looking. You won't find it.

The British Cemetery is a very real part of the island, and you can visit and enjoy the memorial plaques as I've described them in the book. It is maintained by the local Coast Guard station based on Silver Lake.

The jobs I've given various law enforcement groups in this story are valid to the extent that they further the story I wanted to tell. I made every effort not to stray too far afield, but my purpose in this story was not to create a documentary on police organization and procedure but instead a good read. If you enjoyed my tale, then I've done what I set out to do.

www.ingramcontent.com/pod-product-compliance
Lightning Source LLC
Chambersburg PA
CBHW051131030726
47504CB00004B/813